ALSO BY HARRY CONNOLLY

The Twenty Palaces Series:
Twenty Palaces
Child of Fire
Game of Cages
Circle of Enemies
The Twisted Path

The Great Way Trilogy:
The Way into Chaos
The Way into Magic
The Way into Darkness

Standalone Works:
A Key, An Egg, An Unfortunate Remark

*Bad Little Girls Die Horrible Deaths, and
Other Tales of Dark Fantasy*

Spirit of the Century Presents: King Khan

One Man

A City of Fallen Gods novel

HARRY CONNOLLY

RADAR AVE
PRESS

With thanks to Dashiell Hammet

CHAPTER ONE

On the day after the summer solstice in the year 403 of the New
Calendar, Kyrionik ward-Safroy defe-Safroy admir-Safroy hold-Safroy
attended his own funeral.

As a noble family, the Safroys were expected to hold two ceremonies.
One would be private, reserved for family, close political allies, those in the
High Watch who thought it prudent to show respect to a member of a
rival faction currently out of power, and however many of Kyrionik's
former friends his mother felt obligated to invite.

By tradition, it should have already happened. Somber guests would
have worn their mourning whites. Servants wearing hoods of muslin gauze
would offer each a cup of bitter tea, to represent grief, followed by drams
of honeyed brandy, which represented happy memories of the loved one
who had passed. After a few moments of silence, polite guests would talk
about family, friends, newborn babes, aging parents—anything concerning
the way people live their lives—to remind the grieving family that life
goes on. Impolite people would try to talk business.

Kyrionik's mother was a former member of the High Watch, the parsu
of the Safroy family, and a rich, influential woman. She was always surrounded
by impolite people.

The private ceremony was ordinarily held at home, usually in a garden
or courtyard. For the Safroys, that meant everyone would be high enough
on the slopes of Salash Hill that the family could mourn in direct sunlight,
without the unpleasant tint of the light from Suloh's bones. Perhaps
they'd gather in the east hall, with its floors made from smooth white
marble imported from Koh-Gilmiere. Or maybe on the southern deck, with
its skywood and commanding view of the sea. Or the gardens, where
Kyrionik and his brothers used to—

No. Those memories were from his old self. The one who lived among the wealthy, high-born Salashi. That man was long gone. Kyrionik had a new name now.

Now he was Kyrioc, child of No One, which marked him as lower than a commoner. He was an orphan. Unlike the high-born Kyrionik, poor Kyrioc had no family, no titles, and no inheritance.

But he did have an obligation.

The public funeral for hapless young Kyrionik was being held in High Square, at the southernmost end of the Upgarden deck, and Kyrioc, child of No One, stood in the long, long line of complete strangers waiting to pay their respects.

Kyrioc could not have attended the private ceremony without revealing himself. Without reclaiming his old name. The idea of reuniting with his family, of the joyful tears, the celebrations, the calls that he explain where he'd been and what had happened…

What he'd done…

And they would embrace him. His hands, responsible for so much death, would touch his mother's small frame. They would feel her warmth and movement. Her breath. Her life.

Just the thought of it made him flinch and close down. He shut his eyes and stopped shuffling forward with the rest of the line. He could hear screaming, as fresh in his memory as if he'd heard them that morning. Then he remembered burning figures running through the jungle at night, then the darkness itself coming to life, and the sound of steel on flesh, and the smell of blood, and—

"Good sir?"

Kyrioc jumped, hand reaching for a weapon he no longer trusted himself to carry.

The woman who had spoken was a Free-Cities merchant. She'd dressed in an open green linen robe over cream-colored tunic and trousers. They complemented her bronze skin, setting her apart from the dark-brown faces all around her. Instead of a hat, she had pinned a small block of perfumed wax atop her rather ordinary bun. It had barely begun to melt into her hair, but the sharp, flowery smell was overbearing in the still air.

Her right eye was surrounded by a web of scars and was dark brown. Her left eye was hazel. If she could afford to replace her eye, she probably did not spend much time around people like him, but funerals bring together the high and the low.

She was gaping at him. He lowered his hand.

"You stopped walking," the woman said with more kindness than he deserved. "Are you all right?"

"I'm sorry, good madam. Bad memories."

"Ah. I thought you were grieving, and that perhaps you knew the deceased personally."

Kyrioc wasn't sure how to respond. "I would have been a stranger to him."

The line was still shuffling forward without them. Kyrioc mumbled another apology and hurried to close the gap.

For the day, Kyrioc had worn simple black trousers with a black cotton tunic and vest. They were the funeral clothes of a poor man—a man with disfiguring scars and shaggy black hair hanging in his face—and they were supposed to let him blend in with the crowd.

High Square, where the Safroys awaited the long queue, was nearly two blocks away. Kyrioc could *not* let himself fall into a reverie again, not if he was going to hide himself in this long line of stitches.

He wished he could summon his cloak of mirrors, but that was impossible in the midday sun.

Kyrioc looked up and down the street, checking for Safroy guards. There were none this far from the square itself. Instead he saw city constables, private shop security, and the usual flash and bustle of the main street of the Upgarden deck.

Here at the southern end, with High Square and the terminus of The Freightway nearby—and with the gate to The Avenue just behind him—Upgarden was at its most luxurious. Not only were the streets themselves constructed from pale, beautiful skywood, so were many of the stores. This close to High Slope, the shops sold only the finest goods from around the Semprestian: silks from Carrig, spices from the Free Cities, furs from Katr nomads, jewels from Koh-Benjatso, Koh-Gilmiere, and Koh-Kaulma. If there was a piece of finery with the poor taste to have been made right there in Koh-Salash—or anywhere along the shores of the Timmer Sea—it was sold downcity, where the shops were made of ordinary wood and people walked about in the pale orange like of Suloh's bones.

The deck was little changed from the days when Kyrioc roamed there as a teenager. As the Safroy heir, he had been welcomed into every store, tea shop, and cafe with a broad smile. Silks had been draped over his shoulders, pastries set before him, and rings slid onto his fingers, with the bill to be delivered to his family later, naturally.

But that boy, the one who was gone from the world forever, had not been able to see Upgarden as the orphan Kyrioc did. Local merchants paid such high taxes, and they served such a precious clientele, that a pair of city soldiers—not even constables but soldiers—stood at every intersection. And because the wealthy could never be reassured enough, each shop employed at least one private guard.

To Kyrionik, heir to the Safroy wards, holdings, titles, and treasury, they were friendly figures he could make sport with. To Kyrioc, child of No One, they were a deadly threat.

Standing beside carved decorative panels in the shop doorways, children dressed like little dolls beckoned to anyone who flaunted fine fabrics or jewelry. If the shop lacked customers at the moment—and with this long queue of commoners in the street, business was slower than usual—the owner stood behind them, their thoughts turned inward as they calculated the cost of this intrusion.

Kyrioc looked around. Young Kyrionik had been too pampered to recognize the hunger in their eyes. Smiling or blank-faced, they had always looked at him the way a street cat stares at an injured bird, because no matter how many jewels they wore, or how much gold they earned, it was never enough.

An elderly woman stepped out of a perfumery, followed by a long train of servants bearing packages. She suddenly declared, "What *is* this parade of scraps and scavengers?"

Kyrioc turned his gaze toward the deck. The bouquet in his hand crumpled as he gripped the stems too tightly. A long, shuddering breath released some of the tension in his chest.

Being recognized wasn't the only danger. Revisiting these streets and shops was almost like returning home, and in the coming weeks, he might be tempted to return. To haunt the planks and squares like a ghost of his former self. Then, inevitably, he would be recognized, and then—

But that wouldn't happen. As far as Kyrioc was concerned, his old self— that reckless young noble who had done so much harm—was dead in every way but the one that mattered the least.

Moving with the queue, he came to the end of the street and descended a few steps into High Square. His soft-soled boots were quiet against the skywood. At the far end of the square was the domed roof of the Temple of Suloh. It wasn't even as large as the smallest of the Upgarden shops, but this was only the very top of the tower. Beside it were stairs and plankways leading down into the lower decks of the city.

Then he moved far enough into the square to see Suloh's colossal shoulder blade jutting up through the cluster of shops and villas on the next street over, the orange crystal glowing even in midday. No part of the gods' skeletons stood higher, except for Suloh's skull, which had been hauled to the top of Salash Hill long, long ago.

At the western end of High Square were a dais and a broad set of stairs leading up to it. Both had been built, extravagantly, from skywood. The

Safroys would be standing up there, on display. Constables, bodyguards, friends, and loyal allies would fill the stair between them and the procession, but the family would be at the top.

Kyrionik's mother would be there.

Kyrioc did not look up.

As the parsu of a noble family with a sizable sail, his mother would stand in the highest place. And every stitch in the family sail—along with the many others who hoped to join the sail—would pass below in a slow, mournful procession, leaving a flower by the marker for her fallen heir.

The Safroys would likely not even look down at the commoners passing below. Kyrioc would not look up.

Live, your virtue, and remember us to your mother.

He flinched at the memory but did not close down. Not this time.

Kyrioc had not come for his mother, or his brothers, or his father. He had not come for the circle of friends and sycophants around them. He had not even come to see his own monument, which was finally right before him, a simple stone pillar with the Safroy bull and the flower of ice carved at the top. It was surrounded by flowers, none of which were joined in a bouquet as his were. The traditional roses, lilies, and daisies were there, of course, but so were numerous other flowers, all meant to show honor to the memory of that lost heir.

He had not come here for that, either. He'd come for one reason. He'd come to repay the terrible debt he owed, because he knew no one else in his family would even acknowledge it.

Kyrioc laid his bouquet of thirty red poppies before his own monument.

* * *

AFTER THE THIRD HOUR spent standing at attention, watching the clouds float lazily above them, Culzatik ward-Safroy defe-Safroy admir-Safroy hold-Safroy's feet felt swollen. Pain ran up his legs like a pair of stockings.

But this was for Kyrionik. The four of them—Mother, Father, Billen, and him—would stand through the day and the night if it was required. No one would ever say they'd shirked their duty, not for this.

They'd waited nearly eight years for this Mourning Day. The first tears had come when they realized Kyrionik would not return from his First Labor, and there had been more in the years since.

Not here, though. No Safroy would shed a tear in High Square in full view of the common folk, no matter how deep their grief. They were not even supposed to look at the stitches as they shuffled by the monument.

But Culzatik was so bored with looking at the clouds, he did exactly that.

That was when he saw his big brother.

At least, the man looked like Kyrionik, vaguely. He was walking away from the monument. His shaggy black hair was a mess and his black cotton tunic and vest were threadbare, but there was something about the way he moved...

No, it *couldn't* be.

"You there!" Culzatik shouted, shocking everyone, including himself. "Constable! Stop that man in the black vest!"

The shaggy-haired man glanced up, and he seemed to change in some subtle way. His features blurred and his clothes momentarily swirled with color, but the effect vanished almost immediately.

That could only have been magic. Failed magic, but magic nonetheless.

The man couldn't be Kyrionik, not with that monstrous scar, but the line of his jaw on the other side...

Instead of collaring the scarred man, the constable stationed at his brother's marker stared up at Culzatik as though he'd been slapped awake. One of the Safroy guards strode forward to do it for him, seizing the wrist of a woman in a green robe.

A few stitches cried out in fear and the procession of well-wishers surged away, splitting into three different streams as they fled for the stairs out of High Square. Culzatik, normally as sharp-eyed as a hawk, somehow lost track of the man in the black vest, but he'd been mixed in with the group heading for the exit to the northeast.

A guard with a brush on his helm—one of the family lieutenants—slapped the first guard on the spaulder and he released the woman. "On me," the lieutenant said, and took off running. Six Safroy guards followed.

On impulse, Culzatik staggered down the stairs, aching legs balking at the sudden movement. He had no real idea what he was doing or why. He only knew that he couldn't hang back. That shaggy-haired man with the scar wasn't Kyrionik. It was impossible. Yet he found himself clumsily shoving through the crowd at the bottom of the stairs and running after his guards.

Mother called his name, but he didn't acknowledge her. If *he* didn't know why he was doing this, what explanation could he make to her?

"I want him alive!" he shouted.

Aziatil was right beside him, running with an easy stride while he still labored to work the stiffness from his legs. There was no one he would have trusted more to capture this scarred man than the slender, fair-skinned Free Cities woman beside him, but she was his bodyguard. She didn't open doors, carry packages, or leave his side to shackle downcity fugitives.

Constables blew whistles, and answering whistles sounded from blocks away. Any moment now, the Undertower lifts would be halted and the ramps and stairs out of Upgarden would be blocked.

Culzatik was not the most athletic young man—especially compared to the family guards, who could not sneak out of Father's exercise sessions—but he wasn't wearing steel armor, either. Eventually, he caught up to them. The lieutenant glanced back. "Your virtue," he said.

The fellow had distinguished himself during Culzatik's First Labor. Tyenzo, child of Tylinus, was his name, and Culzatik felt a twinge of pride at having remembered it. Beneath Tyenzo's steel helmet, sweat ran down his face in fat drops. The midsummer heat was awful, and they were suffering.

But that's what they were paid for.

"I want him taken alive," Culzatik repeated.

"Yes, your virtue. He'll probably be collared by the constables. If he'd run directly north, he would be going for the lifts, but the only way down from the eastern edge of the deck is The Freightway, which the constables have already shut down."

Tyenzo had a commoner's idea of Upgarden, because he only passed through on his way to the Safroy compound. The people who lived and shopped there knew the south end of the deck had half a dozen ways—

"There!" one of the guards shouted, and they all turned east.

Culzatik followed them up the stairs at the edge of High Square and back into the streets of Upgarden. He felt a jolt when he saw the man they were running toward—shaggy hair, black vest—ducking into an alley, but in the next moment, he knew it wasn't the fugitive.

At their approach, the man spun around. He was too short, too thick, and had no scar on his face.

"Don't try to stop me! Don't you try!"

The far end of the alley held only open space. They'd come to the very edge of the Upgarden deck, and the man intended to jump.

Culzatik didn't give a shit about some commoner's suicide. "You. Go away."

"Yes, your virtue," he answered. The unscarred man could have simply stepped over the edge, but he shuffled into the street instead. Tyenzo warned him about hitting someone below. Why not go to the hospital, where his death would do some good?

Culzatik moved toward the edge of the deck. There was no wind today, but he still gripped the side of the building.

Koh-Salash was a young city, founded just over four hundred years earlier. Fleeing Lost Selsarim, Culzatik's ancestors tried to make landfall in many places around the Semprestian Sea, but they had been driven away by archers, fire, and fleets. Only here, at the Timmer Straits, in this forbidden and forbidding place, could they make new homes.

But to live there, they had to build their homes within the skeletons of two dead gods, each three miles long. Living above them on High Slope, it was easy to forget their true scale.

Yth lay beneath, her back to the mud. Suloh lay atop her, ribs on her ribs. Hips on her hips. Just as they were when they were killed.

And the Upgarden deck, constructed around Suloh's glowing spine, stood nearly four thousand feet above the stony beaches of the Timmer.

The nearest deck was Dawnshine, just two dozen feet below, but it didn't extend this far east. The fugitive couldn't have simply dropped down to it.

Culzatik looked south. His view of Yth's skull below was blocked by buildings. Turning north, he saw the back of a shop that extended beyond the edge of the deck, then underneath it.

It was a private passage down to Dawnshine. The shop owner couldn't have cut a stairwell through the skywood deck to the level below—it was *skywood*—but they could go around it.

Culzatik suddenly realized he'd been there. It was a back entrance to a Dawnshine casino that Father had once dragged him to.

The constables were blocking the *public* stairs and ramps out of Upgarden, but did this shabby fugitive know the deck well enough to…

"Follow me." Culzatik sprinted up the street, his skin tingling. He found the building easily, although he had not visited in three years. It was a hat shop with high double doors and a sensibly neutral carving of the flower of ice above the door.

As he was about to enter, Aziatil blocked him. Culzatik felt a flare of annoyance, but it passed. Of course he shouldn't be first through the door.

Tyenzo stamped up the stairs through the doorway, advancing in the stance Father had taught them to intimidate unarmed citizens. His shield was high, his sword held above his head with point forward. The other guards followed, mimicking his stance.

Culzatik went in right behind Aziatil. She did not take her hands from her long knives.

The guards advanced through the empty shop. Culzatik craned his neck to look into the back room, where the passage down to Dawnshine was hidden. The door stood open. The elderly shop owner was visible.

Then the old man moved sideways suddenly as if shoved, and Culzatik caught a glimpse of the fugitive. His shaggy black hair made it impossible to see any part of his face but his mouth, which was fixed in a tight-lipped frown.

Tyenzo shouted, "On your knees! Get on your knees right now!" The guards leaned forward to intimidate him into surrendering, but nothing about him suggested—

Without warning, shadow enveloped the fugitive, swinging around his body from both sides and meeting in the middle like a pair of weighted window cloths falling closed. For the briefest instant, where the man had stood, there was only a slash of darkness.

Despite the summer heat, a chill of fear ran down Culzatik's back. "Let's go."

Darkness billowed from the scarred man like smoke.

Magic again, but this time it did not fail.

A moment later, Culzatik was back out in the street, Aziatil close behind. Another squad of six Safroy guards came jogging up. "In there, your virtue?" asked the armored woman in front. He nodded, but she approached the door without entering.

"What the fuck is that?"

Impenetrable shadow filled the room. The guards looked at it, stepped back, then began looking up and down the street as if they were about to run. Culzatik couldn't blame them.

"Hold positions," he ordered. "Tyenzo's people are inside. Be ready to seize anyone who tries to escape."

They did. Culzatik would rather have ordered them to join the fight, but Mother had taught him never to give an order that would not be obeyed.

Then the darkness retreated like water draining from a bath. Culzatik followed it inside. "It's fine," he said to his bodyguard. "It's over."

The fugitive was gone.

In his wake, he'd left the Safroy family guards in disarray. Two were sprawled on the floor, clutching twisted knees. Two more lay unconscious. Shields and swords lay scattered around the room.

By the fallen gods, who was this man?

"I cut him," a guard said. He was holding a sword with blood on the point. "He caught my arm and stopped me just as I was cutting him."

Tyenzo, crouching in the corner beside the shop owner, struggled to stand. He removed his hand from his lower back. His palm was covered in blood. "It wasn't him you were cutting."

Culzatik knelt beside the shop owner. He was unharmed. Maybe the fugitive had shoved the man aside to protect him. "Do you recognize me?" The old man stared with wide eyes and said nothing. "No? It's all right. It was a long time ago. Did you recognize *him*?" The old man shook his head. "Did he take the key?"

9

To this, the shopkeeper had no answer.

"He cast a spell on us," Tyenzo said as he slumped to the floor.

Culzatik moved to the center of the room. "No, he didn't. A spell must be spoken aloud, and his lips weren't moving." There. He lifted the hidden latch, but the trap door was bolted from the other side.

Which was probably for the best, considering.

"Your virtue," Tyenzo said, his face turning pale. "What should we say happened here?"

Culzatik had long considered himself an accomplished prevaricator, but for the moment, his wits failed him. They'd gone in pursuit of a single fugitive, and look at them. The truth would make the family guard look like incompetent clowns.

"Anything you like," Culzatik said. "I wasn't here. Just don't mention that the man used magic. We'd have the whole city in an uproar." No one would try to capture the scarred man alive if they thought he knew spells, and Culzatik still wanted to talk to him.

He and Aziatil started back toward High Square.

Who was that scarred asshole? And why had Culzatik run after him? It had been pure impulse, and impulsiveness was not a worthy trait for the new Safroy heir.

High Square was empty. The stitches had fled, which meant the service had ended prematurely. Because of him.

Culzatik flushed with shame. So much for never shirking his duty.

The Safroys lingered near the monument, surrounded by their guards, attendants, and a few lingering well-wishers. Mother was talking with a tiny, elderly Carrig wearing the stiff, scarlet bonnet of the Kings' Tower Apostles. After a brief handclasp, the Carrig glanced at Culzatik, then shuffled away. Two Safroy guards accompanied her.

Why was a Carrig heretic standing for the Safroy heir?

Father noticed him and tapped Mother's shoulder. She turned, and her expression made everyone else shrink away. "Culza, what have you done?"

"Mother, I—"

"What's the matter? Were you bored without a book?"

"*Mother.*"

His tone deflected her anger. She laid one strong, slender hand on his arm "Culza," she said, her voice still tight. "I know you loved him, but—"

"Mother, I *idolized* him."

Father came up behind her, and the expression on his face was pitiless.

"He's been gone more than seven years," Mother said, "and we must prepare *you* to take his place." Of course. She couldn't let a day pass without implying that she didn't think he was ready. "What have I told you about the family sail?"

Culzatik knew the answer. If there was one thing he was good at, it was his lessons. "'The parsu fills the sail and does most of the work. Eighty percent of your time will be spent doing things for the stitches who owe their loyalty to you. But when you ask the sail to make a change, the effect will be powerful.'"

"No," Mother said. Her tiny, close-set eyes looked as black as the fugitive's magic. "Never show weakness. Not to your friends. Not to your enemies. Especially not to your fucking underlings."

This conversation needed to be over. "Yes, Mother." He turned toward the constables. They looked as though they would have paid good silver to be anywhere else. "Did any of you see the man I wanted captured?"

A constable stepped forward, removing his steel helmet out of respect. He might have been the handsomest man Culzatik had ever seen. "I saw him, your virtue. His hair was black and much too long, and he had a scar on his left cheek as if he'd been savaged by a dog. I saw nothing amiss in his behavior. He laid this at the monument." He held out a bouquet of red poppies. Culzatik took it.

"He's still at large," Culzatik said, "I want him brought to me alive." It was ludicrous. He had not—*had not*—seen his older brother running from his own funeral. Beating six of the family guard in a fight, while saving the life of one.

Doing *magic*.

It was impossible. Still, Culzatik would have no rest until he saw the man up close.

Before his mother could speak again, Culzatik bowed to her. "On my honor, I saw a knife in his hand," he lied. "I feared he would disgrace the funeral with bloodshed."

She did not believe him for a moment.

"You heard my son," she called to the constables. "Your duties at the service are done. Bring that man to the south tower for questioning." The captain of the constables nodded.

Culzatik saw that the Safroy family investigator had come to make a report. She didn't look happy.

He turned his attention to the bouquet. Why red poppies? Kyrionik wasn't a soldier. And why… He counted them quickly. Why thirty of them? It didn't make sense.

By the fallen gods, who was that man?

CHAPTER TWO

Two days before:

*   *   *

A TYPICAL SHIELDSDAY EVENING on the two Apricot decks was like a lodestone for pickpockets, con artists, tar dealers, and even the occasional gang of kidnappers. They were drawn to the crowds of restless young merchants, sailors on leave, and careless teenage nobles the way rats were drawn to larders. Which was why constables were stationed everywhere. The ironshirts of Koh-Salash were not the cleverest humankind in the world, but they didn't have to be clever to swing a truncheon.

Tonight was not typical. Tomorrow was summer solstice, which marked the end of the year. The day after that would be Mourning Day, a day to honor the friends and loved ones who had passed on since the previous solstice. In short, a time for the Salashi to celebrate their achievements and contemplate their regrets.

Which meant the Apricot decks would see more than the usual high spirits. There would be more of everything, except restraint.

But not for Onderishta, child of Intermala, one of the city's highest-ranking investigators, and the unofficial operative for the Safroy family. Tonight was a work night, and while Onderishta was part of the bureaucrat class and drew a government salary, it was Lanilit parsu-Safroy defe-Safroy blah blah-Safroy—and, to a lesser extent, her family—who chose her assignments.

Onderishta's superior had explained everything on the day of her promotion. As one of the wealthiest and most powerful families in the city, the Safroys could turn government staff into personal servants—unofficially, of course—when the need arose. As it turned out, the need arose constantly. Safroy errands kept her busy through all her work hours and many of her private ones, too.

Not that Onderishta minded. It was a better job than most, even if it meant she was once again spending a Shieldsday—and holiday—evening sitting in a cafe on the edge of the High Apricot promenade without the company of Zetinna, her wife.

The only thing that could have made her job better would have been if her work actually accomplished something beyond the narrow interests of her noble parsu. Koh-Salash was a fucking sewer, and it really should have been the work of inspector bureaucrats like her to clean out all the shit.

By law, all bureaucrats were required to wear gray while on duty, and Onderishta wore green calf-length trousers and the multi-patterned vest of a reveler, with a discreet gray stripe on the lapel. But down here, an hour past sunset, when the only light came from the parts of Suloh's ribs not blocked by the Upgarden and Dawnshine decks above, no one could tell.

Drums began to pound in the platform hall across the promenade, and revelers cheered. Behind the slender wooden rail, crowds began to dance and sway as high-pitched flutes joined in. Beautiful shirtless boys walked the edge of the platform, selling watered-down brandy from a tray. Business was brisk despite the early hour.

Not a typical Shieldsday.

Onderishta watched groups of young women—and the young men who trailed behind them—hurry for the entrance. Most of the women had green, red, and black designs painted on their arms, hands, and nails, but few of their male pursuers made the effort. What had been sacred in Lost Selsarim had become mere ornamentation in exile. Not that it mattered. Selsarim was gone. They were all Salashi now.

The roof of the platform hall was nothing but stretched, bone-white canvas, with a few holes to allow light in and body heat out. The parts of the hall far from one of the canvas holes were dimly lit by paper lanterns. It was just bright enough inside to recognize the face of your friends and to see the spatter of brandy stains on the cloth above.

Sailsday's Regret was only open one night a week, but they made the most of it.

It was owned by Harl Sota List Im, the most important ganglord in Koh-Salash, and according to Onderishta's employer, this was the likely spot for tonight's exchange.

What, exactly, was being exchanged had not been shared with her, which was annoying. No, more than annoying, it was infuriating. Unfortunately, as a commoner, it wasn't her place to show her feelings to the family who doled out her assignments, not if she wanted to keep her job.

Onderishta glanced around the promenade. There were the usual sit-down drinking places like the one she was in—although hers, being built against the eastern edge of the deck, offered a cool sea breeze. That was why they charged triple for their weak tea and cheap brandy. Nearby were body-painters sitting on their mats, shops that sold roasted strips of everything from cow to mouse, privy shops, and of course the alleys that ran between them all. Respectable citizens kept to the promenade. Addicts—stains of white tar on their faces visible in the distance—and kids in street gangs loitering in the alleys, giving the city constables a wide berth. The ironshirts in their gleaming steel did their best to keep the peace, for what it was worth.

She spotted a huge figure leaning against a pillar. The man's face was not visible, but she could see a maul strapped to his broad back. Presumably, he was a bodyguard for one of the dancers. Mauls were popular weapons for intimidation, and only certain classes were allowed to carry long weapons.

Two ironshirts in full armor appeared at the top of the deck stairs, silhouetted by the glowing bones behind them. Onderishta immediately had a bad feeling about them, and she quickly realized it was well founded. They scanned the promenade and moved toward her as soon as they spotted her.

"If you salute me," she said as they came near, "I'll have you both reassigned to latrine duty."

The nearest soldier, a tall woman with a crooked nose, had already begun to bend her elbow. She froze in place. Onderishta stood and sighed heavily as she fished her token from beneath her tunic.

"We don't need to see your identification," the second soldier said. He was a squirrelly-looking little guy. "We know—"

"You're going to look at this token as though you're searching for someone." Onderishta handed it over. "Then you're going to hand it back, and do the same with three other well-fed middle-aged women on the promenade, preferably ones with a bit of gray on top like me. You're going to act as though you're searching for someone specific but can't find them. After that, you're going to go into the Sunken Drum, find your captain, and explain how close you came to ruining my surveillance. Now give my token back and stop treating me like your boss."

The woman with the crooked nose suddenly leaned in close to Onderishta, as though about to threaten her. When she stepped back, she had Onderishta's tea cup in hand. She gulped the contents and tossed the cup back onto the table with contemptuous carelessness, then strolled away.

Prickles ran down Onderishta's back. By the fallen gods, she'd told the constables to stop treating her like the boss, and they'd done it. If she wanted to maintain her disguise as a common bystander, she had to take that insult in silence.

As the cafe owner rushed to bring her a fresh cup, all the while clucking his tongue at the *rudeness* of these young constables, Onderishta watched them harass another older woman with the same sullen disdain.

It had been a good piece of improvisation. She'd have to remember that constable.

Fay Nog Fay, her second-in-command, was standing beside a stall that sold long strips of something that was supposed to be lamb. He pulled a blue scarf from his sleeve and wrapped it around his neck.

That was the signal. Onderishta sat back just in time to see Second Boar push through the crowd.

Ten years ago, there'd been a whole crowd of street kids who chose the "Boar" name, a crowd of cousins, friends, and cousins of friends. Paper Boar, Rainy Boar, Copper Boar…they were quite the sizable young crew. They were led by a gigantic kid with wild hair who called himself Front Boar because he stood in front of all the others when there was danger. Of course, standing in the front—like trying to claim a tough-sounding name the way their cousins Iron Boar and Steel Boar had—was a good way for a kid in a street gang to make a target of himself. He did not last long.

Second Boar was his younger brother but he grew up to be, if anything, even larger than Front. He stood nearly six and a half feet tall, with massive shoulders, arms, and gut. He looked more bull than boar, even with that big bald head, but he was smart and tenacious enough to rise within Harl's organization, although that meant he'd left the other Boars behind.

In this heat, most people wore trousers that barely passed their knees and vests without tunics, but Second had dressed like a magistrate: long black trousers, white tunic, green vest, untied green sash. Still, no matter how distinguished the clothes, no one could have mistaken him for anything but a criminal, not with that face.

Revelers gave him a wide berth as he strode the promenade. A pair of lithe young women in silk vests edged toward him carefully, smiling as they offered him a taste from the jug they carried. He brushed them off. Our boy Second was not easily distracted from his assigned task.

Rueful grins on their faces, the young women headed toward the Sunken Drum, but not without an apologetic glance at Onderishta first. Selsarim Lost! Who trained these people in undercover work?

As Second turned to survey the growing crowd, Onderishta lifted her cup to her mouth to hide her face. Last year, she'd sicced the ironshirts on him once before, had him dragged to the south tower, and interrogated him about Harl's business. If he recognized her now, he hid it well.

When she looked up, she saw him touch the left side of his vest to reassure himself something was there. Perfect.

He entered the platform hall with little more than a nod to the gate man—prompting a halfhearted groan from those who had to pay—then plunged into the crowd.

Fay Nog Fay went in right behind him.

Onderishta stood. She was already unhappy. Fay was supposed to signal that the exchange had been made by taking off his scarf again, but Second was late and the crowds early. She couldn't see Fay or Second Boar amidst the dancing bodies.

* * *

RULENYA, CHILD OF RASHILA, thrust her hands in the air, feeling the pounding of the drums through her whole body. She loved coming to Sailsday's Regret, loved the bounce in the wooden platform, but most of all she loved the kettledrums. This was her element. This was what she worked all week for.

"It's like I'm going to fucking war!" she shouted at whatshisname, the guy who was paying for tonight. Haliyal, that was it. Haliyal did as he was told. Haliyal had brought a jug to her stall before the evening began so she could get her wobble going. Only a fool tried to start a drunk on the overpriced swill at a platform hall.

"Sure, baby!" Haliyal shouted back. A boring answer from a boring guy.

As the years wore on, the guys had become less fun. They had less power and more desperation. The really hot ones barely gave her a second glance. Rulenya was still beautiful, but nobody stayed young forever. She just needed to keep whatshisname from getting what he wanted too early, because then he'd stop buying drinks.

"MORE!" she shouted as another boy circled the rail. Haliyal shoved through a circle of girls and returned with two cups. She took both and downed them, to his clear delight. They were stronger than expected. She cheered. He cheered. She threw the cups toward the outer edge of the canvas roof, knowing they'd fall into the pouch at the rim to be collected, rinsed, and filled again.

None of the idiots here were as drunk as she was. She was drunk enough to jump, drunk enough to dance with wild abandon, drunk enough to cheer at the warlike kettledrum beat. When she collided with other dancers, she was drunk enough to risk relieving them of petty trinkets like combs or bracelets, because these people were nothing but helpless petals. She was even drunk enough to fuck this boring guy with the desperate smile, once he'd bought a few more cups. She was drunk enough to feel sure she could give him what he wanted without coming down with another Long Hangover.

What she wasn't, though, was drunk enough.

A huge, meaty hand landed on Haliyal's shoulder and shoved him aside. He turned, fists clenched, until he got a look at the man who shoved him. He was dressed in green and black, wearing sash, vest, and long trousers on the sweaty platform, but his bald head and scarred knuckles marked him as one of Harl Im's heavies. Haliyal raised both hands in a placating gesture, but the big man didn't seem to notice.

The big guy's hand pressed the bottom of his vest against his gut. Rulenya had picked enough pockets to know what that meant. He was carrying something valuable.

"Come on!" she shouted, pulling her useless date—her walking wallet—into the big guy's wake. Haliyal didn't like it, but she kept him dancing and moving along. Suddenly, it wasn't enough for him to buy the drinks. They were listening to war music, and if wanted to have her, he would have to plunder.

"I can't challenge that guy," he shouted, and she rolled her eyes.

"Of course not! Look!" She turned and rubbed her ass against his hips, and they both saw the big guy pull a folded leather packet from his vest and pass it to a skinny little guy with three rattail braids on his forehead. The little guy passed back a coin pouch. "*Him* you can challenge. Let's go to fucking war!"

The two gangsters turned away from each other. The big guy continued moving away toward the rail, but the little guy pushed his way right toward them. Haliyal did just as he was told. He danced and spun until the gangster with the little braids had just passed him, then he punched him, hard, behind the ear.

The man staggered against Rulenya and she righted him quickly, turning him so his back was to Haliyal, who had already disappeared into the crowd. Rulenya glanced at the big gangster, but his back was to them. As the big man moved away, he revealed a pale, foreign-looking little guy who was flinging his blue scarf into the air in time with the beat. He looked like an idiot, but something about his expression made her wary.

She tucked the folded leather packet into her trousers and vanished into the crowd.

* * *

ONDERISHTA NEEDED STILTS.

Her second had vanished in the crowd. She approached the entrance with the captain and a pair of constables, glaring up at the gate men. They glared back. During business hours, the platform hall could deny entry to anyone they pleased, even the city constables. This was one of Harl's places, and he was the only gangster in the city with a parsu's protection. If Onderishta ordered her soldiers to push through that gate without cause, she would have to answer to the High Watch.

A third gate man had come to reinforce the usual pair, and all carried hatchets in their belts. Harl's people were usually smart enough to leave their weapons alone when dealing with ironshirts, but her own people kept their hands on their truncheons, just in case.

Tiptoeing, Onderishta tried to peer through the crowd, but it was pointless. The dance floor was three steps above the promenade. She couldn't have peered over the heads of those revelers if she'd stood on a chair.

Just then, the tail end of Fay's blue scarf appeared above the heads of the crowd. It snapped upward as though he was aiming at a fly, then it snapped upward again.

The captain saw it too. She quirked her head at Onderishta. "Is he signaling, do you think?"

"He must have taken it off to fling it into the air, right?"

"So," the captain said uncertainly, "that's the signal?"

Onderishta suppressed her irritation. "Let's move. And there's our boy."

She pointed to the hulking figure of Second Boar as he emerged from the crowd. At the same moment, the captain blew her whistle and her ironshirts surged forward.

The gate men were smart. They left their hatchets in their belts, extended their arms and shouted in protest. They wouldn't fight constables, and they wouldn't threaten them—no one wanted another Downscale War—but they could stall so the criminals they protected had a chance to get away. If they did anything more than that, the ironshirts could treat them like belligerents and start breaking bones.

The constables formed a wedge and pushed through, slapping the gate men's hands aside with leather gauntlets. The music faltered and stopped. Dancers spilled over the railing like a flood breaching a seawall, fleeing in a panic. More ironshirts left their stations around the promenade and rushed toward them.

Second Boar walked to the rail and stopped. People were watching, and running away was undignified for such a big man. He had a rep to consider. The dance floor was nearly empty, and Second strolled calmly toward the gathering ironshirts.

The constables lowered their shoulders and tried to knock him down, but Second braced and cast them aside. The screams of the panicked revelers mixed with the shouts of her ironshirts. The ironshirts leaped on him—three, then four, then five—all shouting at him to drop to the ground. Instead, he planted his feet and twisted his body like a wrestler, slamming constables against each other and pitching them to the floor. He did not give a single fuck about being labeled a belligerent.

Enough. Onderishta took two running steps, leaped upward, then brought her considerable weight down on the back of Second Boar's left knee.

He toppled sideways, bringing the constables with him. They knelt on his arms and ankles, and he finally gave up the struggle.

Onderishta stood over him. "Hello, Second. It's been a while."

His only answer was to glower at her. Fine. The pocket on the left side of his vest bulged a bit. A coin purse. She opened it.

There were five golden Harkan regents inside. The diameter of each was longer than her middle finger. One of the ironshirts whistled. This was enough for Onderishta to buy the city block that she lived in.

"Never knew you were a thief," Second Boar said, "Onderishta, child of Intermala."

So he knew her full name! She was sure he meant it as a kind of threat, but she wasn't impressed. "Second Boar"—best to pretend she didn't know his real name—"you'll get these back if you come along peacefully and we don't charge you with a crime."

"No law against carrying coin, is there?"

"That depends on what you just sold." The platform was almost completely empty now. The band gathered around the hat they used to collect their tips, muttering over the contents. By now, Fay should have had the courier—and the item Second had been carrying in the left side of his vest—in hand.

She didn't see him, and that made her nervous.

To the captain, she said, "Take him to the south tower. I'll want to talk to him there."

One of the constables hurried toward her. "Your boy says there's a problem."

Of course, Fay Nog Fay was no boy. He would turn thirty in less than a month. His small, lithe body, not so different from the tray boys selling cups at the rim of the hall, made people underestimate him. Also, he did not have Salashi blood, so the constables were not inclined to treat him with respect. At least they no longer called him "good sir yellow," which had been intolerable.

As Onderishta hurried toward him, she could see that he was very angry.

"I lost the courier and the package both," Fay said, his fists clenched at his side. "I was right there for the exchange, but the big oaf turned suddenly and knocked me into the crowd. By the time they stopped shoving me around, the courier was gone, like a fucking ghost." He shook his head. "I wrecked the whole operation."

Although Fay kept his chin up, his cheeks were flushed. His pale Carrig complexion—how was his skin tone supposed to be yellow?—showed embarrassment so easily.

"The fault isn't yours," Onderishta told him, and she meant it. The fault was hers. The operation needed more bodies, but who could she have recruited? More young women who shrugged apologetically at her?

Fay was the only one she trusted to perform his duties competently, and soon he would be promoted to lead his own unit. In fact, it would have happened already if he'd been of Salashi heritage. Where he would find qualified people of his own, she had no idea.

"I'd recognize the courier if I saw him again," Fay insisted. "I saw his face."

Onderishta moved to the rail. She had a decent view of the promenade, but nothing immediately caught her eye. Some of the revelers who had been driven from the hall lingered nearby, watching. Others moved to other platforms, or food stalls, or privy shops.

But she saw no furtive movements, no little clusters of people excited about what one of them was holding, no crooked grins of contemptuous triumph.

The new Safroy heir had given her this assignment, and he'd stressed its importance multiple times. He'd wanted that package, whatever it was, intercepted.

He wasn't going to get it. Not tonight.

"Fuck."

* * *

SOMEHOW, HALIYAL SEEMED TO know where Rulenya would slip out of the platform hall, because he was there, waiting. Or maybe he was just lucky. Fine. It didn't matter. Rulenya was willing to share the score, whatever it was. She swung both legs over the rail and gestured at the nearest tray boy. Haliyal bought again, but this time he kept one for himself. His hand trembled as he drank.

They moved with the crowd, putting Sailsday's Regret far behind them. Haliyal clutched at her arm until she showed him that she'd snatched the leather packet.

"That was—"

"Bold," Rulenya said. If she'd let him finish the sentence with *stupid* or *risky*, it would have ruined the mood. They'd faced the enemy and triumphed! They'd robbed a gangland heavy like he was a pretty little petal waiting to be plucked. Shouldn't they celebrate?

"You have very deft hands," he said, absentmindedly checking his own purse.

She laughed. "Of course!" Raising one hand, she pretended to hold a slender brush. "How else do you think I paint such intricate designs?"

There was a paper lantern at the entrance to a privy shop, and they strolled toward it. A smart thief would wait until they got home to open the packet, but then Haliyal would want her right then and there, without spending another knot on her wobble, and the Long Hangover would still be sniveling in her bed.

Besides, she was drunk enough to take a risk.

Standing very, very close together, Rulenya opened the leather pouch.

Inside was an ear. It was the most perfect little ear you could imagine, like the ear of a child. Smaller even than her daughter's, maybe.

But this hadn't come from a child of humankind. It was not brown, but bluish-white, and the skin reflected the lamplight with dozens of tiny flecks of color.

"Oh, fuck," Haliyal muttered.

Then she realized what she was holding. It was an ear from one of the glitterkind.

"Selsarim Lost," Rulenya said. "We're fucking rich."

CHAPTER THREE

There were no gardens in the Woodgarden deck, and as far as Kyrioc could tell, there never had been.

Nestled snugly inside the midpoint of Yth's rib cage, Woodgarden was a long crescent that connected both free ribs by way of the collarbones, and it was one of the oldest decks in Koh-Salash. Once the refugees from Lost Selsarim discovered the properties of the skywood growing out of those bones, they must have fallen on it like starving children on a long-abandoned larder. That first harvest must have made them rich, even if they were still learning how best to exploit this godly treasure.

But those days were long gone, and the wealth created from those early harvests had found its way elsewhere. All that remained in Woodgarden were the ancient plankways, decks, and buildings built to accommodate those original workers.

There was still skywood to be cut, still growing just as slowly as it always had, but now it was chained off. Private guards made sure that only the approved woodcutters, working for the approved owners, harvested the bounty of a dead god who had once benefited all.

As the fortunes of Woodgarden shrank, so had its dignity. There were still hardworking men and women living in the cramped apartments built upon the ribs, but they were fewer every year, just as there were fewer tea shops, bakery stalls, private tutors, and buskers. Every year saw more elderly folk sleeping on the planks, wild kids no one could control, and jobs for private guards willing to dole out bruises and broken bones with glee.

Control of the skywood that grew here had been seized by a few noble families, admir-Something and defe-Nobodycares. Wealth flowed uphill to them, and the only thing that trickled back down was sewage.

Kyrioc, child of No One, had learned Woodgarden's secrets well over the past year. He had returned to Koh-Salashi quietly, like a criminal. In truth, he would have preferred to go anywhere else: the disputed Harkan plains, the Free Cities, the lavish Carrig ports. He couldn't. He'd made a promise.

So, he'd wandered through Mudside, the darkest part of Koh-Salash, which the light of sun—and of the murdered god of the sun—rarely touched. In this city, the poorest did not even have a right to see the sky. If someone else had the money, they could just build a new neighborhood over yours, replacing day-, star-, god-, and moonlight with a network of sewer pipes that were supposed to be sealed against leaking. And if they built it from skywood, you couldn't even daydream about burning it down.

Kyrioc had settled in Woodgarden. Down in Mudside and other low places, people lived in an inescapable shadow economy of crime and exploitation. In so-called respectable parts of the city, Salashi lived and worked under the watchful eye of the city bureaucracy. Woodgarden fell in between. There was honest work to be done, but it meant living among thieves.

Horizontal shafts of golden light shone between the buildings. Downcity, sunrise was the brightest time of the day, because the sunlight slanted from the east and reached far into the interior. As the sun rose, the shadow of the decks above threw people into gloom.

Kyrioc walked down the broad plankways to the market. He preferred the early hours, when vendors were too busy setting up their stalls to chat. He bought three buns, a triple order of boiled rice, and a bundle of purple carrots. After a moment's hesitation, he spent extra for a loaf of fresh bread and two small crocks of preserved fish.

The florist was next. Red poppies. Thirty of them, which he was buying a day early to make sure she had plenty in stock. She was startled by the order. She muttered that the next day would be Mourning Day, yes, and she'd ordered extra poppies and daisies and lilies and roses, of course, but if her very first sale was thirty, well my goodness, she wasn't sure if she was truly prepared for the season, and...

Kyrioc endured her nervous chatter without meeting her gaze and she quickly lost momentum. He paid, then waited while she tied the bouquet into three equal bundles. When she handed the flowers to him, he accepted them with his left hand. She glanced down at his discolored flesh and offered a rote condolence. He was already walking away before she could finish.

At the market entrance, two groups of boys challenged and insulted each other, their hands on their hatchets. They were fifteen or sixteen, old enough to fight from the walls or rigging but not old enough to understand what was at risk.

Nearby shopkeepers pulled their goods back into their stalls or closed their shutters. Brawling street gangs were bad for business. The constables who were supposed to be patrolling this part of the deck must have been sleeping off a drunk, and the private guards hadn't arrived yet. Someone needed to step in before violence erupted.

Kyrioc kept his head down and hurried up the plankway toward home.

The shop where he lived and worked was inside a four-story building constructed against the most vertical part of Yth's last free rib on the eastern side. The structure was mounted on three thick trunks of skywood sawed off at the edge of the foundation and scarred so they could not be sawed further. No door barred entrance to the building atrium, which extended from the floor to the open space in the roof, although there was damage to the jamb where hinges had once been mounted. Kyrioc slipped inside, then climbed the stairs to the third floor.

As on every floor, three businesses overlooked the atrium, with six small apartments on either side. There was nothing on the northern wall but shuttered windows. Older residents said that, when the building was new, Suloh's dull orange light shone onto all of Yth's bones and into their homes, too. Since the deck for Low Apricot had been built above, light had become scarce. The opening above the atrium could have been boarded over for all the good it did now.

Kyrioc climbed to the third floor. The central shop sold cheap brandy and even cheaper whisky, with a quiet but very lucrative side business distributing white tar. The shop on the eastern side had been shuttered. The former owner sold skewers of roasted meat, but her love of tar made her nod off beside the fire too often. The landlady finally lost patience and confiscated her equipment. It wasn't legal, but tar heads rarely had the coin to go to the magistrates. Now the shop stood empty.

On the western end of the building was a pawnshop. Kyrioc wasn't the owner. He was the sole employee and the occupant of the tiny attached room. The owner kept a cot for himself in the storeroom for the rare occasions when he turned up. More often, he was out in the city on extended benders, drinking himself blind, returning only when his purse was light.

Which meant the shop was Kyrioc's to run. Most of their stock came from petty thieves eager to go next door for a jug—or something stronger—but there were also mothers desperate to make their rent, street thugs hoping to buy their way into a better occupation, and gamblers sure their luck was about to turn around.

Those who came to buy were a higher class of people, or believed themselves to be. They had jobs and clung desperately to Woodgarden's fading respectability. All they had to do was pretend they didn't know where their purchases came from.

Kyrioc unlocked the heavy front door, entered, then shut and barred it. The owner, Eyalmati, lay snoring in the back room. Kyrioc gently shut the storeroom door. Better not to wake the old man if he didn't have to. In his tiny chamber, he set the bouquet in the remnants of yesterday's clean water. Then he returned to the shop and slid open the shutter on the barred window. Open for business.

The first few hours of the day were typically a busy time. Snatch-and-grab thieves and alley thugs liked to unload the night's loot as quickly as possible, but this was his second summer solstice in the shop, and just like last year, Kyrioc had only one seller.

It was Riliska. She appeared at his window only a few minutes after he opened, pressing her small, dirty face against the bars. "Good sir, I have something for you. It was a gift from a noble lady!" Her high, bright voice rang in the dim hall.

"You worked last night?" Despite himself, Kyrioc felt a faint glimmer of happiness at her company.

Riliska was only nine years old. Her mother, Rulenya, was a talented hand painter in the traditional style, but she'd already been thrown out of three high-end shops in Upgarden and Dawnshine for her drinking.

Last spring, she had given her brushes, paints, and blanket to Riliska. The girl set up a station near the constables, who were sometimes willing to shoo thieves away from her while she painted people's hands and nails. Strictly speaking, it wasn't begging—begging was illegal—but she wasn't being paid for her sophisticated skills.

Not that Rulenya cared, as long as there were a few coins to be had at the end of the night.

"I did! I did this nice lady's thumbnails, and after she paid me, she offered me a set of finger chimes as a tip! She had a little box of them, some copper, some silver, some wooden ones that went *clack clack*. I didn't like those. Listen to this!"

She lifted her hand. She had a pair of steel finger chimes, and when she struck them together, they made a high, clear, beautiful tone.

Kyrioc had heard better. "Pretty."

"So? How much will you give me for them?" She dropped the finger chimes into the tray. Kyrioc slid them beneath the barred windows.

He examined them quickly, feeling a familiar stony gloom returning. It was unlikely that a noble of even the lowest rank would own finger cymbals. More likely they came from a merchant's daughter with a few cheap gifts from suitors in her pockets. These probably cost three silver beams from a stall in Low Market. Kyrioc could probably get half a beam for them. He set a tiny silver coin in the tray. "One silver whistle."

"One?" she protested. "Only one?"

"You shouldn't steal things."

She didn't try to correct him. "But these sound great! Try them!"

Kyrioc snatched up his coin and dropped the cymbals back into the tray. "Your choice."

She pouted, then nudged the cymbals toward him. He dropped the coin in the tray, tossed the cymbals into the box of goods he would take to Low Market next week, then recorded the transaction in the ledger. Just one more stolen object circulating through—

"Good sir, I don't know why you're so mean to me."

Kyrioc stopped writing. He'd just treated this little girl like one of the snatch-and-grab tar heads who hung on his bars, breathing their corpse breath onto him. She was just a dirty kid in a tattered shirt. A good kid, too, considering the way her mother was bringing her up.

It wasn't like she was going to buy herself a twist of white tar with the money he gave her. She'd be lucky if her mother didn't take it.

He knew better than this. Kyrioc unwrapped a corner of the loaf, letting the bakery smell fill the air.

The little girl's stomach growled loud enough for him to hear. "Do you have *fresh bread*?"

Kyrioc stood, unbarred the shop door, and let Riliska inside. He barred the door again and shuttered the shop window—no other customers were in sight—then led her into his chamber. She followed quietly, keeping her hands at her sides, while he set the cloth sack of food on the table and removed the bouquet from the bowl of water.

"Wash your hands," he said. "Face, too."

"Thank you, good sir," she said brightly, then did as she was asked. While she scrubbed, Kyrioc fetched two small bowls and filled them with rice. Then he tore the loaf in half and gave her the smaller piece. He also gave her the smallest carrot and one of the crocks.

Riliska pulled up her chair and sat opposite. The first thing she picked up was the bread.

"Eat everything," Kyrioc said.

"Except *that*." She held a flat palm over the carrot. *Stop right there.*

"Haven't you eaten carrots before? They're a little bit sweet."

That made her curious. She held it sideways and nibbled at the middle.

Her eyes lit up.

Once the carrot was gone, she opened the crock and dipped the bread inside. When Kyrioc was her age, he'd hated preserved fish, but he'd been fed by servants and could eat all the meat and salt he wanted.

She glanced at his discolored left hand, then the scar on his face. "Good sir, were you a soldier?" He didn't answer. "Sometimes, I hear people talking about you. They aren't always nice. Were you a heavy? Some people think you're in hiding because you killed someone. Are you an assassin? Do you work for smugglers from Carrig?"

Riliska had asked these questions at his table before. Kyrioc did not eat with her often—Rulenya had forbidden it—but today was a holiday, and he'd suspected the girl would have no one to look after her. It seemed he was right.

Still, if she was caught here, eating at his table, Rulenya could make a scene and the landlady might demand Eyalmati send him away. Eyalmati himself didn't mind the girl's company—only a month earlier, he'd stumbled drunkenly into the room and joined the two of them for a late dinner—but no one wanted to risk pissing the landlady off.

But if she was hungry, he fed her. If she was dirty, he gave her water to wash. If she had questions, he listened. It was nothing, almost literally the absolute least he could do to interact with the world around him in a way that didn't involve the exchange of coin. She spoke to him, and he could answer without having to hold his temper in or startling in fear or rushing away with his skin crawling.

It was the only part of his day—of his entire life—that he actually enjoyed.

But these were the only questions that he didn't answer, for her sake.

"It doesn't matter what the neighbors say," he said. "What do you think? Do you think I'm a heavy? Do you think… You're not afraid of me, are you?"

It surprised him how much he cared about her answer.

"Well…" She hesitated, and Kyrioc had a sudden awful certainty that she would say *yes*. Instead, she said, "You don't exactly look like a *respectable* person." She put extra emphasis on the word to show her pride in it. "That's why you're here in Woodgarden, right? Because there are some respectable people here, but they're the worst. But that's okay. Mom says we're not respectable either."

Riliska smiled at him, and he felt a sudden, absurd rush of gratitude toward her. He glanced down at his bread and tore off a piece.

"Is this the place where glitterkind come from?"

A chill ran down Kyrioc's back. "What do you mean?"

"Well, some kids were saying that glitterkind are kept in gardens so they'll grow."

"And?"

"Well, the name of this deck is Woodgarden, which makes it sound like it was a really nice place once, and those kids said that before the upper decks of the city were built, glitterkind were just lying around where anyone could take a nibble. Do you think that's true?"

"What I heard," he said, "is that glitterkind need sunshine and grass to grow. There's no grass in Woodgarden."

That disappointed her, but her mood rallied quickly. She held up her left hand. "I've learned to make yellow." The nail of her pinky had been painted yellow, with a few slender red lines. It took him a moment to realize the lines suggested the face of a wise, smiling cat.

"I didn't know yellow was possible," Kyrioc said.

Riliska's eyes were bright and her smile broadened. "It's a very rare color. A shop in Upgarden started offering it weeks ago, and everyone wanted to know how it was made. Her competitors offered her gold, or even the means to sell her color overseas, and some people had her followed everywhere, or even tried to have her collared. Do you want to know how I worked it out? *I watched*. I snuck into her shop while she was arguing with the soldiers about her warrant. Her rafters were full of clutter, so I hid up there and waited. Before she went to bed, I saw her at her bench. Everyone thought she was buying mushrooms because she liked to *eat* them, but only I figured it out."

"She was making the color from mushrooms?"

"Yep! A special kind."

"Where did you get the mushrooms to make your own?"

She looked cagey for a moment as she tried to think up a likely story. "I bought them, of course. With tip money."

"You shouldn't steal."

There was a loud rapping against the shop shutter. "It's probably no one," Kyrioc said. He went into the shop, leaving the door to his room ajar, then slid the shutter back.

It was Rulenya, still drunk from the night before.

"Why aren't you open yet? Does your boss know you're still sleeping in? Well?"

"There's no business on the solstice holiday," Kyrioc answered wearily.

"There's me," she snapped. "I have business, but I suppose I'm nobody." She passed him a Harkan wedding robe, made of bright red silk with a pleated flannel lining. "You be careful with that! No stains."

She surprised him by accepting his first offer. He gave her a claim token. She had five weeks to buy it back, or he would take it up to Low Market and get a nice price for it. Although, considering the seam work and the fabric, Dawnshine might be more appropriate. It would be worth the trip. "Five weeks," he said. "Is that all?"

She began to lay things in the tray: A jade comb. Two steel knives, one with a spiked knuckle cover. Bangles made from copper and cheap, cloudy glass. A bronze ring. A tin flask.

Plucked from those too drunk to protest, no doubt. She'd had a productive holiday.

"Where's Riliska? Didn't she come by here yet?"

"You saw the shutter was closed."

His evasion only seemed to anger her further. "You better not be keeping her in that room of yours. If I find out you're messing with my little girl…" She craned her neck to the side and saw that the door to his little room was slightly open. "Who's in there with you? Open that!"

Kyrioc moved toward the door and opened it slightly. Riliska was nowhere to be seen, and neither was the meal. He pushed the door open all the way, letting Rulenya see the tiny table with a single bowl.

He closed it partway again and returned to the window. She seemed mollified, and a little resentful that her accusations had not been born out. "If you touch my daughter, I'll slash you. You won't even know it's coming."

"I'll give you five silver whistles for the lot."

It was an insulting price, but she surprised him again by accepting it. As he was marking the items in the ledger, Rulenya made smacking noises. The booze must have been wearing off.

She offered him a crooked smile. "You look like you can handle yourself. I like that in a man. Why haven't you picked up some of the silver in your boss's drawer and bought me a drink or two? I don't mind a scar if the brandy's flowing."

He paid her, slid the shutter closed, and sorted the items.

The sound must have stirred Eyalmati, because he stumbled out of the storage room and rummaged through the cash box. "Where's the rest?" he demanded, his words slurred.

Kyrioc stared at him. "It's Last Day. The solstice. You know how business is on Last Day."

Eyalmati shrank away from that look, then grumbled as he shuffled toward the hall. He'd left one whistle and three knots in the cash box for Kyrioc to finish out the day, and there was no telling when he'd be back.

Once the old man's wooden heels had thumped down the stairs, Kyrioc opened the bottom drawer, lifted the false bottom, and took out enough money to see him through the morning. Then he placed the Harkan robe into the five-week box at the back of the store room.

Everything suddenly seemed extraordinarily vivid—the glittering edges of the knives, the faces of the tiny statuettes, the rough steel surfaces of the tools on the shelf. It all seemed to be closing in on him, and he could hear the sounds of a faraway jungle. Human screams mingled with weird shrieks and—

No. No. Those were just memories. He was safe now. He was alone, with barred windows and doors—not to mention an entire city and miles of open water—between him and that place. He'd left those dangers behind.

But not their echoes. Kyrioc took deep breaths until he was able to unclench his fists.

He found Riliska standing at the table, the bundle of red poppies in her hand. A tiny flower was tucked through one of the ragged holes in her tunic. Her smile was bright and cheerful. "Don't they look pretty next to my skin?"

Before he could think about it, Kyrioc snatched them from her. "Don't take other people's things."

His hand trembled, and he felt sick to his stomach. He crossed the room and set the flowers back in the bowl of water.

Riliska followed. She slid the flower from her tunic and put it in with the rest, her tiny face downcast.

CHAPTER FOUR

Onderishta interrogated **Second Boar** through the night, but it was pointless without the package—whatever it contained—to hold over him. The sun had barely risen before upcity advocates battered at the gate, warrant for his release in hand. Harl's parsu had moved quickly. Second Boar must have been higher in the organization than she'd thought.

The warrant had been signed by Rueljun parsu-Lorrud ward-Lorrud defe-Lorrud admir-Lorrud hold-Lorrud, a respectable head of a respectable—but mostly apolitical—noble family. What's more, he must have been awakened in the middle of the night to do it. Not that she needed yet another fucking reminder that Harl wielded power beyond his station in life, but there it was, nonetheless.

Fay suggested they hold on to Second by pretending there was an error in the warrant, but the tower captain would not hear of it—especially, as she said, since they had no actual evidence of a crime. When Second Boar left, she looked relieved to be rid of him.

Onderishta followed Second out onto the Spillwater deck. She'd switched from her multicolored vest to a gray one and had put on a low, square cap. Uniforms were their own kind of armor.

"I had no idea you were so high up the slope," Onderishta said lightly. "Harl must think a lot of you to get you pulled so quickly."

"The eye must think a lot of me, too, to collar me for no reason."

Was this banter? Onderishta didn't think the big thug had it in him. "How did you win his trust?"

That was the end of the banter. He was smarter than he looked.

Onderishta stopped walking beside him. Next time. Next time.

* * *

TIN PAIL KNEW THE blow was coming but she didn't brace for it. She didn't roll with it, either. She just took it.

Rumor had it that Harl had been deadly with a hatchet in his younger days, but today, he was a sporting man. Today, he held a hammerball paddle.

They were on the roof of the club he owned—at least, he acted like he owned it, but he acted like he owned the whole city, so who could fucking tell—and Tin Pail was forced to kneel at the edge. Behind her was a four-story drop—high enough to kill or cripple her but not escape. Not that she cared to try.

Harl set a hammerball on the tee beside him. They were hollow, with some sort of animal bladder at the center, covered with yarn and leather, and sealed with rubber, making them fast, and light, and stiff enough to bounce hard if they hit hard.

Harl's first shot struck her just above the navel. She gasped at the pain and reeled, almost tipping back off the roof.

The only other sound came from Paper Mouse, her top lieutenant. He cried out in fear when he thought she might fall. Tin's bodyguard stood off to the side, his face impassive. He did exactly what he'd been told to do, which was nothing.

Harl sneered. He snapped his fingers and one of his heavies set another ball on the tee.

Tin Pail leaned forward, making her face impassive. She would not reel back at the next shot. If Harl wanted to kill her, he was going to have to throw her off, because fuck him.

The second ball struck the bony part of her right hip. Was he aiming for her crotch? She kept her hands at her side and made no noise this time. Harl fucking Sota List Im was not going to see her flinch again.

The third ball grazed her ear as it went by, and the pain from that one was different but no less intense. The fourth ball struck her right cheek just below her eye. This time, she reeled—she couldn't help it—but straightened herself quickly. The pain was disorienting and she thought her cheekbone might be broken.

"You are a fucking moron," Harl said in Carrig. His next shot glanced off her right bicep.

Tin Pail took it without complaint. Paper Mouse had the common sense to be staring shamefaced at his feet, his three front braids hanging over his eyes. Her wild-haired bodyguard stood near the rack of hammerball paddles—Harl kept several close in case his heavies needed to ruin someone's day—staring out across the city.

The sharp *crack* of paddles against balls echoed. All around them stood practice lanes for the local hammerball courts, and Harl was dressed in the thin, eggshell-white cotton trousers and tunic of a player. His feet were bare as if he'd just come off the grass, and his pale Carrig skin had obviously not been touched by the sun in weeks.

He laid the paddle on his shoulder, but Tin quashed the hope that her punishment was over. His hair was kept short and neat, and his chubby cheeks made him look like someone's kindly merchant uncle. He didn't even carry a knife or a hatchet anymore.

That air of respectability had been purchased with more than gold. It had taken blood, too. Salashi blood, like hers. "The lot of you are fucking morons. Imbeciles! All you had to do was make the exchange—to *take* what I was *giving* you—and you fucked it up."

The roof door swung open with a creak, and a gigantic man lumbered through. Tin Pail knew him well.

"You!" Harl waved the newcomer over. "Second Boar, you made the pass?"

The big bald Salashi shrugged. "There was no mistake, boss. I made the pass."

"You!" Harl gestured at Paper Mouse. "You speak Carrig?" Paper nodded. "What happened? How the fuck did you lose my package?"

Paper glanced at Tin, then looked at the floor.

"Well?"

Tin said, "I told him not—"

The boss whirled on her. "I'm not asking you! I'm asking him!"

"I told him not to speak," Tin said. "I'm in charge, so I'm responsible."

"Well, well," Harl said. He looked around the room at his heavies, all dressed like sober, respectable magistrates, all staring at her like hungry dogs. Few were Salashi. Most, like Harl, were foreign friends. Carrig. "Someone who knows how to run a crew. Why don't you answer my question, then? What the fuck happened?"

"He was attacked and robbed in the crowd." Tin kept her voice neutral. Any sign of what she really thought about Harl's plan to make the switch would piss him off further.

"Then you sent the wrong man!" Harl's eyes bulged and his cheeks wobbled as he shouted.

He sighed, lifted his paddle, and looked down its length. Tin glanced at her bodyguard, but he was still. Harl wasn't ready to kill her yet.

But he wasn't done talking, either. "I can't believe my uncle exiled me here, to live among these shit-eaters. These *refugees*." Tin Pail's back stiffened, but Harl didn't seem to notice. "You have no idea what's important and what isn't. No idea how to behave among your betters."

While watching hammerball volleys below, Tin Pail's bodyguard absentmindedly picked up a game paddle. While Harl continued his tirade, Second Boar lumbered toward him. Her bodyguard glanced up at his approach and set the paddle down. Second snatched it out of the rack anyway, shaking his head at the stupidity of the world. Her bodyguard turned toward him, the silver chimes in his red beard ringing faintly, but he had been ordered to do nothing, and he followed orders.

Harl pointed at Paper Mouse with his paddle. "This little shit rag lost my package, but you know what? I don't blame him. He's nothing. He's just another dumb, horny ape climbing through the branches of this blasphemy of a city." He stalked toward Tin. "I blame *you.*" Harl pressed his forefinger against Tin's head and pushed, making her lean toward the edge. "You trusted him with this job. *You.* That makes you responsible for this fuck-up. Tell me your name."

Tin Pail felt a chill run through her. Everyone became very still. "Tin Pail," she said.

"I don't mean your stupid street name. Don't you Salashi use *Stupid, child of Stupider*? *Lazy, child of Useless*? Don't you and your brother work for me? Tell me your real name."

"My real name is Tin Pail."

"That's what I thought you'd say. Get out. Take your dumb, horny ape and your sweaty, stinking northerner. You have three days to find my package, contents *intact.* Second Boar, go with them." Harl gave his paddle to one of his boys. He didn't need it to threaten people. "If you don't have my package by then, you might as well throw yourself into Undertower. It'll be an easier way to die than what I have planned for you."

In the street, Tin Pail spat into the gutter. Her blood was bright against the skywood deck.

Her bodyguard—she still couldn't bring herself to say his name aloud, or even think it—offered her a linen cloth, almost certainly stolen from Harl's club. She wiped her lips clean, then tossed the cloth aside.

A few passersby gave them guarded or suspicious looks. One didn't throw bloody cloths in the street in Upgarden, not unless you wanted to risk a fine. One also didn't wander the streets with a wild-haired Katr barbarian as a bodyguard. The cosh tended to notice that sort of thing.

Not that it mattered. Fuck the cosh. The people in the Upgarden decks were petals waiting to be plucked. They were nothing.

"First, we go to Low Market," Second Boar said. "The thief will want to sell, and we should put out the word what will happen to anyone who buys."

Tin Pail waved him off. "Do what you want. I'm going to get my brother first."

She found Wooden Pail exactly where she expected him to be, in a Low Apricot brothel called The Pelican Baths. He was wearing nothing but his steel necklace and his crazy smile. Tin figured he must have just woken up, because the girls were still asleep.

His smile faded when he saw his sister's face.

"What the fuck happened to you?"

"It went wrong last night, and Harl is pissed."

"I should have been there."

"Yes, you fucking should. Get dressed."

Wooden padded naked across the room toward the mannequin where his clothes were hung, but before he touched them, he fixed his hair in the mirror.

Tin went to the balcony and looked down at Low Market, which was directly north and below the Low Apricot decks. It was also open to the sun—at least, the upper parts were—having been built into Suloh's and Yth's massive pelvic girdles.

Second Boar could do as he pleased. Her people were already there, visiting full hospitals, canvas stalls selling medicinal tea, and everything in between. If their thieves were smart, they would stay far away from the Low Market decks. But they weren't smart. They'd stolen from her.

Wooden joined her on the balcony, wearing white silks trimmed with gold. He hadn't just been whoring. He'd been shopping, too. Ah, well, if they didn't find this ear for Harl, it wouldn't matter how much he'd spent.

Unless…

Wooden strapped on his long, slender knife, and his crazy smile returned. "I see you have a new boy in tow. One of Harl's?"

Tin started toward the door. "He is. Where we're going next, we'll need him."

CHAPTER FIVE

Sailsday's Regret was usually shuttered on Sailsday. Patrons took their regrets elsewhere. After closing, a little old woman swabbed away the sweat, blood, and brandy, tables were brought out, and the spot became an ordinary—if somewhat spacious—tea shop.

Not today. Today was Last Day, and the tea shop tables were still packed away. The platform hall would be a true platform hall again tonight, and once again, the crowds would be huge.

In fact, some had already begun to celebrate, laughing and drinking on the promenade, getting their hands painted, or shopping for a tunic to dance in.

So, the staff of Sailsday's Regret was quite busy loading casks of brandy and prepping for the evening when Second Boar lumbered in and pulled the manager aside. They spoke for only a few minutes, then Second returned to Tin Pail and her people.

For such a big man, he had an oddly high voice. "I'm going into the office, but Harl wants me to stick with you. Don't leave High Apricot without me." He went into the wooden building at the back of the platform and shut the door. The big gorilla was probably taking a nap.

The manager sent one of his cleaners on an errand. The only words Tin could make out clearly were *Low Market*. Clearly, Second Boar wasn't going to take on that mission himself. Tin was surprised. She hadn't pegged him as the type to give orders.

Tin gestured for the manager to approach. The manager bustled over, looking annoyed until he noticed her expression and the way her hand was resting on the hammer in her belt. He smiled and bowed.

They spent the afternoon pulling tray boys aside as they showed up for work. All were eager to help. None had seen anything useful.

In between those conversations, she had little to do except drink tea with Wooden and imagine the terrible things she would do to the thieves when they caught them.

* * *

FAY NOG FAY NERVOUSLY drummed his fingers on the tabletop, waiting for Second Boar's crew to do something interesting.

He'd tried to sleep when Onderishta ordered him to, but after three hours, he'd jolted out of a dream in which the constables collared him and presented an order—from the High Watch, no less—that he be shipped to the slave pens of Carrig.

It was stupid thing to be afraid of. Onderishta assured him that she couldn't get along without him and would never let him be taken away, but he'd lived his whole life enduring little reminders that he did not belong.

At least he didn't carry a slave's brand. His parents were the ones who'd fled their homeland for a new life. They were the ones who wore long sleeves in all weather to hide the slavers' marks. They were the ones who'd spent twenty years futilely applying for skin graft surgery to remove them. As for Fay, not only had he never set foot in Carrig, he'd never even left Koh-Salash. He might have looked like a foreign friend, but in his heart he considered himself Salashi.

He stood out among all these dark-skinned people. He knew that. He also knew some thought he ought to be kicked out of the bureaucratic service to open a position for one of the "Heirs of Selsarim."

His only real protection came from Onderishta, and he had just fucked things up for her when he'd lost the package Second Boar sold.

So, there he was, sitting in Onderishta's spot in the tea shop across the promenade from Sailsday's Regret, brooding about how vulnerable he was, when Second Boar returned with a crew of hungry-looking heavies.

Plus one wild-haired Katr barbarian.

While the heavies milled around, giving each other hard looks, the barbarian stood at the edge of platform and stared out at the crowds. Most passersby wouldn't meet his gaze for more than a moment, but he did not hesitate to stare at anyone, even the glowering ironshirts at their posts.

Fay didn't meet his gaze either, but the barbarian stepped over the rail and crossed the promenade, heading straight for him. Despite the summer heat, the man wore a long coat with a fur collar—the Katr loved their fur. They displayed it like jewelry in any climate. At least he had the sense to go without sleeves. Fay would have bet good silver coin that, under that long coat, the barbarian wore some sort of illegal long weapon.

The man came up the short stair and walked directly to Fay's table, then sat opposite him without invitation. Fay couldn't hide his surprise at being singled out. Did the man know he was an investigator, or was he looking to chat with another non-Salashi?

The owner approached nervously. He knew Onderishta well and would send a message if Fay was in danger. The intruder said nothing. He just laid a coin on the table and tapped the empty teapot beside it. The owner scooped up the money and, with a worried look at Fay, retreated to the kitchen.

It was rare to meet humankind with blue eyes, but the barbarian had them. To his surprise, Fay found them beautiful and a little mysterious. The barbarian's red hair and beard were matted and untidy—the result of deliberate neglect—but he was handsome in his own way: broad-shouldered, muscular, and covered with tiny scars.

The tea and an extra setting arrived. The barbarian refilled Fay's cup, then his own. They sat in silence, drinking their tea and regarding each other. Fay could not sense contempt or admiration in the Katr's expression, just a sullen, casual regard. He had no idea what the man thought of him, although he didn't imagine it was flattering.

The silence went on long enough that it became weird, and Fay wondered if he had been enlisted in some sort of competition to see who would give in and speak first. Since Fay didn't care one whit about any game except the one he and his boss were playing with Harl, he yielded and said, "Thank you for the tea."

The barbarian nodded. A faint chiming came with the movement, and Fay realized the man had tiny bells tied into his unkempt beard and hair.

"Are you lonely?" Fay was not usually interested in men, but exceptions could be made, especially if it helped Onderishta's case.

"A true man is never lonely," the barbarian answered in his thick, harsh accent.

Fay rolled his eyes. The worst thing about dealing with criminals every day—aside from the fact that they'd cut out your guts for a laugh—was that their macho bullshit was so fucking boring.

"True men just hide it better than most."

That earned a laugh. The barbarian lifted his cup in salute. "Sometimes, what others believe to be true about us is all the truth that matters."

Interesting. "My name is Fay Nog Fay. What's yours?"

"I am called Killer of Devils."

Fay couldn't hide his surprise. "That's not a street name."

"No, it is not." The barbarian set his cup down and leaned back. "Too boastful for your local street rats, yes? In Katr, our true names are spoken only when we are children at our mother's breast and adults beneath the bedcovers. Our community gives each of us a public name for the rest of the world. A name we earn."

"Do you have a lot of devils in your country? To kill?"

"They come often. They build houses beside our watering holes, fences across our grazing land, and towers atop our holy sites."

"Ah. And now you've come to a city full of devils. But here, you're the foreigner, right?"

Killer of Devils nodded. "That is true. I am now the foreign devil, but few here seem to mind."

Fay felt the sting of that, as though this foreigner had been reading his thoughts and knew he had been made welcome where Fay was not. "What work do you do?"

Shit. He'd wanted to change the subject and had pushed too fast. If he was going to ingratiate himself with someone in Harl's organization, he couldn't afford to be clumsy.

Killer leaned forward. "You know the answer to that question, just as I know who you are and what you do, Fay Nog Fay. You have no secrets here."

The hair on the back of Fay's neck stood on end. Would staking out Sailsday's Regret be the mistake that got him killed? Onderishta didn't even know he was here.

Fay held himself very still. He wasn't a fighter, but he could run like a—

"Do not run." Killer held up his hand, then refilled their cups. Once again, he seemed to be reading Fay's thoughts. "You have nothing to fear from me. In fact, I come to you in hope that we might benefit each other."

Fay kept both feet flat on the floor. If the barbarian made a move for him, he'd drop to the floor and roll under the rail. "In what way?"

Killer set down his cup a little too hard, then leaned forward and lowered his voice. "I know you are searching for a certain package. Do you know what is inside it?" Fay didn't answer. "Neither do I. However, if I find it before you do, I may decide that I want nothing to do with it. If I needed to get in touch with you, to tell you where and when you could locate the package, how would I do that?"

Fay took another sip of tea and did his best to keep his expression calm. They didn't have the package either. Whatever was being transferred had been snatched by someone else.

And they didn't know who.

"Why would you want to give this package to me?"

"I am not, you understand, a criminal by nature. It might be to my benefit to alert you to its location."

"How so?"

Killer drained his cup and set it on the table with another bang. "Do you understand how honor works among my people?"

Fay shrugged. "Let me guess. What you do matters less than what people think you do."

Killer sighed. "I seek an end to obligations that I find onerous. I would prefer to return to my home. There are no mighty enemies here for me to fight. This city"—he gestured to the glowing bones down the long plankway—"is cursed. No humankind should have settled here, inside the corpses of two gods murdered while they were fucking. Yth's corpse should not have been desecrated by the cutting of skywood. The light from Suloh's bones was not meant to illuminate every back-alley whore and cutpurse.

"This land is *traifa*—forbidden. Four hundred years of blasphemy is the only legacy of Koh-Salash, and when doom comes, it will come swiftly." He saw something in Fay's expression that made him smile briefly, but he quickly became sullen again. "Perhaps you do not agree. It does not matter. I long for home. You long to break the hold foreign criminals have on this city. I believe that means we have common interests. Is that enough to convince you I am not trying to deceive you?"

Fay shrugged again. Of course it wasn't. "Sure. Why not? Tell me who you work for and how they get white tar into the city."

The barbarian's morose expression darkened. "I am not a spy. I am not an informant for the eye. You will either allow me to contact you at the time of my choosing, or we must farewell."

Fay sipped his tea to give himself time to think.

The most obvious way to pass a message was through the owner of the tea shop they were sitting in, but he wouldn't want the city's criminal network to know the proprietor was that friendly with the city's bureaucrats, especially the investigator branch. "In Low Market, there's a woman named Shah Til Shell who sells Carrig carpets. Her stand is near the northern end of Undertower. Give her a message, and I'll normally get it within the hour."

Killer nodded and stood. "I will return to my comrades and report that I recognized you and threatened your life. You should leave this deck immediately."

The tiny bells in his beard chimed as he turned away.

* * *

AT FIRST, TIN PAIL suspected the tray boys were playing with her. They seemed so eager to please but had nothing to offer. Eventually, she realized they saw her as a gateway to a supposedly easy life. A heavy's life.

But no one had seen the exchange or the robbery. No one had seen a pickpocket at work. No one had even seen someone they *suspected* of being a pickpocket.

Her bodyguard—she wished he would accept a proper Salashi street name, but he absolutely refused—stepped up close to her and spoke quietly. She could barely hear him over the music. "Arrangements have been made."

Good. No foreign friend was going to run her out of Koh-Salash. This was her city. *Hers.*

Before she could respond, the manager brought her a cup of the hall's cheap brandy. She'd spoken to all the tray boys from the night before, he told her, and the guards, too. If there was nothing else, the manager needed to open. The musicians had arrived—which Tin already knew because those fucking drums were giving her a headache—and they were turning away customers. Tonight would be one of the busiest nights—

The musicians! Tin knocked the cup of brandy to the floor as she pushed by him.

They were on a small stage, just four feet above the crowd. To the drummers, all seated, the customers were a sea of bobbing heads, but the flute players stood during the show.

It turned out that none of the musicians had seen the handoff or the robbery, but a flute player had recognized a pickpocket among the customers.

"Why didn't you call for me?" the manager cut in.

"By the time I recognized her, soldiers were pushing through the gates and everyone was screaming, and you vanished to I don't know where!" The flute player's words were slightly slurred and his eyes hooded. Tin suspected he'd taken a taste of white tar before the performance.

The manager drew himself up. "Well, I couldn't let myself get collared!"

"Shut the fuck up," Tin said to him. She turned back to musician. "Tell me everything."

"I've been trying to remember her name. She was a good fuck when she was sauced, but she could be mean, too. She got caught filching on the dance floor and the manager barred her, what, two years ago?" He turned to the manager. "Remember? She offered to do you if you changed your mind."

"I do remember." He turned to Tin. "She was about my height, dark complexion, oval face, large eyes, a pretty girl. Full-blooded Salashi. Someone should have recognized her, even after two years."

With a place like this, the manager and the musicians were probably the only staff still working here two years later. Still, Tin dared to hope. "What about that name?"

The manager shrugged. The flute player said, "Alenya?" in his thick, uncertain voice as though he was guessing. "I only saw her for two weeks, maybe. Once she was barred from the hall, she stopped coming around. Plus, I don't know if I should even mention this, but she could be pretty mean."

"Where did she live?"

"Oh. Huh. We always went to my place for our fun. I live above a tavern in Woodgarden, and she said she was nearby but my place was nicer than hers. So, I don't know. Plus, I think she took stuff from me, but you know, I knew she would."

Tin Pail could hear the customers growing restless behind her, but that was tough shit for them. "That's not enough. I need more."

The flute player snapped his fingers. "She painted hands. I almost forgot about that. She worked in some shop in Upgarden, but only for a couple of days. She's not really the society type." He shrugged vaguely. "That's all I know."

Tin looked at Paper and her bodyguard, then led them to the rail.

Woodgarden. Pickpocket. A hand-painter. *Alenya*. It would be enough.

* * *

SCUT WORK. THAT'S WHAT the foreign heavies in Harl's organization gave him. Bullshit messages to deliver, guard duty in the middle of the night, and worst of all, fetching meals.

No matter what his mom thought, Cold Sunshine was not enthusiastic about being drafted into Harl's organization. He'd liked being in a street gang with his friends, hanging on the corner, joking with the girls, maybe filching a purse or two. They'd called themselves the Quick Ones, and most of the shit they pulled was petty kids' stuff. Cold himself had never gotten caught. He knew his Spillwater neighborhood like his mother's kitchen and had so many ways to escape the cosh that no constable ever saw the same one twice. It was fun.

It couldn't last. The cosh started to notice his tricks, and it was never good for the cosh to notice you. Plus, he was getting too old for kids' stuff. He was nineteen now, and he wanted to get away with grown-up stuff.

Cold Sunshine wanted to kill someone.

The idea had come to him four years earlier as suddenly as a bridge collapse. To slide his knife into someone's heart, feel their blood flow over his hand, see the expression on their face…

It had given him an instant hard-on. The thought haunted him for weeks until he decided he had to act on it. He waited in a dark alley for another member of his own gang—a guy he mostly liked, which made things even more exciting—and took the point to him.

Or tried to. His strike wasn't fatal, and it was so dark he couldn't even see his friend's expression, which was the whole point, really.

Luckily, his friend didn't see him, either, because the uproar that followed that knife strike was chaotic and terrifying. Not only did their leader swear to hunt down the attacker, but the Quick Ones nearly started three different gang wars. Cold himself watched two members of the Lower Deckers get their hands broken and their teeth kicked out because they were caught buying buns on the wrong side of the plank. Finally, Cotton Stair sent people to look into it, mainly to blunt the rage of his gang.

No one ever suspected Cold himself, and the whole thing was too terrifying to risk again.

But he still wanted to take the point to someone very badly. If Koh-Salash had been at war, he would have joined the military, but in peaceful times, soldiers just stood on the walls and talked about how drunk they'd get on Shieldsday. He'd have joined the cosh if they killed more people, but they were afraid of starting another Downscale War.

Even signing on with Harl, which everyone had always expected, seemed iffy. Heavies killed people, sure, but usually, they had orders first. You had to move high up the slope for a job like that. If Cold was going to kill someone without taking the point himself as punishment, he was going to have to earn the trust of his higher-ups. He'd need an assignment.

That looked like a long shot under Harl, who gave the most difficult and dangerous jobs to Carrig.

It didn't help that Cold himself was so short and slender that he was often mistaken for a kid. The top heavies among Harl's people were generally bulky, muscular types with intimidating glares. Cold was sure that a quick, sneaky knife in the dark would be just as effective—maybe more effective—but he was so far down the slope that he didn't dare suggest it.

He was returning to Sailsday's Regret with a crock full of the thick, salty porridge those Carrig assholes like to eat. It had cost six copper whistles, and not only was he not going to be paid back, the assholes wouldn't let him eat with them.

These were the dues he had to pay, and they sucked. He just needed a chance to prove himself.

When he set the crock in front of the platform hall manager and his two heavies, the elder, Nal At Isp, caught his arm. "Do you see Second Boar over there?"

"Who? I know the name, but…"

The heavy sighed and stood. Cold followed him to a table where a huge Salashi man sat squeezed between two tables. He was the biggest asshole Cold had ever seen, and while he was dressed like a magistrate in fine green cloth, his scars left no doubt that he was a street thug.

Cold felt a tingle at the thought of what they might ask him to do.

Nal cleared his throat. "Second Boar, this is the guy. He can help." Nal turned to Cold and leaned in close. "No killing."

Goosebumps ran down Cold's back. Could this asshole read his mind?

But Nal was already walking away. When Second Boar spoke, his voice was surprisingly high, like a child's. "Why did he say that last thing?"

Cold answered honestly. "I don't know, good sir. I have never taken the point to nobody. Never been told to."

Glancing around the table, Cold saw that a wild-haired northern tramp was sitting with them, although he had the arms of a dockhand. Beside him was a guy with three braids on the front of his head who was barely older than Cold, then a handsome, smirking creep with a steel chain around his neck, and a stony-eyed woman who looked enough like the creep to be his sister.

There was something about the last one that caught his attention. Not that there was anything special about her appearance. She was average in every way, from her hair to her clothes, but the way she looked at him gave him a chill.

"And you won't today, either," Second Boar said. "The northerner scared off the eye who's been following us around, but he put two constables on us. They're sitting in the opposite corner, in their street clothes. See them?"

Cold walked to the counter, then returned with a fresh pot of tea. "I saw them," he said. "With the haircuts."

"Draw them off," Second Boar said, "without starting another Downscale War."

Cold went into the back office, wondering where people got these ideas about him. How could they tell he wanted to kill someone?

Still, no big deal. He fetched an old wash bucket, pissed in it, then carried it into the cafe and dumped it into the constables' laps.

"Fuck you, assholes!"

The room erupted in laughter. Red-faced, the cosh leaped from their chairs, toppling their table and everything on it.

But Cold was already at the rail and running. Not too fast, though. If he lost them too quickly, Second Boar wouldn't have time to get away.

He heard their feet stamping on the platform, and he laughed as he ran.

CHAPTER SIX

Riliska slid her apartment door open just in time to hear the slap.
She went still, her stomach fluttering, and made her expression grave. Bitter experience had taught her that no one wanted to see a smile on her face after a fight. No one wanted to see her at all.

Usually, when her mother had people in their rooms, Riliska would slip back outside, but tonight, there were shapes moving on the plankways that made her nervous. Her paint set wasn't worth much, but she knew people didn't always steal things because they were valuable. Sometimes, it was simply because they could.

Riliska could hear her mother's voice in the other room. "This was my idea! Without me, you'd have nothing to sell. Why I shouldn't get half?"

"You must be crazy."

Riliska didn't know that voice, but it was male. She crawled under the table and sat in the back corner, making herself as small as possible. Sometimes, her mother's male guests were nice to her, giving her a copper knot or a piece of fruit, but that was rare. More often, they looked at her as though she was proof of some mistake they'd made.

This one sounded angry, and the angry ones sometimes pulled Riliska's hair or slapped her face. She tried to decide if she'd be safer on the plankways.

"What do you think *you* can do with it?" the male voice demanded. "Turn it into coin? Don't make me laugh. The first person you approached would gut you like a hog and take it. Then where would I be?"

"Shitting your skirts like a—"

There was another slap, this one so loud that Riliska jumped. Then another. Then another.

"Haliyal." Her mother's voice sounded small. "Haliyal, stop."

"I'm going to give you one day to bring back my prize, baby. Hear me? One day."

The bedroom door slid open, and a man emerged. Riliska could only see the side of his face from below, but she'd seen his type many times over the years. He was a little bit handsome and a little bit strong, but was mostly mean and dumb. Her mother sometimes called guys like him "fuddled." Riliska had no idea what that meant, except that he'd never be powerful or clever or important or stick around.

He could still be dangerous, though.

She kept so still, she didn't even breathe. He didn't notice her. He just slid the door open and snatched the last bun off their tiny counter. He took a deep bite, then left with the remainder.

Riliska crawled quickly from her hiding space and went to the counter. There was nothing else to eat there. The fuddled man had stolen her supper.

Heart sinking, she turned to her mother sitting on the mat beside her open door. Maybe she could buy something before all the stalls closed, even though the stalls in Woodgarden never stayed open this late. Night had fallen, and what little glow Woodgarden got from Suloh's bones was—

"Go outside," her mother said, looking at the floor. The side of her face was swollen. "Go play." She slid the bedroom door shut.

Riliska went to the doorway and opened it a little. Someone down in the lobby on the main floor had a lantern, and the shadows it cast swept across the walls on the higher floors.

Men's laughter echoed up the stairs. Not safe.

She crept back under the table.

* * *

RULENYA SLID THE DOOR shut, then pushed a piece of broken crockery aside so she could sit on her stained mat. She hated it when one of her guys hit her, but she hated it even more when the Long Hangover saw it. Why couldn't that fucking kid find someplace to play? Why did she have to haunt these rooms like a hungry ghost?

And that shitbrain Haliyal... Rulenya laid her hand on her swollen cheek. By the fallen gods, she hadn't been hit so hard in months. Someday, she would find a man who would hit others for her instead of hitting her for himself. A man who didn't look at her home—and her—with disgust.

There was no noise from the front room. Good. The Long Hangover must have gone out to play. Rulenya swept aside a tray covered with crumbs and old bones, then picked up a piece of folded satin. Carefully, she laid it on the mat, unfolded it, and examined the contents.

It was the tiniest cut from the glitterkind ear that she could make with the tiny bronze knife she kept for scraping down her dyes. It was smaller than a bead of rain on a waxed plank. It was smaller than a flake of chapped skin she might bite from her lip.

But she'd heard such stories… How it took away pain. How it healed injuries—not diseases, but even missing limbs or ruined organs could be replaced. How fucked-up was that? Her own heart could be cut out and a dead man's put in its place, and she would go on about her life.

Would that make her a different person? A kinder one, maybe, if the heart came from a kinder person? One who spent more time at her brushes and fixed little meals for her daughter, the way mothers were supposed to?

She nearly laughed. Her own mother had fixed meals every day, and had beaten her black and blue. Every meal had been another chance to scold and punish, but no matter what the old monster did to control her, Rulenya had only grown wilder.

A new heart wouldn't change her. It would just be something new she could consume.

Uncorking a jar, she took a long drink. Brandy was her preference, but wine did the job in a pinch. The hours when she was sober were long and sour ones, and sometimes they brought the urge to grab Riliska and leap from the deck to the dock flats below. Her mother thought she drank too much? Well, it beat the alternative.

At least she was not like those tar heads. Sure, a tar high was *amazing*, but she didn't mess with that shit anymore. She'd never sink so low as to become like *them*.

But a piece of glitterkind? Even by the pale lantern light of her filthy squat, colors flashed from it like tiny reflected pinpricks. She couldn't possibly become addicted to this, because there was so little of it and she was about to sell the rest anyway. Even if it was supposed to be powerful in very tiny doses.

Maybe she should cut the tiny piece in half?

Rulenya scooped the whole paring onto her pinky and pressed it against her tongue. Hesitation was for losers. She had to grab hold of every pleasure the world offered. What if Haliyal came back and killed her? What if she died thinking about this high she *might* have had?

The tiny flake made a slight tingle on her tongue, but it was so faint, it might have been her imagination. She swallowed, hoping that some kind of rush would hit soon. If she was going to risk a tiny cut that even a shitwit like Haliyal might notice, she'd better get something for it.

A moment later, her whole body seemed loose and boneless. She slumped to the floor with a small, helpless cry.

An odd feeling like nothing she'd ever felt before welled up inside, making her feel huge and diffuse, like the ghost of a giant. There was nothing physical about this rush, no sour stomach, blurred vision, or lightness in the head. Instead, she just felt large, and powerful, and so serene that she was without want or fear.

Rulenya cried out in pure joy, her voice high and squeaky like a child's. She had never felt such contentment before, had never felt so complete.

By the fallen gods, she was going to ride this feeling until the very end, and then, when the pawnshop opened again, she was going to get the rest of that ear back and vanish with it. She'd just walk into the jungle, or swim to Vu-Timmer, or something—anything—to experience this again. And again and again and again.

Then, when her supply was all gone, she would be ready to die.

* * *

RILISKA CROUCHED IN THE darkness beneath the table. Something terrible had happened to her mother. Riliska hadn't dared to open the door, but the sound that came from their shared bedroom terrified her. No humankind could make that noise. It was part shriek, part song, part joy. Something Else was in there with her mother.

She imagined herself flinging back the door with the force and confidence of a hero. Whatever she'd find there, whether it was a hungry shadowkind, one of the ghostkind clad all in black armor, or even a bloodkind that crawled up from the depths of Mudside, she would shout STOP AND GO AWAY, and the power of her voice would terrify it so much, it would leap through the shutters into the night and never return.

But Riliska would never risk it, because what she was most afraid of was that there would be no intruder in their bedroom. She would open that door and find only the usual filth, and her usual mother lying in it, writhing on the floor in the grip of some new drug.

Her mother's voice squeaked, then held a long high rasping note. Riliska laid both hands over her ears, but nothing could block that sound or the way it made her feel.

* * *

KYRIOC TOOK HIS BLACK tunic, vest, and trousers from the narrow shelf above his bed. All were brand-new. He hung them on a length of hemp rope, wet a soft-bristled brush in the bouquet water, and carefully brushed the fabric. He'd worn finer clothes—the robe he'd slept in as a bedwetting child cost more—but this would do.

Today was Last Day, the longest day and shortest night of the year. Tomorrow would be Mourning Day, the first day of the new year. It was also the day families would mourn those who had been killed the previous year, or who had been missing so long that they could be legally declared dead.

Goosebumps ran down Kyrioc's back. He could see Aratill's bloody face in the moment before he died as though it was happening all over again. And that face wasn't the only one. One after another ran through his thoughts, each as vivid as if they were in the room with him.

He suddenly realized that he'd been standing, motionless, in his room for... Actually, there was no way to tell how long he'd been standing there. He tried to clear his thoughts and set to work again.

When Kyrioc returned to Koh-Salash from his disastrous First Labor, he'd sought out the families of those who had not returned with him. They were not hard to find, but he couldn't bring himself to approach them. He felt like a thief who had stolen something he could not return, and really, what could he have said?

The situation was impossible, so he did nothing.

But the Safroys planned a public Mourning Day service for their eldest child and their entire sail—along with those who hoped to join the sail—was expected to attend. With luck, Kyrioc could hide in the crowd, pay his respects to that lost thirty, and slip away without—

There was a knock at the door.

He glanced through the shutters and saw that night had fallen. No one would be looking to do business now. He threw the bolt and opened the door a crack. Riliska stood in the hall, looking up at him with an anxious smile. He opened the door all the way and stepped back.

Eyalmati's bed was empty, but Kyrioc didn't think it worth the risk of putting Riliska there. The old man's benders usually lasted three or four days, but he was unpredictable, and if he returned early, blind drunk, he might fall on her.

So, he put the table away and laid out the spare mat, then fetched an extra blanket from his trunk.

She lifted the hem of her tattered shirt and wiped at the dirt on her cheeks. "I won't be here long, good sir, I promise. Just until my mom finishes mixing the stinky paints and dyes for tomorrow. I don't want you to get in trouble."

"You won't."

"And I've decided that I'm not going to steal things anymore, good sir. You're right about that." He didn't respond. Riliska's stomach rumbled so loudly that he could hear it across the little room. She laid her hand over her tummy. "Sorry."

Kyrioc put away the mat and blanket again. Then he took out the table and set it with the last two carrots and sole remaining bun. The little girl's smile broadened and her chatter became livelier. She washed her hands and face without being asked, carefully removing the poppies from the bowl first, carefully replacing them afterward.

She tore into the food, smiling with delight when she discovered the bun had sweet fig paste in the middle. Kyrioc wondered if she'd eaten since he fed her that morning, and wished he'd bought more. When she finished, he cleared the platter and set the table aside. This time, she helped him unfold the blanket.

"You have a nickname, you know. The landlady's nephew says he heard it in the market and out on the decks. I've heard it, too. Do you want to know what it is?"

Kyrioc rolled a blanket to make a pillow for her. "What is it?"

"*The Broken Man*," she said. Kyrioc thought he should have some reaction to this, but he couldn't imagine what it should be, so he said nothing. "Or sometimes just *Broken*, I guess. I said it wasn't very nice, and he threatened to throw a stone at me, but that doesn't make any sense. Where's he going to get a stone out here on the plankways? He'd have to throw a coin or something, and I'd let him, because then I would catch it and it would be mine. Good sir, do you want to know what my nickname is?"

"Tell me." Kyrioc turned from the mat and took a clean cup from the shelf. The wooden pitcher had a little water left in it. He poured until the cup was half full and set it on the floor beside Riliska's mat.

She'd fallen silent. He saw her expression, then pulled out a little stool and sat against the wall, giving her his full attention.

That prompted her to speak. "It's *Long Hangover*. Isn't that funny? Mom says that most hangovers last until lunchtime, but I'm a headache she's had for years."

Kyrioc was still for a moment, then gently tucked her in. "Get some sleep."

"Good sir, I promise I won't stay too long."

"Sleep."

As he went to his own bed, Kyrioc heard her say, "The Broken Man and the Long Hangover. It sounds like a funny play. I've never seen a play, good sir. Have you?"

Kyrioc didn't answer. Riliska sighed in the growing dark.

For once, Kyrioc's night was not full of flame, shadow, and death. For once, he fell into a deep, dreamless sleep.

He woke in meager daylight. The mat he'd laid out for Riliska was empty, the blanket folded and placed on top. It wasn't folded well, but it was folded. The water from the cup had been drunk and the remains of last night's fig roll was gone. He refolded the blanket and put the mat away.

Eyalmati had not returned. Kyrioc moved a few silver whistles and a silver beam into the drawer so the owner could refill his purse without bankrupting himself—assuming he returned to the shop today, which was doubtful. Mourning Day was an excuse for drink even among those who did not drink every waking hour.

The only light came from sunshine reflected off other buildings along the plankway, but it was enough to see the outlines of his empty room. He'd spent long hours there while Eyalmati was passed out in the supply room or wandering the city. Before this moment, he'd never felt lonely.

Kyrioc put on his funeral clothes. It was time to go up to High Square, where his family would be standing beside his own memorial.

Taking up his red poppies, he locked the shop up and went into the streets. Already, crowds of people in their funeral best gathered on the planks, making the solemn journey to a private or public affair. Many of them, he knew, would visit several ceremonies before sundown.

Tragedy was not just the parent of grief. It was the parent of toil and duty as well.

Glancing eastward, he saw bright sunlight. The sky must have been cloudless or close to it.

Upgarden would be full of people today—not just those who wished to curry favor with the Safroy family, but their servants and private guards as well. Kyrioc would have to be careful, and in this bright light, he would not be able to use his cloak of mirrors.

Head down, he joined the sluggish crowd moving toward the lifts at Undertower.

CHAPTER SEVEN

The year 395 of the New Calendar, eight years earlier.

* * *

KYRIONIK WARD-SAFROY DEFE-SAFROY admir-Safroy hold-Safroy stood at the bow of *Fair Season*, hearing sails snap behind him. The wind on his face was called the Parsu—or among his own people, Parsu the Deliverer. It was the westerly that had carried the Salashi people to safety when the ghostkind drove them out of Selsarim. And now he was sailing westward again.

But not all the way back home. Not yet.

He couldn't help wonder how this year's Parsu, which the captain and her crew worked so hard to tack against, compared to the Deliverer itself, almost four hundred years before.

According to Kyrionik's childhood history lessons, when Selsarim fell, the Parsu had been blowing unusually hard. The journey across the ocean—which normally took three months—finished in two. Many refugees survived the trip who would have died the year before or after.

They might have thanked the gods, but the gods were all dead.

So, once they were established in their new land, the heads of the noble families—in their humility—took the name *parsu* for themselves. The common folk pledged to a particular noble family and reliant on them for political favors, loans, or mediation with the bureaucracy were known collectively as a sail, and individually as stitches. But what good was a sail without a wind to fill it?

Someday, Kyrionik would be the Safroy parsu. Once he finished his First Labor, his mother would present him to the High Watch. Until then...

He raised his mailed fist, offering a challenge to the world. Everything was going perfectly.

"Your virtue," a gruff voice said, "take that steel off."

No one but Aratill would have spoken to the Safroy heir that way. Even though Aratill had explained many times that wearing armor throughout the day made a warrior stronger and quicker—had made Kyrionik wear it during long hours of exercise and scholarship—he would not allow it at sea. And, as Kyrionik's weapons instructor and bodyguard, he had the authority to make the young noble obey.

"What about Shulipik?" Kyrionik asked. They glanced midship, where Shulipik tuto-Beskeroth stood beside the mast, his helm beneath his arm. His steel breastplate gleamed. The sea air blew his long braids, and his short glaive, taken from a ghostkind ranger in single combat, was strapped to his back. The shaft rose behind him like a pole stripped of its flag.

What about Shulipik? Kyrionik had meant to suggest that Shulipik was a celebrated warrior, so perhaps Kyrionik should emulate him. Instead, the question had sounded childish and petulant, as though Shulipik had been served a bigger slice of cake. He wished he could unask it.

"Let him play the fool," Aratill said, too quietly for the man to hear. "He is not my charge, nor would I want him to be. My charge is a sixteen-year-old child of the nobility who has more courage than sense. I've seen ships pitch suddenly from an unexpected change in the wind or from the thump of a hungry beast hoping to shake loose a meal. If you are dumped into the waves, I'd like you to bob at the surface long enough to be pulled out again."

Kyrionik sighed and unhooked the plate, feeling slightly embarrassed. Shulipik hadn't just put on his breastplate. He wore spaulders, upper and lower cannons, and more. He was a warrior of great renown, and he looked the part.

In contrast, Kyrionik had just been scolded on the deck in full view of everyone. He shed the plate and mailed gloves, handing them to a servant. "Prudence, Aratill, child of Araphin. How many times have you tried to teach me this lesson?"

"The time for bold decisions will come soon enough, your virtue. This is *your* First Labor, not his. You command here."

"With your consent."

"No, your virtue. I advise—in my fashion—but you are the one who leads us. Our lives rest on your judgement. That's what truly separates you from him, whatever his skill at arms."

That and his ghostkind weapon. But Kyrionik didn't say it, because he knew his instructor wouldn't laugh.

Still, he hungered for what Shulipik had: renown. And he would have it if this First Labor succeeded.

Which it would. Why doubt himself?

The captain emerged from her cabin with Selso Rii, their guide on this trip. They stood together on the deck, framed by dark wood of a type Kyrionik didn't recognize—his own home was made of pale skywood and paler stone. The captain was the same height as the guide, but she stood as straight as an oak, while he was a slender reed that bent under the force of her attention. Kyrionik almost laughed at the sight.

Oblifell joined Kyrionik and his bodyguard in the bow. "Our captain seems less happy every day."

Aratill and Oblifell clasped their scarred hands together. The former was stocky, scarred, and tall, while the latter was stocky, scarred, and short, but they were a fine match. Clasping hands was the only affection the husbands allowed themselves on a mission.

"She's been paid, hasn't she?" Kyrionik asked.

"She has," Oblifell said, smiling crookedly, "and it was an exorbitant fee. But treasure provides no luxury to the dead."

"She has thirty loyal Safroy troopers aboard," Aratill interjected quickly. "She'll keep to her agreement."

It suddenly occurred to Kyrionik that Oblifell's remark about treasure and the dead might have been directed toward him. He stared out ahead of the ship. Vu-Dolmont, their destination, still lay beyond the horizon. They'd been at sea for six weeks. Could they have missed it? Sailed by it in the night?

"Aratill, do you think this trip is wise?"

"Your virtue, that's a question you should have asked me half a year back. But I've known you for most of your life, and I knew your First Labor would be a challenge."

Every child of noble birth took on a First Labor at the age of sixteen. For many, it was a task of civic improvement: founding a school in the farmwilds, an orphanage in Mudside, or repairs to the downcity plankways and decks. Some took on intellectual pursuits. Kyrionik's' younger brother Culzatik was only fourteen, but he was already planning to take a team of scribes to the libraries of Koh-Gilmiere—which were rumored to have codices that were hundreds of years old—and return with a more complete history of Selsarim.

But for those who planned to one day stand as the Steward-General of all of Koh-Salash, their First Labor were supposed to be feats accomplished with sword and spear.

The most common Labor was for a young noble to sail up the Timmer to the northern farmwilds and kill bandits. When he was fourteen, Kyrionik undertook a trip like that. He'd brought his steed, his lance, his sword, and his desire for fame. He planned to accomplish what most young nobles undertook as their First Labor, but he would do it two years early.

It had been a repulsive slaughter worthy of no renown at all. Most of the bandits were starving farmers bled of their coin by a grasping local steward. Few knew how to fight, most fled, and those desperate enough to turn their billhooks against mounted, armored men died quickly.

Kyrionik himself had killed one man. The fellow tried to flee, but Kyrionik rode after him and called for his surrender. The man might have done so, except that Kyrionik's voice cracked. When he realized he was facing a boy in full armor, the bandit flew into a rage and charged, his axe held high. Kyrionik reacted as he'd been trained, with shield and sword.

It had been absurdly easy. Shamefully so. Even now, two years later, he could still remember the bandit's final expression. He swore then that his own First Labor, when it came, would not be to ride out and murder the poorest and most desperate of his own people.

His mother had been impressed when he announced his plan to build a tower in the Harkan borderlands, one that would secure a working port and establish a permanent Salashi outpost in the south. After decades of civil war, the mighty Harkan throne, built by the Ancient Kings themselves, had become little more than a monument. Stability and trade would be welcomed by the local Harkan farmers and crafts folk, and bring wealth to Koh-Salash.

It was a bold plan. Risky. It had earned him the cautious approval of the nobles who visited the family compound to curry favor with his mother.

But it was fake. For his real First Labor, Kyrionik had something more daring in mind.

The captain approached. Her hair was clipped short and her face deeply tanned. She was probably around fifty years old, close to Aratill's age. Although this was supposed to be Kyrionik's mission, she addressed his bodyguard as much as him. "I expect we'll dock at Vu-Dolmont by midmorning."

"When will it come into sight?" Kyrionik asked, glancing ahead of the ship.

"It has already, your virtue." The captain pointed off the starboard side, to the north. Kyrionik turned around and he saw it, a broad, squat, hazy gray mass on the northern horizon.

"That's Vu-Dolmont?" Aratill asked.

This time, it their guide who answered. "It is," Selso Rii said. He cringed from the look the captain gave him. It was not his place to answer questions. Wringing his hands nervously, he stepped back against the rail.

"Captain, I wonder if I might ask a question of you," Kyrionik said, then plunged forward without waiting for permission. "Wouldn't it be faster to sail on a beam reach and approach directly?" He kept his tone light, as though this was a classroom and she his tutor.

Still, when she answered, it was with a tone that suggested his remarks were tiresome. "We dare not approach so directly because the waters here are treacherous. There are pillars beneath the waves that would tear out our hull, and *Fair Season* is not maneuverable enough to pass through safely, even if we traveled under broad sunlight. According to your guide's pirate map, we'll have to sail beyond and approach from the southwest at broad reach. With luck, we will sail into the bay at Childfall without incident."

Fair enough. "Thank you, captain, for sharing your expertise."

She bowed, glanced at Aratill—who pretended not to pay attention—then left to speak with her first mate.

Selso Rii stepped forward nervously. "Not a pirate map, your virtue. We were never pirates. Never that."

Oblifell looked at him with undisguised disgust. "Smugglers, then."

Rii addressed Kyrionik as though he had spoken. "Your virtue, we were traders. Humble folk in search of our way in the world, such as fortune and the law provide."

"What concerns me," Kyrionik said, "is the accuracy of your map and your story."

Selso Rii stepped closer. "The map is good, your virtue. The captain has said that it matches her charts. She has said so, your virtue. I think you may have heard her. I hope you have, your virtue. I also hope my humble map might add slightly to her charts, if it's not too bold of me to say, your virtue. And I would hardly have come all this way, among such stern, dangerous fighting folk, if I had not told my story true. I will keep to my part of the bargain."

"And I mine. If you lead us to our prize, and we sail safely away with it, I will see you brought to a Salashi hospital and made healthy again."

Selso Rii absentmindedly touched the thin cloth cap over his balding pate. Beneath it was a growing cancer, common enough in a man exposed too long to the sun. "Your virtue's word is as good as a chest full of golden coins, of course it is," he said, as though he suspected otherwise but didn't dare admit it. "Of course it is."

Aratill took hold of Rii's upper arm and began leading him away. "You just be ready to come ashore with us tomorrow."

"Ashore?" Rii squeaked. "Good sir, what do stern fighting folk like yourself need with a man like Selso Rii? Will you need someone who is handy with a mop? Or a needle and thread?"

"Of all the humankind on this ship," Aratill said, "only one has ever set foot in Childfall itself and survived. I want that man with us."

"But good sir—"

"Our arrangement," Kyrionik interrupted, "was for you to lead us to the spot."

"And I have, your virtue!" Rii sounded offended. "I have! The map is clearly marked."

"If all I needed was a crude smuggler's map, we would have left you in that tavern in Spillwater. Our arrangement was that you would lead us to this prize. If you renege, I will be disappointed but not surprised."

Selso Rii's mouth twisted with resentment, and he bowed low, where his expression could not be seen. "Oh, no, your virtue. I would never want you to be disappointed, your virtue. Never that." He backed away.

Aratill watched him go, scowling. "That one is not to be trusted," he said gruffly.

Kyrionik snorted. "I picked up on the subtle clues as well."

Aratill and Oblifell both barked out a loud laugh. Everyone on deck turned to look at them, and Kyrionik felt a flush of pride.

He glanced northward again at the distant island. "It doesn't look like much, does it?"

Just before sunset, the captain changed course, and sailors doubled their efforts, untying ropes and letting out slack. Their sails swelled, as did their speed. Kyrionik's mother loved the open ocean—had, in fact, captured two pirate ships sailing out of The Free City of Koh-Alzij for her First Labor—but he'd never felt the same call. But he had a healthy respect for the difficulty and complexity of the work.

The first mate climbed up into the bow. "Dinner is served in the captain's mess, your virtue."

Kyrionik knew when he was being asked to make space for working folk.

At dinner, he, Aratill, and Oblifell discussed the next day's itinerary with the captain. Shulipik, who had removed his armor for dinner, also joined them, although he had little to say.

Could the ghostkind have followed humankind this far and settled on the island? Aratill thought that unlikely, but the idea cast a pall. The reports that the island was infested by bloodkind or shadowkind were not taken seriously. Bloodkind were well known in Koh-Salash—they had lived in abundance on Salash Hill before humankind drove them underground—and not greatly feared. Shadowkind were rumored to be in all sorts of places, but for hundreds of years, they had been nothing more than rumor. Sensible folk believed they had been left behind in the west, if encroaching ghostkind armies had not destroyed them.

It was the ullroct that everyone was concerned with. There was little doubt that one had once lived on Vu-Dolmont. The Harkan people had tried to settle the island fifty years before, but a single ullroct had destroyed the settlement. Kyrionik had studied the records carefully—what he could access in Suloh's Temple, at least. For the benefit of the others, he repeated once more what he'd learned.

The settlement had been established with a garrison of three hundred soldiers and a work crew twice that number—many with their families—dropped there by a small fleet of ships. After six months spent clearing the lowest plateau and building a walled town upon it, a "creature of iron and flame" emerged from the jungle. It destroyed the settlement, driving the people to the ships. Those that could not make it, children included, were driven off the cliff onto the rocks below.

Some sources claimed The Harkan throne provided a glitterkind to the settlers, but that seemed extremely unlikely. If there was one on the island, it had to have been there when the settlers dropped anchor. Since it was common knowledge that ullrocts destroyed glitterkind on sight, it would take a wild stroke of luck for them to arrive at the island and find it still there. Still, Selso Rii had seen it, and not long ago.

Their meal finished, the ship's steward cleared the table and the captain laid out the map. Vu-Dolmont was an irregular blob forty miles across at its widest point, with a high, curving ridge that ran from the northwest to the southeast. There were no beaches, nor did it have a rocky shoreline that could be approached with a skiff. The entire island was surrounded by cliffs, the lowest being the edge of the western plateau where Childfall had been founded. Beyond the settlement, the land rose sharply to the ridge. The Childfall plateau and the ridge behind it were perhaps fifteen percent of the island's total surface. No one knew what lay beyond.

Their main concern was simple. Was the ullroct still living on the island fifty years later? And if so, what did that mean for the prize they'd come to find?

Because four years earlier, Selso Rii had been part of a landing party desperate to find fresh water and wood to repair their ship, and he had looked deep into the jungle and seen a spray of rainbow colors there.

The people of Koh-Benjatso did not hide their glitterkind behind high walls and locked gates. They were kept in public squares, among the finest greenery the city can provide. Selso Rii had seen sunlight reflect off of glitterkind skin many times in his life. In that distant city, the creatures' healing magic was cultivated in secrecy, but creatures themselves were displayed like temple monuments.

And on that day in the ruins of Childfall, Selso Rii had happened to be standing in just the right spot, at just the right time of day, to see that same flash of light and color that he'd seen hundreds of times before in his home city.

Perhaps the ullroct was dead. Perhaps it was still there but hadn't yet found its prey. Perhaps Selso Rii was lying for reasons of his own, or simply mistaken and there was no glitterkind there, waiting to be plucked out of the jungle like pirate treasure.

Tomorrow, they would find out.

The sun rose to reveal that the waters around Vu-Dolmont were infested with hunting jellies. The captain ordered baskets of shit prepared. For months, the whole crew had been relieving themselves into clay pots. Now those pots were strapped into tightly woven baskets, cracked with a hammer, and hung over the sides.

Aratill was amazed. "This drives off hunting jellies?"

The captain's expression was grim. "Usually."

Stairs had been carved into the cliff face leading from the water to the plateau above. It was only seventy feet, but Kyrionik still found the height forbidding. Even though the day was a calm one, the captain wouldn't bring *Fair Season* near the cliff face. The landing party had to approach on a skiff, six at a time. Aratill insisted they carry their armor in packs, and that Kyrionik come in the next-to-last boat, which he did, although he thought he would be more comfortable on the broken stone stair inside his armor rather than feeling the weight of it pulling his shoulder.

His skin tingled. He'd never faced real danger before—not when he faced the bandits, or competed in the dueling yard, or raced his stallions. Not *real* danger. Not like this. It was intoxicating.

"What was this settlement called before it was destroyed and renamed?" he asked as he negotiated a crumbling switchback. "I assume the Harkans picked something more optimistic, but I couldn't find it in our records."

"I'm not sure anyone knows." Aratill answered.

"Probably erased for political reasons," Oblifell said. "We've never been friendly with Harka."

Kyrionik glanced down at the churning green water and the rocks just below the surface. A person might survive a leap from the top of the cliff, but only if they hit the water in exactly the right spot. His own cousin, the Imsyel heir, had drowned after jumping from a third of this height, striking a rock and breaking his back.

He glanced up and imagined men, women, and children leaping into the air above, hoping that the fall would be luckier than the thing chasing them. *Children.*

"Why 'Childfall' then?" Kyrionik shifted his pack higher. "If so many people leaped from the cliff and died, and so many were children, shouldn't it be 'Childrenfall'?"

"Because," Oblifell said, "one dead child is tragedy enough. The death of a single child is like the end of the world."

Something in his voice suggested there was something important behind Oblifell's words. The older Kyrionik got, the more complicated other people seemed to be. This was something he should ask the older warrior about someday.

Just thinking about it spoiled the tingling thrill of the adventure they were undertaking. He turned his attention to the stairs and climbed in silence.

Childfall was moments away.

CHAPTER EIGHT

B *efore leaving the empty* casino, Kyrioc summoned his cloak of mirrors. Dawnshine earned its name because it was built so close to the Upgarden deck that it received daylight only in the earliest hours of the day. It was now midafternoon, so Kyrioc was safely out of the daylight and could call up his cloaks.

He moved with the crowd. No one paid him any attention. Whenever someone did glance his way, they did not see a scarred man in black clothes. He wasn't sure what they saw—it would be different for each of them—but it would be unremarkable.

He followed the crowd toward Undertower and caught the lift down.

Kyrioc circled the lift platform to stand in the shadow of the central shaft. Despite his stillness and his reluctance to make eye contact—which helped him avoid attention and therefore aided his cloak—his heart was pounding in his ears. He wanted to stampede through the crowds. He wanted to leap over everyone's head. He wanted to shout his throat raw.

He'd seen his family. He wasn't supposed to look up, but when his younger brother shouted, *You there!* Kyrioc had done what reflex demanded and looked Culzatik in the eye.

Kyrioc stepped off the lift at the Shadetree deck. It was upcity from Woodgarden, but this Undertower lift didn't connect directly. Shadetree was widely considered a "safe" district. It was mainly a residential space for tradefolk, laborers, and merchants with modest ambitions. The buildings down there did not need carved skywood panels hung above the lintels. They were constructed from real wood harvested in the north, and the figures—sails, stalks of wheat, cresting waves, owls, or leaping fish—were carved directly into the building.

The lift had been slow, and Kyrioc could not maintain his concentration forever. Dropping his cloak of mirrors, he hurried south along the boulevard. Shadetree was not known for street thieves, but its axe handle–wielding citizen patrols could be so much worse.

The fastest route back to the anonymity of the pawnshop led through Gray Flames, but that was the home of the city's administrative bureaucracy and it was thick with constables. Kyrioc doubted word of his pursuit would precede him, but he'd also thought he could slip through his own funeral unnoticed. The safer path was the longest one.

His heart was still thumping. For the past few months, he'd spent long hours in the pawnshop, learning to suffocate that response with stillness and remorse, but it was never far below the surface. As he moved farther into the deck, in this place where sunlight rarely shone, he thought he heard a familiar birdlike chittering from the darkened alleys…

No. It couldn't be. It was just his imagination filling the shadows with memories.

Still, he readied his cloak of iron and hurried on.

Kyrioc passed into the busier, more public part of the deck. Most everything was closed for the holiday, of course, but a few cafes were open. The people working there, as well as most of the customers, were mostly light-skinned foreigners. They probably observed the funeral customs of their homelands and had no use for Mourning Day.

Some people didn't wait to grieve.

Suddenly, the unfocused anger drained out of him and he stopped in the center of the promenade. He hung his head, letting his shaggy black hair cover his face.

All he'd wanted to do was honor those who had died in his place, but he'd only brought chaos. The faces of his guard came back to him, along with the sounds of fires in the jungle and the screams of the dying.

Eventually, a woman stepped out of her tea shop to ask if he was okay, and Kyrioc could only nod and walk on. He knew the way home from there.

It took nearly an hour to make his way back to Woodgarden. At the top of the ramp that connected the decks, he stumbled onto a mini-caravan of mule-driven carts loaded with barley. The guards traveling with them carried shields emblazoned with the Safroy bull. They turned westward onto a boulevard without taking notice of him.

The Safroy family owned warehouses in the darkest, westernmost end of Shadetree, but they were typically rented out to small businesses. Why would Mother—he meant *the Safroy parsu*—store a shipment of grain there instead of the safer warehouses in The Folly?

Unless she was preparing for a siege.

But the problems of a noble family had nothing to do with a commoner like Kyrioc.

Back in Woodgarden, the young street toughs who haunted the plankways were absent. Maybe they had lost a few of their own this past year and stood vigil for them. The only people out were the ironshirts—who were always on patrol, holiday or no—and families moving between Mournings. A few vegetable shops were open, but their goods looked picked-over.

He passed around one of Yth's abandoned temples to an intersection outside his building. There he heard a loud slap, then a shrill voice. Three people stood in a little circle. Two were constables, who were listening to a woman with her back to him. He didn't know her, but he knew the type—a woman in a tattered robe who was outraged, *outraged*, at the state her neighborhood had sunk to.

"What do we pay taxes for? Huh? Why are we paying your salaries when you can't even keep these little thieves down in Mudside where they belong?"

She shifted position, revealing a boy of about ten who was probably her son. Beside him, in the center of the circle, was Riliska, child of Rulenya. There was no bright smile on her face now.

"What are you doing in this district?" the woman shouted. She slapped the back of Riliska's head. "You're probably not even Salashi, huh? Right?" She struck the girl again. Riliska hunched down, trying to make herself as small as possible.

One of the ironshirts laid her hand on the woman's shoulder. "Good madam, you must stop hitting that little girl."

The woman ignored her and shoved Riliska on the side of her head. "Don't you glare at me! Didn't your mother teach you not to stare at adults?"

"Calm," the constable said. She turned to Riliska. "Did you take this boy's wax tablet?"

Riliska looked up. She hesitated a moment, then, in her small high voice, she said, "I thought it was mine."

The boy shoved her. "You liar! You don't have a tablet!" He tried to slap the side of her head but she flinched away, and he struck her shoulder instead.

The constable moved to interpose herself but the boy's mother reacted first, yanking him back. "Don't touch her! If she's from Mudside, she might have a bloodkind mark." She turned to the constables. "Have you searched her for bloodkind marks? You know they send these little thieves upcity to rob decent folk. Have you checked?"

The ironshirt rolled her eyes. Her partner stood nearby and did nothing but stare into the distance. He looked bored. The first addressed Riliska. "Are your parents nearby? An adult would help settle this dispute."

Riliska looked directly at Kyrioc, as if she'd known he was standing there, watching. She hesitated a moment, then nervously raised her arm and pointed.

Right at Kyrioc.

A chill ran through him. They would ask his name. They would ask where he lived and worked.

Then they would make a report. If news of his flight from the constables in High Square made its way down there, these two ironshirts would remember.

Kyrioc's careful anonymity was about to be shattered.

* * *

CULZATIK FELT THE SAFROY family attendants and guards watching him, but there was little he could do. His brother's public memorial had been cut short and it was his fault. Thank the fallen gods Essatreska had decided to be a bitch and skip the ceremony. He would have to endure her smirk later, but right now, in this place, she would have been unbearable.

Aziatil, his bodyguard, moved close, standing between him and the rest of the city.

That fellow had looked so like Kyrionik, but that was impossible. Culzatik's older brother had left for his First Labor nearly eight years before, and he'd never arrived at the port in the Harkan borderlands. Anything could have happened to him. There had been no serious storms that month and pirates seemed unlikely, considering how many Safroy troopers were on board, but there was always fire. Fire aboard a ship could be deadly. For months, Culzatik had obsessed over the reports of other vessels between Koh-Salash and Harka, but he'd found no news.

And then, finally, he'd realized it didn't matter. Kyrionik, the elder brother he'd looked up to and loved, was gone, and there was nothing to be done about it.

But if he really believed that, why had he run off during the funeral service?

He clenched his narrow fists in front of his chest, trying to expunge the heavy shame growing there. While the rest of Koh-Salash had been out drinking and dancing on Last Day, he'd stayed at home, scrubbing at his ink-stained hands so he would be presentable for this funeral. Still, the marks lingered.

Onderishta came near. The night before last, she and her team were *supposed* to capture the delivery man, courier, and—most important of all—the package they were exchanging. According to the rather cryptic note she'd sent to him, they'd failed. Culzatik knew she was still working on it—she hadn't spent her Last Day drinking and dancing, either—but the look on her face was not triumphant.

"I assume the news is bad," he said.

Onderishta nodded. "We still haven't recovered the package, your virtue."

Damn. "What happened?"

She described the handoff and how it went wrong. As he listened, he heard only confirmation of what he already suspected. The fault was his, not hers. He had not shared his suspicions about the package in question, largely because they were only suspicions.

However, if he *was* correct about the contents of that package, a lowly pickpocket was running loose in the city with a prize worth two or three fully loaded cargo ships. At least.

A prize that, possibly, could destroy his family.

It was vital that Onderishta recover it first. That package would not stay secret for long.

"So far," Culzatik said, "the only people who know about the theft are the thieves themselves, you, and the parties making the exchange. If you follow the parties, they might lead you to the pickpocket."

"Yes, your virtue. My second has already given the order, but the belligerents were expecting it. They've dodged one team, but we'll pick them up again soon."

"Ah," Culzatik said, feeling his face grow warm. "Of course you're right. And I don't say that because you need to be assured that you're right, but to acknowledge that I have, quite foolishly, trodden like an amateur into your field of expertise. I apologize. Er... How did they manage to lose your team?"

"With a well-thrown bucket of urine, your virtue."

Culzatik had absolutely no response to that. The very idea... It would never have occurred to him that such a thing was possible, and he suddenly felt very sheltered. "Yes. Well. What further steps have you taken?"

She said, "That no one spotted the pickpocket before they acted suggests that they were most likely freelance and small-time. That means they'll be looking for a buyer. We have a network of fences we can contact, your virtue, but it's pointless to approach them unless we know what was stolen."

"I have nothing more than suspicions."

"Then share them with me, your virtue, so that I can make informed decisions." When he hesitated further, she said, "One of the belligerents approached Fay about this package, to offer its location, maybe, if it turns out to be serious trouble. But I can't make that deal if I don't know what it's supposed to be."

Culzatik glanced around. Aziatil, of course, stood close, her hands near the long knives she wore at her belt. Others—family guards, constables, influential stitches in the Safroy sail, and even friends of Kyrionik he had not seen in years—milled about, moving in and out of earshot.

"You're right," he said, "but we can't talk about it here." Onderishta had worked for his noble family for many years, and Culzatik admired the control she had over her expression. Still, at the moment, she couldn't quite disguise her crooked half-frown. "I promise you," he said, anxious that she should continue to take him seriously, "that you will understand once we've had a chance to speak privately. Come to the family compound in one..." Culzatik glanced at his mother and father. His mother was speaking to a crowd and his father was standing silently behind her. Both were staring directly at him. "Better make it two hours. It will all make sense then."

"As you wish, your virtue." She bowed slightly and left.

All that remained was for him to run the gauntlet of his own family.

Billentik approached him first. He and Culzatik were already of equal height, although Billentik's chin still held nothing more substantial than peach fuzz. Already broad-shouldered, he was likely to grow taller even than Kyrionik had been. In a year—or perhaps less—Culzatik would have to look up at his younger brother.

And if the boy had idolized Kyrionik, he was less deferential to the family's book-loving second son. "Did you really see a commoner with a knife? Be honest."

Be honest. Culzatik glanced at him, keeping his voice mild and his body language relaxed. "Little brother, if you're going to be stupid enough to question the word of a family member, have the sense to do it in private."

Billen blinked and stepped back. Unless Culzatik changed the dynamic between them, soon his little brother wouldn't back down at all.

But he couldn't think about that at the moment. Now he had to face his mother.

As always, she was surrounded by aides, power brokers, and the heads of the bureaucratic machinery of the Salashi state, many of whom seemed more frantic than usual. She wasn't even a member of the High Watch anymore, but apparently Koh-Salash would collapse if Lanilit parsu-Safroy ward-Safroy defe-Safroy admir-Safroy hold-Safroy took a day to mourn her dead son.

Father had no knack for kind words and careful diplomacy. He had only a strong sword arm and the instinct to strike first. Those traits had served him well in his younger days, when raiders from the Free Cities tried to sail through the Timmer Straits. However, as he passed through middle age, his impatience and quick temper made him a liability in city politics. He no longer spoke to anyone outside the family if he could help it, and when the Safroys threw parties, Mother no longer bothered to make excuses for his absence.

Culzatik approached. His mother was explaining that her son had just saved a mourner from a knife attack. His father turned his head from side to side, always watchful, without ever looking at anyone in particular. If not for his fine clothes, he could have been mistaken for Mother's second bodyguard.

She snapped her fingers. The aides bowed and began to lead the others away. She strode toward him.

Many times in his life, he'd overheard jokes about the way she looked: too skinny, too much nose, too little lip. These were traits Culzatik had inherited from her, and he felt their physical similarities made a bond between them. She had never shown evidence of a similar feeling.

"Your father and I are going into seclusion, since we are not permitted a public ceremony for the son we lost. You will go into the dueling yard and practice your swordplay. For too long, you have been neglecting your exercises. You ran across High Square, in full view of the stitches, like a crippled old man. Think of it as a kind of meditation."

"Yes, Mother. If the constables do catch the man in the black vest, I want to speak to him."

"I've already had a private word and called the search off." Before he could protest, she said, "It's Mourning Day, Culzatik, and you have... On second thought, no. Go home to the dueling yard. Tonight at dinner, you can explain what could possibly have prompted you to give one solitary fuck about a commoner being knifed. Go."

He went.

* * *

ONDERISHTA HATED GOING TO the Safroy compound. As laborious as it was to write out a detailed report and arrange for a messenger, it was still faster than going herself. Still, when her parsu—or in this case her parsu's heir—called, she had no choice.

Two hours. She hurried into the south tower and checked the status of their current operation. The news wasn't good. The constables Fay had assigned to follow Harl's people had not found them again, and now she had nothing to go on.

If only the Safroy heir had not insisted on his secrets. The young man was smart enough—and had worked hard for those smarts, despite his comfortable upbringing—but if he'd been a commoner looking for an apprenticeship, Onderishta wouldn't have taken him on. He acted as if he knew as much as she did.

It occurred to her that she was angrier than she'd realized. She took the tower lift to High Square, crossed to a cafe, then treated herself to a honey cake she couldn't really afford. The Safroy heir would learn. It might take him a while, but he would learn, especially with his mother Lanilit teaching him.

Her treat finished, Onderishta crossed to Hillside Boulevard, the broad promenade that ran along the western edge of Upgarden, with exclusive shops—and the private security that went with them—on one side and Salash Hill on the other. This was the only way into High Slope.

Only noble families—the wealthiest and most powerful—were permitted to live in the High Slope neighborhood. There were few business transactions that required the Steward-General's approval, but buying a family compound in this most exclusive neighborhood was one of them.

The Safroys, of course, were one of the founding families of this city, and while every noble house waxed and waned in power, the Safroys had never fallen far enough to lose their home above the city.

And a privilege it was, too, because unlike the other neighborhoods of Koh-Salash, High Slope was built on solid ground.

Years before, while sailing to the Free Cities in the fruitless pursuit of a blackmailer, Onderishta had seen the city of Koh-Gilmiere from the water. It surrounded the bay like a blanket laid across rocky ground. Not *flat*, exactly, but thin.

The residents of Koh-Salash had built their own city like a massive, complicated maze within the bones of the dead gods. Blasphemy, many called it, but if the doom of the godkind was to fall on them for their lack of reverence, that stroke was more than four centuries delayed.

It would come, someday. Doom and failure came to all, eventually, whether as revolution, war, or pestilence, but when Koh-Salash collapsed, the long-dead godkind would take the credit.

For now, the city was a noisy, chaotic place. The wealthy, who wanted nothing to do with the stink and shout of the poor, had taken the land on the hillside above Suloh's corpse, where the sun could shine on them directly and there was nothing under their feet to make a noise louder than worms scratching through the earth.

By those standards, the citizens of Koh-Gilmiere—and every other city in the world—lived like Salashi nobility. A curious thought, but Onderishta brushed it aside as she always did. She loved her city. She loved the chaos and the mess. It energized her and gave the investigator bureaucrats tremendous job security.

Onderishta reached the gate. A wall of skywood separated the edge of the uppermost platform from the hill above. According to the High Watch, this wall had been built as a final circle of protection should the city ever be invaded, but that didn't explain why it was as densely patrolled as the massive city wall below. The sentries kept the thieves out, the skywood formed a break against fire, and the noble families slept peacefully through the night.

The constables that checked her token against their ledger were tall and clear-eyed. They were nothing like the stumblers assigned to her units—discarded to her units, more like. Someday…

They found her name in the ledger and she was admitted onto The Avenue. She sidestepped the servants rushing downcity on their errands, then looked up. And felt a chill run down her back.

The Avenue was made of granite cut from a cliff face at Vu-Timmer, shipped by barge and mule all the way to the top of the city. The blocks fit together neatly, even after three hundred years. Surely, someone had replaced broken stones or shored up eroding soil, but Onderishta had never seen anyone doing that work. As far as she knew, it maintained itself, as if it had been created by one of the spellkind.

This part of Salash was steep, which meant The Avenue was full of switchbacks. Along the outer edges, iron posts had been erected, each topped by a lantern with a little wick and a pot of coconut oil. This was not the only street in the city to have artificial lighting after sunset, but it was probably the first.

Those switchbacks made the journey much too long for anyone with real work to do, so shortly after the road itself was finished, the High Watch commissioned a set of granite stairs that ran straight down the middle of those bends and turns. Everyone took the stairs if they had a choice.

Onderishta wasn't daunted by their height or steepness. She was Salashi, born and raised. She climbed stairs and ramps all day, every day. No, it was the sight at the top of the stairs that gave her a chill.

There, crowning Salash Hill above her—above the entire city—was Suloh's skull.

From this angle, she could only see the upper and lower jaws. Many teeth were missing, and the inside of the mouth was not shadow but a glow of pale orange. One had to move far away to see the whole thing.

And since it belonged to a being that once stood three miles tall, that skull was nearly two thousand feet high. On a clear night, it could be seen for hundreds of miles out in the Semprestian and the Timmer Seas.

Onderishta glanced at it, then looked away, then glanced again. Normally, the city's decks blocked any view of the sky, let alone the top of Salash Hill. When she was in Upgarden or the higher platforms of Low Market, buildings on the street or the steepness of the hill hid that skull.

But she couldn't visit High Slope without getting chills.

Which was silly, really. She lived among godkind bones, walked on them, read by their light, knocked on doors made from skywood harvested from them. But inside the city, their sheer size hid their true nature. That wasn't possible here.

Zetinna sometimes laughed at her, wondering how someone so sensitive had become an investigator, and Onderishta took care to hide her discomfort from everyone else.

Perhaps what really troubled her was that someone—or something—had pulled off Suloh's head and stuck it all the way up there, more than half a mile from his corpse. No humankind could have done it. That skull had to weigh thousands of tons.

It must have been the Ancient Kings of the Walking Towers themselves, and Onderishta could imagine no reason for it except as a show of power and a promise that—having murdered the gods themselves—they would return someday.

But this was not something a lowly bureaucrat needed to fret about.

The Safroy compound was not at the top of the Avenue, but it was near. It sat on a plateau at the very edge of the third switchback from the top of the hill, in the southernmost part of the city, where the view showed Vu-Timmer and the Semprestian Sea beyond. Above the entrance way was the engraved symbol of a bull's head. While the white paint on the stone walls was maintained with painstaking care—as were the walls of every noble family—the engraving had been allowed to weather and fade as if to demonstrate just how long it had hung there.

Onderishta approached the gate and found, as expected, an elderly woman waiting. Unlike most of the families on High Slope, the Safroys put a servant—too weak for other work—at the entrance to their home to welcome guests, rather than a guard to intimidate them. The guards stood just out of sight, their blades bared.

"How are you, Pinagrath, child of Eldograth? Knees still bothering you?"

The servant bowed. "I am well, thank you, good madam." She

unlatched the gate. "May your troubles lose track of you in this humble home."

Onderishta bowed in return—but less deeply—before entering. In the antechamber beyond, she gave the guards her knife, then allowed herself to be searched.

They were polite but professional. She'd been called there many times, after all. Another servant in a long white robe waited for her, and when she was judged safe, he led her through stone halls, past frescoes depicting ships on stormy seas, and warriors fighting atop walls at the edge of an abyss, past basins of clear water on small tables, and the slow-running fountains from which they had been filled, past busy servants and nervous supplicants, past the quiet strumming of harp music and the loud clash of wooden practice swords.

Culzatik awaited her on one of the many verandas of this hillside home. It was not a large space, but it did connect to the family library, and the Safroy heir had turned it into an office of sorts, working from a small skywood desk. At the moment, he was covered with sweat, and there was an iron practice sword leaning against the wall. The pommel of the pretend sword, the skywood desk, and the lintel above the entrance to the library were all marked with the Safroy bull.

"Oh, good," Culzatik said. "We have much to cover, so I'm glad you're early."

Of course, Onderishta was exactly on time. "I live to serve, your virtue."

Aziatil glanced at her, then looked away, her hands far from her knives. The only other person on the veranda was a soft-bellied young man with long hair hanging in his face. His attention was fixed on a book, and he did not seem to notice her.

"Selsarim Lost, Ulfender," Culzatik said to him. "Wake up."

The pudgy young man raised his eyes. "Sorry. Hello."

"Good day, your virtue," Onderishta replied. Ulfender admir-Shelti hold-Shelti had been Culzatik's lover since he was old enough to take one, but Onderishta did not understand the appeal. If an overstuffed couch cushion could squint, that would have been Ulfender.

"We still have a bit of time, I think," Culzatik said. He stood. "Would you like to see the family glitterkind?"

CHAPTER NINE

Riliska had seen Kyrioc when he was sad or quiet, but she had never seen him like this. He looked as though she had snitched on him to the cosh.

"Good sir!" the constable called. "If you would, please?"

Riliska looked again at his expression and dared to hope he would come for her anyway.

He didn't. Kyrioc turned on his heel and slipped between two buildings without a backward glance.

"Good sir? Good sir, are you…" The constable turned toward Riliska. "Is that your father?"

Riliska looked down at the deck again so she would not have to look the grownups in the face. She expected another slap, but it didn't come. The woman said, "Send this one downcity where she belongs." Then she seized her son's elbow and dragged him down the street.

The thought that the cosh might drag Riliska off to Mudside brought up a wave of panic. It wasn't fair! She and her mother had lived in Woodgarden for three whole years. She didn't even know anyone down there!

But how could she prove it? She couldn't lead the cosh to her mother. They might collar her. Then Riliska would be truly alone, just another orphan in a city full of them.

Time to run. But simply thinking that thought made the cosh behind her seize her arm roughly. How did he know what she was thinking?

"Don't bother." The first ironshirt took off her helmet and scratched at her shaved scalp. She glanced at the spot where Kyrioc had vanished, then shrugged. "The bitch walks away, we get to walk away." Laying her hand on her truncheon, she looked down at Riliska. There was no kindness in her expression. "I suspect we'll be seeing more of you in the coming years."

The ironshirt didn't just release Riliska, he shoved her. She stumbled and nearly fell onto the dirty planks. The cosh strolled off, not seeming to give her another thought.

A terrible anger welled up inside her. The way that horrible woman had treated her, just because she'd picked up that tablet. The way the cosh had shoved her, as if she was nothing. The way Kyrioc...the Broken Man...

She stood and clenched her fists, wishing she had something to throw or smash. She wanted to stamp her foot and shatter the plankways beneath her. She wanted to swing a gigantic axe and cut Yth's ribs like paintbrush bristles. She wished she was an immortal warrior like one of the ghostkind, so she could draw a gigantic sword and cut down everyone who had ever been unfair to her.

Wishes and fantasies ran through her head like rushing water, and they did nothing but make her feel helpless. She was just a little girl in a dark city with no one to protect her.

For a moment, Riliska was tempted to follow Kyrioc into that narrow space between the buildings, even though it was gang space. There was nothing back there but one of Yth's abandoned temples, anyway. What was he going to do, pray to dead gods?

A white-haired man leaned on the post of his vegetable stall, staring down at something in his hand. Should she grab something from him and run? Even though midday had passed, she hadn't eaten yet, and the whistle she'd gotten for her chimes lay hidden in her room. She couldn't go home. She would almost rather be grabbed by the cosh again than hear more of those sounds from her mother.

But that white-haired man knew her name. He could set the cosh on her mother if he wanted to.

I suspect we'll be seeing more of you in the coming years.

She moved close, tempted to do it anyway. Just grab something, anything, and get in trouble. Real trouble. It would be a relief to get it over with.

She suddenly realized Kyrioc was beside her. He'd appeared out of nowhere like a ghost.

"Riliska, do you think I'm a bad person?"

The scar on his cheek was bloodless and ugly. It was the ugliest thing she'd ever seen. It was so horrible that she couldn't speak, and she felt slightly ill that she'd ever eaten a meal with that face right across the table.

There was something in his expression that she didn't like.

He said, "You said you wouldn't steal anymore."

She snatched a pair of carrots off a shelf and ran.

* * *

CULZATIK COULDN'T HELP IT. He got a childish satisfaction at the look of surprise on Onderishta's face. Maybe it was unworthy of the heir of a noble house that dated back to Lost Selsarim, but he took his pleasures where he could. Besides, he suspected she didn't think much of him. This might raise her esteem.

Or not. It didn't really matter.

When Ulfender heard Culzatik offer a tour of the family wards, he did something Culzatik had never seen him do before. He snapped his book shut and sat upright in one fluid motion.

"Oh, I'm sorry, baby," Culzatik said to him. "This is business."

Ulfender looked as though he might protest, but instead, he shrugged and returned to his book.

Culzatik led Onderishta into the library, then pushed aside a bookcase to reveal a secret door. There was no handle. He knocked three times, then two, then four. A moment later, a guard wearing the Safroy bull on his breastplate pulled the door open and allowed them entry.

Before them lay the southern atrium. Trees grew comfortably in the rich soil of the hill, and short grasses grew between them. A small pile of artfully arranged stones disguised the spout of a fountain, and a thin trickle flowed down a rock-lined gully into a small artificial pond.

But it wasn't the atrium that seized Onderishta's attention. It was the glitterkind within it.

There were three of them. In some ways, they looked very much like humankind. They lay upon the grass as if sleeping—their eyes were shut and their mouths open as if they were about to snore—although of course they were utterly breathless and soundless.

They were also naked, sexless, and white-fleshed—but not with the pinkish white of the Katr barbarians. This was a bluish white, like the marble of his mother's favorite table. Nothing about their breasts, shoulders, or hips suggested gender. To Culzatik, they looked like slender, spindly children of five or six.

Except for one thing—two were over ten feet from heel to crown, and the other was just above fourteen long.

But the most striking thing about them was the trait that gave them their name. Where daylight touched their skin, tiny facets in their flesh threw off sparks of color. They glittered in every color of the rainbow.

Onderishta said nothing. She simply gaped. And why not?

Culzatik touched her arm and led her toward a stone bench at the southern end of the atrium. Aziatil stayed close. "There's no need to trim the trees or cut the grass," he said. "The glitterkind themselves keep the plants from overgrowing. It's been theorized that they siphon off a certain amount of the plants' vitality to sustain themselves. They thrive only when left outside among greenery, where the sun and the rain can touch them."

She lifted her head toward the arching bars overhead. "That's why the bars are in place?"

"They're not really bars, just painted to look like dull steel. We used to have an iron cage overhead to protect our wards from thievery, but it turned out that it attracted lighting strikes. This new cage is skywood. It's not cheap, but it's as hard as stone and it won't burn."

"And you paint it to resemble iron so potential thieves will bring the wrong tools."

Culzatik smiled. "Exactly so."

Onderishta stared at the creatures. "They're beautiful."

"I'm glad I can show them on a sunny day."

"Thank you, your virtue. Seeing this delights me, but I assume I'm here so I will recognize glitterkind flesh in the future."

Culzatik raised one ink-stained finger toward the far corner. "Do you see the wood and canvas rigging? Those are the scales the bureaucrats use to weigh our wards, to be sure we don't sell healing magic on the black market. You see, glitterkind are like water. When a portion has been slivered, it does not show."

"What do you mean, your virtue?"

He held up his left hand. "If I were to cut off the last joint of my pinky finger, it would be gone forever. Anyone who looked at my hand would see the scars and the missing joints. It could only be restored through magic."

"Are you saying the glitterkind can grow back missing limbs?"

"Not precisely. As I said, they are like water. This shape you see before you—" He gestured toward the sleeping figures. "This is the shape the creature assumes. It is always this shape, and if some outside force acts on it, the ward returns to this. If you cut one ounce of glitterkind flesh from the end of their small finger or from that mass atop their heads that's shaped like hair, the severed part would keep its shape, but before the day was out, the ward would be whole again. The creature's flesh would have—and I apologize, but this is the best way to describe it—would have slowly flowed into that space so the ward would appear whole again."

Onderishta nodded. "But the glitterkind itself would still be one ounce lighter."

"Yes. The change to the creature as a whole might be imperceptible, but if you weighed it on one of those scales, it would be one ounce less than before. As long as the portions are slivered in very small increments and iron never touches the creature's body—just the touch of iron will burn and scar them—they remain hardy and strong. Our main task is to sliver them more slowly than they naturally grow."

Onderishta's voice became quiet. "Is that what you suspect that package contained? Did you send me out to recover an ounce of stolen glitterkind flesh before the theft became public?"

"No!" Culzatik said. "Our security is excellent, and all three of our wards are weighed weekly. We're very careful."

"Have you been accused of selling black-market magic?"

Culzatik sighed. "Not yet." There was a commotion from the front of the house. "I think that's our cue," Culzatik said. "Let's move quickly."

The guard opened the door for them and they hurried back into the library.

"I still don't quite understand what you are asking, your virtue. If you thought there was a handover of—and I can't believe I'm saying this—of black-market glitterkind flesh—"

"Suspected," Culzatik interjected. "I only had a vague suspicion."

"Even so, we're talking about a crime on a par with treason. If you had shared your suspicion about the exchange—"

"Yes, of course, you're correct. I had my reasons for withholding that information, but I can see now that I was wrong. I apologize."

That seemed to mollify her. In truth, Culzatik had two reasons to keep his suspicions to himself. First, he was afraid Onderishta would overplay her hand, bringing in so much security to acquire the package that she would spook the courier and lose their only chance at it.

The other was that he was afraid to be wrong. The other noble families might have voted his mother out of the High Watch, but she was still widely respected. If Culzatik earned a reputation for being impulsive or unreliable, Safroy stitches would move to more stable sails, and his mother's political faction would restrict him to a role as an advisor or aide. In short, it would weaken his—and his family's—position.

The incident at Kyrionik's Mourning Day service was embarrassing enough.

They returned to the veranda just in time to receive Essatreska admir-Phillien, Culzatik's future wife.

* * *

ONLY YEARS OF DISCIPLINE kept Onderishta from rolling her eyes when Essatreska admir-Phillien swept into the room.

Her jet-black hair had been pinned to a small wooden frame to make it point upward with the characteristic bulge and curl of a candle flame. Set within were several rings of multifaceted glass beads, which reflected the daylight in a pale imitation of glitterkind flesh. Her frilled white robe was pinned with an assortment of golden brooches. One, above her left breast, bore the leaping fish of the Phillien family. The others were decorative but nondescript.

Her face had been carefully painted, with white lines radiating from her eyes like sunbeams, and a tiny red fish on her right cheek. The hand she extended to Culzatik had been painted with intricate, dizzying designs, and her nails were a bright yellow. The color did not complement her, but Onderishta knew it was rare, new, and expensive, and fashion had always valued those things above merely looking good.

This wasn't the first time Onderishta and Essatreska had met, not that the young woman would remember. A year before, Culzatik had requested a dossier on her, and Onderishta had followed the girl for a month. In an unlucky coincidence, they'd engaged in an extended conversation about the location of a certain shop in Low Market.

The job, and the dossier, had been rather dull, but Culzatik had been pleased and nothing further was said on the matter. Essatreska glanced at Onderishta without any sign of recognition.

Then, as now, Onderishta felt an unaccustomed stirring when she saw the young woman. Betraying any sort of interest in her would be absurd, but beneath all that paint and artifice was a woman who was as beautiful as a goddess. And she knew it.

Entering with her was Bedler of Koh-Alzij, her bodyguard. He was just over six feet tall, broad as a temple door and almost as solid. He was rumored to have once been a bard—a rumor he started himself, which was carefully noted in the dossier—before entering the tournaments, but now he followed the eldest Phillien daughter from one shop to the next, scowling and laying his hand on his maul when the Wrong People got too close.

Culzatik's bodyguard, Aziatil, had entered the tournaments in the same year as Bedler. Aziatil had placed almost at the bottom, ranked seventeenth, while Bedler had earned third place. Nevertheless, when it was Culzatik's turn to hire a bodyguard, he had chosen from the bottom of the list.

Aziatil remained stoic, but Bedler allowed himself a contemptuous grin when he saw the slender young woman.

Essatreska curtsied, her painted hand extended. "Thank you for receiving us, my betrothed."

"Thank you for visiting," Culzatik replied, clasping her offered hand and bending over slightly. "I'm sorry you missed the Mourning Day service."

"Too painful," she said, her expression miming a show of grief that was undercut by every other thing about her. "Kyrionik was important to me. Losing him… I cared deeply for him."

Kyrionik's betrothal to Essatreska was more of a business deal than a love match and everyone knew it. When he failed to return from his First Labor, the Safroy and Phillien families had reassigned the contract to the new Safroy heir, and the bride-to-be did not hide her displeasure about this new arrangement. Kyrionik had been an athlete, a fighter, and a bit of a daredevil. Frankly, Onderishta thought he was a brash young idiot. But girls made excuses to be near him and boys looked up to him. He had magnetism.

Culzatik didn't.

"So many times," she said, "I dreamed of being his wife. I'm afraid I might have run out of the service in tears. As you did."

If this remark stung Culzatik, he didn't show it. "Of course," he said, smiling sympathetically. "You're a very sensitive person."

Essatreska's delicate nose wrinkled slightly at this, as though she was not sure if she'd just been insulted. "I must also ask you to delay the remainder of your bride price until the fall. It just seems…disrespectful, somehow."

That was a surprise. Even Aziatil blinked double-time. But all Culzatik said was, "If it would make you happy, my betrothed, I am pleased to do so."

"Hmm. I did not expect you to agree so readily. Is the Safroy family having money troubles? I hear so many rumors."

This time, Culzatik did not respond at all. He simply smiled, holding Essatreska's gaze in his, and let the silence play out.

"Hello, Ulfender," she said, her voice chilly, "what have you been up to?"

He looked up. "Studying the text of *The Lai of Shulss and His Dragon* to help Culza find evidence that it shares an author with—"

"I don't care about that," Essatreska interrupted.

Ulfender turned his attention back to his book. "And yet you asked."

A frosty silence fell again. After a short while, Essatreska shifted uncomfortably, then glanced around the room. "You Safroys stick a bull's head on everything, don't you?"

"Pardon me!" called a voice from the hall. It was a man's voice, reedy and anxious. "Pardon me, my goodness, please."

Bedler pivoted to allow an older man into the room. He was about fifty and had perhaps been handsome in his youth, but his face had gone pouchy and his expression was anxious. His white robes, the proper color for nobles on Mourning Day, were brand new but not especially fine. It seemed the family clothing budget was being spent on the Phillien daughter. "Culzatik, my boy! It's so good to… Essatreska, what are you up to *now*? Culzatik, I'm *mortified* that we were not at the service today, honestly. It was impossible to make *anything* happen at home this morning. I swear, their mother was able to corral my girls, but without her I'm helpless—"

Culzatik clasped the man's hand. "Ponnalas, it's good to see you."

"It's good to see you, too, my boy. I heard about the commotion at the service. For what it's worth, I think you did the right thing. If only people weren't so panicky… But still, all life is sacred, yes?"

"Absolutely," Culzatik said with every semblance of sincerity.

Ponnalas gestured at their funeral clothes. "This must be terrible for you, even after nearly eight years."

"Every time I think I've put it behind me, I discover I haven't."

"The uncertainty must be most difficult. When my wife passed, I was right beside her. I knew my world had changed forever in that moment. But for you to wait so long without knowing for sure. I confess I still hope that he will return again, alive, with an amazing story to tell."

"In quiet moments," Culzatik said, "so do I. Then I could return to him his position in the family and all the other aspects of this life that are rightfully his, and I could return to those that are rightfully mine."

"Your library, yes? And perhaps a position in Suloh's Tower, studying the history of Lost Selsarim?" Culzatik nodded, and Ponnalas laid a friendly hand on his shoulder. "I am sorry, my boy, so very sorry about today. We owed it to your family to be there, and I have come to apologize in person. Your parents are in seclusion, but I'm glad I can say this to you, at least."

"Accepted. You are always welcome, Ponnalas. Is Caflinna with you?"

"She would not leave her rooms. She and her sister…" He glanced back and saw that Essatreska had already left. "Lately, they can barely look at each other. I can't decide which is more troublesome."

"When you return home, please tell her that I acquired that copy of the final volume of *The Kings of Koh-Benjatso and Their Wars*, and I'm sure she would like to read it."

"Thank you. That really is most kind. Most kind. Now I should go."

"I'll show you out." Culzatik turned to Onderishta. "Just a moment." He left.

A welcome silence settled onto the veranda, broken only by Ulfender carefully turning pages. Onderishta went to the balcony rail.

The day was hot and the sun bright, but a cool breeze blew up the hill from the water. The air was clear and fresh in a way that air inside the city could never be, even when the winds were strong, and Onderishta studied the sensation so she would remember it. The veranda was positioned to face almost due south. Very little of Koh-Salash itself could be seen, and as much as Onderishta loved her city, so much green and blue was soothing.

Vu-Timmer lay far below, bustling with small, sail-less craft. The great body of water beyond, the Semprestian Sea, was full of merchant trading vessels, some sailing northward into the strait, where the Salashi people would collect their due, or else outward to other lands, having already paid the Steward-General's toll.

By the fallen gods, it all looked peaceful from up here. Was there anything more deceptive than Salashi lands from a distance?

Culzatik returned. "I'm sorry to delay you here, Onderishta, child of Intermala, but I wanted to show you directly what I'm facing."

"Your betrothed hates you."

"I wouldn't say that," Culzatik said with a rueful grin. "She thinks I'm beneath her. She thought Kyrionik was a husband worthy of her, but she thinks a marriage to me is demeaning. Her problem is that we have already paid her family a substantial bride price, and Ponnalas admir-Phillien cannot afford to pay it back."

"So, she intends to cause a scandal so she can cancel the marriage contract and keep the bride price already paid."

"Plus whatever additional wealth and influence her family can acquire when my mother is hung for treason and our properties dispersed."

Onderishta nodded. It was a vicious plan, but she was an investigator. She'd seen cruelty beyond imagining. She didn't have it in her to be shocked anymore.

"Thanks to the dossier you prepared," the young man continued, "I have spies in the Phillien compound. According to reports, Essatreska believes she's about to locate the Lost Ward."

This again. Onderishta stoicism failed her. "There have been rumors of a Lost Ward since I was an apprentice. Those rumors have never panned out."

Culzatik shrugged. "The Phillien sail is not large, but there's money in it. According to my reports, two of her stitches paid for cosmetic surgery, getting their skin grafts on the black market. Essatreska believes the Lost Ward is real. Frankly, I think she's right."

"Your virtue, the Lost Ward is a child's fable. There have always been rumors of black-market healing magic. It's just wish fulfillment."

"What if it arrived only recently, within the last few years? Decades of unproven rumor would mean the bureaucracy would not take the rumors seriously, and black-market trade could continue in secret."

Onderishta turned back to the sea and sky. Anything was possible, but this wasn't the first time she'd heard this particular conspiracy, and it had always turned out to be a waste of time. Perhaps one of the reasons Culzatik kept his suspicions about the package a secret was because Onderishta would have brushed the job off to her second and spent the evening at home with her much-neglected wife.

"Your virtue, I think it's time to start this story at the beginning."

"Fine. Six months ago, I received a message from a pawnbroker down in Low Market that she had a book to sell me. It's a disreputable place, but it's the only shop willing to fence stolen books, largely because they can sell them to me."

"If we shut down that fence, your virtue, thieves would have nowhere to sell books and would stop stealing them."

"Experienced thieves would stop, but amateurs would not. Book thieves are usually students about to flunk out of Suloh's Tower or disgruntled servants, and if they discover too late there's no way to turn them into coin, they burn the evidence of their crime. My way, the books are preserved and I return them to their proper owner, after I've made a copy for myself."

Regretting her interruption, Onderishta said, "A sensible plan, your virtue."

"Aziatil and I dressed in nondescript clothing and hurried through the city. As we came into view of the shop, we saw Bedler of Koh-Alzij walk out. We were some distance away and he did not notice us in our common clothing, but he was unmistakable. After conducting our usual business, I pressured the broker to tell me why Bedler had come to see her. It took some doing, but she finally admitted that he was trying to arrange medical treatment outside of a hospital. She said she turned him away, and we believed her.

"Since then, he's been visiting the decks of the city, trying to get in contact directly with Harl Sota List Im, but without much luck."

"He's lucky he's not dead."

"He can fight," Culzatik said with a shrug. "The tournament proved that. For whatever that's worth. Anyway, Essatreska has done her best to recruit her servants and stitches into the search, but it was only recently that they heard Harl was entrusting one of his lieutenants to set up their own black-market medical operation."

"But your virtue, a black-market hospital? It doesn't seem possible."

He spread his palms. "Now you see why I was reluctant to share my suspicions. But let's assume that Essatreska's source, which I haven't been able to identify, is correct and the gangs of Koh-Salash think they can get away with it."

"They would need glitterkind flesh. That was the exchange I was supposed to break up."

"It was. I'm sure Bedler was there and he intended to steal the package for Essatreska."

Onderishta suddenly realized she'd seen Bedler there, outside Sailsday's Regret. Not his face, but that figure stood out in a crowd. "Maybe he did, your virtue. My people have been trailing heavies all over the city, but if we'd known, we would have collared that asshole immediately."

"He doesn't have it," Culzatik answered. "Essatreska and I have been betrothed since our parents realized that Kyrionik wasn't going to return, because the union of our families makes business sense. However, the contract couldn't be *legally* transferred until the Mourning Day Service after he disappeared, more than seven years ago. Tomorrow it becomes official, and she just asked me to delay payment of the final installment of the bride price."

"She's still stalling."

"Otherwise, her play would have hit us yesterday, the morning after the package was acquired."

"*If* the package was a portion of glitterkind, your virtue," Onderishta said.

Culzatik nodded, conceding the point. "If. It's possible that it was white tar or the deed to a copper mine, and Bedler is the pickpocket, and your second is chasing a figment of my imagination."

"But you don't think so."

"I don't."

"The real question is, where do they get their information? Harl doesn't just kill gangsters who sell him out. He skins them."

Culzatik shrugged. "So far, my spies haven't heard Bedler name his source, but getting this information isn't as difficult as it sounds. For us, anyway. Heavies on the street would never talk to the eye or the cosh, but a noble family's flunky with some money to spend? That's different."

Hmf. Onderishta wasn't pleased to hear that, but she filed the information away for future reference. "So, you want me to collar Bedler with glitterkind flesh in his pocket?"

"No. Please, no. Remember when I told you that iron will burn glitterkind flesh? Well, every ward in Koh-Salash has been branded with a special mark that identifies the family charged with its care. I believe Bedler of Koh-Alzij carries a tiny iron brand with him. If he were to get his hand on a piece of glitterkind flesh, even for a moment, he could lay the brand onto it. Arrest him then—"

"And this Lost Ward would appear to be Safroy property."

"Precisely. That's not a scandal. That's treason. Among all the terrible things that would happen to the Safroy family, my mother would get the pitch and flame just like a common murderer. All of Koh-Salash would turn up to watch. That's why I need you to find this Lost Ward first and get it somewhere Bedler can never reach it."

Onderishta nodded. It made sense. The idea that there really was a Lost Ward still made her skeptical, but she would have to look into this carefully.

"You need more people," Culzatik said, "but I'm afraid it's not going to be the specially trained soldiers you've been asking for." He removed a token from his pocket and pressed it into her hand. "On my authority, take these two apprentices under your guidance. Don't make that expression."

"I have no expression, your virtue."

"The expression is inside your mind. I can see it there. These two are smart and will work hard. They can also run and scout for you."

Onderishta thought back to the two young woman who were supposed to be working undercover. "I need trained, experienced operatives, your virtue, who can fight when necessary."

"Yes, I've read your reports—"

He was interrupted by a gentle knock on the door. That same white-robed servant padded into the room. "Your virtue, your noble father requests your presence."

"Shit. I'll be along shortly," Culzatik said. To Onderishta, he said, "For the moment, these are the best I can do. However, once this matter is settled, everything will be different for you. I have plans for you, Onderishta, child of Intermala." He hurried to the door.

Onderishta was thunderstruck.

Plans? She was already where she wanted to be, doing the work she loved. What did this boy know about her life or *her* plans?

More importantly, what was he going to order her to do?

The servant gently cleared his throat. Of course. She left Ulfender reclining with his book and descended into the city once again.

* * *

KYRIOC KNEW IT WAS the wrong thing to say as soon as the words were out of his mouth. He'd treated her like an addict or a pickpocket. Again. Why was it so fucking hard to show a little kindness?

He took a pair of silver whistles from his pocket and approached the counter. "Two carrots and a pair of those fig buns, plus the two carrots she took."

The old man set the device he'd been working with on the counter. It was a series of interlocked wooden links. A simple puzzle. He made change. "She's a good girl but she's always out on the street, running around all alone like an orphan. Why don't you spend more time with her? She deserves better."

Kyrioc took the food and went into the street. Riliska was gone.

The complaint about the wax tablet had seemed like such a small thing. At worst, the constables would have scolded her and sent her home. Nothing important had been at stake. For her.

But that was his perspective. Riliska was a little girl. Those slaps and insults must have made her feel powerless. And in that moment, she'd turned to him for protection.

He returned to his building and went to the third floor. Riliska wasn't there. In fact, the hall was empty but for three boys with dirt on their faces and challenge in their eyes. They were couriers used by the local gangsters, but Kyrioc couldn't guess why they were there.

They hadn't seen Riliska—or wouldn't admit to it—so he ventured out into Woodgarden again. If the old shopkeeper was correct, the girl was often out in the neighborhood, but he had no idea where her favorite places were, or where he might find her friends.

...running around all alone.

Kyrioc had survived for years as a trapper and a hunter, but here, in this city, he'd never learned to track people by the signs they left. He wasn't even sure it was possible with so many people tramping over the wooden decks.

All he could do was return to the last place he'd seen her and walk street to street, alley to alley. If she was hiding behind a barrel of trash or sitting on the landing of a stairwell, he would find her. If she'd gone indoors, he would not. Not until she emerged again.

Night fell before he saw her again. She had ducked down the same alley he'd used when he had walked away from the constables, and was sitting on a low wall outside the abandoned temple. Her sandaled feet kicked at the marred but intricate carvings of branch and vine along the rim.

Kyrioc made sure to scuff his steps when he approached so he would not surprise her. She glanced up, then turned resentfully away. Raised voices came from within the temple. It was the sound of boys at celebration, boasting in that sacred place to brace their fragile courage.

Moving close, Kyrioc held out the sack of carrots and stale buns. She took it, but she wouldn't look at him.

He was right. He had hurt her badly. Possibly worse than he could really understand. "I'm sorr—"

"I embarrass you, don't I?" The question startled him. "That's okay. I'm used to it. The other kids in the neighborhood like to pretend I'm not here, and so does the tutor Mom hired for me. Once she realized Mom wasn't going to stand over her every second, she started acting like I was a piece of furniture."

Kyrioc kept silent so she could have her say.

"That stupid cow back there, with her stupid son, tried to tell me I didn't belong here. She wanted to throw me into Mudside, where no one would ever see me again. But what you did was worse. You can't just treat a person like they're real one day and then later act like they're not. That's too mean. You have to pick one and stick with it. Okay? If you don't, it's too hard for me to know what to do.

"Maybe I *should* go down into Mudside. Isn't that where the thieves come from, and the little bloodkind, who sneak into the nursery and night and feed on babies? Maybe I could become like the bloodkind and come back for that kid in the dark. Maybe down there in the dark, I could... Mom says that we're cursed. Not just us, the whole city. She says this is a cursed place and she thought we would all be dead by now."

By the faint light of Suloh's bones, shining through a gap in the decks above, Kyrioc could see tears on her cheeks.

"Sometimes, when Mom gets really drunk, she says we should die. She says that would be easier than living this life. *Never let anyone near you. Better to be dead.*"

A chorus of cheers erupted from the temple, followed by jeering. Riliska took a deep, shuddering breath.

"It's okay, though. It's okay. Even though I'm mad at you right now, I'm not going to hate you. I can't. You're nice to me sometimes. More than my mom is. If I let myself hate you, I wouldn't even have that."

Clutching the sack to her chest, Riliska leaped off the wall and ran through the refuse of the alley. Kyrioc watched her go, then he sat on the wall in the dim light. The teenage boys inside the temple continued to sing and boast, their voices slurred with drink, but for Kyrioc, they might have been a continent away. He could hear nothing but the pounding of blood in his ears. And he could feel nothing but the churn of shame and anger within him.

Hurting people seemed to be the only thing he was good for.

* * *

RILISKA RAN HOME AND saw that her door was standing open very slightly. She slipped inside quietly in case the fuddled man had returned. A strange humming came from the back room. Riliska recognized her mother's voice but not the tune. If it was a tune at all.

"Mom?"

Goosebumps ran down Riliska's back. Something bad was happening, but she knew her mother's voice. She had to go to her.

Riliska slid the bedroom door open. She was not surprised to see a man in the room with her mother, but she hadn't expected to see her mother tied up and gagged. Her mother's skirt was torn, revealing her long brown legs. The man held a fistful of her hair.

Her mother wasn't humming. She was screaming through her gag.

The man looked at Riliska, and any thought of helping her mother vanished. *STOP AND GO AWAY*, she'd imagined herself saying, but now that the moment had come, she understood how powerless she was and how empty and silly her words would be.

The man's eyes were wild, and his smile was huge. She'd seen scary smiles on scary people, but never like this. He wore silk finery and a steel chain around his neck, like one of the fashionable partiers outside the platform halls who came to her to be painted.

He gasped in a mocking way, then pretended to be ashamed, then smiled again. He was clowning, but not for her.

Riliska could not look away. He was younger than she first thought, and he was handsome.

But in his crazy smile she could see that he enjoyed other people's pain.

He held up his thumb and index finger, then pressed them together as though his hand was a tiny pincer. Then he moved his hand to mother's face and, with his tiny pincer, pinched her nostrils.

Mother struggled and kicked. She sucked air into her mouth, but the gag was large and tight, and her eyes showed her panic. She was suffocating. She was being murdered right here in this room.

Goosebumps ran down Riliska's back. Was she really seeing this? Was this really happening in this very moment? Even though she knew she should run, she could not move. That horrible smile, so rigid and cruel like the grin of a carved wooden puppet, held her transfixed.

Then, with a sort of peekaboo expression of surprise, the man released his grip, and Mother desperately inhaled through her nose, her ribs heaving and her nostrils flaring.

Then she screamed through the gag. This time, it didn't sound like humming at all.

The man with the steel chain did something Riliska did not think possible. He smiled even wider than before.

A hand clamped on Riliska's shoulder. She could hear little chimes behind her, like the ones she'd sold to Kyrioc, only smaller. The hand on her shoulder was large, and rough, with ugly red hairs sprouting from the knuckles.

Another hand covered her eyes. Now she couldn't see what was making her mother scream, and if the red-haired man thought that was kindness, he was so very wrong.

CHAPTER TEN

Onderishta glanced at the token Culzatik had given her. It was for the Academy levels of the tower at the south end of the city. In theory, it would grant her access to Suloh's Tower. In theory.

The double doors ahead of her were arched and banded with iron. Two guards, leather scourges in hand, stood outside. They wore no armor other than burnished helm and breastplate, and their shields were faced with gleaming steel. They rarely drew the swords at their hips, but she expected they had been polished just as brightly. Their expressions made clear that they did not have an easygoing attitude about their duties.

The Academy was not a bureaucratic institution, after all. It was Suloh's temple.

The paving stones around the temple entrance were the boundary. No one was to cross from the paler wooden deck except on temple business, under pain of a lash. A guard noted Onderishta and the token in her hand, and stepped forward to greet her. She handed him the token. He examined it in the lantern light, returned it, and let her pass.

To a new visitor in Upgarden, Suloh's temple would look like little more than a bungalow. The dome roof was only four feet above the top of the door frame, with a few narrow, crooked pipes to act as chimneys.

The other guard knocked. The door swung open onto a dimly lit chamber as large as the bungalow itself, where a second pair of guards admitted her. Onderishta's boots rang as she stepped onto the metal grate.

Extending down several thousand feet was the main part of Suloh's Tower, which grew wider the farther down you went. Warm air rose through the grate. Below, in rings down the inside of the tower, were books upon books, one row after another, down through the many levels of Koh-Salash.

And suspended in the center of the shaft were long, narrow, pointed crystals, each glowing with a faint orange light. They were Suloh's teeth, pried from his skull centuries before, and they looked like the fangs of a gigantic serpent.

Before they were destroyed, the godkind had been predators.

Far below, the tower was much wider to accommodate the libraries, laboratories, barracks, suites, classrooms, and more. That was where she was headed, but it was too far to see.

Onderishta took a deep breath, trying not to think about the height or the fact that she was standing on a trapdoor. It was the third line of defense for this entrance. If the guards didn't like the look of a visitor, they could pull a lever and drop them into an iron cage. Most were freed after an interrogation, but not all.

Like religious zealots everywhere, temple guards could be fickle about how they treated people, but Onderishta must have caught them after a meal. The captain actually smiled politely before he unbarred the inner gate. Then he took her iron knife.

She would have to come all the way back up if she wanted it back. Still, she knew better than to protest. She started down the stairs.

The lift, a flimsy-looking corkscrew of a platform that barely held two people, passed her going up, then came back down again. Miraculously, it was empty. She stepped on. Suloh's Tower was as tall as the city of Koh-Salash itself, and while she had climbed stairs and ramps her whole life, it was a long, long way.

But where were the people? No one was dusting the shelves, or hunting for a book. The place was eerily quiet. It was only after she passed the first study rooms that she remembered what day it was. Students and tutors alike were away, mourning their loved ones.

The hall outside the main offices were deserted except for a girl of nine sweeping a corridor. The child obligingly led Onderishta through a maze of offices to what appeared to be the sole occupied desk.

An elderly man crouched by his window, quill fluttering as he scratched out a letter. There was a stack of correspondence at his elbow.

"Goodness, what is this?" he asked, irritated. "Can't a fellow get some work done on a holiday? What is it?"

"A token." Onderishta handed the tile to him. He squinted at it, then sighed.

To the little girl, he said, "How is your sweeping coming? Almost finished?" She nodded. "Good. Finish up and we can go down to the kitchens. I asked Cook to prepare extra fig buns just for us. Now run along."

The girl sprinted away.

"She's not supposed to be running in the Academy, but...herm...I'm not supposed to be telling her to run, either. Must break that habit someday. She's a good child, especially when you consider where she came from. One of our orphan students. Tested in, as they do. You really need top scores to make it by that route, but even so, those students always seem to be damaged in some way that wealthier children aren't. I'm Flustice tuto-Beskeroth."

"Onderishta, child of Intermala, your virtue." They shook hands. The old man's grip was fragile, but his eyes were alert.

Flustice stood and stretched. After a brief groan, he doddered toward the door, waving for Onderishta to follow. "Looking for apprentices, are you? Orders from some noble or other." He squinted at the token again. "Safroys, eh? Hmf. Must be important. You're lucky you caught me here. Most of the tutors and staff... Well, you know. Makes this the perfect time to get work done. No *interruptions*. Usually. Sometimes, I think the worst place to get any work done is at work."

"I don't keep many office hours."

"Hrm, yes. You're the investigator. Don't look so surprised. We haven't met, but I know who you are. We keep sending you apprentices and you keep sending them back!"

"The bureaucracy has many demanding jobs, your virtue," Onderishta said, falling back on her standard response, "but only a few will get you killed if you make a mistake."

The old man snorted. "Hah! Spare me. Just last week, an apprentice perished while inspecting the city wall. Collapsed scaffolding. Two months ago, another fell from a plankway...or he was pushed. If you want to talk about *dangerous* work, what about going to sea? Piracy is the least of it..."

Onderishta tuned him out, annoyed that he was making the risks of working as an investigator or constable seem ordinary. What did this old bookworm know about the dangers she had to face every day?

They arrived in the main office and Flustice approached the log book. It rested on a pedestal in the middle of the room, already open. He flipped pages.

"Hrm. The first number on this chit is for a young woman. Another orphan, although she's not here today. Mourning a friend who was still trying to scrape by on the streets. She's smart but too restless for serious study. Perhaps that's what you're looking for. Still, it's always nice to have the burden of one of our charity cases lifted early. Let's see about this second number, then. A boy this time, also thirteen years old. I don't recognize his name, which probably means he's nothing special, for good or ill."

"When will they return to the Academy for their studies?" Onderishta asked. The old scholar turned slowly in a circle until he found a window. It was shuttered. "It's late."

"Ah. Hrm. They're due back at sundown, although no one respects curfew on Mourning Day. But they might return tonight for a meal."

"When both arrive, send them here." Onderishta took a slip of paper and wrote brief instructions on how to find her little house in The Folly. "I'll see that they're fed. Work begins tonight." She turned to go.

"One moment." The old man leaned on the book with both elbows, staring at her intently. "Hrm. You're a handsome woman of comfortable size. What do you say we get together with a cup of tea sometime?"

Shit. Onderishta had thought she's left this sort of thing behind her when she'd passed her fortieth year. This old scarecrow with the worthless noble title should *definitely* have put it behind him. She suddenly wished she had given him Fay's address instead of her own. "I have a wife, so no."

"Ah, well." Flustice shrugged and began to fill out a work form. He had nothing more to say to her.

* * *

EVENTUALLY, KYRIOC'S THOUGHTS RETURNED to the real world. He wasn't sure how much time had passed since Riliska left him, but the boys inside the temple had gone quiet. Maybe they had moved on. Maybe they had drunk themselves unconscious. It didn't matter. Their Mourning Day was over.

But Kyrioc owed one more debt.

The plankway outside his building was empty except for a shuttered and secured delivery cart parked at the rear. Most likely it was a small, mobile brothel, a common-enough sight in this neighborhood.

But when he entered the lobby of his building, he saw that was empty too. Kyrioc's senses went on full alert. The landlady made a sack of copper knots every night from poor folk in need of a safe, dry place to sleep, and the lobby was always full of men who had spent their days lugging cargo up The Freightway.

Not tonight.

Kyrioc made his way to the third floor. The lock he'd placed on the shop door had been cut and cast aside. Then he heard a slight scrape of flesh against wood and looked down the length of the hall.

Huddled in a dark corner was a malnourished boy of about six. Was he a courier awaiting a job or had he been posted as a lookout?

Kyrioc opened the door and slipped into his rooms, summoning his cloak of shadows. It wrapped around him tightly, engulfing his whole body.

His cloak of iron was nearly invisible and could turn sharp edges like a suit of armor. Unlike a suit of armor, it faded slightly every time it was hit and took tremendous concentration to maintain.

His cloak of mirrors disguised his appearance, but it worked only in crowds, and only if no one looked too closely at him. Just as the cloak of iron faded from repeated blows, the cloak of mirrors faded from sustained attention. Unsurprisingly, his years on Vu-Dolmont had not given him much chance to practice this particular magic.

It was his cloak of shadows that he had used most often and had nearly mastered. It wrapped him in impenetrable darkness through which only he could see, and nothing could shrink or weaken except bright light.

In fact, none of his cloaks worked in daylight, which was hardly a surprise, considering where he'd learned to summon them. If Kyrionik's Mourning Service had been held downcity, he might have passed unnoticed through the crowd, wrapped in his cloak of mirrors.

The interior door to the pawnshop had not been broken open, but the door to his rooms had been. Someone was in his living space.

A short, slender man with three rattail braids on his forehead stepped into the doorway, followed by a bull of a man in magistrate's clothes. Both held lanterns with the wicks burning brightly, and his shadow retreated from them.

Kyrioc let his cloak dissipate in the yellow light. Both men were Salashi, but that was the only trait they shared. The one with the braids was maybe twenty-four, but he'd retained the dumb, careless swagger of a teenager. The big one behind him had muscle, but he lumbered like an aging ox.

Kyrioc took his leather coin purse from his belt and offered it. "Take the coin and go. I won't call the constables."

The little one laughed. "You have something that belongs to my boss." He drew a knife.

* * *

IN THE STREET OUTSIDE the pawnshop, Killer of Devils sat at the reins of the delivery cart. Wooden Pail, one of his employers, was inside the cargo box, whining about the bloodstains on his silks. Killer kept silent. The Pails had not hired him to care about finery. Besides, the young man was winding down.

At least he'd stopped beating the woman in front of her daughter.

He looked up at the side of the building. Lantern light was barely visible through the shutter slats, but it was moving around.

Paper Mouse was taking too long. Why have thieves on the payroll if they couldn't grab what you wanted and get out quickly?

The lights from the room grew brighter, then something struck the shutters so hard, one flew off its hinges and crashed into the street.

The light retreated from the newly exposed window. Wooden Pail slid back the panel between the driver's shelter and the cargo compartment. "What the fuck was that?"

Killer of Devils slid out of the cart, sprinted into the building, and vaulted up the stairs. On the way, he slid the blade of his sword from beneath his long, sleeveless coat.

One of the Pails' beetles—the young children they used as couriers—waited for him on the third floor, pointing at the broken doorway. Paper Mouse stood in the entrance facing the room, his lantern trembling in his hand. His other hand was empty. Killer moved beside him.

In the apartment, Second Boar lay on the floor beneath the broken shutters. He did not move, but he was still breathing.

The third man in the room was a tall, lean, shaggy-haired Salashi in black. A terrible scar covered his left cheek, as though he had been mauled by hounds. When he looked at Killer of Devils, his still, sorrowful expression did not change, even when he saw the bared ghostkind steel.

Killer glanced at Paper. The little thief lifted his chin toward the scarred man. "Shit got complicated."

Again? But Killer did not say it. A warrior didn't scold his fellows in the face of the enemy.

The scarred man said, "Go." He did not move—in fact, he barely looked at them. Killer could sense tension and readiness in his posture, but it was all defensive. It was Killer's holy gift to know what others were about to do before they did it. This man wanted to do nothing. "The constables don't have to be involved. Just go."

The scarred man had taken Second Boar down without receiving a visible mark, but he was speaking the words of a coward, not a warrior. And yet, Killer could sense no fear in him. Like so many things in this awful city, the contradiction bewildered him. "We will go when we have what we came for. Rulenya, child of Rashila pawned something here yesterday. A Harkan wedding robe. We want it."

"That's one full week's interest on top of the loan already paid," the scarred man said. "Six silver whistles in total. She has appeared in person to close out the loan, and she'll need the chit. Loss of the chit will cost a copper knot."

"A copper knot?" Killer shook his head, making the chimes in his beard ring. He leaned back out of the doorway and waved to the beetle. The boy scampered close. "Go downstairs and tell good sir that the shopkeeper needs to see the woman and that he expects her to pay."

The scarred man still had not moved. They stood that way a short while, staring at each other.

"A copper knot," Killer finally said, feeling more murderous and morose than he had been in a long time. That was what a human life was worth in this cursed city. The meanest coin of all. "You want to see her?"

He nodded toward the broken window. The scarred man leaned over Second's still form and looked out.

* * *

KYRIOC RECOGNIZED THE NORTHERNER'S ghostkind steel immediately. There was no point in calling up his cloak of iron, not against an edge like that. The Katr hadn't made an overt threat—hadn't even lifted his weapon—but baring that blade was threat enough.

He leaned over the unconscious thug and looked into the street below.

Beside the delivery cart stood a wild-eyed young man with a long steel chain around his neck. He unlatched the cargo section and, drawing a long, slender knife, dragged someone into view by their hair.

It was Rulenya. She was bound and gagged, and even at this distance, Kyrioc could see she'd been beaten. The wild-eyed man smiled with such exuberant malice that Kyrioc thought he was about to cut her throat while he watched.

"Six whistles?" the sullen Katr said. "A copper knot? You would throw away their lives for that?"

Their lives?

"Mom!"

Riliska lunged out of the cart and tried to bite the hand holding the knife.

The smiling creep was too quick for her. He elbowed her forehead without letting go of Rulenya's hair, knocking the little girl into the cargo box.

"Don't hurt them!" Kyrioc's back was exposed to the thugs behind him, but he didn't care. "Don't hurt them."

The braided heavy sighed. "Then get on with it."

Moving with a desperation he hadn't felt in months, Kyrioc unlocked the shop, then pulled Rulenya's Harken robe out of the five-week box. When he reemerged, the barbarian had attached a short spear handle to the hilt of his sword, turning it into a true ghostkind glaive. Kyrioc tossed the robe to the Katr, who passed it to his companion.

The little gangster unfolded it with a flick of his wrist, then began to squeeze the fabric along the seams. It took only a moment to find what he was looking for. He tore the cloth apart and pulled out a small, flat leather pouch.

Kyrioc could not see all of the pale, tiny thing the heavy removed from the pouch, only the top edge. When the gangster lifted the lantern to shine it onto his prize, the light made it glitter in many colors.

CHAPTER ELEVEN

The heavy with the three braids shot one last venomous look at Kyrioc, then sprinted down the stairs.

There was no mistaking what he had. These gangsters had acquired a piece of glitterkind…or, worse, had a whole one hidden somewhere in the city, and they were cutting pieces from it. Large pieces.

Nothing was more dangerous.

Someone needed to kill these assholes, but it wasn't going to be him.

"You have what you came for," he said. "You don't need the girl or her mother anymore. Set them free."

The courier reappeared. The Katr bent low so the child could whisper to him. His morose expression didn't change. He just listened, then shooed the child away.

With a sudden movement, he lunged into the room and extended his arm, thrusting his glaive into the throat of the big man lying unconscious on the floor. The big man shuddered once, then became still.

Kyrioc remained utterly still, ready to move if the Katr's attention turned his way.

The northerner wiped his blade on the dead man's respectable clothes, then stepped back, holding his weapon in a relaxed low guard. Kyrioc watched him carefully—eyes, hands, hips—anticipating a second stroke. None came.

"You have what you came for," he said again. "Set the girl and the mother free."

The barbarian shook his head, making little chimes ring again. "Those hostages have not been ransomed. Not yet. If you want them back, you will have to do more. Stay. You will hear from us again."

He stepped back out of the doorway. A moment later, the lantern light moved away.

Kyrioc summoned his cloak of shadows and, enveloped in darkness, moved silently into the hall.

The Katr was moving quickly but not running. He'd already reached the first landing. Hidden by his cloak, Kyrioc moved to the top of the stair, ready to leap down and knock the barbarian through the rail. If the fall didn't kill the man, it would certainly break bones. Then Kyrioc could free Riliska and her—

The Katr suddenly stopped, raised his glaive, and looked straight at Kyrioc. For a moment, Kyrioc thought the man could see through his cloak of shadows, but no. The barbarian's gaze was unfocused, his expression confused. He couldn't see Kyrioc, but he could obviously sense danger, and he knew where it came from.

Kyrioc kept perfectly still, shrouded in darkness, waiting for the barbarian to lower his guard. He didn't. The Katr descended the stairs slowly, never turning his gaze away from Kyrioc's position.

There was no way to drop down on him without risking the point of that ghostkind steel.

Whoever this northerner was, he was dangerous.

Once the barbarian reached the second floor and passed out of sight, his footsteps sped up again. Kyrioc followed silently, cloak in place. By the time he reached the lobby, the front door was swinging closed.

The barbarian was already in the cart. He snapped the reins. Kyrioc sprinted after, his cloak dissipating.

As the cart jolted forward, its back doors swung outward, revealing Riliska and her mother huddling in the dark. The girl's gaze met Kyrioc's for the briefest of moments before the doors swung shut and the latch engaged.

Kyrioc ran harder, spurred on by the terror on Riliska's dirty face and the sound of her fists pounding on the wood. He could still catch up if the horses were slow to reach their gallop.

They were not. This part of the plankway had a slight downward slope, and the horses responded with a quickness that came from extensive training. Kyrioc watched the cart roll northward on the broadening avenue, moving deeper into darkness.

The road followed the curve of Yth's rib cage, then split in two. The larger avenue went down to Low Market, a part of the city that never slept. The narrower path rose toward Low Apricot, and then High Apricot.

But Kyrioc had already lost them in the gloom. The sound of the hooves was still loud, but the way they echoed made it impossible for him to follow. They could be headed anywhere in the city. Anywhere.

He couldn't chase them on foot.

Kyrioc needed to stop and think, which meant he needed information. He had to find someone to tell him where they laid up overnight and where they might take the girl.

He returned to find his building empty. The young couriers were long gone.

Water began to flow through the gaps in the deck above. It must have started raining. Kyrioc fetched a stale fig bun from his room. It was a suitable bribe for a starving street kid. He put it into his pocket and returned to the streets.

* * *

ONCE THEY WERE CLEAR of Woodgarden, Killer of Devils slowed the horses. Outside of High and Low Apricot—and Low Market, obviously—the streets were mostly empty at this hour, but it was still illegal to race carts inside the city. Tin Pail hated paying bribes because Killer let her brother get in trouble with the law.

As if that thought summoned him, the slat opened and Wooden Pail's eyes glared at them. "What the fuck happened back there? It was just one guy?"

Killer nodded.

"What the fuck is wrong with you, Paper? You can't handle one guy? He's a fucking petal!"

"Boss, he—" Paper wiped sweat from his forehead. After the screwup at Sailsday's Regret, he knew letting himself be disarmed by a *pawnshop broker* might get him pitched over the edge of a deck. "You should have seen him, boss. He didn't seem like a petal to me. He was so fast… He took out Second Boar like that." He snapped his fingers.

Wooden rolled his eyes. "Psh. Second Boar."

Killer had no love for Paper Mouse, but if the little thief took the point, he might be replaced by an even bigger fool. "He did not react when I drew my glaive. He did not flinch when I cut Second Boar's throat."

Wooden Pail did not seem to understand what he meant, and when he did not understand, he suspected he was being insulted. "So, he's not a pawnbroker, then? Is that what you're saying?"

Killer shrugged. "What I am saying is that I do not know what he is."

"Fuck it." Wooden sighed. "Whatever he is, he's our arrow. I just need Tin to string the bow."

* * *

"YOUR PEOPLE FUCKED IT UP."

Tin glared at the doctor. Didn't she have enough bullshit to deal with already? And now this...*addict* talking back to her.

The doctor wore the traditional white hospital robe. On someone else, it would have been a sign of status, but Elberish tuto-Sienvet glistened with sweat and grime. Her hair—cropped with a dull knife, apparently— sat in a greasy tangle atop her head. A dull expression haunted her like a curse.

But Tin had learned that behind the white tar stains and half-closed eyes was a sharp, practical, and ruthless mind that did not give a fuck what people thought of her.

Tin glanced at the three heavies leaning against the wall. They were Caps, having come up from a street gang she'd absorbed three years ago. If they were good for anything beyond drinking themselves stupid and swinging a heavy stick, she hadn't found it. "How did they fuck it up?"

The doctor shuffled over to the apparatus that Tin had spent nearly a third of her savings to acquire. "I told them the inside of the glass case had to be completely sterile. It wasn't. I told them that the fire under the distiller had to be kept low to avoid splash contamination, but they stoked the fire anyway. I told them the water they started with had to be as clean as possible, preferably fresh rainwater. I don't know where the fuck they got this. Maybe they drained it from a privy shop or something. When *I* told *them* what was necessary, they rolled their eyes, then half-assed the work so they could get back to throwing dice."

Elberish tuto-Sienvet was used to throwing her weight around. Before she'd been stripped of her credentials and turned out to feed her addictions on the street, the doctor had been a star surgeon in a clinic down in The Folly. Clearly, she was used to people who craved her approval. "My people take orders from me," Tin said.

"And therein lies the problem."

Tin looked at the glass tank the doctor had said she needed. It brimmed with water, along with the first of the humankind donor organs they'd collected. "It looks clear enough to me."

"This," Elberish said, pointing to a minuscule spot of grime on the rim of the tank. "And this. And this. And more besides. That speck of green fuzz floating in the corner would be enough to ruin everything you'd collected so far."

"*Would be*? Are these organs being preserved?"

The doctor looked astonished. "No, they certainly are not. Not in this setup. I don't know who you have slivering portions for this broth, but tell them to enjoy a night off, because this shit isn't ready."

More delays. Tin laid out a lot of money to set up this scam, and it was going to take a while to show a profit. If it took too long, she wasn't going to be able to pay her people, the cosh, or her suppliers. She had expenses. "When? When does this start to earn?"

"Not tonight," was the doctor's only answer. "Look, you are never going to run out of idiots who burn the skin off their backs or get stabbed in the kidneys. But you will, someday, run out of this." She pointed at the oiled leather packet that contained Tin's glitterkind ear. "I'm not going to waste my time and your money on contaminated parts."

Tin nodded, running the calculations in her head. She could afford to lose tonight's profits, even if nothing else she was planning worked in her favor. But life was made out of catastrophes, and a new one could come any time. Money and influence were the best shield against them, and it made her a little sick to know that she was bleeding both for a project that might not pan out.

She turned to the three Caps, still waiting by the iron-banded door. "You three are going to fetch three buckets, and you are going to scrub them cleaner than you've ever cleaned anything in your life. Then you're going to pass the buckets to the left, and scrub them again."

"With soap?" the one called Crooked asked.

"Yes, with fucking soap. What the fuck do you think? Then you are going to fetch clean water in those buckets, and not from a barrel in a fucking Spillwater tannery. Understand? Take it from someplace upcity. When you get back here, you"—she pointed directly at Crooked—"will scrub that entire tank, inside and out—with soap—while you two scrub the still and the pipes. When you're done, you'll switch up and do it again."

"Yes, boss," they said.

"Check each other's work. Before we start up that fire again, this pain in the ass will check it. If she complains, *I'm* gonna have a fucking complaint. You don't want that."

While they set to work, Tin strode to the table in the corner. A little wooden shingle with a smear of white tar rested on it. It had the familiar greasy sheen and stank like rotten tomatoes.

Like most criminals trying to climb the slope, she preferred to keep the tar itself away from her heavies so she wouldn't lose too many to addiction—and away from herself in case some captain of the cosh was overcome with ambition and raided her. But she needed the doctor, and the doctor needed the high.

Tin took the shingle and headed for the door. She didn't have to order the doctor to follow. They crossed into the main part of the warehouse, then down the ramp to the front counter where they did business with the public.

"Get in."

She gestured to the tall iron cage beside the counter.

Elberish's expression changed from worry—no addict liked to see someone walk away with their drug—to near panic. "But I'm doing everything you—"

"*Get in the fucking cage.*"

The doctor hurried inside. Tin slammed the door shut, then locked it, placing the padlock key on the counter. Then she set the shingle on the floor and rested her hammer on the corner. One of her people might be stupid enough to pass the shingle to a prisoner, but not one of them would fucking dare move her hammer.

"I don't understand," the doctor said, forehead beading with sweat. "I was only warning you that you were going to throw money away."

Tin Pail leaned close. "It was the way you warned me. Remember back when you were a hot-shit doctor? Remember the way the cleaning staff talked to you? That's how you talk to me."

Elberish tried to reclaim some of her dignity. "You can't do this without me."

Tin actually laughed aloud. Fucking petals. "I keep you by holding your tar for ransom, but I could do the same with another doctor by ransoming their kid, and that new doc wouldn't stink like a fucking flophouse. Open your eyes, or one of your old colleagues is going to see their six-year-old child thrown into that cage with your bloated corpse. Because nobody cares about you. Nobody cares about anybody."

* * *

IN THE HOURS THAT he searched, Kyrioc could not find a single courier. He did find a pair of constables stationed at the high point of a plankway from the lower decks. He tried to explain that he'd seen a woman and her daughter kidnapped by gangsters, but when he mentioned the piece of glitterkind flesh, they snorted in disbelief, drew their truncheons, and threatened to throw him into a cell for the night.

The constables were not going to help him.

He returned to his rooms. Eyalmati was not there, but the corpse was. Kyrioc tried to imagine what his name had been and why he'd been killed.

But he couldn't force himself to think about it. All he could think about was Riliska and the look on her face as the doors closed over her. It had been a look of acceptance, as though she knew it was her fate to be chewed up and spat out by this city. Frightened but not surprised.

He barred the doors and windows, then sank to the floor in the darkness. The coppery smell of drying blood wafted over him. The sound of rainwater draining through the city in little waterfalls droned incessantly.

Another trance came over him, a dreamlike parade of past sins and terrible violence that slowly became an actual dream of the horrors of Vu-Dolmont, although in his dream, Riliska, child of Rulenya, was with him in the ruins of Childfall. He tried to convince her to flee into the jungle, but she assured him that when Death came, she would gladly sacrifice her life for his.

He woke with a start at the sound of pounding on the barred door. It was the landlady. She'd found the shutter in the street and was shouting that she would not be paying for repairs. Kyrioc did not respond. Eventually, she left, cursing at the ingratitude of tenants.

A glimpse through the broken window showed that the sun was shining on other parts of the city. He immediately grabbed the fig bun—which had been stale yesterday when he bought it—and devoured it like an animal. The habits he'd learned while he was "dead" were returning. Food was fuel for his inner fire, and he couldn't let it burn low, not if he was going to ransom Riliska.

Soon, the northerner—or one of his couriers—would contact him. If running their errands meant the release of Riliska and her mother, he would run them gladly. *You have something that belongs to us.* Rulenya had been stupid enough to steal from gangsters. It was bad business for criminals to forgive someone who stole from them, but Kyrioc was prepared to do whatever they asked, and keep doing it, until mother and daughter were free.

Maybe, while he was working for them, he'd learn where Riliska was being held. Then, all he'd need were his cloaks.

He glanced at the panel that covered his secret hiding place. No, just the cloaks. Nothing more.

Kyrioc filled his belly with water that tasted like dust and food that had no taste at all, and he crouched in the darkest part of his apartment. He did nothing but quiet his breathing and quiet his mind and quiet the sudden jolts of anger that made his skin prickle and his heart race.

The knock, when it came, was light but insistent.

Kyrioc went into the shop and slid back the shutter on the cage window. A little boy of about seven stood against the far wall, putting as much distance between himself and the window as he could. His clothes were better than Riliska's—someone was looking after this child—but his eyes had a hunted look.

"I'm being watched. If you do anything to me, the Pails will see that you won't get what you want."

Kyrioc nodded. *The Pails.*

"There is a ship called *Winter Friend* docked beyond the wall. Speak to the bosun. His name is Dry Wave."

The child sprinted away. Kyrioc closed and barred the shutter. He moved the cash box behind a hidden panel that Eyalmati knew about, leaving the money he'd set aside for his employer for any thieves that might break in. The landlady ought to have the lock replaced by morning, but just in case…

He touched the hidden panel that only he knew about. Would he need the weapon within? Was he ready to be that person again?

The thought made him sick. No, he wasn't ready to return to that, and he didn't need to. There were always knives in a pawnshop. He took two from the three-week shelf. One went into his belt, the other into his boot.

It occurred to him that this was the first time he'd taken anything from the pawnshop that Eyalmati hadn't explicitly given him. Yes, he'd kept operating cash hidden from his boss, but he never spent it on himself, nor had he taken any of the pawned items from the shelves before.

He would return them when all this was over, if he was still alive. Eyalmati would probably never know. He noted them in the log book anyway.

Kyrioc brought the shutter into the shop, and met the landlady's nephew as he brought a replacement for their damaged padlock. The boy locked the metal gate. Kyrioc took one of the keys from him, then watched the boy run off to complete his other errands.

He almost gave the key back. What was the point? It was just another thing the man with the steel chain could loot from his corpse. He had no illusions about the sort of people he was dealing with.

It didn't matter. He would do whatever they demanded, then he'd take Riliska and her mother to safety.

And if the Pails betrayed him, nothing in this cursed world would save them.

CHAPTER TWELVE

T *in Pail had a* lot of work to do, as always. Dumb motherfuckers always thought being a heavy was as easy as a noble's life: sleep late, do a deal in the afternoon, take the point to someone over dinner, spend the rest of the night throwing dice and whoring.

In truth, Tin hustled as much as any Low Market merchant. More. Arranging deals, bribing cosh, paying off the fucking foreign friends up the slope…it all took careful planning. And if a merchant made a bad deal, all they'd lose was money. Tin gambled with her life. Always.

And then there were the people who worked for you. If a shop employee turned out to be a thief, call the constables. If they were lazy, turn them out. If a shopkeeper hired some asshole who wanted to gut the owner and declare themselves the new shopkeeper…well, Tin had never even heard of such a thing.

But every shitwit the Pails took on was treacherous, lazy, and sticky-fingered. She spent nearly a quarter of her time watching over her heavies, making sure they were so afraid they wouldn't dare fuck with her.

She had two dozen grown men and women living out of her purse (the beetles didn't count) and she sort of trusted three of them. Her brother, Wooden, because he was her brother and he was smart enough to know he needed her. Then there was her bodyguard, with the name she didn't even like to think about, let alone say aloud. He was bound by his barbarian code of honor to do her bidding, and judging by what she'd seen of his godkind magic, if he wanted to betray her, it would have happened already and she couldn't have done shit about it. All she could do was thank the fallen gods that he was stupid enough to follow his ridiculous code.

Finally, there was Paper Mouse. He wasn't a fighter. He wasn't a thinker. He didn't have ambition. What he did have was loyalty and an ability to follow basic directions without getting greedy, a trait that put him head and shoulders above the rest of her crew.

Unfortunately, he'd let pickpockets steal their package. Then he got disarmed by a petal who worked a pawnshop. Apparently, she could trust Paper to be loyal but not to get the job done.

For today's work, no underlings could be trusted. Tin and Wooden stood alone outside the city wall, beneath the awning of a cart that sold meat pies. Both were drinking hot tea and watching *Winter Friend* tied up at dock.

The beginning of the year was not a busy time at the trade ends of the dockyard. The parsu-controlled section was a never-ending succession of wheat barges and ore shipments, along with other staples needed to keep the people of Koh-Salash alive, but until the fall harvest, most freelancing ships sailed deeper waters.

But even without a full complement of ships, the docks were full of smugglers, pickpockets, greedy-eyed cosh, and the odd mercenary, all hunting their next coin.

Wooden swallowed the last of his pie and set his empty tea cup aside. "That's him."

The pawnbroker was still dressed in funeral clothes, with shaggy black hair hanging in his face. Paper had described a terrible scar on the left side of his face, but she could only see his right side. Tin did see that his left hand was an odd color. His face and right hand were the same rich brown as any Salashi, but his left was a dark orange, as though it had been imperfectly dyed to match.

"Sooner than I expected," she admitted. He must have come straight to The Docks without trying to enlist the help of a friend or hire a bodyguard. She wasn't sure what that said about him. Was this really the guy who spooked Paper? He looked like a petal.

The broker found *Winter Friend* easily enough, then tracked down the bosun. Dry Wave had clearly just woken up—he liked to drink while in port—and did not immediately give the man what he wanted. It was better that way, to make it seem as if they were haggling. The cosh wouldn't think there was anything suspicious about haggling.

"He doesn't like that," Wooden said, as though teasing a child. Tin saw it too. The broker's body tensed and his hands clenched into fists.

Then Dry pointed to the cart, and the man in black walked away from him.

Then, like a fucking moron, the bosun turned and looked directly at Tin. As though he'd quickly realized his mistake, he let his gaze wander this way and that, as though he wasn't looking at anything in particular. The shitwit.

One of the beetles sat in the cart. When the broker approached, the boy climbed down. Tin and Wooden were too far away to hear them, but their beetles knew to say what they'd been told to say, or else: They were being watched. The boy wasn't to be touched. Take this cartload of potatoes to Low Market and find a Carrig fishmonger named Unt Fal Nam.

The beetle started to run, but the man motioned for him to stop. Tin saw that the courier was skittish, but he waited. The broker spoke briefly, then the boy nodded and ran off.

The beetles knew better than to scurry directly to their boss, so the Pails would have to wait a while to hear the broker's message. While they refilled their teapot—and Wooden spiked it with a shot of brandy—they watched the man in black walk a circuit of the cart. It had tall sides and was sturdy, but it didn't have the roof and locks of the secure cart they'd used last night. Those made the cosh suspicious. Burlap sacks full of potatoes had been piled all the way to the rail, and the man shifted a few at the top to make sure there were more potatoes beneath. Then he climbed underneath to examine the undercarriage. Finally, he tied down the canvas cover to protect the cargo.

After that, he went to the front and petted the nag in her harness. He took a carrot from his pocket and fed her while gently stroking her flanks and murmuring a few words. Then he climbed onto the cart and flicked the reins gently, steering the nag toward the ramps to Low Market.

"Yes!" Wooden hissed, grinning like an idiot. "The arrow leaves the bow."

The skin on the back of Tin's neck prickled. Not once had the broker looked around The Docks for a familiar face. He hadn't brought a bodyguard. Maybe he'd sent a spy ahead to track the movements of the beetle who'd spoken to him?

Tin couldn't see anyone who looked likely to be a spy, but she was still antsy when the courier crawled out from behind the cart and sat at her feet.

"What's his message?"

The beetle wiped his nose. "Boss, he said he wants the next courier to tell him where and when he can pick up the girl and her mother."

Wooden let out a guffaw. "He's got a lot of balls, making demands of us!"

Tin slid a copper knot off the edge of the table. The beetle snapped it out of the air and scurried away. "He's being careful." She didn't like careful people.

* * *

KYRIOC KEPT THE CART in the center of The Freightway, passed through the city gates, and turned sharply to the right.

Not fifty yards inside the outer wall was a second, smaller wall. Behind that was Mudside, the most dangerous district in the city, where natural light was rare and constables even rarer.

Between those walls were numerous stairs and plankways that led up into the city. Kyrioc stayed on the largest, The Freightway, which hugged the outer wall and led north to Low Market.

It had been more than a year since Kyrioc had been outside the skeletons of the gods. Selsarim Lost, they were big.

The city wall itself was a hundred feet high, and while it was the highest city wall in the world—built as it was of skywood rather than stone—it was nowhere near high enough to block the view of Yth's massive wooden skull. The back of her head was sunk partway into the mud, but the edge of her eye socket still stood more than fifteen hundred feet above the ground. It wasn't a human-shaped skull, not really, but it was close enough to be unnerving.

From this angle, most of her head was concealed by her humerus and collarbones, as well as the glowing crystalline ulna and radius of Suloh's left arm, where it rested beside her shoulder.

Suloh's skull, of course, could not be seen from down here.

After half a mile, he rose above the wall that caged the residents of Mudside. Kyrioc glanced down into the district and saw the back of Yth's rib cage sunk so deep in the mud that only fifty feet of wooden bone was still visible. Between the ribs he saw hovels in the black mud. No people were visible. No bloodkind, either.

The city wall continued north for three miles, following the curve of the landscape and the gods' bones. But the wall was only a hundred feet high, and Yth's skeleton, even sunk into the mud, was many times that. And of course, lying atop the wooden bones of Yth were the glowing crystal bones of Suloh. Those rib cages loomed over him like a gigantic cliff, three-quarters of a mile high.

Legend said that, someday, the gods would awaken. Or the Ancient Kings would return. Either way, doom would finally come to Koh-Salash and its people.

But that was not today.

The nag trudged up the ramp. Once the midday heat arrived, many Salashi would seek a shady place until afternoon, but Kyrioc couldn't risk that.

The largest portion of The Freightway turned away from the wall and angled up to the top of Yth's arm. Once there, some seven hundred feet above the earth, it turned northward again.

The nag balked as they neared the first equestrian fountain, so Kyrioc led her to drink. When she finished, he gave her another half-carrot, and the horse nuzzled his cheek. He patted her flank, then took up the reins again.

When the sun was fully overhead, many servants and trades folk crouched at the edge of The Freightway and draped a cloth over their head. Others kept trudging uphill, sweating beneath their burdens. A few walked along with water jugs and little cups, selling a few swallows of clean water. The road crossed Yth's elbow joint and arced upward toward the place her pelvis met Suloh's.

The road passed through the entrance to Low Market, and Kyrioc was inside the gods' bones again.

The gate was made of pennants, ribbon, and slender poles. All were welcome. There were no weapon checks and no one was turned away because of the way they dressed.

There were armed guards, though, a great many of them. Most were ironshirts, but a good number sported the orange and black of the merchants' private corps, a crowd of bullyboys who kept the poor in their place and sent the sticky-fingered away with cracked skulls and shattered wrists.

Kyrioc held the reins lightly as the nag passed beneath the white ribbons, then the nag took the upper passage. It seemed to know the way better than he did.

In Low Market, progress was halting and maddeningly slow. Cart drivers stopped in the center of intersections, cursing at anyone who blocked their path. Pedestrians wandered blithely through traffic, forcing drivers to pull up short. Hawkers in shop doors—some at the very edge of the road, some leaning over the platforms above—bellowed into the crowd about the astonishing quality of their wares, and the ruinous prices at which they were offered.

The road led upward through decks, mini-decks, and platforms toward Salash Hill at the western end of the city.

Since Kyrioc started working at the pawnshop, he'd made many trips to Low Market, but he preferred to come after sunset. The stores were still open and their cashboxes were full. Also, there were fewer people and they were more cautious. There was none of this jostling and cursing, with each person demanding everyone else make room.

Kyrioc breathed deeply and thought about Riliska. She needed him, and he would not turn away again. Not for anything.

He glanced upward and saw Suloh's massive hip bones looming above them, glowing even in sunlight. God's shining asshole. If he had endured seven years in exile, he could endure this.

Traffic was so slow, Kyrioc had time to study each shop sign minutely as he searched for Unt Fal Nam's name, but it wasn't until he'd reached the upper western end of Low Market, where shops had been constructed outside of Suloh's skeleton on the actual rocky ground, that he found it.

Kyrioc turned the nag toward the front counter, forcing their customers to make way. Then he climbed down and told the elderly woman roasting eels over a coal bed that he had brought her potatoes.

"Get the fuck out of here, shitwit!" she screeched. "We don't serve potatoes. I'm not paying—"

A cry came from the back room and she stopped speaking. An old man hurried out of the back and offered Kyrioc a small sack. "Please, good sir. Here, good sir. As requested. Always happy to do a favor for the Pails. Your joke about the potatoes was very clever, good sir."

The old man seemed anxious to be rid of whatever was in that sack. Kyrioc accepted it. The old fellow bowed several times, retreating slowly without turning his back.

Nothing on or inside the sack suggested where he should go next. As far as Kyrioc could see, the sack contained nothing more than a roasted salmon fillet wrapped in seaweed, with onions and apples. The old man smiled fearfully, anxious for Kyrioc to leave. If he had additional instructions—or news of where Riliska and her mother would be released—Kyrioc thought he would have volunteered it.

He led the nag to the fountain at the southward turn in The Freightway.

There were no child couriers in sight. Kyrioc set the sack on the bench beside him and dug through it. He removed the apples and broke them apart. Nothing. He tore the roasted onions open, too, but they were also empty. He offered both apples to the nag. The onions he threw away.

Then he peeled the seaweed off the salmon. The meat was charred in the Carrig style.

Pulling it apart, he found a small leather packet, well-oiled and carefully folded, no longer than his little finger. Kyrioc picked at the knot until it came loose.

Inside was a pale, viscous substance that stuck to the oiled leather like glue. Kyrioc lifted the sack to smell it, and his suspicions were confirmed. It was white tar.

He closed the packet and tied it carefully with a knot that would be easy to undo, then slipped it into the inner pocket of his vest.

The salmon looked delicious, but Kyrioc wouldn't have risked a single bite, not if there was a chance it was tainted by the tar. He suddenly remembered the apples, then leaped from the driver's seat to check the nag. The beast had no signs of trembling and its eyes looked normal. Good. Tar was dangerous enough when smoked. The nag might have dropped dead if she'd eaten too much.

Kyrioc purchased a fig bun from a walking vendor with a tray full of them hanging from his neck. He ate it slowly. No couriers approached. He moved the cart away from the fountain and sat quietly on the driver's bench, reins in hand. He waited.

It was two hours before full nightfall when the next courier appeared. This time, it was a little girl. "Deliver the cart and the meal to a man in Upgarden. He spends his afternoons in the hammerball courts at the edge of Cloud Square—"

"I know it."

That surprised her, but she continued. "His name is Harl Sota List Im. Make the delivery at the dinner hour, just after full dark. Don't be late."

"What about my friends?"

The girl slowly backed away. "They said… They said I should answer if you ask."

"I'm asking."

"Two hours before midnight, you will find your friends at a tea shop across from Sailsday's Regret. Do you know where that is?" Kyrioc shook his head. "It's in High Apricot. It's easy to find. The tea shop is a favorite with bureaucrats and the cosh, so your friends will be safe while they wait for you. Don't be early to meet them, and don't be late with your delivery."

Kyrioc nodded. She sprinted away.

* * *

FAY NOG FAY HAD developed a taste for bone broth a few years back while his mother was sick. Now he thought about her, and how long it had been since he last visited, whenever he drank a bowl.

He'd been scouring Low Market for hours, trying to track down someone, anyone, shopping glitterkind flesh. He'd already spoken to everyone he thought were the most likely buyers, then to their competition.

Next were the people only a fool would approach, but that was a long shot. But first, he'd checked with his auntie across the plankway to see if any Katr warriors had come to visit. No such luck.

She noticed him staring and waved. He waved back.

So, Fay sat alone in this broth shop, drinking from his bowl. Did he really think the stolen package would just be *handed* to him like—

A boy in tatters sprinted toward Shah's shop. Children rarely approached his aunt. They preferred to beg for food, not carpets.

Fay watched them speak briefly, then Shah pointed directly at him.

Lifting the bowl to his mouth, Fay drank the rest down quickly. Whatever message this child was about to deliver, he wouldn't have time to linger.

* * *

KYRIOC DID NOT HAVE much time to get to Cloud Square. Upgarden was well above them, and the poor nag had already done a heavy day's work. Kyrioc climbed out of the cart and walked before her to lighten her burden and urge her onward.

Still, the rhythm of the nag's clopping hooves slowed, and they faced a tide of people and carts flowing in the other direction. Most were working folk heading to their homes on lower decks. Others were delivering stale or outdated goods to secondary shops for the evening trade in Low Market. All blocked his way.

Worse, The Freightway did not go directly from the high western edge of Suloh's hip to the nearest of his free ribs, where the Upgarden deck began. Instead, it struck out toward the god's spine, crossing a great deal of empty space, then connected with the Dawnshine deck below Upgarden's eastern edge. From there, it touched Upgarden almost at High Square. Kyrioc had to urge and cajole the horse every step of the way, and he wished he'd bought more carrots.

By the time he reached Cloud Square, the flow of workers had ebbed. Still, they barely arrived on time.

The courts were in the same place they'd been when he'd played there as a boy. Hammerball wasn't typically a young person's sport, but Kyrioc's father said the game would make his sword arm more accurate, so Kyrioc and his friends had taken lessons.

It hadn't worked out. The other club members didn't like loud noble boys jeering each other's strokes, and they were made unwelcome in subtle ways. Besides, some of the men lounging outside the courts made them uncomfortable. Kyrioc wasn't sorry when his friends decided not to return.

It was only now, a decade later, that he understood. Those lounging men were heavies.

He led the nag down the long alley to the stables around back. When a stableboy ran out, waving him off, Kyrioc said he had business with Harl

Sota List Im.

The boy stopped immediately. An older boy behind him ran into the building. Kyrioc waited.

Moments later, three men and a woman emerged. The men were of a kind—hard expressions and soft heads, old scars on their faces and new flab on their bellies. The woman was different. She had the crisp look of a court manager, with a tidy red vest and black pants.

"Harl Sota List Im is waiting for this delivery," Kyrioc said. "The Pails sent me." Kyrioc had heard that street name twice, but he had no idea who it referred to.

The manager recognized it. "Search him."

Two of the thugs stepped forward and ran their hands roughly along his arms and torso. They found the knife in his belt and took it. "Cheap shit," one of them said as he examined it. He was right, too.

Now that they'd found the weapon they expected, the search was over. "I'll take you to one of Harl's lieutenants."

"It has to be Harl himself."

"If you waste Harl's time, he'll cut off your arms. You know that?"

"Yes."

She shrugged. If Harl made a mess of him, she wouldn't have to clean it.

CHAPTER THIRTEEN

The year 395 of the New Calendar, eight years earlier.

* * *

ON THE WESTERN PLATEAU of Vu-Dolmont, where Childfall had been founded, Kyrionik expected to find an empty square in the Harkan style, with ancient paving stones and a handful of decrepit stone buildings around the rim. Instead, it was jungle. The paving stones had been uplifted by tree roots, and not one stone from those buildings rested atop another.

Fifty years had turned an abandoned village into wilderness again.

Afternoon was well upon them, and Kyrionik was increasingly frustrated by delays. *Fair Season* had approached Childfall at a snail's pace, and the skiff had been a tedious way to transfer soldiers and gear to the island. Then, by the time the troops had crossed over, climbed to the top, and donned their armor, it was past time for a midday meal.

Kyrionik was tempted to urge them to hurry, but Aratill was watching him. Kyrionik took a deep, calming breath. He was the leader—that was the whole point of a First Labor, after all—and a leader had to know when to sprint and when to walk. It made no sense to skip meals when they had a long, uphill slog ahead of them.

Still, he couldn't calm himself. He finished donning his armor—with Aratill's help—then took his portion of sea bread and stood at the edge of the makeshift camp.

The ground sloped gently upward. Somewhere beyond all that greenery, the slope became much steeper. And somewhere up on those slopes was his prize. He hoped.

When their meal was over, the soldiers formed a defensive line of shield and spears. They'd been issued the shortest spears from the armory in the cargo hold, which was a sensible choice considering the terrain, and one Kyrionik would remember for the future. He buckled his helmet on.

Selso Rii stood off to the side and adjusted his cloth cap. Of course, he had no armor, but he had been given the stretcher cloth and twelve-foot poles to carry.

"Be silent with those," Shulipik tuto-Beskeroth snapped as he walked by. Then Shulipik approached Kyrionik and Aratill. His glaive was in hand now, and his braids were hidden beneath his helm. If he seemed restless on the ship, here on the island he was still and watchful. "Your virtue, a brief search of the plateau has revealed nothing unusual. We thought we might find a track though the jungle and scorch marks on the plants, but there is none. There seems to be no sign of the ullroct."

Kyrionik was pleased that the older man addressed him and only him. "Your virtue," he said in return, showing equal respect even though Shulipik's family were barely nobility at all, "we know little about such creatures, and with luck, we will learn nothing new today."

For a moment, Shulipik's expression showed something Kyrionik did not recognize. Distaste? Disappointment? Contempt? Then the older man's expression returned to its usual stoicism and he turned away.

Kyrionik caught his arm, steel on steel. "Your virtue, did you… Did you come on this trip because you wanted to fight an ullroct?"

Aratill suddenly became still and gave them his full attention.

Shulipik stepped close to speak in a low voice. Kyrionik had always been considered tall for his age, but the warrior loomed over him. "No, your virtue. Not at all. But if chance turns that way…"

His voice trailed off and he looked over Kyrionik's shoulder, as though seeing something of great import on the horizon.

Aratill spoke, his tone accusatory. "You hope to add to your fame."

"Fame matters little to me now, although once it was my guiding star. I am nobly born, yes, but my father is poor. We live like beggars on a scholarly endowment from more influential families. The work of scribes and academics never suited me, so I hoped to improve my family name other ways: first renown, then an influential marriage, then enough land to become hold-Beskeroth, or even to win the defender's title as a defe-Beskeroth." Shulipik stared into the distance. Kyrionik knew he had more to say, but he couldn't think of a way to draw it out.

Silence did it for him. Shulipik said, 'Then I hurried out into the world and everything changed."

Kyrionik's mouth had gone dry. This was a story he wanted to hear. "You slew a ghostkind."

For several months, Kyrionik had entertained the idea of meeting a ghostkind ranger in single combat for his First Labor. He knew they were tall, strong, and brutal, with skin like dirty ice and ears like the blades of a knife. He also knew what it would mean for a young Salashi noble to slay one of the creatures that had driven his people from their homeland. He couldn't imagine a greater achievement.

But he'd been only twelve. Once word reached his mother about his plan, she sat him down and explained that a First Labor was about service to the Salashi people, not personal glory. He swore to her, at the breakfast table, that he would choose a different task.

Still, Kyrionik hoped to test himself against his people's greatest enemy someday.

Shulipik nodded. "I've slain three." Aratill made a disbelieving grunt but Shulipik did not seem to care. "The second and third were at the same time. I faced them together, and afterwards, I was terribly wounded. I lay bleeding on the ground beside one of my enemies. My red blood mixed with his silver, and we spoke for a while, just two of our respective kinds, dying slowly on a grassy hillside far above the Timmer Sea. What he said changed me, and then he died, and then I was alone, and then my companions found me…"

Shulipik hesitated. Kyrionik waited for him to continue.

He did. "Your virtue, I have slain three ghostkind. I've slain five bloodkind, when they ambushed me in a pack. Of my slain humankind enemies, I've lost count. Then there are the bears, hunting jellies, and other beasts of the wild that I have turned my blade against. The glitterkind do nothing but lie insensate beneath the open sky and cannot be fought. The shadowkind are always rumored to be in places where you are not. The spellkind vanished when the godkind died, and none now remember them. The Ancient Kings of the Walking Towers have abandoned their thrones to us, lesser beings though we are, while they roam distant places in this world or some other. If we are to believe the Kings' Tower Apostles, the Ancient Kings will return in my lifetime—"

"They've been saying that for centuries," Oblifell interrupted.

"One moment, your virtue," Aratill said. "You're hoping the Ancient Kings will return soon so you can *duel* one? These are the beings that murdered the gods. That blasted the flesh from their bones."

"That's what the legends say. According to those same legends, their return is long overdue. I don't 'hope' they return, but if they do, I am ready to face them."

Aratill and Oblifell glanced at each other, their expressions carefully neutral. Shulipik noticed but continued talking as though it meant nothing.

"I hold no great lands, no wealth, and have found no wife of my own. What was supposed to be a path to greater things is now an end in itself. I have measured myself against the dangers of the world, and with every successful test, I feel diminished.

"So, no, I did not come here to find fame against a legendary enemy. But should the worst occur, I will be the one to face it. Alone. That's why you brought me, and it's why I have come. If you can understand why I must do this, please explain it to me, because I do not." He bowed. "Your virtue."

The hairs on the back of Kyrionik's neck stood on end as Shulipik moved to take the point of the front rank.

Oblifell stepped forward, watching Shulipik's retreating back. "Who is that guy kidding? Can't find a wife of his own? Please. With that patter, he could almost have me." Aratill gave him a look. "I said *almost*."

Oblifell's attempt to relieve the tension soured Kyrionik's mood. He watched Shulipik form up. By the fallen gods, Kyrionik could learn something from that man. "I'm glad he's not pitting himself against us."

The last six to appear at the top of the stairs were not his own people but crew from *Fair Season*. Their prize would likely be too heavy to carry down to the ship, so before scrounging for supplies, the crew would build a boom.

Kyrionik waved Selso Rii to him. "Where does the glitterkind lie?"

They stared at the island as though they could see through the green. Rii rubbed his hands together. "From here, your virtue, I dare not guess. I saw the flash while collecting water beside a ruined mill. From that spot, I will be able to point the way."

"Lead on."

After a few minutes of hiking up the hillside, Kyrionik wondered if it would have been wiser to leave their armor aboard ship. Even with the ocean breeze blowing across his back, he was sweating miserably on the slope.

Steel clanked against steel. The soldiers' tread was heavy, and no matter what Aratill said to them, he could not completely squelch their groans and complaints. Only Oblifell, moving among them, man and woman alike, could make them hold their tongues.

"What did you say to them?"

"Subtle motivation, your virtue." Then he moved on.

The answer annoyed Kyrionik. Oblifell was one of his instructors, wasn't he?

But then he remembered where he was. This was his First Labor. If the troops were making too much noise, it was his fault for not controlling them. If they were wearing too much armor—or just the wrong kind—that was also his fault. He could have ordered them to do otherwise.

It was time for Kyrionik to stop standing behind the shields of his instructors.

Still, even with their voices silent, the soldiers' tramping was loud, and the wind carried the sound into the jungle.

"Hsst!" Selso Rii came back a few steps into view, waving his arms. "Here is the stream, your virtue." The flow he pointed at was little more than a trickle. It would have taken hours to restock *Fair Season* from it. "It will lead us to the mill."

He hurried toward it. The troops followed.

The ground quickly became extraordinarily steep. Soldiers slung their shields and moved among the trees, bracing their boots against the trunks and scrabbling across bare roots. It was unpleasant work, and Kyrionik began to worry about the return trip. Assuming they found a glitterkind, how would they carry it down to the plateau?

Shulipik hurried by. Even in full armor, with his glaive on his back, his movements were quick and sure. Kyrionik marveled at his athleticism. It was rare to meet someone more agile than him. Had the warrior really talked about challenging an Ancient King to a duel? The idea had a wonderful, reckless madness to it. He tried to copy Shulipik's climbing style, but Aratill whispered to him to stay within the perimeter.

Shulipik caught up to Selso Rii and forced him to stay within the perimeter, too. Until they had found their prize, the guide was too valuable to risk.

They had not traveled far when the first soldier fell. The clatter of his armor—and in his cry of pain—resounded in the jungle. Kyrionik hurried down the slope to the spot where he came to rest. Oblifell was already there.

Kyrionik recognized him immediately—they'd sailed up the Timmer Sea together two years before—but for the life of him, he couldn't remember the man's name. Oblifell believed it was no worse than a broken ankle, and the injured man apologized profusely. Kyrionik accepted and told him it was unnecessary, then assigned two others to escort him back to Childfall. The climb continued.

It did not take long to find the old mill. It could not be far from the village itself, obviously, and had been built at the edge of a little waterfall. The wheel was long gone, but the pond remained alongside the old foundation. One of the soldiers spotted a series of stone blocks that led back down the hill from the right-hand side of the site.

They were obviously stairs, leading down to the village, and although they were overgrown, they would have made an easier ascent than the trackless jungle slope.

Kyrionik summoned Selso Rii. "Where were you standing, and where did the flash come from?"

"Ah, yes, your virtue. I was back quite far from the pond, you see. Near where the ground slopes away again. And..." His voice trailed off as he looked around. He oriented himself to the foundation, trying to recreate the memory. Then he raised his hand. "There, your virtue."

The direction indicated lay almost directly across the pond and high up the slope, which became steep once again on the far side of the pond. There were a few groans from the soldiers. Only Shulipik and Selso Rii seemed as eager for the climb as Kyrionik himself.

"Aratill." Kyrionik kept his voice low, but everyone heard and awaited his word. His bodyguard followed him around the edge of the pond to the ruined foundations of the mill.

A slender tree had fallen across the decrepit stone stairs, and a thicket of bushes had grown around it. Approaching, Kyrionik could see the stone steps that led down the hill. Shulipik and the front ranks of their shield line ought to have found those stairs, but at the same time, Kyrionik should have expected them to be there. He should have tasked a squad with searching for them.

Aratill waved over two of the nearest soldiers and ordered them to clear the way. "It will make for an easier descent, your virtue."

"Assuming it goes all the way down, but that's not what caught my eye. Look." He pointed through the slender thicket. There, partially hidden by fallen leaves, were more stone steps, leading up the hill.

"Well spotted, your virtue."

More soldiers started clearing the way. Aratill scowled up the hill. The path was steep and the stones broken in some places, missing in others, and simply crooked everywhere else. "Where does it lead, I wonder? Another mill?"

Shulipik stood at Kyrionik's shoulder. "Not for a settlement this small. I expect the original inhabitants found the same prize we seek and went to some trouble to create easy access to it." He smiled. "It's a good sign. Permission to scout ahead, your virtue."

Kyrionik felt a flush of pride at the warrior's approval. "Granted, your virtue. But keep within sight of the soldiers at the front and, if you would, take two for support."

"I prefer to go alone." Shulipik set one boot on the tree trunk as it was being dragged away, then leaped onto the hillside. He scrambled upward, his hands grabbing for purchase.

Oblifell ordered soldiers to follow in pairs.

Aratill gave Kyrionik a doubtful look. The boy shrugged. "If these stairs don't lead where we hope they do, we can backtrack and ascend another way."

But the older man frowned and said nothing more.

When Shulipik reached the top of the long, broken stair, he stood still. There was no sign of celebration and he did not wave to call them forward. Kyrionik's heart sank.

But when other soldiers joined him at the top of the slope, they raised their hands in the air in victory. Some even cheered, until Oblifell struck one across the back of the helm. That ringing blow silenced them all.

"Keep your distance," Kyrionik called. Selso Rii cast aside the poles and cloth and scrambled up the hill, passing everyone in a mad rush to the top. "Good sir, keep your distance!"

Shulipik noticed Selso Rii's approach. With one pivot, he caught the back of Rii's neck in a steel gauntlet and pinned him against a slender tree.

The soldiers made way for Kyrionik, of course, and when he reached the top of the slope, his heart leaped.

The stone stairs led to the rim of a shallow depression in the side of the hill. It was perhaps one hundred feet across and was filled with small green growing things and sunlight.

As well as five glitterkind. Five!

They looked much like the creatures he'd grown up with in the Safroy compound back in Koh-Salash. They were naked and sexless but otherwise very like humankind in shape. They even had something that approximated long hair, although it was made of the same flesh as the rest of their body. Their skin was pale white with a faint bluish hue, and streaks of darker blue ran through it like impure marble. And, overlaid on that pale flesh, were thousands of tiny facets that threw the sunlight off in a thousand different colors.

The creatures reflected so many flecks of colored light that they practically glowed in the daylight.

And of course, they were asleep. Glitterkind spent their entire lives in a state like a coma. As far as Kyrionik could discover, no one had ever seen one of the creatures wake for any reason, even when they were slivered.

And why should they? No animal would willingly taste the creatures' flesh, and no plant dared to burrow into one. They simply lay in the sun, drawing life from the nearby greenery and growing.

Aratill took his helm off and wiped the sweat from his bald scalp. "Your virtue, the stretcher we brought—"

"Is not large enough," Kyrionik finished. "I've never seen glitterkind of

HARRY CONNOLLY

this size. I had not even imagined it."

The nearest of the creatures was at least twenty feet long from heel to crown, and that was the smallest. The other four were approximately thirty feet long.

By the fallen gods, they'd have to come back with a larger ship. Ships. New glitterkind had not been discovered for three hundred years. The last one was in the distant farmwilds north of the Timmer Sea during the Salashi people's long expansion into Katr.

Shulipik's voice was hushed, and he watched the trees at the edge of the depression with restless care. "Your people are ward-Safroy, are they not, your virtue?"

Noble families who bore the title *ward-* had been entrusted with one or more of the glitterkind. The Safroy family cared for three of the creatures, protecting them, making sure they thrived, and sharing out their flesh to those whose medical needs were great—at a tremendous profit. Bringing five more back to the city would make the price of medical magic dip, but if Kyrionik's family controlled *eight* of the creatures...

"They are," he answered. "One of our wards is not even fifteen feet long, and it's considered an utter marvel. Aratill, our prize is greater than we expected, and we are lucky to have brought so many hands, and to have found these rough stairs. The stretcher should be sturdy enough to carry the torso, but we'll need to make another for the legs."

"Now I wish I'd brought our long spears." Aratill rubbed his chin. "We will risk the noise of cutting trees, and twist vines to make the bed. How many will we carry?"

"Just one. The small one, if we can call it that without laughing." Kyrionik sighed. "I wish we could bring more, but they wouldn't fit on the ship, and we can't store them in the cargo hold out of the light. It's dangerous. Remember that no iron is to touch glitterkind flesh."

Aratill nodded and began to arrange things. Kyrionik was grateful that he didn't ask for more detail, because he had none to offer. Glitterkind were dangerous, that much he knew. How and why creatures that lay in the grass unmoving were dangerous remained unclear. Kyrionik had tried to learn more before this trip, but even idle questions asked in a casual way raised suspicion, and he'd been forced to give up.

While the soldiers got to work, Kyrionik briefly found himself with nothing to do.

It was working. He could scarcely believe it, but his mission was turning into a success, and when he returned with a new glitterkind for his family's compound, he would have pulled off a First Labor greater than anyone had managed since his people had settled Koh-Salash.

119

Best of all, he wouldn't have to kill anyone to do it.

"Your virtue, if I may…"

Selso Rii stood beside him, wringing his weathered hands. "What is it?"

"Perhaps your virtue would allow me to take my reward here and now, while—"

"No. That won't be possible."

"But your virtue, there is enough flesh here to restore a defeated army. I would not even take from the creature you bring home. Just a thumb knuckle from one of the big ones…"

Kyrionik thumped his spear against the ground. "A thumb knuckle? Good sir, you have a growing blemish on your scalp. A bit of transplanted skin would be enough to preserve your life, and for that you'd need a bit of broth. Less."

"Transplanted? My olive skin would be marred by a patch of dark Salashi brown. My face—"

Kyrionik waved him off. "My own grandfather lived for many years with a patch of pale Carrig skin on his arm. If it's good enough for him, it's more than good enough for you."

Kyrionik turned away, and Selso Rii took hold of his spear arm to stop him. The noble spun swiftly, raising his gauntlet to strike a blow, but the old sailor was already cringing away, his empty hands upraised.

"Your virtue, I apologize for daring to touch such a fine young warrior as yourself, but your virtue, I fear that the terms of our agreement are unclear."

"There's nothing unclear. You have led me to our prize, as promised. I will see you healed to full health once we return to Koh-Salash, as promised. Or do you doubt me?"

At that moment, Shulipik stepped up beside Kyrionik, his hand on his dagger. Kyrionik realized, with a little thrill, that he could have the sailor slain with a word. His thought immediately went to the expression of the "bandit" he'd slain, and his thrill turned to ice.

Selso Rii bowed even lower without lowering his hands. "I do not doubt your word or your honor, your virtue. I would say the same in any port in the world, even if I were not facing your strong young spear arm and your noble companion with his ghostkind weapon that could slice poor Selso Rii apart like butter." He caught his breath. "Your virtue. My only concern is that, in keeping your word to me, you may find the cost dearer than you knew, and I would not want you to have a single regret, not when a humble word from myself could have given you fair warning."

Every word out of the sailor's mouth made Kyrionik feel wearier. "Explain."

"The name *Rii* comes from the Elderspeak, your virtue, one of the ancient tongues of humankind before we were driven from the west. Like *khan* or *autarch*, it means *king*. My ancestors were kings of Thelmagypica, a land of blowing sands, rich delta farmland, and gold mines of fabulous wealth. All taken by the ghostkind long before the fall of Selsarim.

"Your virtue, I am a humble man of proud lineage, and I believe I am the last of my line. The petty machinations of powerful men—mere merchants, your virtue, not men of noble birth like yourself—would see an end to the names of the kings of the west. Only glitterkind flesh can prevent this, and no transplant will do. Your virtue."

Kyrionik had lost the thread of the conversation somewhere. He turned to Shulipik, whose expression had turned grim. "He's saying he's been castrated."

The sailor clenched his hands into fists. As shocking as the revelation was to Kyrionik, hearing it spoken so plainly had embarrassed and angered Selso Rii. The sailor recovered himself quickly, unclenching his fingers and letting his shoulders sag. "It is a terrible burden to bear, your virtue. Shameful."

Kyrionik looked back and forth between the two men, utterly at a loss for words. He'd taken his share of cuts while sword-fighting, of course, but the idea of feeling that very specific sort of pain down in—

"In the Free Cities," Shulipik said, "they castrate rapists."

Rii bowed even lower, but this time, he turned his face to the ground. "Your virtue, I swear, I *swear* that I never—"

"It doesn't matter." Kyrionik's skin was crawling. This should have been his moment of triumph, but Selso Rii had shit all over it. "Whatever crime you've committed, I made a promise I will have to keep. I must be the instrument that undoes the punishment you received, whether it was just punishment or not."

The sailor looked up, a faint glimmer of hope in his expression. "I knew you were a man of honor, your virtue. But my reward does not have to be subtracted from the prize that you bring home! That is the humble point I seek to make. A sizable piece from one of the *others* would benefit us both."

"And you would not have to wait for your cure, yes?" Selso Rii bowed his head, but his smile vanished when Kyrionik continued. "Absolutely not. Do not interrupt me again, good sir. No one will be getting a piece of glitterkind flesh before we return to Koh-Salash. Glitterkind magic is dangerous, and it's risky to cut one. We do not have the tools for the job." In truth, Kyrionik carried a slender bronze scalpel in his boot, but it was for dire emergencies only. "Or the skill."

121

Suspecting that his lie was not convincing, Kyrionik leaned forward and scowled. "One of my own, a soldier who stood at my shoulder two years ago in the midst of battle, has broken his ankle. If he has to wait to be ministered by a skilled healer, so do you."

Selso Rii stood for a moment with his jaw muscles throbbing. He clearly had much more he wanted to say, but he did not dare. He recovered himself, bowed politely, and thanked Kyrionik for his fair consideration. Then he skulked into the trees to make room for working soldiers.

Shulipik glowered at him, then went back to watching the jungle for threats. Kyrionik wondered what he would have to do—or endure—to train himself until he had a similar habit. "If that scurvy-ridden old backstabber has royal blood in him," Shulipik said, "I'll eat a rat."

Kyrionik shrugged. "We have hosted former kings in our family compound. You shouldn't offer that wager unless you think rats a delicacy."

Shulipik smiled again without turning his gaze from the surrounding trees.

"I don't think there's an ullroct on the island," Kyrionik said. "Everything I've read about them says they destroy glitterkind on sight, and these are just lying out in the open."

"Perhaps." Shulipik glanced at Selso Rii. "I'll keep watch over that one."

The new poles were cut without incident, although twisting and tying the vines took longer than expected. The afternoon had started to fade when the soldiers lifted the closest of the glitterkind onto the stretchers.

The creature's shoulders were so broad that its hands had to be draped across its midsection and bound at the wrists. Kyrionik felt a twinge of regret at that. He's been taught that glitterkind healing magic was sacred, and the creatures should be treated with respect. Still, it was only temporary, and better than dragging its wrists on the jungle floor or, worse, bumping it against steel armor.

They also had to wrap their cloaks around it. When it came to a choice between risking permanent scarring from the accidental touch of steel or temporarily blocking the sunlight, Kyrionik chose the latter. Glitterkind survived nightfall, didn't they?

It required fourteen men and women to carry it, seven on a side, four each by the torso. Tucking his gauntlets into his belt, Kyrionik preceded it down the rough stair. If it began to slide forward on the stretcher while they carried it on the steep slope, he wanted to be in position to brace it.

Great gods, but it was huge. The head alone, lolling off the front edge of the stretcher, would have stood from Kyrionik's knees to his collarbone, and the mouth was big enough to bite him in half. The thought made him shiver despite the heat.

Aratill arranged for a small contingent of soldiers to lead the way down the stairs, while Oblifell and Shulipik organized the rear guard.

It was difficult work, and Kyrionik twice had to brace the glitterkind when the stair became too steep. Still, things were going well. If the crew at the cliff had finished the boom, their prize could be aboard before sunset.

Kyrionik tried to imagine his mother's expression when she saw what he'd brought home for his First Labor. She had been an Elder under a previous Steward-General, but maybe some portion of the renown he was about to win would help her return to her place in the High Watch. It was only fair, after all. She *deserved* it. Maybe she'd even be elected Steward-General.

When they reached the ruins of the mill, a great wordless cry sounded from the top of the hill. It was a deep, bellowing sound, full of pain and fear. Then there was another, then another.

The massive head of the glitterkind on the stretcher twitched. With a cry, Kyrionik jumped back into the edge of the pond.

The creature's eyes snapped open, its mouth gaped, and it began to bellow, joining the chorus atop the hill.

"Don't drop it!" Aratill shouted, his voice booming in the jungle. There was no more need for secrecy, not with this awful choir. The glitterkind voices seemed to reverberate within Kyrionik's rib cage and skull—inside his very thoughts—and filled him with a terrible emptiness.

Several soldiers swore against their fear, and Aratill called for double time. They did, leaving Kyrionik standing beside the mill pond like a lost child. He peered up the slope to see what was happening, but the greenery was too thick.

The stretchers snaked down the long crumbling stairs, allowing Aratill to approach Kyrionik. The bodyguard had already drawn his sword and his bull's-head shield.

A sound like ice water cast onto red-hot iron resounded from the top of the slope, and a column of pale white light shot into the clouds.

CHAPTER FOURTEEN

When *word came that* the Pails' messenger had arrived, Harl Sota List Im was composing a letter to his sister.

Harl was a rich man. Not the richest in the city, certainly not, but he had enough money that the most precious coin he could spend was his time. And he did not want to spend another minute carefully composing and sending a reply to his fucking sister. For the third time.

He figured that the letter she'd sent to him, barely enough to cover one side of a sheet of paper, had taken a full day to write. In it, she begged him to visit her children—even though her only child was already making a killing as a jewel trader in the Free Cities—and to see Mother one last time before she passed, even though their mother had been dead for fifteen years. She told him he'd spent long enough in a doomed foreign city. She *implored* him, more forcefully than ever, to come home.

It was, Harl knew, a warning. His sister's husband was a committee officer in the court of the Amber Throne, and he must have told her a secret. It wasn't something she could say openly in a letter, but the meaning was clear.

Carrig was preparing to invade Koh-Salash.

There had been rumors of war for years, but if the Carrig fleets were preparing to sail in the coming spring, Harl's sister might have tried something like this.

What she didn't understand was that his venerable uncle had already ordered him to stay.

Harl had spent the last year compiling blackmail material on the members of the High Watch that he could use to foment conflict among the ruling class. He'd acquired warehouses in neighborhoods built of ordinary wood that would be prone to arson and fire. He'd sent laborers into Mudside to dig "foundations" that could easily be turned into tunnels.

He'd even stockpiled little packets of white tar for upcoming Sword and Spear Day. His venerable uncle had not ordered this, but Harl figured free samples on the holiday meant to honor Salashi soldiers would mean more addicts among the ranks and fewer fighting troops when he withheld their drugs on the day the invading fleet arrived.

But of course, none of this could be put onto paper, either. His sister was worried that he would be innocently caught up in a coming battle, without understanding that he had a role to play in it. And if she kept sending increasingly urgent letters by sea, someone was going to notice.

He needed to make her stop, and it wasn't a task he could entrust to a clerk.

So, when the heavy at the door said the Pails had sent a courier to return his lost property, he was almost grateful.

"Show him in."

In Harl's experience, you could judge a gangster by the people they employed. Smart people hated working for cowards and fuck-ups. They wanted bosses who could put coin in their purse and protect them from the cosh.

Harl had the best people in the city and, not surprisingly, considered himself the sharpest boss in the city. He'd have to be, to last fifteen years at the top of this shit pile. Tin Pail's flunkies, on the other hand, impressed no one at all. Especially that northerner with the stinking fur around his grimy neck.

So, he was surprised to hear that she'd sent someone rather than deliver it herself.

When the Pails' messenger was led to his lounge, Harl stood beside the counter, comfortably relaxing beside the remains of his supper. The fellow had already been searched downstairs, of course, but Harl's bodyguards did it again. They liked to grab other people's flunkies and shake them around a little.

The man had a knife sheath on his belt, but it was empty. He was allowed to enter.

Harl's first thought was *I am not impressed.*

The messenger was taller than average, but not by much. Harl himself was often the shortest guy in the room, and in his experience, again, the tall ones were more confident than they should have been.

This one, for example, didn't show any of the tics that suggested he was trying to hide his fear. Smart criminals knew Harl's reputation and were nervous when they met him. Therefore, *stupid*. This guy's shaggy hair hung in his face. *Careless.* His clothes were all black, as though he'd just come from a funeral or was trying to dress like a villain in a play. *Trying too hard.* He was also younger than Harl first thought. His posture and expression—not to mention the scar on his face—made him look older, but he was still a young man, not even thirty. *Inexperienced.*

Then Harl looked at him again and noticed the defiance in his eyes.

Was it possible that the messenger had steel to back him up? Who had the Pails sent?

"Come in, come in," Harl said in Carrig. "Tell me about the delivery."

The man approached, taking a position on the other side of the counter, as he was supposed to. His gaze shifted from figure to figure: Harl himself, the heavies nearby, the room, the balcony, the rail, the other exit. His face remained impassive.

Harl didn't like to be kept waiting. "Well?"

"Are you ready to let them go?" the young man asked in Carrig. His voice was a little rough, as though he didn't speak often, but his accent was excellent. It was almost better than Harl's. "That was the deal."

Let them go? Did he mean let the Pails live? Or were they planning to flee the city? A sudden chilly anger cleared Harl's thoughts. "Deal? There's no deal here, except the one I've already offered." If the stranger recognized the threat in Harl's voice, he didn't show it. "Return what's mine, and *maybe* I won't have you skinned alive!"

The stranger's hand shot inside his collar, then slapped a small leather pouch on the counter between them. He moved so quickly that Harl's bodyguards barely had time to uncross their arms.

"What's this?" Were they stupid enough to send a glitterkind ear to him personally? Here? And how had his people missed it?

Harl untied the package and peeled the oiled leather back. White tar. There was enough here to hang every person in this building, even the ball boys.

From somewhere very close, he heard the flat, repetitive gong of the constables signaling a raid.

* * *

KLUNG KLUNG KLUNG KLUNG. Onderishta had been pleased when Fay Nog Fay asked to man the gong. This was his tip, and she trusted him to lead.

It was risky, though. Harl Sota List Im was the big boss of organized crime in Koh-Salash, reporting to no one but his Carrig masters overseas, and he'd played that role for years. To survive that long, he had to be wealthy, smart, and connected. If this raid was a bust, Onderishta's bosses would not trust her to try again.

But Harl was also the man responsible for flooding Mudside and

Spillwater with white tar, for running protection rackets in Low Market, and for a thousand other crimes, large and small. The bureaucracy wanted him.

And with Fay's tip that he would be personally accepting a delivery of white tar, the bureaucracy might get what they wanted.

The ironshirts rushed into place. Two donkey carts were dragged into the alley that led to the stables, then flipped onto their side. No horse could jump that barrier.

One team hit the front doors while another entered through the adjoining tea house. Were there other ways out? Onderishta wouldn't have been surprised, but in the last decade, she'd bribed eight different employees to draw a map of the courts for her, and none had included secret exits or escape tunnels. Plus, the Upgarden decks were made entirely of skywood. It would have been easier to dig a trap door through solid granite.

Mirishiya ran around a corner of the building, a mob of employees following close behind. "This way, quickly!" she urged, even as the constables moved in and pressed the forefront of the mob against the building.

She approached Onderishta, smiling with crooked teeth. This was the first of the apprentices from Suloh's temple, an orphan child who'd grown up as a sneak thief in the downcity plankways. "It worked just like you said," she said, beaming. "I urged them to follow me to safety and ran them into your nets. Go again?"

Trillistin, the second apprentice, was at the back of the mob, telling them there was no point in running. He was the other apprentice Culzatik recommended, but she had no idea why. He seemed a fine boy but nothing special.

Crowds gathered. Shouting voices echoed against the buildings, and every few seconds, a belligerent fell to the ground and cried out that the cosh were beating them. It was chaos. The boy gawped at it all.

Onderishta rapped a knuckle on the top of his head, and he gave her his attention. His hair was close-cropped like the child of servants that he was, and his eyes were wide and nervous. Although he and Mirishiya were the same age, he stood a head taller, no doubt because he didn't grow up half-starved. "Both of you stay with me. You did fine work, but this is just the staff. Harl's thugs would have taken you hostage."

Today was the day. She was about to collar Harl for possession of white tar. His sponsors among the noble families would not dare protect him this time. This collar would stick.

And without Harl, dozens of tar sellers downcity would be stripped of their protection.

This wasn't the work Onderishta's noble sponsor had given her, but to her mind, it was the work she was *supposed* to be doing. For once, she was going to make life in this city better for everyone, not just the Safroys.

All they had to do was catch the bastard.

* * *

AS SOON AS KYRIOC saw Harl's reaction to the oiled leather packet, he knew he'd walked into a trap. Worse, he *was* the trap, sprung to catch more important prey.

Harl's eyes went wide. "You do this to me? *To me?*"

He squeezed the package in his soft little fist, tar oozing from the ends, staining his pants where it dripped onto him. Then he threw it at Kyrioc.

It was a good throw. An athlete's throw. Kyrioc was faster. He batted the leaky package away with his elbow.

Harl took a deep breath. *"Sh'chee-yon—"*

Kyrioc threw himself to the side before Harl reached the final syllable. He couldn't hear it—no human ear had ever heard all the spoken components of a ghostkind spell—but he recognized it immediately.

This time, he was not fast enough. A rush of invisible power flew past him, but the edge washed over his face like a blast of oily smoke from a furnace. A blinding light and terrible pressure flashed against his eyes, then it was gone. He stumbled over a low piece of furniture and fell hard.

Hands seized him. Someone kicked his legs, preventing him from gaining his feet. Someone else grabbed a fistful of his hair. Kyrioc couldn't see who was doing it or where the attacks were coming from.

He was blind. His eyes stung, and tears streamed down his cheeks. Harl's spell had taken his sight away.

Kyrioc raised his hands in a defensive posture, only to have them kicked away. He needed to escape. He started to call up his cloak of shado—no, his cloak of iron.

But he couldn't focus. Too much chaos, too much shouting, too many hands pinning his arms and pulling at his hair while punches and kicks slammed into him. Then someone pulled his hair so hard that his head tilted back, exposing his throat.

There was only one reason for them to do that.

This was the end.

Finally.

"Stop!"

The attacks stopped. There was still shouting from the hall and the courtyards below—still the sound of the constables' gongs—but while those distant noises were growing closer, this room fell still.

"The magistrates will need to tie a noose around someone's neck for all this tar. He's the one who brought the bundle, so he's the one who'll swing."

There was a brief pause. Whatever vicious blow Harl's thugs had been about to deliver never fell. Instead, they hoisted him to his feet, dragged him across the room, and threw him over the balcony rail.

* * *

FAY SHOUTED, "NO BLADES, no blades!"

The constables didn't need to be told, but he wanted the heavies to hear the order being given. *We won't escalate if you won't.*

So, blades remained sheathed. Truncheons had been drawn but not swung. Heavies stood in the hall with their hands out, shouting at the constables to hold up, explain themselves, slow down, but the words blended together into an incoherent chorus of raised voices. The ironshirts, truncheons forward, pushed their way through the doors and up the stairs, the heavies offering only enough resistance to slow them to a crawl.

If Harl had a secret way out, they were giving him time to reach it.

Fay turned to Onderishta. Her expression was grim. She shouted something several times, but her voice was lost in the din. By the fallen gods, the noise was awful.

A sudden escalation in the shouting made him look up. Harl had appeared at the top of the stairs, and there was a smear on his right pant leg—Selsarim Lost, it wasn't just a smear. It looked like a piece of white tar.

If they captured Harl with contraband on his clothes, he would swing for sure, and Fay would be the one tying the noose.

The thought gave him goosebumps. He was making enemies today— powerful ones—but his father had told him a person could judge their worth by the enemies they made.

Fay smiled, his thoughts both grim and happy, and *pushed*.

* * *

NOTHING FOCUSED THE MIND like the feeling of falling though open air. Kyrioc curled up, relaxed his muscles, and called up his cloak of iron.

He did not fall far, and he struck soft, yielding wood rather than the stone-like skywood of the Upgarden decks. The impact still knocked the breath out of him and splashed a puddle of rainwater onto his face, but his cloak of iron blunted much of the impact.

But not all. Any armor, magical or mundane, could only do so much.

Kyrioc felt his sleeve soaking up the rainwater, and he rubbed the wet linen against his eyes. The stinging bright light faded slightly. He rolled over and pressed his face into the puddle, then opened his eye.

A spell. Harl Sota List Im had cast an actual ghostkind spell.

No wonder he was in Koh-Salash. Spellcasting was a capital offense in pretty much every civilization on the Semprestian, but in Carrig, they put your whole family to death, just in case.

Kyrioc washed out one eye, then the other. The water neutralized the magic, growing warmer as it leeched the spell away, but the puddle wasn't enough. He needed a full basin at least.

He could see blurry shapes and colors. He blinked and blinked again, trying to force his own tears to flow harder. It helped, but not fast enough. The tinny clangs of the constables' gongs were getting closer, and so were the shouting voices. Kyrioc rolled onto his back and nearly fell off the edge of the platform he had landed on.

He caught the scent of horses and horse shit.

A door banged open, then Harl's voice ordered someone to block a hall with furniture, which was followed by the sound of a door slamming shut and latching into place. Kyrioc looked over the edge of the roof but couldn't see anything moving. Harl was below with the horses out of sight.

And he might know something about Riliska. If not, he would know other things, like who the Pails were and where they laid their heads at night.

Kyrioc swung himself over the edge of the building and dropped down to the deck. His vision had cleared enough to see Harl—blurry but obviously him—climbing into a saddle. The stableboy was beside him, boosting him up.

"Kill him," Harl said.

The boy drew a knife from his belt. Kyrioc still couldn't open his eyes all the way, but he had blinked away much of the spell's effect, and he knew immediately what the boy's posture showed: body tilted, right arm held low, left bent close to the body. Someone had taught this kid how to fight, probably the bored heavies loitering around the place.

The boy feinted as Harl gained his seat and dug in his heels. The horse took off and the boy hopped to the side, putting himself between Kyrioc and his fleeing boss.

Then he lunged. It was a brave move—and well executed—but he was just a boy. Kyrioc sidestepped and slapped him on the side of the head.

Not too hard, but the knife clattered against the skywood deck. The boy staggered and fell into the hay.

Harl rode for the alley, which was the wrong choice. That way led to the street, straight toward the ironshirts, and the buildings pressing in on either side gave him no options except to go forward or retreat. Maybe he expected help from them, either because they were on his payroll or hoped to be. Maybe he wasn't thinking at all.

Kyrioc snatched the boy's knife off the deck, but Harl turned the corner into the alley before he could throw it.

The nag still stood where he'd left her.

The boy had not taken the rig off her. She was still attached to the carriage. For a moment, Kyrioc no longer felt bad about that slap. He dunked his face in the horses' water trough, then opened his eyes. The water wasn't clean, but magic was its own contamination, and he'd take horse slobber over a spell any time. When he stood again, he could see pretty well, but the nag was spooked. He took up the reins, making soothing noises.

She backed up, her cartload of potatoes moving across the mouth of the alley. He could hear shouting from the street, and Harl's mount let out a whinny. Hoofbeats approached. Kyrioc knew Harl had met the ironshirts in the street and was now retreating.

The back of the cart struck the building opposite, completely blocking the alley entrance. Kyrioc bounded into the cart and stood atop the potatoes, his arms held high and wide.

A good, strong horse could have jumped the cart, and Harl's horse was fine indeed, even if the rider looked uncomfortable in the saddle. But even a good horse will balk when a man jumps in front of it, arms splayed.

Harl's mount halted, head dipping low and rear lifting up. Harl lost his seat and went over the horse's neck.

Kyrioc sidestepped the falling body, but one of the burlap sacks ruptured under his foot, and he fell forward, striking his head against the wall and landing beside Harl's mount. Harl himself plowed into the burlap sacks, breaking the far side of the cart and spilling the potatoes everywhere.

Harl's horse did not trample Kyrioc. It backed away, skittish. Beyond it, a swarm of constables sprinted toward them, eyes wild, voices yelling.

Harl stood. There was a bloody mark on his forehead and he held his left arm close to his chest as though it was broken. He ran into the courts.

The nag reared and kicked. A terrible rotting smell came from the cart, and the horse shied from it.

Kyrioc couldn't let Harl escape if he was going to find Riliska and her mother. He vaulted over the cart and landed on a burlap sack on the other side.

And stopped.

At his feet lay a dead body, half wrapped in a shroud. Harl must have knocked it from the cart when he broke through the side.

Kyrioc couldn't move.

Couldn't speak.

He could only stare.

Ironshirts ran toward him, shouting and waving truncheons, but they fell silent when they saw the body too.

It was an adult woman, flayed from the neck down. Where her stomach should have been was just an empty cavity. Her scalp had been removed, leaving only exposed bone. Her eyelids sat sunken over empty sockets.

He had not just delivered drugs for the Pails. Not just. He'd also brought Rulenya, child of someone he did not know, mother to Riliska.

A woman stood beside him. Her gray vest marked her as a bureaucrat, and the exertions of the day had left her graying hair in disarray. Kyrioc assumed she was the investigator in charge of this raid.

She'd been the first at his side and the first to notice Rulenya's corpse.

When she looked up at him, there was an icy hatred in her gaze.

"Take him," she said.

CHAPTER FIFTEEN

Onderishta climbed the stair and joined Fay at the tower window.
The raid had been his chance. If they'd caught Harl with the incriminating evidence his source said would be there, Fay would have been, briefly, a hero. He would have immediately been offered a promotion into a position like her own—city payroll, private masters.

Or he could have moved to a different part of the bureaucracy: the diplomatic bureaucracy, so he could visit relations in Carrig, or regulate goldsmiths, where the bribes were said to be life-changing, or as an aide to the High Watch, where he would be a whisper away from the most powerful nobles in the city.

But Harl had slipped away. His men had been rounded up by the dozens, but the boss was gone.

White tar had been found in the building—smeared into a sofa, as a matter of fact—but there was no way to prove the boss was involved, because they hadn't collared him. Fay and Onderishta had taken their shot, and they wouldn't get another.

Their only result was a corpse that implied a crime no one wanted to admit was possible.

"I like coming up here," Fay said. "I like real sunlight."

Onderishta didn't speak.

He sighed. "That informant sent word that we should move on Harl and I did it. Like I was taking orders. I wanted Harl so much that I didn't even consider that I might be…" He looked down at his empty hand. "That body…"

Onderishta gave him a moment to compose himself, then she said, "You examined her?"

He shuddered slightly. "I did. In the years I've been working for you, I've seen a lot of corpses, but I've never seen anything like that. She hadn't just been flayed. Her insides had been taken out. And her eyes. Do you think Harl is running a black-market hospital somewhere in the city?"

"I've heard new rumors of a Lost Ward loose in the city."

Fay drummed his fingers on the sill. "A day ago, I would have rolled my eyes. This shit *just doesn't happen*, but… Is there any doubt that Harl would cut people up for parts if there was money to be made?"

"No." Onderishta told him about her meeting with the Safroy heir and his suspicions about the package exchange they'd missed in Sailsday's Regret. She even told him about the possible plot to frame the Safroys for treason.

"So, the white tar we found at the hammerball courts wasn't from the package we missed in Sailsday's Regret? My Katr informant with the bells in his hair either didn't know what was being passed—which I don't really believe—or the white tar was planted, or your noble boss has it all wrong. I'm hoping it's the last one, but if Harl is deep into black-market medicine, we need to jump on it."

Except there was no aspect of life in Koh-Salash more scrupulously regulated than healing magic. Replacing eyes, livers, skin…all of it was bound by careful procedures and bureaucrats who were not only the most rigid, self-righteous human beings on the face of the earth, they were given full authority to regulate each other, too. The lowest of the low could thoroughly audit the accounts of the head of the department, and if they expected to be promoted someday, they did.

So, if Harl was selling body parts, either he had bribed every regulator in that department, or he had found a way to do illicit medical magic right under their noses.

Either way, they would have to ask awkward questions of some very powerful, very unpleasant people.

She said, "Tell me about the extra man."

That was how they were referring to the asshole who'd delivered the corpse—and, presumably, the drugs—to the hammerball court. *Extra Man*. It would have made a decent street name, although Onderishta imagined it had already been used, probably more than once.

"Patrols haven't recognized him yet. The other knuckle-busters has been named and tagged, at least with a street name, but not him."

"An out-of-town contractor?"

"He looks Salashi to me." Fay shrugged. "He could be someone Harl brought in from the farmwilds for a special job."

Onderishta had made note of him: young, shaggy black hair, dark brown skin like her own, except for a discolored hand. In fact, he looked like Harl's thugs, wearing black like a villain in a play.

Except he lacked the swagger. Most gangsters liked to strut, especially when they'd been collared. It was practically a competition with them.

The extra man did none of that. He stared at the wall as though he could see through it, and he wouldn't talk. "He hasn't offered a street name, either."

Fay grimaced. "He irritates me. These guys love to tell us their stupid made-up names. But not him."

"Which brings us back to the possibility that this is a setup," Onderishta said. "It's wildly unlikely, but if your foreign informant was acting on his own, he might not know the rule. Maybe he didn't realize that gangsters knife people who set the cops on them, no matter who they are. Someone—and by *someone* I mean that northerner with the bells in his beard, maybe—wants to get out from under Harl's thumb, so they drop some white tar and a collected corpse into his lap. The extra man was supposed to slip away—or he was expendable—and the constables swoop in when they're told to."

"Like employees." Fay noted Onderishta's expression and said, "Sorry. Okay. We swoop in but Harl has a secret exit no one knows about and blows the informant's plan. It's possible, I guess, but how long has Harl been the big boss? Twelve years?"

"Fifteen."

"Shit. That's a long time to consolidate power. Plus, his lieutenants love him. He's made them rich enough."

Onderishta couldn't hold back a rueful smile. "Rich enough? No such thing."

"He also has the backing of the Amber Throne. My informant looked like a capable guy, but he was running with Second Boar and a bunch of faceless nobodies. Do we know anyone with the guts and ambition to defy the city's top ganglord, all the lieutenants he's paying, the noble family that supports him, *and* the Amber Throne?"

"No one who isn't already in this room."

That made Fay laugh. "It seems farfetched to me, too." He snapped his fingers. "What if this extra man isn't a heavy?" Fay asked. "What if he's hospital staff? Or even a full-fledged doctor who lost his license?"

The thought hadn't even occurred to her. "My instinct says no," Onderishta answered, "but fuck my instinct. That seems more likely than some internal revolt among the heavies. We have apprentices at hand. Let's send them to every hospital in the city. This asshole seems pretty memorable to me."

Fay clenched his fists. For a moment, Onderishta thought he might throw a punch at the wall. "Shit. We almost collared Harl fucking Im."

"Giving up?"

Fay's fists immediately unclenched and his self-pitying expression vanished. "No. Never."

Trillistin appeared at the top of the stairs, gasping for breath. He must have run a long way, because there was sweat streaming from his close-cropped hair.

Onderishta had to wait for him to catch his breath. The temple kept their charges at their writing desks, and most of them were as soft as caged veal.

The delay became annoying. "Have the constables identified our mystery man?" she asked.

"No," the boy gasped. "But one. Recognized. The woman."

* * *

IN THE YEAR BEFORE his First Labor, Kyrionik ward-Safroy defe-Safroy admir-Safroy hold-Safroy had been well known to the constables of High and Low Apricot. Mainly, they knew him as a boy trying too hard to seem older, and they'd laughed at him. When he got into trouble, they dragged him back to the Safroy compound and received a few silver whistles for their trouble. He'd been a lucrative side job for them.

No one recognized him now. Whether it was the hair or the scar—or that he was supposed to be dead—Kyrioc recognized many of the faces under those steel caps, but to them he had become Nobody, child of No One.

And thank the fallen gods for that. One of his worst fears had always been that he'd be returned to High Slope—to the Safroy compound. Prison would have been preferable. Work camps would have been preferable.

Hanging would be preferable, and considering his history, hanging was what he deserved.

Rulenya was dead. Kyrioc had done what he'd been told, traveling from the bottom of this corpse of a city to the top, but he had not saved her. He had not even realized that she'd been dead all along.

And what did that mean for Riliska?

The ironshirts had herded all of the arrested thugs—men and women—into the courtyard of the south tower. There, they had been split up. The women were led to a smaller holding area made of stone blocks, and the men brought directly into the base of the main jail. They had been forced to strip—with several of the constables glancing warily at Kyrioc's scarred back and limbs—then led into a stinging-cold bath. The heavies' sullen silence was broken by that icy water, and they began to shout at the blank walls in protest.

But no matter what they said, no one looked directly at the ironshirt in the doorway with his sword—not a truncheon—in his hand. The constables were not playing games this time. The local heavies were brave enough to complain, but that was it.

Kyrioc kept quiet and did as he was told. One of the constables found white tar on his clothes and told him his days as a free man were over. Since he didn't have tar stains around his mouth, he'd be convicted as a dealer, and dealers swung.

He heard that several times from several different constables, and each time, it was like a promise. They were going to cure him of his life.

The ironshirts dragged him into a room and shoved him into a sturdy metal chair. His left hand was shackled into place with a heavy padlock.

By the fallen gods, he'd fought for so long to survive on Vu-Dolmont and finally made his way back to the city, and for what? Why had he bothered? To keep a promise to a dead man he had loved?

That promise had been fulfilled. It was behind him. Done.

He'd failed Rulenya and Riliska, and he didn't have any reason to go on.

* * *

AS ONDERISHTA EXPECTED, THE medical inspector was a real delight. Dressed head to toe in gray, with a high conical hat to emphasize his status, he stood in the south tower council room with his arms pressed against his stomach, as though he was afraid he would dirty himself if he touched anything.

When they had asked his name, he refused to give it. Security reasons, he said. Then he said, "I'm afraid there's no doubt."

Onderishta waited for him to continue. He didn't. She turned to Fay, who looked more confused than exasperated.

"Doubt about what?" Fay asked.

The bureaucrat sighed. "There's no doubt that she's been collected. That much is clear. However, it's impossible that her collected parts were actually *gifted* to a patient."

Onderishta kept her expression neutral. "Please continue."

"I suspect that this woman was murdered this way to *deceive* you into believing she was collected for black-market medical purposes, when in fact she was simply killed for some other reason. Perhaps her gifts were disposed of in a sewer or garbage receptacle. I wouldn't know about that. I just *know* that they weren't used in hospital for a patient's benefit."

They had returned to the idea that Harl was set up. "How can you be so sure?"

"Because they would need glitterkind portions to make the process work, and there are no illicit glitterkind within a hundred miles of Koh-Salash. Because the systems in place—within the hospitals and without—would preclude illicit trade in stolen organs." He straightened the collar of his robe. "I wouldn't allow it."

"I see." Onderishta sat on the corner of her desk and folded her arms. "You don't think it's impossible because your people are too honest and too smart."

"Whether you're able to believe it or not, yes. This Harl Im must have ordered it as a ruse."

"By the fallen gods," Fay said. "A *rooz*."

"And why do you think Harl Sota List Im, a gangster with connections to the parsus themselves, would stage a murder this way?" Onderishta asked. "When he could have made her disappear into one of the sausage shops he owns in Low Market?"

"Sausage shops?" The bureaucrat turned pale beneath his big, ridiculous hat.

"Understand me," Onderishta said quietly. "You may know your field very well, but you don't know mine. Harl is a prominent stitch in a noble family sail. The Lorrud sail, to be specific. That means he's protected by some of the most powerful people in Koh-Salash. To keep that protection, he has to keep his business—the murders, the drug smuggling, the extortion—at arm's length.

"So, the idea that Harl himself ordered this girl collected then left for us to find—*to deceive us*—is laughable on its face. Harl has no reason to create a scandal.

"Of course, one of Harl's enemies might have left the corpse there, but you have to ask why it was collected first. To get *you* involved? Or us? No, the criminals in this city keep their distance from Gray Flames—the cosh and the eye—out of a sensible self-preservation.

"No, the only reason to collect this woman before she was dumped was because there was money in it. That's all. That's how these people operate."

To his credit, the inspector bowed slightly. "I apologize. Of course you know your field better than I do."

"Accepted. So. This woman was collected, so her parts must have made it into the market. You're here to tell us how it's being done."

"It's impossible."

"And yet, we have a body on a stone slab downstairs, so it's happening."

"It can't be happening. It's impossible."

"Let's pretend it isn't."

"But it is."

Fay looked at Onderishta, his smile crooked.

"I'm sorry," the inspector said. "I know it *seems* like I'm being obstinate, but I'm just explaining the facts. It's impossible for any black-market organ trade to operate in Koh-Salash. It just is."

"All right," Onderishta said, "let's talk about this perfect system of yours."

The inspector scowled. He hadn't liked the word *perfect*, but he didn't object to it. "Certainly. I'll do my best to be thorough but concise. First, despite what you may think, gifting isn't that common. It isn't vanishingly rare, but it's nowhere near as routine as it ought to be. Each gift comes from established social organizations. Usually it's the Temple of Suloh, but sometimes it's Yth or one of the smaller temples. Other times it's a fellowship or lodge set up by a noble family."

That was a surprise. "A lodge?"

The inspector waved a hand. "Among the other benefits of paying a fortune to join a club led by one of the richest, most powerful families in the city is that they'll help you arrange, and pay for, a transplant if you're injured."

Fay cut in. "And they'll collect you when your time comes."

"Well, yes," the inspector said without blinking. "When your time comes, of course. The flip side of receiving gifts when needed is that one must be willing to provide them when appropriate. If one Intends to benefit from a system, one should expect to pay into it as well. And, frankly, not every lodge member is willing to enroll in such a benefit."

"Not until it's too late, right?"

"Exactly. And that's why the system can't be gamed, exploited, or cheated. Each of these donors has a record at the temple or fellowship. Those records can be checked, and they come from reputable people, with a unique mark on every tank. The mark is transferred to the accompanying paperwork, which is written on a distinctive paper that we fashion ourselves, to prevent forgeries."

The inspector was going too fast, assuming they knew too much. "Family's mark?"

"Yes, the ward-family. The nobles. Each infinitesimal piece of… Okay. Gifts are collected when the donor passes. It has to be within the hour for most body parts, but never mind. The gift, whether it's an organ, an eye, or a sheath of skin—and healthy skin is always in high demand—is placed into a tank of water that's been seeded with a tiny portion of glitterkind flesh. The glitterkind magic in that broth preserves the gift and readies it for the recipient's body. Each ward-family is responsible for the care of their glitterkind charges, and they're weighed with incredibly sensitive instruments *before* and *after* portions are taken."

"What about glitterkind procedures that don't involve transplants?"

"Impossible," the inspector said, then caught himself. "I'm sorry. They're not impossible, obviously. They happen on very, very rare occasions. Vanishingly rare. Transplanting healthy organs requires a tiny amount of glitterkind flesh. Regrowing damaged or amputated tissue requires almost a thousand times more. It's incredibly expensive and only used when a transplant would do no good. Special permission is required, and not even the Steward-General would be guaranteed such a treatment."

A procedure that used a thousand times the normal dose of glitterkind flesh would be the perfect opportunity to skim. Fay must have been thinking the same thing, because he jumped in with a question of his own. "Have you ever overseen that sort of procedure? Where glitterkind flesh is used but there's no transplant?"

"Not in the eighteen years that I've been doing this work," he said. "It's really only... Hmf. Let me speak plainly. It's only used for brain injuries and castrations. With the former, they're almost never approved. With the latter...they do not happen often through mischance, and the medical system is not in the business of undoing criminal punishment, whether doled out by a Salashi magistrate or a foreign one."

Onderishta nodded. "About those family marks, I assume the marks are noted when the...donations arrive at the hospital."

"Correct, unless the gift-giver was collected at the same hospital as the recipient. That's the preferred way to handle things. But sometimes the donation is shipped in, and it's always authenticated with the ward-family mark."

"Each has their own?"

"Exactly so."

"That woman was killed this morning at the earliest. If her...donations had been put in a transplant tank, how long would they be viable?"

He didn't like that question. "She wouldn't... Was she a member of a licensed social organization?"

"Let's assume we're going to find out that she was."

"Well, you see, the collections would typically remain viable for anything from a week to a month. Skin lasts longest. Eyes decay fastest. But there's a minimum period, too. The organs need to be suffused with glitterkind magic before the operation can go forward. That's at least an hour for the eyes, liver, heart, et cetera. It can take a full day for the skin."

"So, the skin grafts won't happen until sometime tomorrow, but it could be anytime within the next month?"

"Typically," the inspector said. "But I assure you, this is all hypothetical. There would be no way to get a murder victim's parts into the collection procedures without alerting the medical inspectors. It just isn't possible."

She'd gotten all she could from him, for the present. "Thank you, inspector. Later this week, I'm going to send some apprentices to your office to look over your records. Have them made available."

He scowled, then caught himself. He was a man who could command the attention of the High Watch, possibly the Steward-General himself, but he couldn't let people think he was hiding something. "Of course. I hope I have been helpful. Good luck with your investigation." He left.

"No one is in greater danger," Fay said, once the door had closed, "than the fool who thinks themself completely safe. I can think of two different ways to corrupt his perfect system, and that's just off the top of my head."

"That's not what concerns me. Did you notice how quick he was to suggest that the whole thing was meant to mislead us? It didn't sound like the first time he'd said that. It sounded rehearsed."

"What are you thinking?"

"Send someone to the other towers. I want to know if they've found other bodies like ours, and if the office of medical inspections convinced them it was some kind of hoax. Let's also get a couple of constables up here. I want them out of uniform so they can follow the couriers making these deliveries. I want a rundown of how they operate, how often, what times of day, the whole thing."

"I'll take care of it."

"Do we know where the victim lived?"

"Woodgarden."

"While you're arranging that tower errand, send up my new apprentices. Then find me two pairs of Woodgarden constables. I want to see where this woman lives and how she's connected with Harl."

* * *

"EVERYONE ELSE HAS TOLD us their street names. Why haven't you?"

The ironshirt stared across the table at Kyrioc with half-closed eyes. He looked bored, as though he didn't care whether he got answers to his questions. He'd stripped off most of his armor, leaving only the leather jerkin and the truncheon at his belt. His iron chest plate and helmet hung on a peg behind him.

Two armored constables slouched in the doorway, looking like they thought a little violence would relieve their boredom.

Kyrioc said nothing.

"We know that woman was alive when you skinned her," he said. "We can tell by the way she bled. You know what I'm going to do? I'm going to ask to be excused from my shift on the day you appear before the magistrates. They are going to be so very eager to sentence you. They burn murderers, you know. Pitch and flame."

Kyrioc said nothing.

"It's a sight. They don't set up big wooden pyres anymore, because that's how the Katr like to send off their heroes. Too honorable. Now they just coat your balls with this sticky, oily jelly and jab you with a lit torch. It takes a while, too. Yeah, I'd like to see that. I like to see condemneds' expression the first time they breathe in raw flame." He leaned in and lowered his voice. "But it doesn't have to be that way."

Kyrioc said nothing.

"I bet you didn't kill that woman on your own, right? Probably someone ordered you to do it. I'll bet it didn't even seem real at the time. I'm willing to give up my afternoon's entertainment—watching you burn alive in front of a jeering crowd—if it means catching the *real* criminal. Your cooperation could help you, too. Magistrates have been known to send low-level guys to the work crews."

Kyrioc said nothing.

"But you can't wait. You need to help us now, while we can still catch the person who made you do it in the first place."

You can't just treat a person like they're real one day and then later act like they're not. That's too mean. You have to pick one and stick with it.

Kyrioc closed his eyes. This interrogator had done this patter too many times. Like an actor who had played a part for too long, he was going through the motions, and when Kyrioc was finally ushered out of the room and the next ushered in, he'd go through it again. Probably word for word.

Because Kyrioc wasn't real to him. Kyrioc didn't matter.

"I could help you," the constable said. "You're not the one we're after. You're an errand boy. We're aiming for your boss. You..." He let his voice trail off, but that sounded well rehearsed, too. "My brother used to work for Harl. I don't tell people this, but my older brother ran errands, beat guys up, threatened their kids... Selsarim Lost, I loved him, but he was bad all the way through. I tried to convince him to get out, but even when things were going wrong, he couldn't. 'Pinochin,' he said, 'there's no getting out for guys like me.'

"You don't have to burn like a fucking spectacle for a jeering crowd the way my brother did. Tell us what we want to know about Harl, and I'll see that you're sent to work in a camp far away where no one will know you.

New name, everything. Wouldn't you rather trim grapevines in the warm sun than burn alive?"

Kyrioc said nothing.

Riliska was dead.

"You think Harl is loyal to you? He'd knife you to get out of a dull conversation. Be smart. Take the chance now, while you can. Because if you're anything like my brother, you'll beg for it when it's too late."

She had to be dead. Didn't she?

The interrogator leaned close, his voice low. "I couldn't help him, but I can help you."

Kyrioc looked him in the eyes. Help wasn't a terrible idea. If Kyrioc told his interrogator everything he knew, would the constables go after the Pails, whoever they were, and hit them with the pitch and flame?

He doubted it. No one was going to tell this investigator what he wanted to know, because if the man himself wasn't on Harl's payroll, one of the other constables would be. Anyone who talked wouldn't live through the night, and then what would get done?

Nothing.

If these Pails were going to get payback, he was going to have to do it himself.

"You're still alive now, but the magistrates are going to turn you into a pile of ash in front of a jeering crowd of drunks. Is that what you want? To die soft? To die humiliated?"

You can't just treat a person like they're real one day and then later act like they're not.

"Harl Sota List Im," Kyrioc said. His voice was raw because he hadn't spoken in hours. "That's what you care about."

"That's right," the interrogator said, startled. "He's the only one we care about. He could die in your place."

Kyrioc closed his eyes again. For so long, his only goal had been to survive. That was the task. That was the promise. Survive.

But everything had changed. He'd returned home, and what he'd found was a different city from the one he left. A city that ground up little girls to nothing. This city—his city—threw them away like they were worthless.

He realized then that he'd assumed Riliska and her mother had been killed together. He'd pictured it in his mind: Riliska's face still and gray, eyelids sunken over empty sockets, her tiny body flayed. But he hadn't seen it. He didn't know for sure.

"Alive," Kyrioc said to himself, quietly. "Alive."

"That's right," the interrogator urged.

Kyrioc had *assumed* Riliska was dead, and that was just another way of pretending she wasn't real.

For so many years, survival had been his only purpose. He'd dragged his grief through the long hours of the day like heavy chains, and what good had it done? What good had it done for anyone?

That little girl needed him. She was real, and he was not ready to give up on her. Not yet. He would find her, alive or dead, survival be damned.

He moved slightly, rattling the chain binding his wrist. "I swore never to tell anyone," Kyrioc lied. "Can I write it down?" He lifted the manacle.

The interrogator hesitated, then glanced at the two ironshirts in the doorway. Both were young fellows with thick necks and heavy shoulders. The interrogator stood. He was ten years older than the constables at the door, but he had the same imposing build. Kyrioc did not.

He smiled and took out the manacle key.

CHAPTER SIXTEEN

Haliyal moved through Low Market* carefully. Not that Low Market was especially dangerous, but like any place, if you weren't careful, you weren't alive. The way he saw it, that was the magic spell the dead gods laid on Koh-Salash. That was its special enchantment—it turned living humans into dead ones, and all it needed was a desperate addict with a rusty blade to work its spell.

But he knew his way around. As a kid, he'd hung out on the plankways with his cousins. Like every kid, they were as dumb as freshly carved tombstones. They used to run everywhere, fight with their fists, and filch stuff from food stalls. Petty bullshit, but it made them feel fast and free and clever.

Then they got old enough to notice girls. Suddenly, it wasn't enough to steal a few plums. They needed coin. That was the best time of Haliyal's life. Stealing shit. A little dealing. They were barely fifteen years old and they were on their way up. Red Apricot herself had said she was watching their little gang. He'd had *hope.*

Then Haliyal had gotten sick. In a tiny room at the back of his mother's building, he woke only long enough to drink broth. It took three whole weeks for his fever to break, and it was more than a year before he was strong enough to go out.

By then, his cousins were all dead. They'd come to him while he was bedridden, all excited about their plan to rob a neighborhood tar dealer. Haliyal wished he had tried to talk them out of it, not because they would have listened but because he felt so guilty about his enthusiasm for their stupid plan.

He thought about his cousins every day.

When he was well enough, his mother found him a job and he took it. There was no point in going back to the plankways all alone.

And now there was this thing with the Package. He'd thought Rulenya would be a little bit of fun—someone to pour brandy into until she was ready to come back to his place—but they had stumbled across the biggest score ever.

It made him nervous, to be honest. It made him feel vulnerable. Where could a thief fence a piece of glitterkind? Magistrates branded white tar dealers weekly, which was petty bullshit compared to this. This was magic. It was worth a fucking fortune.

He had one problem and it couldn't be solved. How to convert that ear into coin. He'd hit on the idea of asking around for a black-market transplant for himself, to identify potential buyers, but no one would admit to knowing a way to get one. He'd asked after Red Apricot, but she'd taken the point three years before. He'd even gone all the way up to High Slope to find a noble family with *ward* in their names, to see if there would be a reward or finder's fee for recovering the piece, but he couldn't get past the guards at the wall.

In fact, the whole thing had turned into a mess, and Haliyal was ready to go back to his job sharpening saw blades. Probably the best thing to do would be to walk into the nearest hospital, find the bureaucrat in charge, and say he found it. Maybe he could get ten sails as a finder's fee. Maybe—

"Pardon me, good sir, but would you help me, please?"

Haliyal was startled out of his reverie. An elderly woman stood at the intersection of three plankways, and yeah, she was addressing him. "Me?" he asked, feeling foolish. The street-smart kid he'd once been was long gone.

"If you would, good sir," she said, perfectly polite. "My nephew wrote me a note, but I can't see as well as I used to." She held up a sheet of cheap paper.

Although it was past sunset, Low Market was well lit by Suloh's hip bones. The old woman stood far from the shadows on a well-traveled street. She was dressed nicely, like a merchant's wife, with the makeup, painted hands, and jewelry of a girl fifty years younger. Haliyal guessed she'd been beautiful once and refused to stop putting in the effort to maintain herself. Her every movement was stiff, as though she was in pain.

And she was all alone.

Haliyal thought briefly of his grandmother, who had sat with him for many hours while he was bedridden. This woman had nothing in common with his gran except age and infirmity, but he could spare her a moment in this open public place.

He approached. She held up the sheet of paper. No wonder she couldn't read it. He could barely see it himself. As he squinted down at the curving lines that didn't look much like Selsarim script, he heard a carriage pass behind him on the road, and a door unlatch.

Before he could turn around, Haliyal, child of Hyordis, felt a heavy blow strike the back of his head. The last thing he saw before darkness took him was the little old woman's face, which did not betray a trace of surprise or concern.

* * *

IT TURNED OUT THAT the constables in the south tower only worked sections of Woodgarden. The woman who recognized the corpse knew her as a pickpocket who'd been thrown out of several platform halls in High Apricot. Another ironshirt had called her "Woodgarden trash." No one recognized her, so she must have come from the northern parts of that deck.

Onderishta led Fay to Woodgarden to find locals who could help. They crossed the imaginary border between south and east tower jurisdictions, where the constables needed only the barest description before they could provide her name and the building where she lived.

The hall outside her apartment was cleaner than expected. There were three shops on the center mezzanine but they were all shuttered and padlocked. Fay tried the gate on the pawnshop window, but it wouldn't budge. He followed the landlady to the victim's apartment.

Rulenya, child of Rashila, lived in a pig's sty. Onderishta had smelled worse places, but usually they included a rotting corpse. The floor was covered with discarded clothes, stained bedsheets, and broken crockery. A hand-painting set leaned against the wall in the corner. It seemed their victim had a day job, too.

"By the fallen gods, I had no idea things were this bad!" the landlady cried, but she wasn't very convincing.

"Stay in the hall," Onderishta told her. Fay strode fearlessly inside, and Onderishta followed. The ironshirts moved into the doorway and did nothing but look disgusted. "This is going to take all day. I should have kept my new apprentices handy so they could manage this for us."

"If you'd have brought those two here, they wouldn't be your apprentices anymore." Onderishta was about to concede the point when Fay picked up a set of tiny shoes from beneath the table. Children's shoes. The victim had a kid.

"Put the kid on the list of people to find."

* * *

RILISKA SAT IN THE dark and did as she was told. She kept quiet. She kept still.

She may not have learned her letters from the tutor her mother hired, but she'd learned something from her mother's guests: never test a stranger's patience. It was impossible to tell when they would suddenly have none, and sometimes they didn't punish kids the way a parent would. Sometimes, they beat her the way they'd beat an adult.

Riliska couldn't bear that, not when she was so far from home with no idea where her mother had gone.

She'd been loaded into the carriage like a crate, and she tried to be as still as one, even as she was bumped and shaken by the carriage's noisy springs. She didn't even look up at the shadowy figures around her.

Then the carriage slowed and two of the men lunged through the door. Riliska shut her eyes, but she heard the sound of leather hitting flesh, and a man's awful grunt of pain.

Footsteps rushed toward her and she had to peek. The two short, well-muscled men were half-shoving, half-carrying a third toward the carriage. At the same moment that Riliska saw his nightmarish expression—tongue lolling, eyes rolled back—she recognized him. He was the fuddled man who had beaten up her mother.

He was tossed into the box, almost falling directly onto her. She wondered if she should feel happy to see him receiving some of what he'd given out, but she didn't. She couldn't. He looked helpless and ruined.

A moment later, she felt herself shoved out of the carriage. She fell onto the hard skywood deck, blinking in the sudden orange light of Suloh's bones as the carriage rolled away.

Opposite her stood an old woman with no expression at all. The smell of perfume hung about her, and the painted designs on her hair and nails were clumsy and smudged. A moment passed. Then another. The woman's expression never changed.

Goosebumps ran down Riliska's back. She didn't know where she was, but she wanted to be somewhere else. Surely, she could outrun an old woman wearing too many clothes.

She had to chance it.

"Do you want me to take you to your mother?"

Riliska froze in place. Her mother? She felt the lie in the woman's words, but she decided to believe it anyway. It only made sense that they would return her to her mother. Who else would bother to look after a Long Hangover? Besides, Riliska could run away from this woman anytime, which meant she wasn't a captive anymore, which meant she didn't really have anything to be afraid of. Maybe.

The woman turned away and started walking. If she had tried to grab Riliska, or had ordered her to come along, Riliska would have run away. But she didn't. It was Riliska's choice to follow or not, and that surely meant that this smelly old woman would bring her to her mom.

They walked along the broad road to a set of circular stairs. The old woman lumbered up into the darkness and Riliska followed. Shadows lay everywhere. The glow from Suloh's bones was blocked by the decks, plankways, and avenues of Low Market. The smell of overturned chamber pots grew stronger, and when the breeze shifted, she caught a whiff of rotting fish.

But this was where she needed to go. But the old woman knew where the man with the steel chain and the crazy smile had taken her mother, and of course it would not be someplace respectable.

The woman left the stairs and led Riliska across plankways between old, disused warehouses. In the spaces between the buildings, intermittent streams of filthy water flowed from the deck above, but whether it was spilled sewage or just a shopkeeper mopping their floors, Riliska couldn't tell. Drums thrummed from above.

The old woman suddenly turned to a door and drew out a key. There were no markings on the building except an engraved panel showing two buckets hung from the same hook. Riliska followed her inside.

The room looked like a tiny shop. One side had a counter, but the other walls were covered with shelves. On the shelves were hundreds of tiny, unpainted wooden dolls. They had oversized bubble-heads and hollow recesses for eyes, and their tiny arms were outstretched as though barring the way. Riliska thought they looked oddly threatening. She hurried around the counter to catch up with the old woman.

The next room was dark and full of workbenches set with different sorts of saws and drills. They were ominous in the dim light.

The woman climbed a flight of cramped stairs. Riliska didn't like the look of it. Not at all.

"If you don't come up, you won't see your mommy."

It was a lie. Riliska knew it was a lie, but she couldn't stop herself. She climbed the stairs.

She had been separated from her mother most of the day, and that felt wrong. It was past time to see her again. Besides, who was she to second-guess a grownup? She was just a kid. What did she know about where the man with the crazy smile might take her mom?

Once she'd reached the top of the stairs, Riliska could see that the room beyond was dark. There was a single window at the far end, with the faint yellow-orange glow of Suloh's bones filtering through the dirty glass. Was her mother sleeping? She crept into the doorway, and the awful smell...

Just as Riliska was about to back away, the old woman shoved her. She stumbled into the room and the door slammed behind her. She heard a bolt being thrown.

"Let me out!" she shouted. She threw her weight against the door and pounded at it with her tiny fists. "Let me out! Let me out!" But the door didn't even rattle.

She'd known her mother wasn't here, but she'd come anyway.

There was movement in the dark behind her, and Riliska stopped shouting. She could see silhouettes moving in the room, rising off the floor like hungry ghosts. The old woman's footsteps retreated down the stairs. Whatever was in here, Riliska was trapped with it.

Hands reached up and caught hold of her wrists, her legs, the hem of her tunic. She squealed in terror at the unexpected touch. She found she could break free easily—the hands were small and not terribly strong—but there were too many of them.

It was then that she realized they were shushing her. Their hands were grimy but their voices were desperate. They were saying *please*, and when Riliska heard their voices, she realized they were children like her. From the sound of it, some were very young. She had woken them up.

She let herself be pulled down onto the lumpy mats in the dim, hellish light. She let herself be shushed. And that was all it took to become one of them.

CHAPTER SEVENTEEN

Onderishta could have kicked herself.

She and Fay were rummaging through the mess in the dead woman's apartment when she spotted something among the shards of a shattered jug. It was a claim token from a pawnshop.

"How many pawnshops in Woodgarden?" she asked the nearest constable. Onderishta's work took her all over the city, but most of her time was spent in the very wealthy neighborhoods or the absolute poorest. Woodgarden fell between.

"Ah…" he answered, then looked toward the ceiling and began to count on his fingers.

"A baker's dozen," said a second constable, "now that the Silver Purse burned down." She was nearly Onderishta's age and was still wearing chest plate and helmet.

Onderishta lifted the little wooden disk. "This claim token doesn't have an address, just an indecipherable mark. I haven't seen one like this since I was an apprentice." She had a good idea where it was from, but smart investigators didn't jump to conclusions. "Anyone recognize it?"

The young constable sighed as though he was making a confession. "That's Eyalmati's place."

"The one in the hall?"

He nodded. "My father used to…"

"You don't have to explain anything you don't want to," Onderishta said. "They've been closed all day, haven't they?"

The older constable responded by wandering farther into the hall, toward the pawnshop itself. Onderishta followed. She and Fay had already spent an hour in Rulenya's building, both searching the hall and talking to her neighbors. The gates had been locked since they arrived. "Eyalmati is his name? Where's he likely to be?"

The older one said, "On the floor of some tavern, with vomit and an empty purse beside him. He's been drinking himself to death for years and goes on three- or four-day benders."

"How does he stay in business?"

"He's got a guy now," the woman said. "Weird one. The neighbors call him the Broken Man."

"Oh, him!" the young ironshirt exclaimed. "I never liked that one, with that scar."

Onderishta looked at Fay. Fay looked back. "Describe him," Fay said.

The woman, perhaps reading their look, kept her mouth shut. The young man said, "Tall. Slender. Shaggy hair that hangs in his face. The morose type. He never talks, and hates to make eye contact. And he's got a horrible scar on his left cheek, like he was bitten by a shark and then burned with acid."

That was when Onderishta could have kicked herself.

She turned from the apartment door to the pawnshop grate. There was no more than six paces between them. Everything she'd wanted to know about their mysterious prisoner had been within spitting distance all day.

"He started here about a year ago," the older constable said. "Eyalmati says his name is Kyrioc, child of No One."

Onderishta pointed at the younger constable. "Get that fucking landlady down here with a key."

She arrived with an aggrieved look on her face, but one glance at Onderishta's expression convinced her to remain silent. She unlocked the gate.

The stench of rotting flesh billowed through the open door.

Directly across the room, surrounded by a pool of dried blood and a torn Harkan wedding robe, lay the corpse of Second Boar.

Onderishta felt Fay grab the back of her vest and pull her out of the room. She let him, realizing belatedly that she'd automatically started toward the body.

Fay ordered the constables to search the rooms. They paused to buckle their helmets, looking at each other in a way Onderishta recognized well. If the killer was still inside, this might be the day they died. They went anyway.

There were no killers in the shop or the connected rooms, no more dead bodies, and no live ones, either. Fay and Onderishta entered. The landlady didn't have a key to the secure part of the shop, but it took Onderishta less than a minute to find the false wallboard where the spare had been hidden.

There were no corpses in the storeroom, either. The place looked clean and orderly. A scan of the shelves showed nothing unusual: knives, tools, cheap jewelry…exactly the sort of thing desperate working people and petty pickpockets turn into coin.

"What if this Broken Man," Fay began, "whoever he is, was a distribution point for white tar? This would be a good cover, with people coming and going. Maybe the pickpocket was his woman and sold the tar for him on the sly. Make the daughter a courier, maybe."

"You figure she's his daughter?"

"Landlady says she's nine or ten and he's been working here less than a year, but maybe they know each other from way back."

"It's fine to develop theories and to try to see how the evidence fits, but we have too many anomalies here. We're not at that stage yet."

Fay shrugged. "Am I missing something?"

Onderishta pointed toward the pile of cloth in the corner. "Five years ago, a Harkan rebel group took advantage of the general chaos of civil war and 'liberated' the contents of a warehouse. Inside, they discovered stacks and stacks of Harkan robes. It was too much for one ship, so they split their bounty into thirds and sold them to three different captains, telling them they were getting the entire haul.

"One sailed to Ahsala and did quite well. The other two, knowing how much the Salashi love finery and old empires, came here hoping to make a killing."

"I remember," Fay said. "They flooded the market."

"What had once been an extravagant gift for a wealthy woman became commonplace. I still wear mine on quiet mornings."

Fay crossed the room and picked up the cloth. "I had no idea you were such a hedonist. This one's been torn open at the seams."

"Someone hid something inside it. I suspect our dead hand-painter and pickpocket got it as a gift a few years back. When she had to hide her prize, she stitched it up in this robe and pawned it. A clever idea, really."

"Which would make our morose pawnbroker guy…what? A patsy? Or an accomplice?"

Onderishta was about to ask why Fay thought those were mutually exclusive categories when Trillistin charged up the stair and rushed to the doorway. He was not out of breath this time, but his close-cropped hair was damp with sweat.

Before Onderishta could ask why he wasn't hitting the hospitals, he blurted out his news. "There's been a breakout from the south tower," he said.

"A breakout? What do you mean? Did Naufulin show up with a warrant to release Harl's people?"

"No," the boy said. "It was a violent breakout."

That made no sense. It had been hours since the raid. By now, Harl's parsu should have sent Naufulin to the tower with the paperwork for the heavies' release.

Unless word had already reached the noble families that constables recovered a collected body, and now the Lorrud parsu seemed to be withholding his support. Which worked in Onderishta's favor.

Could she have been wrong? Could someone have broken the unspoken rule of the downcity platforms and tried to turn the bureaucracy as a weapon against another gangster? If so, they were either an idiot or a genius. The investigators and constables were a spear with a point at each end.

Still, even the hint of a black-market hospital raised the possibility of scandal, not to mention charges of treason. Even the Lorrud parsu would keep his distance from that.

But if Harl's people couldn't rely on a bureaucratic release from their cells, they might send a force to smash open the cells. Onderishta threw the robe on the floor. "Let's go." She pointed at the landlady. "Keep this locked. No one gets in here unless one of us is with them, not even the guy who owns the business. Keep track of everyone who asks. Yes?" The woman nodded.

They hurried down the stairs. "Casualties?"

"Six," the apprentice said. "No one is dead, but they're hurt pretty badly."

Six! In a way, that was good news. It meant that they hadn't let the prisoners stroll out. They'd fought. Harl must have sent a mob. "How many got away?"

"Just the one."

She stopped on the landing. Fay and Trillistin stopped too. "Just the one what? Harl sent his heavies to rescue one person?"

Trillistin wiped sweat from his face. "Harl didn't send anyone. One of the prisoners fought his way out."

* * *

KYRIOC DIDN'T LIKE THE DOCKS. It wasn't just that, for a short time, he'd lived there as a beggar when he returned from Vu-Dolmont, although most days that was enough. The Docks always had a full complement of ironshirts, and most of them took coin from both their tower and the smugglers they were supposed to collar.

But this was where the constables and investigators expected him to go. Kyrioc had no intention of leaving Koh-Salash, but the people hunting him would expect him to run and keep running until he was far, far away. And the best way to escape was by sea.

So, he expected the ironshirts to be here, watching for him. His cloak of mirrors was powerful magic, but he hadn't practiced it enough. He hunched forward and walked with a limp. There was no way to control what people saw when they looked at him, but if he behaved like an elderly cripple, the magic would fill the gaps. As long as they did not put too much attention on him, the magic should hold.

The man he sought was easy to find. Coming down the plank from *Quiet Speech*, he stood a head taller than everyone else and wore the square hat of a ship's captain, even though he no longer went to sea. His robes were silk, with simple embroidery down one side. Tasteful and restrained, considering his new-found wealth.

He was surrounded by sailors carrying provisions up the plank. Behind him were a chubby, officious little man with a wax tablet and stylus, and two wary bodyguards.

As Kyrioc approached, one of the bodyguards stiff-armed him. If he'd really been a cripple, the blow would have put him down. Instead, he turned enough for the hit to glance off.

"Zikiriam admir-Vlosh tuto-Vlosh," Kyrioc said quietly. "You know me."

Even as he spoke, the bodyguards realized he was not who he appeared to be, and they drew their steel.

"Stop," Zikiriam said without any conviction. Kyrioc let his cloak fall away. "I know a lot of people, grandfa—Holy fuck!" He clutched suddenly at Kyrioc's elbow. "Kyrioc, my friend, I haven't seen you in— Has it really been almost a year and a half since you stepped off my ship?" He touched the collar of his silk robe and glanced at Kyrioc's tattered funeral clothes. His voice grew quiet. "I heard you were working in a downcity pawnshop. You should have come to work with me. I'd have made you a partner. You deserve it. More. By the fallen gods, how are you?"

"I'm being hunted."

Zikiriam glanced around, then led Kyrioc closer to the ship, moving through the stream of sailors to a stack of crates beside a boom. "How can I help? Do you need a place to hide? A berth on a ship sailing today? Whatever you need, ask and you'll have it. I owe you that much."

"I need information from someone who knows The Docks well. How do I find a couple of gangsters who use little kids as messengers and who have ties to the crew of *Winter Friend*? They may go by the street name *Pail*."

"I know the name," Zikiriam said, "but not the people they belong to. If the Pails have ever been on The Docks, I don't know about it. But their heavies and messengers are here every day, watching the ships and picking up cargo. See that dull-looking fellow over there with the scar on his forehead?" The captain nodded toward a man with a slack face, shaved head, and a green magistrate's vest that was too small for him. He leaned over a young boy in orphan's rags as though giving him instructions, then slapped him. "He must be breaking in another new messenger."

One of those two was going to answer all of Kyrioc's questions. He just had to decide which, and what he would have to do to get it. If the child was like the other messengers, he wouldn't betray his bosses easily, and Kyrioc did not bully children.

But that shit-eater in the green vest? Kyrioc knew ways to make him scream.

"Wait a minute," Kyrioc said. "New messenger? Where's the old one?"

There was a shout from a nearby ship. A dockhand shouted something back, but he was too far away to hear clearly.

"There he is," the captain answered, "ducking under."

Kyrioc saw another boy in rags leap into the shallows, then head for the dark, stony space beneath the dock.

Shit.

* * *

OUTGOING: *WINTER FRIEND, QUIET SPEECH, Dandy.*

Incoming: *Street of Gold, Gentle Autumn, Man of Bones, Falling Leaf.*

Jallientus, child of Jalliusha, paced up and down the docks, repeating the names until he was sure he had them. Tin Pail expected a daily report of ships coming and going on each tide, and only Jallientus could be trusted to get it right.

It was easy work in the summer heat. While The Docks were never empty, the real traffic would begin with the fall harvest. That's when he would prove that even though he was only seven—or maybe eight, it was hard to remember—none of the beetles were as trustworthy as him.

Outgoing: *Winter Friend, Quiet Speech, Dandy.*

Incoming: *Street of Gold, Gentle Autumn, Man of Bones, Falling Leaf.*

Jallientus was proud of the responsibility he'd been given. He was proud of the quiet way he moved, and that no one ever seemed to notice him. Proud of his memory. Soon he would give his report to one of Tin Pail's heavies, but he hoped it wouldn't be Little Cinder again. Little's memory was shit, and he tried to blame his mistakes on Jallientus.

Tin Pail knew better, though. When she looked at Jallientus, he was sure she could see how quick and sharp and quiet he was.

Jallientus sprinted beneath a roll of carpet as two deckhands carried it to a cart. Quick. Sharp. Quiet. He'd spotted a sail in the glow of Suloh's bones—these waters were never truly dark—but it steered outward, away from the docks, toward the Timmer Straits.

Fine. A name he would not have to remember.

Jallientus turned his back to the waters. The city wall stood tall before him, higher than any stone wall in the world, he'd been told, and stronger, too, because it was made from skywood. He took an earnest pride in it. No invader had ever breached that wall. The city behind it was well protected, but he, who was nothing more than a gangland beetle, spent most of his days outside of it. *Un*protected.

Of course, the safest parts of the city were the highest ones. Down at the level of the docks, there was all kinds of danger: thieves, tar heads, child snatchers with their canvas sacks, and even bloodkind, if you believed the stories.

Jallientus had never seen bloodkind, but he figured Tin Pail knew they were just another boogeyman story to keep kids in line. The little kids, not him. Bloodkind were supposed to hunt in Mudside and beneath The Docks, but Jallientus had run through the stony muck beneath The Docks many times—on Tin Pail's orders, yet!—and he'd never seen anything scarier than a rat.

If his boss wasn't afraid to send him, he wasn't afraid to go.

Dockhands were unloading *Man of Bones*, and Jallientus recognized one of the men. He hurried near, caught the man's eye, and crouched low. He was a big guy with gnarled hands and gray in his hair, but his expression was kindly. As he often did, the big guy took a fig from the crate he was carrying and tossed it to Jallientus.

Sucker.

As the mate of *Man of Bones* barked out a protest, the boy slipped over the edge of the dock and went beneath. The dockhand spoke with a weary tone. "Better to give him one than have him snatch one with each hand. Besides, he's just a starving little boy."

Jallientus walked quickly away from the water into the darkness beneath the docks, partly so that no one would steal back his treat, but mostly because he didn't want to hear what the dockhand said next. Jallientus didn't need anyone's pity. He had a job, a powerful gangster boss, and a future. Soon he'd have a street name of his own, and he'd spend his days relaxing and his nights doing grownup stuff. Life would be easy—

A hand seized his ankle. He fell onto the mucky stones, striking his elbow and losing the fig somewhere in the darkness. *Not fair.*

He kicked at the hand but it was like kicking stone. Whoever had him was strong. Not a tar head. Not—

Jallientus's hair stood on end and a high whine of fear escaped him. It was a little-kid noise, but as he kicked and kicked, he felt as helpless as a little kid.

Something in the darkness let out a low, hissing laugh. No child snatcher could make a sound like that.

This couldn't be happening. He'd run beneath the docks many times. He'd been *told* to run beneath them. It wasn't his fault that he was here right now with a…

A pair of eyes glowed in the dark. Then the thing's mouth opened, and he could see teeth that shone like stars in the dark. Teeth with two, long fangs with only a dark silhouette behind them. Bloodkind.

The thing sank its fangs into his calf. Jallientus screamed this time, a high-pitched sound that echoed around him.

But there was no one to hear. If Jallientus had stayed near the dockhand, the one who'd pitied him, the man might have tried to rescue him. Then the bloodkind might have killed the man instead.

He could feel the creature's wet mouth on his leg—could feel it sucking blood from his calf. Jallientus couldn't kick himself free, so he reached for the thing's eyes. It straightened suddenly, lifting his foot into the air. Jallientus dangled upside down. The bloodkind was only a little bit taller than him, but it was as strong as a grownup. Maybe stronger.

Jallientus tried to lift his whole body and jam his thumbs into the bloodkind's eyes, but he wasn't strong enough. He wondered if those glowing eyes were hot, like coals from a fire. The light they gave off was cool and blue, and the creature's glowing fangs had pierced but not burned him. Pale and blue and cool, the light was. He'd never seen anything like that before. He scratched at the thing's legs. He pounded his fists on the side of its knee.

He was too weak to hurt it, and it just kept sucking his life away.

His blood made the creature glow, faintly, like a lantern on a faraway ship. He really was going to be killed by a bloodkind—he could barely believe it. Again he saw that for all its strength, it was no bigger than he was, only the size of a child. Now that there was light, he could see that its skin was like ivory, paler even than that Katr. Curly dark hair covered its head, hands and bare feet, and it wore the same sort of tattered, filthy, oversized tunic that Jallientus wore himself.

In the bitter darkness, the creature shone like a beacon.

This creature that was killing him—this bloodkind—was the last thing he would ever see, and it was beautiful.

"Stop."

The whisper came out of the darkness, as if the cold stones had spoken in Jallientus's defense.

* * *

ACCORDING TO CHILDHOOD FOLK tales Kyrioc grew up hearing, the spellkind were able to vanish at will, and the godkind could change shape into anything from a mountain to a raindrop. Whether or not those stories were true, they didn't matter, because the spellkind were gone and the gods were dead.

Kyrioc's cloak of shadows did not make him invisible any more than his cloak of iron made him invulnerable or his cloak of mirrors changed his appearance. All it really did was darken the space around him while allowing him to see normally.

Down in the space below the docks, that meant his cloak intensified the darkness. But it did allow him to see clearly.

"Stop," Kyrioc said again, "or die."

The bloodkind stopped. "This is permitted! We have an arrangement with his elder. It's my turn!"

The little figure puffed out its chest and drew itself up to its full height of three foot nothing. It would have seemed comical if its eyes and fangs had not been glowing.

"Tell me your name," Kyrioc said.

"My name is Mr. Harhand. Now, sir, you tell me yours!"

"You know who I am."

The figure stepped back. Its didn't release the boy or lose its outraged expression, but it gave way slightly. "Darkness."

"I thought your people called me Mr. Darkness, or have you forgotten your manners?"

"Don't you talk to me about manners!" the bloodkind blustered. "This boy's master and I have an equitable arrangement—a contract!—which you have most rudely—"

Kyrioc drew the sword he'd stolen from the ironshirts in the south tower. The slow rasp of steel on leather silenced Harhand. "If you keep talking about your 'arrangement,' I'm going to skewer you onto a length of wood and float you out into the straits. You don't like that, do you? The sun kills your kind, but starlight will make you sick. Until dawn."

"Is that— Is that what you did to my cousins?"

"Walk away, Mr. Harhand. No matter what you hear whispered down in the bottom of the city, I don't hate your kind. If you let this boy go, I'll let you go. But if we have to fight over him, I'll make you wish you'd never left your hole."

Now that it'd stopped feeding, the bloodkind's glow began to fade. It glanced at the starlit water, then back at the boy's leg. A thin trickle of blood ran onto its shining hand. "What am I supposed to eat tonight? A rat? Again? A rat? I've *waited* for this. We made a deal—paid good silver to his employer—and it's *my turn*. Who are you to void a contract between third parties?" It spoke with the wounded dignity of a petty merchant who'd been cheated. "No one delegated a controlling interest in this boy to you! You're nothing special. You're just humankind. You have no rights here. *No right!*"

Kyrioc let his cloak of shadows drop. The bloodkind's fading glow fell on him, revealing the way he crouched awkwardly beneath the deck with the constable's short sword. He held it point forward, a little too high.

Mr. Harhand sneered, dropped the boy, and charged. It slapped the sword out of his hand with that terrifying strength—just as expected—and Kyrioc raised his left wrist in a defensive position.

Bloodkind loved to go for the wrist.

It snapped at his hand, an attack he could have easily dodged, but his cloak of iron was already in place. The creature's fangs struck, but his protective magic held.

Its first reaction was to furrow its brows in confusion. Before it could act further, Kyrioc opened his left hand and wiped the clove of garlic he'd been palming against the bloodkind's ear.

It didn't scream or cry out in pain. It simply sighed as though it had settled into a warm bath, then collapsed.

With the coil of rope Zikiriam had given him, Kyrioc bound the bloodkind's hands and feet. He tucked a second clove between the thing's cheek and gum, then gagged it.

Kyrioc looked around for the sword, but it was nowhere in sight. The bloodkind had slapped it pretty hard. It didn't matter. He didn't really need it.

The boy lay where he'd been dropped. His pulse was fluttery but he was awake. Tearing a strip from the kid's tunic, he bound the bleeding leg. A clean bandage would have been better, but this would have to do for now.

"I have questions for you," Kyrioc said.

"Fuck you." The boy's voice was weak but he sounded like he meant it.

"You heard it. Your boss sold you."

"It was lying."

"You know it wasn't."

The boy began to cry. "I was going to prove myself. I was going to make the boss proud and have an easy life."

"There's no such thing. Answer my questions and you can have a decent life."

"No," the boy said. "No, they'll kill me if I talk to anyone. They said so."

Kyrioc leaned in close. "As far as they're concerned, you're already dead."

The boy thought about that for a moment, and when he spoke again, he sounded alert. "Tell me about this decent life."

So much for gratitude. Kyrioc slipped off his stolen cloak and wrapped the bloodkind in it, covering it from head to toe. Then he slipped the boy over his shoulder and dragged the creature into the shallows.

Zikiriam and his people stood at the edge of the planking, looking worried. Kyrioc climbed the ladder and set the boy on the edge. "This boy needs a job. You should sponsor him at Suloh's Tower, after you've seen to his injury, then take him on. He'll work hard."

With an audible gulp, Zikiriam said, "Suloh's… Do you know what that costs? But I will, if you ask."

"This will help defray the costs," Kyrioc said. He jumped back down and brought out the bundled cloak. "Take this to the tower—don't unwrap it here—and sell it to Fiellas defe-Presse admir-Presse hold-Presse—"

"Er, *Presse*?"

"Yes, she's the Steward-General's granddaughter." He passed the bundle to one of Zikiriam's bodyguards. "She's been studying bloodkind all her life, but as far as I know, she's never had a live specimen."

They turned pale.

"That's your new life," Kyrioc said to the boy. "An education, then a job with a small but growing shipping line. Tell me who your boss was."

"Tin Pail," the boy said woozily. "Are you going to kill her? I hope you kill her."

"Where can I find her? Where can I find the other kids like you?"

"There's a warehouse in Wild Dismal," he said. "The sign above the door has two buckets leaning together."

"Rest." Kyrioc turned to Zikiriam, who stared wide-eyed at the bundled cloak. "Zikiriam. Zikiriam!" The former captain snapped out of his trance. "Take the clove out of its mouth and it will start to wake up. Leave it in too long and it will die. Academics in the tower pay a fair price for the dead ones, so they'll spend a fortune for a live one, along with the means to control it. Go quickly."

Without waiting for a response, Kyrioc dropped back down into the water and hurried into the darkness below The Docks.

CHAPTER EIGHTEEN

O**nderishta did not know** what to expect when she returned to the south tower, but it wasn't this.

Her interrogator had been with her for ten years. The man had a sixth sense about prisoners: when they were about to break, when they would lash out, when they needed a kind word. But when she returned to the tower, she found him lying on a cot. His jaw was broken and he was missing five teeth.

The two ironshirts who'd worked the room with him were local chainball players, lead rippers on the south tower team and captains in an upcity league sponsored by one of the noble families. Each had a broken leg and a broken arm.

There were four more on the other cots. Trillistin was wrong. Seven constables had been injured in the escape.

One man did this. They were armed and armored troops, with shields and truncheons and live blades at hand, and the scarred man went against them with only his bare hands.

Now he was free.

Naufulin, child of Namfalis, one of Onderishta's fellow investigators, strolled through the room as though it was an elaborate performance arranged especially for her. "What sewer line did you crack this time, Onderishta? Because the shit is raining down everywhere."

"I should be asking you," Onderishta snapped. "Did your parsu send a heavy down here to punish the constables for that Upgarden raid?"

Naufulin served the Lorruds, just as Onderishta served the Safroys. And because Harl was in the Lorrud sail, she sometimes impeded investigations against him.

"My parsu hasn't asked me to do anything about the people you collared in that raid," Naufulin said. She sounded sincere, as she always did. "He certainly didn't hire someone to attack your people. He prefers to work within the system."

Which was true. When the Lorruds flexed their muscle on Harl's behalf, they were never this clumsy. Evidence might disappear, magistrates might be bribed, or records altered, but all those were crimes within the bureaucracy. The noble families were creatures of the system. It's what kept them afloat on this ocean of blood and shit.

To break into a tower and brutalize the constables when they could have bribed them? Never.

That left her with a simple question—who the fuck was this guy?

"Besides," Naufulin continued, "I have strict orders to keep out of this mess."

Onderishta kept her expression stoic. She'd guessed right. That murdered woman spooked the Lorrud clan, and Harl was getting by without the protection of his parsu. At least for now.

She pulled Fay aside. "Go to the east tower. Tell them what happened here. Tell them about their fellow constables, and have them triple the watch on that pawnshop. This asshole will go back there. He has to."

Fay went. Onderishta turned back toward her people, but Naufulin was right beside her. "He stole weapons, you know. A constable's sword and knife. It was the last one he injured on his way out, down by the gate. Just broke the man's arms, unbuckled his sword belt, then ran off into Stillwater." Naufulin sighed. "This is looks bad for us, Onderishta. Constables beaten? Having their weapons stolen? This could get ugly."

Onderishta looked down at Naufulin. The woman was clearly enjoying herself. Onderishta wondered how she had survived so long. "It's an ugly world."

The doctors finally arrived, and Onderishta looked after her people.

* * *

MIDNIGHT PASSED. FAY PACED back and forth in the common room of the east tower. Ironshirts, under orders to search every brothel, tavern, platform hall, and gaming room for Harl or his top heavies—or this Broken Man—had returned hour after hour with nothing to report.

But had they found nothing? Or were they taking Harl's silver in exchange for their silence?

Fay carefully examined every expression when the ironshirts made their reports. He saw no smirks, no nervous hesitation, no sign that they were lying. But the fact was that he didn't trust them. Not a one.

If he'd had any idea where to look, he'd have gone into the city himself.

Instead, he waited, and wrung his hands, and wished for news.

* * *

WHEN THE COMMOTION STARTED, Mirishiya, child of No One, was lying in bed, unable to sleep. Her thoughts never stilled in those late hours, and once the others began to snore, sleep would not come. Nights out on the streets had been quieter than this, although she'd spent most of those nights filching from kitchens and had slept through the shadows of the day.

Her fellow apprentice, Trillistin, was the child of some servant family, and she figured he slept in a servant's room up on High Slope. Was it quiet there? She had no idea. She lay in the dark, running her tongue over her crooked teeth. Back and forth, back and forth.

Suloh's temple had been built as a tower, and every wing, laboratory, and dorm hung off that open central space. But for once, as the commotion moved up the stairs, there were no angry hushes or sharp slaps from administrators. No one was quieting this disturbance.

The other apprentices were still struggling awake when Mirishiya slipped into the hall and leaned over the stair railing.

A small knot of people came up the spiral stair, a broad, loose mob crowded behind. Leading the way was a woman she didn't recognize in an academic's robe, and as she passed each level, she pushed bystanders back so that the guard behind her would not be blocked. The guard was carrying something Mirishiya couldn't quite make out. A painted child?

Two more guards came close behind—one was a captain, of all people, and when had anyone ever seen an event so important that a captain left their post during their watch? The other guard carried an orphan child dressed in rags. The orphan's cloth shoes were in fairly good shape, so he was probably a beetle. Behind them was Impilak, child of No One, the boy working the overnight messenger shift.

At the rear was a pack of academics jostling to be near the front of the pack and calling to the woman at the front. "You'll need a good transcriptionist!" "My lab has the best cages in the tower!" "I'm most qualified to make the dissection!"

Mirishiya glanced back at the guard near the front of the pack. He was higher now and she could better see what he was carrying. It wasn't a child and it hadn't been painted. It was the boogeyman of every Salashi kid's nightmares. Bloodkind.

From below, someone shouted "She's not going to dissect a living specimen, you fool!" and Mirishiya felt goosebumps run down her back.

Could the temple academics be reckless enough to bring a thing like that past the iron doors and armed guards?

Of course they would, if they thought they might gain renown within their little community for it.

An odd feeling came over Mirishiya. She worked for the investigator bureaucracy now, and she liked it. Something in this situation pulled at her the way a lodestone pulled an iron needle.

While the academics shouted and the young woman at the front of the procession grimly shoved others out of the way, Mirishiya darted into the pack, caught Impilak by the wrist, and dragged him down the hall into a quiet corner.

The child struggled. "Ow! Stop! I want to see them kill it!"

"They're not going to kill it," she hissed. "They're going to keep it alive and *feed* it."

The boy's eyes grew as big as plums. "Inside the tower?"

"You know I'm working with the investigators now, right? Tell me everything."

* * *

WHEREVER HE WENT IN this city, Killer of Devils felt out of place, but nowhere more so than here. His duties had never taken him north of Low Market before—past the cock and cunt, as the heavies liked to call it, although if the gods once had the parts they would need to fuck, they rotted away long ago.

The Folly, this deck was called. According to the Salashi, it was named this because it was the first deck ever constructed, spanning the distance between Yth's massive thigh bones. This was the site of the oldest plankways in the city.

From his table in a sidewalk cafe, Killer found it unexpectedly pleasant. The neighborhood was crowded with small houses and modest apartment buildings. The streets were lined with cafes and craft shops, and in some spaces, trees grew in large planters. It was a place for the tradesfolk, bureaucrats, and merchants of Low Market to raise families, and after his time in Wild Dismal, Spillwater, and the Apricot decks, he had not realized this doomed city had space for something that looked so much like the little towns of his homeland.

Perhaps someday, when the Pails were dead and his service ended, he would simply walk out of the city, passing through these northernmost decks on his way to the river, so he could be reminded once again what he was returning to.

Unfortunately, unlike the southern parts of the city, The Folly was a sea of Salashi faces. Killer's pale face stood out like a child's tooth on a dark pillow. The only other non-Salashi in sight was a veritable giant sitting in a cafe across the street. He had the look of a Free Cities trader, although he held himself like a bodyguard. In fact, the awkward way he sat suggested he carried something uncomfortable on his back—probably a weapon—so perhaps he was the bodyguard for the expensively dressed Salashi girls chatting at the next table.

The waiter returned to ask about the Katr ale. The owner had ordered a couple of barrels and, while the locals seemed to enjoy it, he wondered what a native thought. Killer chatted frankly with him about the way ales age as they ship, and what alternates the owner might stock instead. It was a pleasant conversation, but it made him even more homesick.

When the waiter asked if he would like something else, he regretfully declined. He paid his bill and left a silver whistle on the table. A generous tip, but Wooden had been explicit that he was there to be noticed.

At the edge of the plankway, he stared at the business across the street. It was a workshop for a family of weavers, oddly silent for the middle of the day. If Wooden's information was correct, one of the few non-Salashi faces on this deck could be found inside—Harl, with a number of his heavies.

Movement in an alley caught his eye. One of the Pails' beetles crouched there, staring.

"Were you the one who found this place?" The child nodded, his eyes wide. "Fine. You will also have the honor of making a report on the next few minutes."

Pedestrians backed away as Killer removed his weapon from inside his sleeveless coat and joined handle to blade, but no one challenged him. He crossed the street, pushed the front door of the weavers' workshop open, and went inside to kill everyone he found there.

CHAPTER NINETEEN

Tin Pail was annoyed.

"Tell me where things stand with Harl."

Paper Mouse had put people on all of Harl's known haunts, and even a few of his secret ones, but no one had spotted him. During the spring, beetles had followed him for two solid months, making note of every mistress, business associate, and host he favored. Now he was in hiding, and he'd run to none of those places.

Even though the cosh missed the man himself, they had obligingly locked up Harl's top heavies for hours. Stripped of his protection, he should have been easy prey.

Tin didn't need to hear what Paper had to say. His expression told her everything. "He's gone to ground and no one knows where. He's smart, boss. He must've had a safe house that he only used for emergencies."

Should have been easy prey.

It wasn't his fault. It was hers. She might have picked up Harl right there in Upgarden, while he was fleeing the cosh. She could have put her people on the street corners and plankways, waiting for him. But that would have showed her hand too soon. Harl would know for sure that she'd put the cosh on him, and if her people missed—and she'd have put money on Harl's heavies over her own any day—he could crush her.

She had planned to take over his organization, not fight it.

Tin pushed past the guard and shoved the iron-banded door wide, stepping into the warehouse doorway. Paper Mouse and a few heavies followed to provide protection, but there was no need. Wild Dismal was her place. What had once been a scattered collection of little gangs were now united under her, because of the blood she'd spilled. The rep she'd built here had caught Harl's eye and led to more responsibilities, more money, and finally the offer of the package.

She would have been happy to serve as one of his lieutenants for a few years, filling her strongboxes with good Salashi coin, before taking Harl's life. But then everything tipped into a privy and Harl smacked a fucking hammerball right into her face in front of her people. She had to move against him. He'd given her no choice.

Tin wasn't delusional. She knew how things ended for people like her. What mattered was how much gold she could grab, how far her reputation would spread, and how many gray hairs she had when some asshole took the point to her.

Fuck it. She'd made her first play and missed. Every moment that Harl still breathed was a loss in her column. So be it. If Harl or his people came for her, she'd be ready. Her hand touched the face of her hammer. When she went down, she'd go down fighting.

She'd make sure no one forgot the way she died.

The front steps creaked as she descended to the streets. No skywood construction here. Most of these buildings had been built from dark woods cut during the clearing of the farmwilds. Most hadn't even been decorated with carvings. It was just thrown together and done. There was some skywood here and there, mainly in the hanging braces that connected to High Apricot above, and obviously the decking itself, but Wild Dismal was a cheap nothing little pocket in the massive structure of Koh-Salash.

In the street, Wooden Pail twirled and thumped his feet in tune with the music from the platform halls on the deck above. There was no one else nearby—no friends, no women, just him, dancing in the fire-lit darkness, hands above his head.

Tin laughed. When the platform halls of High Apricot were booming out their drum and flute, the sound was inescapable. The poor, the miserable, and the crooked either learned to sleep through it, slept during the day, or they went mad.

But Wooden's response to that oppressive, unceasing noise was to dance. Why her little brother had saddled himself with a name that meant "stiff and expressionless," she would never understand. The only thing wooden about him was his head.

She caught hold of Paper's sleeve and pulled him close. "Where is his bodyguard?"

"There," he answered nervously.

She spotted him then, in a shadowy doorway nearby. Here in Wild Dismal, there was no trouble about carrying his glaive openly, with the full handle attached. Tin Pail wanted him to go around armed, and the few constables who wandered through were happy to look the other way in exchange for a little copper.

She'd heard that the Free Cities had adopted the glaive for their armies, but there was no way to copy that good ghostkind steel. No one in all the nations of humankind knew how it was made. All they knew was that they didn't want to face an enemy wielding that edge.

Tin shivered just a little bit. Very few people who made her nervous, but her bodyguard was one of them, even when she was surrounded by her own heavies. The Salashi had godkind magic of their own—not that anyone ever saw the effects of Yth and Suloh's gifts, because they were hoarded by the priests and the nobility—but the talent that the Katr people took from the dead god in the north operated on a whole other level.

"Where have you been? You're supposed to be guarding my brother."

Her bodyguard glanced at Wooden.

"Me. Me. Me," Wooden said. "I sent him away. It's not his fault. It's mine. I needed him to fetch something."

"Well, we don't have time to fuck around," Tin snapped. "We have to find Harl's new hiding place—"

Wooden held up his hand, and she stopped speaking. Few could do that without risking a cracked skull, but her baby brother had special privileges. He turned to the bodyguard. "Show her what I sent you to pick up."

The bodyguard shrugged and picked up a cloth sack from the alleyway behind him. He opened it.

Inside was the severed head of Harl Sota List Im.

"Shit," Tin blurted out. "Nice. Hold on to that. I have need of it. Paper, let's get moving. It's time to make some money. The rest of you, keep those lanterns bright, and clear out these fucking alleys. Treat every drunk you see as a spy for the cosh. Don't kill them, but get them out of here. And double the watch on this block."

It was time to open shop.

* * *

NOTHING GOOD HAD COME out of Cold Sunshine's trick with the bucket of piss in Sailsday's Regret. Nothing bad, either. He didn't know High Apricot as well as Spillwater, but it turned out that he didn't need to. The cosh had run out of breath after only a few minutes and given up the chase. Cold backtracked far enough to see them slip into a public bath, and he knew Second Boar was safe.

After, he went back to running the errands for Nal At Isp, only they had been moved from the platform halls of High Apricot to the brothels of Low Apricot. That was a step down the slope for Nal, and he was sour about it. Apparently, Cold's trick had emptied the cafe, and Nal caught shit for it.

Not from Harl, obviously. The big boss was feeling heat from the eye, and he'd gone into hiding along with some of his most trusted people. Still, his organization had enough lieutenants and sub-bosses that things could run smoothly. For a while.

Like most of the foreign friends, Nal was under Pol Sota Lim llt, the only one of Harl's four lieutenants who was of Carrig descent, but even he was too far up the slope to give a shit. Nal took his orders from the managers of the businesses they protected, and from the plank bosses that kept order in the surrounding blocks. And Cold took his orders from Nal. For now.

Sometimes, Cold imagined the two of them straying near the edge of a deck. One quick shove—that's all it would take—and he wouldn't have to take the point to Nal. The fall would do the work for him. Cold wouldn't be able to touch the blood, which was disappointing, but he might still see Nal's final expression if he was facing the right way. Cold could imagine that mix of surprise and terror—

"What the fuck are you laughing about?" Nal snapped.

"I was laughing?" Cold replied, which was exactly the wrong thing to say.

Nal shook his head. "Gimme that." Nal snatched the jug of Carrig wine from him. His eyes were already bleary. If Nal got blind drunk, Cold would have another chance to recoup his expenses from his boss's purse.

"Got a job for you," Nal said. "There's a petal down in The Shivers buying cups of wine for beetles and heavies. He says he's a pickpocket out of the farmwilds, but I say he's working for Gray Flames. See that he's shoved off, and don't take the point to him."

Cold's desire to stay and pluck some silver from his boss was like a heartache, but he couldn't shirk when he had a direct order. He set off.

In many ways, Low Apricot was like its older sibling. It was filled with platforms, cafes, and taverns. There were even a few platform halls.

But the streets were narrower, the buildings smaller, and the venues seedier. Less of Suloh's light found its way to the people. In its own way, Low Apricot was more dangerous than a place like Spillwater.

Downslope in the city, young criminals were organized into gangs. When they aged out, as Cold had, they either went to work for one of Harl's lieutenants or they got themselves regular jobs and became petals. Once you joined Harl's organization, you were *organized*. You took orders.

But Low Apricot, with its brothels, shitty platform halls, and cheap booze, was like a magnet for young men working in trades or just off the ships. They roamed the deck in packs, getting drunk, looking to get laid or start a fight. They were petals, yeah, but they might beat the shit out of you for the way you looked. Or for no reason at all. And that was the problem. They didn't understand that there were *rules*.

But it was a little too early for those packs to be roaming around, and it was certainly too early for the beetles to be drinking, even the cheap, watered-down piss that was served in The Shivers.

The tavern was exactly the same as the week before, when Cold had delivered lunch to his boss. There were benches along the wall, and battered tables in the center, with little wobbly stools around them. The place smelled of sawdust, sweat, and vomit. In one corner was a group of seven young men huddled around a jug, roaring with laughter. Scattered throughout were beetles, old men, and hard drinkers.

And there was the petal Nal wanted him to roust. He was just a boy, barely more than thirteen, a Salashi kid with close-cropped hair like some kind of servant. Well, that would explain where he stole the money to stand all these drinks.

Cold realized he'd laid his hand on his knife. If there was anyone in the world he would like to take the point to, it was that kid. He didn't even know why. He just didn't like the way he looked.

But not now. Orders.

First, he'd let the kid buy him a few drinks but without really telling him anything. Then, he'd put the fear of steel into him and take whatever coin he had left.

But before Cold could move in, a beefy guy with a green cloth tied across his face pushed through the door and approached the boy's table. Cold didn't like the look of him and kept his distance.

The kid and the beefy guy talked for a long time.

* * *

BY THE TIME KYRIOC reached Wild Dismal, heavies were clearing drunks out of alleyways. The noise and upheaval helped him locate the building with two buckets above the door, but the street was well lit by lanterns and the building well guarded. Men and women circled the property and patrolled the nearby streets. Kyrioc withdrew, then crept forward again.

The lantern light was too bright for his cloak of shadows—he would have looked like a dark cloud floating along the deck. His cloak of mirrors worked in crowds or in spaces where he could pass as someone who was supposed to be there, but this was a nearly empty street patrolled by gangland heavies. They'd even driven off the back-alley drunks. The only cloak Kyrioc would be able to wear was his cloak of iron, and that meant fighting his way in.

For Riliska, he would chance it.

He should have stopped at the pawnshop. The weapon he'd brought back from Vu-Dolmont—but hoped he would never take up again—waited for him there. He could return to Woodgarden right now to fetch it.

But it would be morning when he returned, and Riliska… Anything might have happened to her in that time. Anything at all.

The knife he'd taken from that ironshirt would have to do.

Kyrioc felt heavy with purpose for the first time since his return to Koh-Salash, and a small part of him was overjoyed. Rage had returned. Spark. It felt like a living thing inside him, curling and thrashing.

Now all he needed to do was infiltrate that building and find Riliska. Rousted drunks and homeless, hopeless beggars shuffled past him, muttering resentfully. Kyrioc glanced down the alley and saw one of the heavies moving back into the fire-lit street.

Just as Kyrioc was about to follow, the heavy was joined by another. They muttered to each other, and the new one glanced down the alley at him. Their gazes met, and Kyrioc quickly looked down and backed away. Criminals often pursued and robbed anyone who appeared submissive— they didn't even think about it, they just went—but not this time. They were too busy clearing the neighborhood.

Too bad. Kyrioc could have made good use of the hatchet the man was carrying.

The patrol circled eastward, and when their backs were turned, Kyrioc sprinted across the narrow street into the next alley. There was too much trash—broken crockery, shivered barrel withies, and more—for him to move quickly in the darkness, but he didn't need quickness. Not yet.

When the gangsters had set their lanterns, they'd put them in the middle of the street, to cover as much of the block as possible. That meant the light struck the mouths of the alleys at an angle and only lit the very ends. Kyrioc crept forward slowly, using the reflected light to avoid the trash. The ever-present thump and whine from the platform halls above faded slightly. If the platform halls were closing, dawn must have been near. He edged toward the mouth of the alley and peered out.

The warehouse was there. It took up the whole block, and the sign above the door was freshly painted. The front door had two big, intimidating Salashi heavies standing beside it, and there were two more in the middle of the street. Two civilians pleaded with the heavies at the door for something, but whatever it was, they weren't getting it. They handed over a purse and walked away.

A patrol rounded the block while another approached from the opposite direction. A pair of lookouts peered over the edge of the roof, but Kyrioc couldn't see their hands. Bows were absolutely illegal inside the city for anyone but city and temple guards, but if Tin Pail had control of the neighborhood, that was the place to station archers.

The warehouse looked sturdy, with no windows except slender vents near the roof to let out lantern smoke. The streets were narrow, but not narrow enough to jump from roof to roof, even if he thought he could squeeze through one of those vents.

But everyone was moving in pairs. For his cloak of mirrors to work, he was going to need someone to walk beside him.

Maybe—

"Psst. You there, good sir." A silhouette leaned out of a broken window above and behind him. He couldn't see her, but was an old woman's voice. "That's not a safe place for you to be. Quickly, before they see you. *Quickly.*"

Kyrioc gripped the windowsill and pulled himself up and through, sliding smoothly into the darkness of the room above. No sooner had he settled in than he heard footsteps among the alley trash. Another patrol must have been approaching from the side of the street where he couldn't see them.

He wasn't worried about fighting a heavy or two, but taking them on without a plan meant he might have to fight all of them, and that would give them time to bar the doors. "Thank you."

"Come along," the shadowy figure said. "There's light by the front."

Light from the street shone through dirty windows—she had no lanterns of her own—revealing a rack of iron pots and cooking equipment on one side of the room. The rest was filled with small round tables and low benches. Once, this had been a cafe.

The room smelled like rancid oil and spoiled meat. As the old woman settled into a bench near a window, Kyrioc got a good look at her. Her gray hair was disheveled and dirty, and her skin was sallow. Her grimy arms were so thin, they were nearly skeletal.

He stayed back, in the darkness.

"Are you the reason they increased the guard?" she asked.

"I don't think so."

"Pity. I don't think I could quite manage to stick a knife into one of the Pails, but maybe you could."

He asked the obligatory question. "Why do you want them killed?"

She looked up at him. He must have been little more than a voice in the black to her. If she thought he might harm her, she didn't show it. Perhaps she had moved beyond fear to an acceptance of death, a state Kyrioc had spent many years searching for but had never found. "Me and my daughter had a cafe once. My husband served fifteen years as a loyal stitch of some High Slope big shot, and managed to brown-tongue his way to a loan. We did well, too, because my daughter created a special kind of chewy bun. It was a big hit."

"But then Tin Pail took notice."

"No, it was her brother Wooden. The crazy one. He came every day for a week, stuffing himself and complaining that he had to walk from Wild Dismal to High Apricot for them. One day, his big sister fixed it for him. Her heavies showed up at the start of the day and took everything out of the cafe—the aprons, benches, kettles, everything—and brought it down here. Now her precious little brother only had to cross the street to buy his favorite food, and the Pails' thugs were our only customers.

"My husband went to his parsu to plead for help. Two days later, he was dead. 'Fell from a stair,' they said, but no one was fooled. The Pails and their thugs kept coming. They never paid for anything. It was a relief when they grew bored with us.

"After a week without a single paying or non-paying customer, my daughter borrowed a cart from a friend and began loading our things into it, right out front. Tin Pail walked out of that building across the street and struck my daughter with a hammer. Just one blow, but it was enough. That was four months ago, and…"

"I'm sorry," Kyrioc said.

"They're animals. All of them. The ones who haven't committed murder stand around and laugh while the others do. Meanwhile, I sit here in the dark and starve. If I could knife one, I'd cook and eat them like an animal. I'd savor every bite, too." She looked out the window. "Why have you come?"

"They took a little girl. I want to get her back."

"Your daughter, eh? They have little kids running in and out of that place all the time. She's probably over there. You need a distraction? I could go over there and kick over a lantern."

Kyrioc shook his head. "No."

"Maybe start a fire or make them leave their posts?"

"Do you have a hammer?"

She huffed in disappointment. "They took everything we had when they took the cart away. Everything that could be a weapon, at least. Good steel knives and cleavers. A pair of iron mallets. Quality stuff. Only the pots, cookers and cloths are left."

"A cloth will do. Do they have a special knock?"

"They do, and it changes. One two. One. One two. What are you planning? Kill the Pails? Burn the place down?"

Kyrioc's eyes had adjusted to the dim. He went to the wall and took a long, narrow apron off a hook. It was made of canvas, tightly woven, and dyed some dark color. "I'm just here for the little girl."

"Well, if you get a chance to fuck something up, don't hold back. The universe would be grateful."

A stillness came over him. The idea of seeking out this Tin Pail, whoever she was, and taking revenge for this old woman was so tempting that he'd asked for a hammer without even thinking about it. He had not killed a humankind for a long time, but the idea of visiting the death of this woman's daughter on her killer was a reflex he thought he'd lost.

Rulenya was dead too, and that was on the Pails, along with who knew how many more.

The death of a single child is like the end of the world.

This woman had once had a family, and a parsu, and a business, but misfortune had taken it away. There were thousands like her. Misfortune visited someone every hour of every day.

Koh-Salash was full of people who needed help. Making justice in a place like this would take an army. That's why there was so little help to be had. With so much to do, no one bothered to do anything.

Kyrioc was no different. He couldn't let himself be distracted by the problems of the whole city. The stakes—one orphaned girl's life—were already too high.

First, he'd see that Riliska was safe. Then he'd kill her captors, if he could. Anything beyond that was too much for him to consider. Once he started seeking vengeance for everyone, the killing would never stop.

He laid a silver whistle on the counter. It was more than he would have paid for the apron at the pawnshop. "Thank you."

* * *

WET CINDER HATED HIS NAME.

He'd come up with a little street gang from his apartment building: him, a neighbor kid, and a crowd of cousins from the first floor. When they were brought into the Pails' organization, they decided to take the name *Cinder*. Well, Brisilit decided, because he wanted to be Bright Cinder, and the others followed along.

If only Wet had taken something odd or absurd, like the others. Cold Cinder was still open when his choice came, and that would have been perfect, because it's not really boastful but you still get people calling you

Cold, like *stone-cold killer*.

But the older heavies started calling him "Wet Noodle," and by the time he realized he was supposed to fight about it—he hadn't wanted to rock the boat, just fit in—it was too late. No one took him seriously, and he was stuck doing jobs like this—patrolling around a mostly empty warehouse in the shitty hours of the morning with a drunk.

Worse, the drunk had brought along a flask of brandy—made out of glass in the Free Cities style—and she would not share. He could have taken it by force, but the boss always sided with her women over her men, even if the cause of the trouble was something provocative like not giving him some of her booze.

Crooked Cap slipped her flask back into her pocket and pointed toward an alley with her cleaver. "There."

Wet saw him. Some drunk who couldn't stay away from his favorite alley, probably. Drawing his knife, he stalked forward. Crooked was right behind him, struggling to keep up with her short, chubby legs. Orders were to keep this area clear, and if this vagrant showed the least bit of defiance, Wet was going to cut him as an example to the others. Cutting people felt great.

Gray Cinder. He could have picked *Gray Cinder*.

The figure retreated into the darkness, wood and other trash clattering under his feet.

"You there. Hold." That was what the cosh always said. It worked for them, but not for him. The figure kept moving away, and he was muttering. Wet couldn't hear him clearly, but the drunk's tone was contemptuous.

By the fallen gods, Wet might have had to take that from the other heavies, but he wasn't going to take it from alley trash. Crooked hissed at him to slow down.

He caught up with the figure at the far end of the alley. It was dark here, and for a moment, it almost seemed that the figure was waiting for him.

Good. Wet had always been quick with his knife, and now he was going to show what he could do. No more fretting about the consequences. No more warnings or threats. No more standing by while others made their moves. Sometimes, a person could make something happen because they put everything aside and *just fucking did it*.

He was going to bloody his steel *right now*.

Wet thrust at the still figure, but it seemed to flicker away. A heavy cloth pushed Wet's wrist aside, then wrapped around his arm and pulled.

At nearly the same moment, something struck the side of Wet's face. The dark alley vanished behind a cloud of bright spots. Something struck his knife hand and his foot. Wet lost his hold on his weapon and his balance at the same moment, falling onto a jumble of stinking rags. The blows had come with such terrifying quickness, Wet was sure two more thugs had come to gang up on him.

Crooked came up the alley, swinging her cleaver overhand with a grunted "Yah!" The silhouette barely seemed to move at all, but the blade missed completely. The silhouette's hand and hers were joined together, as though they were going to pull on a rope.

Then there was a flash of steel, and Crooked fell beside him onto the junk pile, her cleaver half-buried in her skull. Her lifeless eyes stared up at nothing.

Death had come. By the fallen gods, he hadn't thought it would be so sudden, but there it was. He hadn't been beaten by a gang of enemies. One man had taken them both, and Wet's only weapon was lost in the darkness and clutter.

The silhouette rapped on a window shutter behind him. Taking advantage of the brief respite, Wet reached across and patted Crooked's jacket, finding the bulge of her flask almost immediately. He stole it, pulled the stopper, and took a long, final draught.

It was the best brandy he'd ever tasted in his life.

When he finished, the silhouette had turned back to him. Wet's eyes were adjusting to the dim, and he saw the man reach to his belt and draw out a little knife.

By the fallen gods, he'd hadn't even bothered to draw his weapon.

"Stay."

The voice barely rose above a whisper. Wet nodded vigorously, then took another pull. The brandy seemed more ordinary now that he might survive a few more seconds.

In the wall above, the shutters opened. A pair of shining eyes peered down at him—hungry, hateful eyes.

The silhouette grabbed hold of Crooked's lapels and lifted her up to the window. A pair of long, bony arms reached out of the darkness and dragged her inside.

Wet shuddered and took another pull.

"Here! What are you shitwits doing?"

High Cap had appeared at the mouth of the alley.

"Tell him everything is fine," the silhouette whispered.

"We chased out a drunk!" Wet called. "Go back to your post."

Wet hated High Cap enough that he was tempted to tell him to fuck himself so he'd come into the alley and get his throat cut. But the silhouette wouldn't like that, and the silhouette was his new boss. High walked away.

The silhouette crouched in front of him. "I'm looking for a little girl. I think she's inside that building. If you help me get her out, I won't cut your throat."

If he did what the silhouette wanted, Tin Pail definitely *would* cut his throat. But that was in the future. Wet didn't even have to consider it. He was already nodding.

The silhouette led him away from the Pails' warehouse, into the next block, then circled around to approach the rear of the warehouse from an alley. The streets were dark, but as they approached a lantern, Wet looked at his attacker.

Which turned out to be difficult. Wet's mind seemed reluctant to look closely, and when he forced himself, he saw a strange doubled image. One was a tall man with shaggy black hair and a horrific scar on his face. The other image was the inky silhouette from the alley.

Magic. Wet shuddered. What could the other guards see? Would Tin forgive him if he told her the killer had cast a spell on him? Shit, no. He almost laughed at the idea.

After only a few moments, Wet felt a knife blade pressed against his back, just above his kidney. They stepped into the street, the stranger at his shoulder.

If he thought the two men guarding the back door, Two Cap and Ash Mouse, would notice a complete stranger approaching, he was disappointed. They glanced at him, then glanced away, keeping bored watch over the street corners and alleyways around them.

The stranger's magic had tricked them somehow. He was already ten feet from them, and they hadn't issued a challenge.

"Another privy trip?" Ash Mouse said.

If Wet said the word *alarm*, they would have readied their weapons and knocked three times, hard and quick, on the door behind them. That let the heavies inside know there was danger. But Wet could feel the knife point, and he hesitated for so long that the choice was made for him.

The stranger's fist shoved him, hard, against Two Cap. Wet tried to drop and roll away, but Two, his face twisted with rage, seized him and wouldn't let go.

Then coppery-tasting blood splattered into his mouth. Two Cap's head sagged to the right, a cleaver embedded in his skull. Wet felt the man's last breath against his face. As Two slid to the ground, his hands caressed Wet's ribs and hips in a mockery of affection. Ash Mouse already lay dead across the doorway.

This was too much. Just because Wet hated most of the heavies in the Pails' gang didn't mean he could do nothing while they were slaughtered.

"There's a coded knock," he said, amazed that he was about to throw his life away for people he despised. Was this how it happened? You suddenly reached the point where you were ready to give your life, even if it was only to give the alarm knock to his sleeping comrades inside?

The stranger yanked his knife from Ash Mouse's eye socket, then gave Wet a look that froze him in place. He raised his knuckle and knocked. One two. One. One two.

CHAPTER TWENTY

Kyrioc did not find her.

Inside the warehouse, there was only one guard. Kyrioc took her out quickly and quietly when she opened the door.

He was killing people again. And he felt nothing.

The heavy helped him drag the bodies inside, then bolted the door. They were in a little storeroom or front office, with a counter and shelves full of wooden dolls with skull-like faces and outstretched arms, as though the tiny figure of Death was asking for a hug.

In Kyrioc's experience, when death came, it was often very, very small: A breaking stair, the vapor from a cough, the edge of a knife like the one he was holding. A tiny figure was exactly the right size for Death, as far as he was concerned.

He pressed that knife against the heavy's ribs and they went deeper into the building.

The cloak of mirrors was tiring him, and his cloak of shadows would have been redundant in this place, so Kyrioc let both rest.

They came to another storefront, but there was nothing on the shelves. The double doors to the warehouse stood unbolted. A ramp led from the entrance to another room, presumably the rest of the warehouse. A counter, some office cabinets, and a padded bench fit for entertaining customers were set against one wall. Beside the counter as an iron cage, complete with a sleeping occupant.

Between them was a narrow flight of stairs. The heavy nodded in that direction. That was where they needed to go.

But they found the room at the top empty.

"I swear," the man said, his palms open as if he were praying, "I swear I swear I—"

"Be quiet. Where else could they be?"

"No place! I don't know. This is where they sleep at night. The boss doesn't let us mix with them, not even to eat. I never even heard of another spot I swear by Lost Selsarim—"

"If your boss killed her…"

"She wouldn't," the man said, his voice almost pleading. "The beetles are useful. She doesn't kill them—they're little kids—and if she did, I would have heard about it. So—"

"Be quiet." Kyrioc had been so sure—*so sure*—that he would open the door, grab Riliska, and flee the building with her. He realized his hands were trembling. "If you don't know where the kids are, who does?"

"The boss? Or her brother? They're in High Apricot, taking control of Harl's most profitable hustle."

"White tar?" The heavy only shook his head, his eyes wide. "Say it."

"Hospital stuff."

Of course. The glitterkind ear, the way Rulenya had been cut apart… "Where in High Apricot?"

"I don't know, I swear. I'm just a guy they put on guard duty at the shitty end of the day. I don't know stuff like that."

High Apricot was a large deck, and even at the dawn hour, there would be a lot of activity. "Okay. How do I find them?"

"There's… You…" the gangster was sweating now. "Wool Cap knows, but he only tells buyers, and they have to pay a fee and have someone vouch for them. All I can think of, you wait for a buyer and then…"

"Then I follow them. Let's go."

Leaving the heavy inside would be a good as murdering him, and that meant breaking his word. Kyrioc returned to the alleyway that gave a view of the front doors. Leaving the back entrance unguarded hadn't caused an alarm. Apparently, no one expected much from the Pails' heavies.

It was not long at all before an elderly woman in an elegant white robe with a silver collar trudged up the middle of the street, a well-dressed Carrig gangster in tow. She looked tired but alert. They were met at the front door by a muscular heavy. The Carrig spoke briefly, then accepted a coin from the woman and walked away. After a brief conversation, the woman paid the heavy a larger handful of coins, then walked away.

Kyrioc could barely hear the heavy beside him. "That's one."

"You can't remember anything."

"What?" The man gaped at him.

"Tell them you can't remember anything."

Kyrioc struck the heavy, hard, on the side of his head. He collapsed like a puppet whose strings had been cut. Kyrioc laid two shallow cuts on his forearms to make it look like he'd gone down fighting, then left him in the trash.

He caught sight of the elderly woman in her robe as she mounted the stairs into High Apricot.

* * *

AFTER THE OLD WOMAN locked her in the room, Riliska lay awake. The smell was awful, and she could hear three different voices whining in the dark. When would her mom come?

Just as her eyes began to close, the door swung open and a lanky man staggered in. Riliska knew a drunk when she saw one. "Scurry, scurry, scurry," he said, over and over, although she didn't understand why.

The other children woke in unsettling silence, as though everyone felt the same fear she did. The kids lined up at the pot, then they were led down the stairs, through a pair of large doors, into the same carriage she'd ridden in.

The only light on the street came from torches and lanterns. She suspected that was the only light this deck ever saw.

The slow clop of the horses' hooves and the gentle rocking of the carriage lulled her to sleep while the other children sat wide-eyed and whispering. Never with her, but never about her, either. She was invisible even to the people who had stolen her.

"Scurry, scurry" woke her again. The children were being unloaded.

As soon as she stepped out of the cart, a chilly breeze blew through her tattered clothes. They had come to the eastern edge of the city, and she could see the starry sky hanging above the black mountains on the other side of the Timmer Strait.

Riliska couldn't help herself. She stopped and stared at the twinkling lights. She'd seen stars before, obviously, but not often. They were beautiful.

A line of torches showed the city wall was only slightly below them. She hadn't realized they'd come so far downcity, and the thought scared her. Low Market lay to the north, while behind and above her was a large deck she didn't recognize. In the dark, it was little more than faint candle lights inside looming shadows.

Where had they brought her? They were near Low Market—she could see Suloh's glowing hip bones—but so far east and south that they were suspended above the empty dirt between the Yth's ribs and hips, apart from the main decks of the city. But they had approached from—

The drunk man flicked her ear painfully. "Scurry, scurry."

Riliska imagined herself flicking him right back with so much force that he was flung from the deck and plummeted into the darkness below. But she knew what defiance brought. She fell in with the other children.

They crossed an empty skywood plaza with shuttered businesses in a half-circle around the southern edge. There was a dry fountain in the center. Once, this little platform might have been pretty, but no one came here now.

Then they crossed a long, narrow plankway to another platform nearly two hundred feet away, which was practically invisible in the darkness. It was a large, multi-story building on a miniature deck of its own. It rested on four long stilts, with a long waterpipe leading up into the western darkness. She'd never seen anything like it.

Riliska's mom taught her to stay clear of unlit buildings because addicts and thieves squatted in them, but her hesitation brought another painful flick on her ear. "The way is sturdy," the drunk man whispered, his words slightly slurred, "no matter how old it looks. Scurry, scurry."

He'd thought Riliska hesitated because the plankway was so long, with only a half-collapsed railing…and she would have, if she'd had a chance to notice. But the other kids were already crossing, and there were no wobbles or creaks from the wood beneath their feet. Skywood. No one else seemed afraid. Maybe they had crossed before, or maybe they just didn't care if they collapsed the plankway and fell into the bottomless dark.

Riliska mimicked them, keeping her eyes on the planks. For the first time in her life, she felt as though a strong breeze might knock her over. One of the girls near the front started crying. No one dared stop walking.

Once safe on the other side, she took a quick count. There were fourteen kids, and all but two were obviously younger than her. The drunk man who kept telling them to scurry was nowhere in sight, and Riliska peeked over the edge to see if he'd fallen off.

There was nothing below them but darkness.

"Let's go!"

That harsh whisper sent chills down Riliska's arms. A sour-faced old man stood in an open doorway, lit candle in hand. The children mobbed toward him obediently.

These were the meekest, quietest children Riliska had ever seen. She couldn't imagine what the grownups did to make them this way, but she hoped she would never find out.

The old man led them into a large entry hall. The dim light of the candle barely touched the walls, but she could hear their footsteps echoing like the inside of a tomb.

"Down that way are the baths," the old man said, like this was a guided tour. "But they've been dry for years, so don't bother. Down there is the exercise room. The caretaker stays there. He doesn't like children. Down that hall are the guest rooms. You'll be sleeping in the beds there."

A few of the smaller kids gasped and exclaimed, "Beds!"

"But not yet!" the old man said before they could run off. "Come this way."

He led them down the stairs and through long corridors into a small room. The walls, floor, and ceiling were lined with flat, gray stones. There was no other furniture, just a pair of racks with long sticks set in them, a couple of doors, and a pile of something yellowish and hairy in the far corner. "This is the spa," the old man said. "Over there is your escape route. Look at it, but don't get close."

The children shuffled past it, and Riliska fell into the line at the end. The hairy mound turned out to be a coil of frayed, knotted rope, and on the far side of it was a hole in the floor. The other children had not approached closely, but she went right to the edge. Below was only darkness.

"If someone comes to attack this building, you lot are to come in here, push that coil into the hole, and climb down quick as you can. Get back to the warehouse in Wild Dismal, and warn the Pails' heavies to come and help. There's an Undertower lift to the west. Clear?" The only answer was silence. "Fine. Go to the pots or to your beds now."

The other children ran to the hall and the promised beds. Riliska stayed. "Sir?"

The old man turned toward her, surprised and a little annoyed. She realized that he had probably been asleep when they arrived, and she was keeping him up. "What is it?"

He didn't hit her, so she dared what the other children had not. "Why are we here?"

"What do you mean?"

"If we're just to escape and call for help, why do you need all fourteen? Why not just one or two?"

"Well," he said, looking uncomfortable, "that's a lot of rope right there, and the coil is heavy. It will take many small hands to push it into the gap. And besides…besides, no one is supposed to know about this place. But should an attack come, well, the more of you there are, the more likely one will make it to Wild Dismal."

Riliska was not surprised or alarmed. Some hidden part of her had expected to hear exactly this answer. Gangland heavies might come, and if they could, they would turn their knives on her and the other children.

Her next question escaped her without thinking if it was safe to ask. "Is my mommy coming?"

The old man sighed as though she'd made a mess he would have to clean up. "I'm just here to sweep the floors, child."

He left.

Riliska could hear the other children settling in. Now that they were on their own, they clearly felt free to chatter and talk.

But they sounded very far away. How much warning would they have if an attack came? Not only would the kids have to make it all the way here, then push in the rope, they'd have to reach the bottom, too. Heavies willing to stab her would certainly be willing to cut through a rope while she was still on it.

She decided to sleep closer to their escape route. Inside the actual room would have been best, but odd breezes made the stone room chilly, and the smell of the "dirt" below—always present in the city—was especially strong. She went through a door for no other reason than the children and the old man had not, and found herself in the bath.

Her mommy had taken her to a bath before, and she knew that there was an open place beneath the tub where fires were lit. She clambered through the stone tub to the far side. The smell of charcoal and old smoke was faint but better than the spa's sewer smell.

It was only when she remembered that the old man had taken his candle with him, and that there should have been no light for her to see, that she realized there was something shining from beneath the tub. It wasn't a fire. Firelight was orange.

Riliska carefully crouched beside the slot and peered in.

Deep inside the gap, lying on the ashy skywood, was a little child, even smaller than Riliska herself. The child glowed faintly in the darkness, skin glittering with a hundred colors.

* * *

NEWS HAD NOT YET reached Harl's platform halls that the man was dead. It was inconvenient but not unexpected. Tin Pail and her brother sat in a cafe across the street from The Flute and Thunder with Paper Mouse, a couple of heavies she sort of trusted, and a single beetle. The guards on the back entrance looked bored. They were attentive, because Harl would never trust laggards with a job like this, but they were relaxed, too.

The cafe owner came by their table again and tried to collect their cups, muttering apologetically about closing time. Paper bared his knife and led the man into the back, explaining what would happen if he kept interrupting.

Before he could return, her bodyguard arrived in the cart, chimes in his beard jingling. He climbed down and approached, holding a bundle wrapped in red cloth. When his gaze met Tin's, he nodded.

They stood from the table and went into the street. Paper hurried to take the bundle from her bodyguard. Tin nodded to the heavies she'd brought along, and they fell back to watch over the street. The bodyguard opened his long, sleeveless, and now bloodstained coat, drew the two pieces of his ghostkind weapon, and joined them together.

That caught the guard's attention. They pulled hatchets from their belts, except for the tall, willowy woman in the back who began to string her bow. There were six of Harl's people—with more inside, obviously—facing Tin Pail, her brother, Paper, and her bodyguard. Harl's people did not look worried.

The shortest of them stepped forward. He was built like a tree stump and sported long scars down one cheek. "Turn around and jump off the edge of the fucking deck," he said. "It'll be a quicker death, and you get to see a glimpse of the night sky before the end. Try to rob us, and Harl will slaughter your whole family."

Tin stopped just outside the range they would have to engage. Paper said, "Harl has murdered his last Salashi kid." Then he lowered the bundle and let the cloth fall.

Harl's head rolled across the planks toward the guards' feet. The biggest of them, and the only one with the pale Carrig complexion, blurted out, "No. No!"

Tin lunged forward. In one motion, she drew her hammer and slammed it down on the top of the Carrig's head. He fell back with an expression that looked almost peaceful. The willowy woman in the back shot an arrow, but Tin's bodyguard blocked it with the flat of his glaive.

"Stop!" the short guard called. "Stop right now."

He looked like he meant it. Tin glanced at her bodyguard and saw him lowering his weapon. If the Katr thought the guy was standing down, that sealed it. She slid her hammer into her belt. Taking his cue, Wooden sheathed his knife.

Tin said, "With Harl dead, you work for me now."

The short guard glanced down at Harl's gaping mouth and gray skin. "All right, I guess. All right." It wasn't exactly a pledge of undying loyalty, but it was the best she could expect. He turned toward the others. "Anyone here love Harl Sota List Im so much they want to fight, without pay, for his corpse?" He waved vaguely at the dead Carrig. "Besides him."

They looked her bodyguard up and down. He wasn't even standing in a guard position. They did nothing.

Tin sighed. This shit was too easy. The fight she'd expected was already over, because Harl's people—some of the best he had, assigned to guard his most lucrative setup—had shrugged off his murder. How many of her own people would do the same when the point came to her? The thought made her want to swing her hammer again. "Open the door and warn the guard inside."

The lead heavy shrugged. "If you're paying our salaries, you're making the call."

"And keep your mouths shut. No one is to hear about this until I tell them."

The people inside were even easier to convince, if that was possible, and the manager's wary submissiveness quickly turned into eagerness to please.

These people thought of themselves as regular working folk. The realization startled and amazed Tin, but it was obvious. They worked a shift, doing the same thing every day, and collected a day's wages. When Tin moved in, they reacted like the staff at a cafe who learned it had been sold. All they cared about was whether they'd lose their jobs. They were practically petals.

It was pathetic.

The manager of the platform hall opened his books for her. The numbers were straightforward and startling. His business earned more than Tin expected, especially since Harl had forbidden prostitution, gambling, or drug trade on the property. The Flute and Thunder was a clean location, except for the sale of human body parts. Suddenly, the endless thump and whine of the music seemed tolerable.

Harl's black-market surgical fixer was a bland, weedy man with a gray bureaucrat's scarf. He stood behind a plain desk in a small back office with a pair of rough-looking but respectably dressed heavies.

Before Tin could ask questions, a new customer was ushered in. She was a well-preserved woman in her sixties, wearing an embroidered white robe with a high silver collar that had been in style ten years before and was now considered conservative.

"It's about my child, you see," the woman said, looking down her nose at the fixer. "He needs a skin transplant, and not a single legitimate facility will perform it. Of course, I'm willing to pay a reasonable surcharge, but—"

The fixer interrupted her with the stoic deference of a funeral director. "May I ask, good madam, what condition he suffers from?"

"Does that really make a difference? I suppose you must know. He's going bald. In fact, he's going bald in the most appalling fashion, and I don't see how I'm ever going to have a grandchild at this rate."

"Of course, we have dealt with such concerns before. Our usual business involves working with those who are gravely ill, but we can accommodate your son's…condition. How old is he?"

"He's thirty-nine."

An unbearable urge to laugh suddenly came over Tin, and she slipped out a side door into a long dark hallway. The old woman's chattering was still audible through the door, which meant the laughter that was about to burst out of her would be heard inside and spoil the deal.

She sprinted—something she hadn't done in years—down the hall until she was right beneath the stage. There, in the shadow of the stairs, she laughed long and hard, releasing years of tension she hadn't realized she was carrying around.

After so much worry over the failed handoff, framing Harl, and hunting him down—after all the risks that came with taking on the most powerful criminal in Koh-Salash—she realized she'd risked her and her brother's life for the coin in the purse of that pampered old woman at the end of the hall. This was where her ambition had led her.

She laughed, and it felt good.

Soon, she began to feel embarrassed and took deep breaths until the laughter subsided. The whole situation was absurd, and a surge of giggles ran through her when she imagined cutting off Harl's scalp for that woman's middle-aged child. Maybe she would have wanted to inspect it first, like a fish in Low Market, so she could approve the hairline.

A flicker of shadow from above finally stifled her laughter, and she glanced up to see a figure in black gliding down the stairs. The music was too loud to hear him, of course, but he descended so smoothly that she suspected she wouldn't have heard him even without the band.

He reached the bottom step. Tin immediately recognized his shaggy black hair and the vicious scar on his face.

She was face to face with the asshole from the pawnshop.

CHAPTER TWENTY-ONE

Tin's first thought was that the pawnshop asshole should be dead. Her second was that he should be chained in a tower while the cosh beat him into jelly. The image made her grin. "Looking for the staff privy, huh?"

He glanced at her, then looked away. "Yes."

"I'm the same way. I had to pay to eat it. Why should I pay to shit it, too? Right? Don't bother with that hallway," she said, pointing back the way she came, "that's for the women only."

"Thank you." His voice was as soft as a serpent's hiss. He rounded the corner toward the far hall.

Time to go.

Tin hurried up the stairs into the narrow, cluttered backstage. Two women, either dead drunk or so tired by the late hour that they could sleep through the thundering music, lay unconscious on heaps of canvas. Tin came to the edge of the stage and looked out.

Her brother was out there flailing his arms and wiggling his hips. As usual, he seemed to have attracted a small crowd of young people. In places like this, someone always found his flamboyant abandon irresistible.

Their bodyguard was not on the dance floor with him, but that head full of wild red hair was easy to spot. He stood at the rail, still blood-spattered but empty-handed. Beside him was one of her heavies, a lean young guy who went by Dry Rain. The heavy was soaked through with sweat and breathing heavily, as though he'd run a long way. She approached them.

"Boss!" Dry had to shout over the music. The nearest musician gave them a look, but Tin had her hand on her hammer, and he turned away quickly. "Someone hit the warehouse!"

That made no sense. "Which one?"

"Yours! The one in Wild Dismal!"

Someone was moving against them. No one was supposed to know what had happened, not yet, but they were already responding. And it couldn't have been anyone working Harl's...no, *her* black-market medical hustle, because they would have had to execute the hit before she showed them the head. "What did they take?"

"As far as we could tell, nothing."

Bullshit. Tin hurried to her bodyguard. "Remember the flunky from the pawnshop?"

The Katr nodded, ringing the chimes in his beard. "The one who did not flinch."

Tin noticed the lone beetle crouching outside the platform, his arms wrapped around his knees for warmth. She signaled for him and he jumped up. "He's supposed to be locked in one of the towers or dead, but instead, he's here right now. Someone sprung him."

"I will kill him."

"No." To the beetle, she said, "Find Paper Mouse and bring him to me."

Selsarim Lost, who could be moving against her? The only people who knew she'd planned to come here were the people she'd brought.

It had to be one of Harl's other lieutenants, and if they were coordinated enough to hit her warehouse and send this pawnshop broker to The Flute and Thunder at the same time, they were all in danger.

To her bodyguard, she said, "Stay with my brother."

They both looked at Wooden, and he noticed. Tin saluted to him, and the signal had its intended effect. He pushed through his throng of admirers toward them.

Tin noticed the manager standing expectantly at the foot of the stage. She drew her hand across her throat and he signaled the musicians to stop playing. They did.

She got a full report from Dry. It didn't make sense. Only three dead, one missing, one beaten unconscious. Nothing stolen or burned. There wasn't even an attempt, as far as he could tell, to enter storage where the white tar and glitterkind ear were kept.

The only thing the intruders did was leave the door to the beetles' bedroom open.

Her beetle came running back alone.

"There's fighting downstairs!" the boy said, eyes wide. "And blood! A man is asking where the beetles are hidden!"

Fuck. They knew. Whoever this asshole was working for, they knew. Tin had planned her move so quietly and carefully, but someone had found out that she'd moved her couriers, along with a dozen heavies, to Harl's secret glitterkind stash. No one was supposed to know that place even existed, but they must have found out. There could be no other explanation for why the asshole was looking for her couriers.

She explained the situation to her brother.

"If they find that place," Wooden said, "we're as good as dead."

He was right. They needed the money from Harl's glitterkind business to keep all of his thugs in line. Otherwise, the Pails would have to face an entire city with a couple of dozen heavies. They'd be swept away like leaves in a stream. The thought made her stomach feel tight.

There was no choice. She turned to her bodyguard.

"On second thought, that scarred man downstairs? Take the point to him."

* * *

WHEN THE WOMAN SUGGESTED Kyrioc head left, he went left. It was clear she wasn't really one of the dancers. For one thing, she wasn't sweaty. For another, no one would try to dance in boots with a steel cap on the toe, let alone a hammer tucked into their belt. No, by her boring clothes and hair, he figured her for a petty white tar dealer trying to steer him away from her stash.

Which was fine. He wasn't interested in tar. All he wanted was to find out where the old woman went and who she was talking to.

There was nothing in the leftmost hall except a storeroom. When he entered it, he could hear a shrill, commanding voice coming through the wallboards.

Kyrioc ran back up the hall, around the bend—the woman with the hammer was gone—and back down the right-hand passage. He did find the women's indoor privy there, but at the very end, he came to a door that was humming with that same shrill voice.

He turned the latch, found it unlocked, and pushed it open. The old woman in the white robe was there, but she was the only one who didn't react to his entrance. She just kept droning on about being no stranger to backroom deals before, and what about seeing the merchandise first, considering the price she was expected to pay.

Across the counter from her were two heavies and one long-faced man with sullen eyes. All three gaped at Kyrioc. The loss of their attention finally made the woman lose momentum and stop talking.

Behind the long-faced man was the man with three little braids hanging on his forehead. Kyrioc pointed at him.

"You. Come here."

The sullen man turned to one of the heavies. "At some point, you're going to have to do what you're being paid to do."

The two men jumped to life and drew their knives. They charged.

A surge of raw emotion welled up within Kyrioc, and his cloak of iron wrapped around him. He lunged toward the charging men, drawing his own knife.

These were not the hapless thugs he'd fought in the alley outside the Pails' warehouse, but it didn't matter. He slipped the first man's charge, caught his wrist, and shoved him into the wall. When the heavy collapsed, his own blade was protruding from just below his right collarbone.

The second feinted low and went high, but before his stroke could fall, Kyrioc's blade had already pierced his throat and withdrawn. The man dropped his weapon to try to staunch the flow of blood, but by the look in his eyes, he knew the end had come.

The long-faced man sighed and drew back his vest to reveal two hatchets. "I suppose I should have done this when the Pails moved in, so fuck it."

"The man behind you hurt a friend of mine," Kyrioc said. His skin was tingling and everything seemed vivid and alive, but he didn't want to kill anyone he didn't have to. He was sick of wasting lives. "He's going to tell me where he put the little girl he kidnapped. That's all I want. I'm not here for you."

The man looked around. The wealthy woman had gone. He drew his hatchets and took up a defensive stance. "You have me anyway."

Kyrioc feinted forward, then jumped back when the sullen man swung at his midsection. When the inevitable overhand right came down, Kyrioc struck the hatchet on the side of the head with the butt of his knife. The weapon spun out of the sullen man's grip.

When the second came in, Kyrioc caught the blade in his bare hand.

He could feel the impact, and he could feel the carefully honed sharpness of the blade, but it didn't break his skin, not with his cloak in place.

The sullen man's look of triumph turned to confusion. Before he could fully understand what had happened, Kyrioc plunged his knife into the side of his neck. He fell to the floor, fumbling at the haft protruding from beneath his ear.

The heavy with three braids was still scrambling over the counter, then landed on both feet and ran for the exit. Kyrioc threw the stolen hatchet, wedging it deep into the jamb and door, pinning it shut. The heavy looked at it with wide, terrified eyes, and then he spun around, knife in hand.

He'd replaced the knife Kyrioc had taken from him with a more expensive one. The blade was serrated and the handle carved from ivory.

It would have commanded a good price at the pawnshop.

Sweat beaded on the man's forehead. When he attacked, fear tightened his swing, and Kyrioc easily caught his wrist and twisted.

He took the heavy's knife and pressed him against the door. "Where have they moved Riliska? Tell me, and I'll let you live."

"Go fu—"

Kyrioc stabbed the blade into his armpit, the steel jamming into his shoulder joint. The heavy screamed, his voice high with pain and terror.

"This is a good knife," Kyrioc said. "I'll bet I could flense your arm to the bone with a blade like this. You could spend a week dying under my care, maybe more if your heart is strong. You know the girl I'm looking for. Tell me where I can find her."

A single sliding footfall was Kyrioc's only warning. He pivoted to the left just as a blade thrust through the space where he'd been standing.

It plunged into the heavy's back, splitting the wooden door from top to bottom.

The red-haired Katr had just tried to skewer Kyrioc with his ghostkind weapon. He looked astonished to have missed.

The heavy's head lolled back. His mouth gaped and his eyes fell shut. The Katr had killed him.

Which meant Kyrioc would have to get the information from someone else. He turned to face the northerner.

* * *

SINCE THE DAY IN the Fiurniss Valley when Killer of Devils accepted the gift of Asca, he had not missed a single stroke and he had not been surprised by another human being. He had surprised himself occasionally, but the celestial magic of the gods—what the Salashi sometimes called *godkind*—meant that he would never misjudge an enemy again.

So, when he thrust his glaive at the back of the pawnshop broker, he had every expectation that the strike would hit home.

Instead, his target had heard his approach and dodged the attack. The decision and action came so quickly that Killer had no time to alter his thrust.

His gift told him the broker was about to grab the haft of his polearm, so Killer yanked it back, freeing it from both the man he had inadvertently killed and the door. Still, the broker was almost quick enough to catch hold. He had to draw back his hand at the last moment to avoid the edge.

An enemy who could move so quickly from decision to completed action—an enemy who could actually surprise him—was not someone to be toyed with. This was not a time for play or posturing. Killer fell back into a fighting stance, his blade held low.

The broker feinted left and went hard to the right. Killer's gift told him the move was a feint even before the man started to move, but the glaive barely clipped his forearm.

The broker fell into a roll and came to his feet with a hatchet. In one, smooth quick motion, he threw it.

Too slow. Killer swept upward with his blade, striking the head of the hatchet and slicing through it. The thick steel head split in two and the pieces flew behind him. His counterstroke…missed again.

His enemy disarmed, Killer tried to bring his glaive to bear, but the haft struck the wall behind him.

The broker took advantage, and it was clear—as if it had not been before—that the man was more than a shop clerk. He slipped inside the length of the glaive and fought with open hand, elbows, knees, and feet. His attacks had real power behind them. Killer had to drop his long weapon to defend himself.

Grim excitement made Killer's skin prickle as he pushed himself to respond. It had been years since an enemy had truly challenged him. An enemy who could dodge his stroke. An enemy who could actually land a blow against him. This one, perhaps, would be the one who would free him from this shameful bondage.

But he was going to have to earn it.

The man was fast, but he could not match Killer's strength and mass. They traded blows, nearly one for one, but Killer believed his strikes took a higher toll. They must have, although the broker did not show it.

Then he caught his enemy's wrist and twisted. The broker, knocked off balance for just a moment, fell against the counter. Before Killer could bring his weight to bear, the man reversed the grip and slammed Killer's forehead against the wood. The world turned bright with pain.

His own knife. His gift working even with spots swirling in his vision, Killer slapped this hand over the knife in his belt, catching it before the broker could clear the sheath. In the struggle, the blade clattered to the floor. Killer threw an elbow that knocked the broker backward. He stumbled over the body of one of the men he had already killed, and in that moment of free movement, Killer fought through his daze and went for his ghostkind weapon.

He caught hold of the haft just as the broker stamped down on the flat of the blade, pinning it to the floor. With a quick twist, Killer released the haft and thrust the blunt end into the broker's gut.

The man staggered, and Killer leaped forward and threw a hard left.

He drove the broker into the corner to hem him in, but before he got close, the broker kicked Killer hard in the stomach. The attack came too quickly to block or dodge. He could only twist slightly to weaken it. Killer fell backward over the same body, but his free hand fell on the other half of his glaive, and when he rolled to his feet, he held both halves in a ready posture.

The broker, crouching unarmed in the corner, glanced at the knife embedded in Paper's body, then took a long, slow breath. Killer realized he was about to see magic. Darkness seemed to billow from him like heavy smoke, and within moments, he was hidden inside a cloud of shadow.

"I knew it had to be so," Killer said to the darkness. "You are like me, blessed with a gift from the gods. Not the paltry gifts of Suloh, so weak that none bother to flaunt them, or the false vitality that comes from the berries of Yth, but something deadly and powerful. Yes?" From the shadow, there was no answer. "And it must have been a god who lies dead within ghostkind lands, because you fight like them. Some godkind in the west, yes? Even after a millennium, there are still celestial corpses lying undiscovered in the world. Which is it? Weyen? Heyest? Not Indib, with that cloud of darkness. Certainly not the god of war."

Killer of Devils realized he was enjoying himself. For the first time in years, he had found a worthy enemy, one whose magic came from a source as powerful as his, and who could give him a real fight. Now, to make everything perfect, Killer was going to cut his guts out or die trying.

Killer said, "I know what you are."

From the depths of the shadow came the stranger's voice. "I know what you are, too."

The tone of the broker's voice was not new. Killer felt that same contempt for the man he had become, and for the circumstances that forced him to serve these masters in this doomed city.

"I thought you might be the one," he said. "I thought you might be the one to free me from my obligation to these criminals, these priests of Heyest, although they do not seem to understand that they are such. But no. I think it will have to be another."

The sound of tiny running feet echoed from the hall outside. It was one of the Pails' beetles.

"Good sir," the child blurted breathlessly, "the cosh are coming. We have to go. Orders, good sir."

Killer cursed silently. He could have killed every constable, soldier, and marshal they sent after him, but he could not protect his employers at the same time. "Yes," he said.

To the shadow, he said, "Another time."

Then Killer's gift revealed that the broker was about to lunge at him. The darkness might have obscured his vision, but it could not fool his magic. Killer threw the handle into the cloud of shadow at head level and, in almost the same movement, swept his sword low through the darkness. The handle rebounded off the walls and rolled at his feet, but the blade came out of the darkness with blood on the tip.

"Good sir!" the child insisted. "Orders!" Killer snatched the handle off the floor and hurried away. He had sworn an oath and could not ignore orders.

* * *

KYRIOC FELL BACK AGAINST the wall, clutching the cut on his left side. His cloak of shadows dissipated.

He'd taken deadlier wounds than this. The cut was shallow and cleaner than any razor could have made. It was about as long as his middle finger, and he thought it had missed his internal organs.

If he was lucky. And, usually, he wasn't. Still, his blood was flowing. Riliska...

Kyrioc stumbled to the body of Paper Mouse and yanked the blade from his armpit. It wasn't much use against a polearm, especially one that could cut through steel like threshing wheat, but it didn't matter. The people who could have told him where to find Riliska were *right here*, and he had fucked it up.

Clutching at his bloody side, Kyrioc lurched after the barbarian and the messenger boy. Someone was going to tell him what he wanted to know if he had to cut it out of them.

Kyrioc staggered as fast as he could to the stairs at the far end of the hall. Behind him he could hear constables shouting. They were close. He hurried up the stairs and found the musicians milling around on the stage. One cried, "Oh, shit!" when she saw the bloody knife, and Kyrioc suddenly had a clear path to the dance-floor rail.

Far down the street, a cart passed a lantern, and Kyrioc saw the barbarian sitting in the back, staring at him. Opposite him was a woman talking to one of the beetles. She snapped her fingers. The beetle leaped from the cart. She turned. It was the woman with the hammer in her belt.

That was Tin Pail. By the fallen gods, the woman who'd taken Riliska had been right beside him.

Kyrioc staggered into the street, sprinting as hard as he could to catch up, but he was still bleeding and the cart was a two-horse rig. It vanished into the city.

His chance to take them by surprise was gone, their boss knew his face, and he'd let himself be injured. He'd wasted his best chance to find Riliska.

The constables came boiling out of the platform-hall stage, roughly grabbing the musicians and the other employees. The last few patrons fled in terror, drawing the ironshirts' attention.

Except for one slender Carrig in bureaucratic gray. Kyrioc recognized him from the south tower.

The beetle ran toward him. "The Pails have a question—"

Kyrioc leaped at the boy and gathered him up in his right arm. Shouts from the platform hall drowned the boy's protests. He raced down the nearest alley while the boy struggled and kicked.

Laying the flat of the bloody knife against the boy's cheek, Kyrioc said, "Behave."

It was nearly dawn, and the alleys were empty. The thieves and pickpockets had already left to sell the goods they stole overnight, and the tar heads had slipped away with their scores.

Before he reached the end of the first alley, Kyrioc knew he could not get far on foot. His heart raced, pumping blood out of his body. Spots floated in his vision. He ran anyway, struggling with his burden.

Kyrioc didn't know High Apricot well, but somewhere to the west was a broad, sloping road that connected to Woodgarden and other districts below. He reached the end of the alley, crossed the street, and entered another. At this time of day, it should be full of vendors making early deliveries to shops all over Koh-Salash. Once he put enough distance between himself and the ironshirts, he had one last chance to find out what he needed to know.

Finally, woozy and desperate, he came to the edge of the High Apricot deck and saw the broad road just below him. The Freightway. But aside from one horse-drawn cart loaded with sheets of tanned leather, the street was still empty. It was too early.

Kyrioc palmed his knife. "Going to Woodgarden?"

The woman driving the cart was gray-haired and narrow-eyed, but what looked at first like a suspicious nature turned out to be poor vision. She moved over on the cart to allow him to sit beside her.

"You don't look so good, son."

The boy sneered. He couldn't have been older than seven. "He's gonna look worse soon. Real soon." To Kyrioc, "I'm going to kill you."

The old woman clicked her tongue in disapproval, but Kyrioc simply said, "I thought you had a message."

"My boss wants to make you an offer. If you tell me who you're working for, she will let you live. If you don't, she will kill you and everyone in your family."

Kyrioc sighed. "I'm not working for anyone. Your boss kidnapped a little girl. I want her back."

The boy smirked. "My boss said to tell you that if you answer with anything other than a name, she'll take the point to you and yours."

The boy reached for the knife at his belt, but Kyrioc plucked it from its little sheath and tossed it into the road.

"All I want is the little girl," Kyrioc tried to keep his voice steady, but the fury was draining away. Nausea flooded him and his hands felt shaky. "Tell me where they've moved those kids. Tell me where you're sleeping now."

The boy stood as tall as he could on the very edge of the cart bench. "I will *never* tell you *anything*."

"Then pass this message on to your boss. Whatever she's building, I can burn it down."

He released the boy's wrist, and the child sprang out of the moving cart. "Fuck you!" the boy screamed at the top of his lungs. "Fuck you!" Then he ran for his little knife.

Colors danced in Kyrioc's vision. Maybe his wound wasn't so minor after all. The woman snapped her reins to speed the cart along. "Son, you sound like you're in some deep shit."

CHAPTER TWENTY-TWO

The year 395 of the New Calendar, eight years earlier.

* * *

THE SUN WAS SETTING in the west behind them, but the column of pale light blasting toward the clouds cast new, eerie shadows in the jungle foliage.

The glitterkind were still crying out their chorus of misery and distress. Though they spoke no words, Kyrionik thought they were sounding an alarm. He could *feel* their panic.

"I'm sorry," he called to no one in particular. He wished he could undo the last six months. Sail to Harka as he'd promised, fight raiders from horseback, oversee the construction of a tower, and secure the peninsula.

But nothing could be taken back. Real mistakes could never be undone.

Aratill rushed toward him. "Your virtue! We—"

Kyrionik leaped up the stairs. Aratill was strong and steadfast, but he was not as quick as an athletic teenager determined to see the danger he had made.

Racing up the slope, Kyrionik grasped at tree roots and half-buried broken stones. Aratill had trained him to never use his weapon as a walking stick, but he did so now, jamming the butt of his spear into the dirt to propel himself upward.

He came to a bulge in the slope and saw Shulipik tuto-Beskeroth once again standing at the top of the stair, once again staring at something ahead. But this time, his ghostkind glaive was in his right hand, and his helm in the other. The force of the great gleaming torrent of light erupting from the ground made his braided hair fly out behind him.

Kyrionik came up beside him, breathing hard. The depression where the glitterkind lay was awash in a terrible white light. The column played on the glitterkind skin in a way that Kyrionik had never seen before, like brightly burning stars of every color. Rainbow beams shone onto the greenery around them.

It was beautiful.

Catching his breath, Kyrionik asked, "Your virtue, what happened?"

Shulipik turned toward him with an expression the younger man could not read. He seemed at once mournful, ecstatic, and transfixed, as though they were watching the end of a tragic play. He almost looked drunk with emotion. "Selso Rii happened, your virtue." Shulipik glanced behind him. Kyrionik saw the man's headless corpse in the green. "I lost track of him, and he secretly cut a portion of glitterkind flesh for his own pack. Look."

He pointed to one of the creatures. Its left hand had been severed below the elbow.

"Too greedy," Kyrionik said. This was why glitterkind magic was dangerous. Greed urged them to cut too deep, and…

And what? Would this column of light sound a warning? Summon help? Kyrionik wished he'd found someone to explain the real danger to him.

"There it is." Shulipik put on his helm and buckled it. He peered into the center of the geyser of light and readied his glaive. "An ullroct."

Aratill caught up to them. His helm was off and his bald head was bright red and streaked with sweat. Kyrionik felt a twinge of guilt at the effort he'd put the older man through. Aratill glanced at the geyser, then grabbed Kyrionik's arm. "Your virtue, you must come away!"

A shadow formed inside the column of light. It stood ten feet tall and was barely a stick figure silhouette in the burning brightness.

Ullrocts didn't prey on glitterkind. They were their guardians.

"Your virtue!" Aratill roared. "Come away or I will carry you!"

Shulipik spun and moved his face inches from Kyrionik's. His eyes were wild and his smile terrifying. "Yes, little noble! Run away! *Right now!*"

Kyrionik bounded down the stairs, sudden fear driving him from both creature and warrior. Aratill fell in behind him, but could not keep up. Once there was some space between himself and his bodyguard, Kyrionik looked back.

Shulipik moved off the stairs into the trees by the side of the slope. Whatever was forming in that terrible white light, that renowned warrior hid from it.

Kyrionik did not have to be told to run. Aratill, his teacher, mentor, and bodyguard, caught up. If the ullroct pursued them—the word *if* felt like a kick in the guts; of course it would—it would reach the older man first.

Kyrionik could not bear that. He did not want to hear him die.

Four soldiers came up the stairs toward them, and Kyrionik met them just above the ruined mill. The nearest one hoisted her spear. Kyrionik had seen her standing guard in the family compound many times. He didn't know her name. "Oblifell sent us to aid you."

Before Kyrionik could respond, Aratill caught up to them. "That thing up there." He pointed up the slope. "Destroy it."

The ullroct had come.

It looked gigantic, perhaps because it was so far above them. It was the color of rusted black iron, and its limbs were as slender as broomsticks. Its feet looked like bends in metal bars, and its hands were wire spiders. One of those spiders held a short length of iron, like a truncheon. Its torso was the shape of an oversized funeral urn—round and narrow at the bottom, round and wide at the top—but its head was as broad and flat as a gravestone. The daylight was still bright but no eyes or mouth could be seen there, yet its footing was confident as it descended the broken stair.

Its every footstep made the ground smoke, and every branch or bush it brushed against began to smolder. Its entire body was enveloped in tiny tongues of flame that were barely visible in the light.

A creature of iron and flame.

Aratill seized the nearest guard. "You swore an oath to protect this boy. Now do your duty and destroy *that*."

The soldier looked Kyrionik in the eyes as if to measure what her sacrifice was worth. Then she charged up the stair, shield high and spear point ready.

A loud scream echoed from high above them, cutting through the droning cry of distress from the glitterkind. Kyrionik glanced up and saw Shulipik tuto-Beskeroth leaping from the stairs at the back of the creature. He hadn't run away. He'd waited until it was below him so he could flank it.

Shulipik brought his ghostkind glaive down onto the ullroct's shoulder with his entire body weight behind the blow.

It ricocheted off.

Shulipik fell against the ullroct's lower back. It toppled, sprawling onto the hillside, spraying dirt and smoke. The soldiers arrived and stabbed it with their spears, but the points glanced off. Shulipik regained his feet and hacked at the back of the ullroct's knee.

A weapon made of ghostkind steel, especially one of the long-handled glaives, could cut through shield and cannon to sever an armored limb, or it could split a steel helm in half.

Again, his weapon bounced off the ullroct's body.

The ullroct didn't appear to be moving quickly, until suddenly it did, grasping hold of the nearest soldier. It lifted the man, armor and all, and he ignited like an oil-soaked wick. The creature raised itself onto its knees, then threw the burning soldier over the treetops as easily as Kyrionik would hurl a loaf of bread.

Shulipik's glaive was notched in two places. Kyrionik had never heard of a ghostkind weapon being notched—had heard it was impossible, in fact. The ullroct stood and raised its other hand. Its truncheon grew longer, becoming like a baton, then a singlestick, then as long as a quarterstaff.

"Your virtue, you must flee. They've sworn—"

The ullroct pivoted and swung its iron staff. Shulipik moved to parry, but he was too slow. The ullroct's weapon sank deep, crumpling Shulipik's breastplate like paper and smashing his ribcage like an egg shell.

"—to defend you, but you waste their lives if you linger."

Kyrionik sprinted down the stairs again, goosebumps prickling his back.

The strange alien cries of the glitterkind echoed through the jungle. There could be no breath behind those voices, because they never paused.

The column of light must have been visible for fifty miles, and the wind blowing into his face smelled of smoke, which was all wrong but his thoughts were whirling and he couldn't understand why.

Shulipik was dead. Everything had gone wrong and it was his fault. He should have kept watch over Selso Rii personally, should have ordered him back to the ship once he'd pointed the way, should never have come here not ever ever ever. His First Labor had failed, and the consequences he would face in Koh-Salash—humiliation, a reputation for recklessness that would make people think him unfit to lead, his mother's political embarrassment—suddenly seemed petty.

The slope became steep and the stairway switched back. Kyrionik leaped through the bush onto the lower set, his thoughts racing. He would order the soldiers to drop their prize and strip off their armor. Their steel spears and swords were useless against the ullroct's iron body anyway. He'd call a full retreat down the side of the cliff. The captain could cast her chamber pots into the shallow waters to drive off the hunting jellies, and his guard could swim to the ship.

The smell of smoke came more strongly. The wind was blowing into his face, but the ullroct was behind him. Had someone built a fire?

The stairs ended at the base of a broad tree that had grown between two ruins. Part of the underbrush had been hacked away, and Kyrionik pressed through the cleared path, raising his spear to keep the point from fouling in the underbrush.

In the center of the ruins of Childfall, brush and toppled trees burned in several places. Kyrionik suddenly heard shouting voices and the sound of metal striking metal. More smoke blew into his face.

He understood what he was seeing at the same moment he saw it before him. An ullroct was attacking the troops in Childfall.

Kyrionik glanced back. Smoke was visible through the trees. The first ullroct was still behind him. This must be a second. He vaulted over a fallen tree and saw the scene in full.

This ullroct was even larger than the other, standing nearly fifteen feet tall, but the flames on its body burned lower than the one upslope. Its iron staff was almost twice its height, and it swept the weapon from side to side, as though driving away wolves.

But it wasn't wolves. It was Kyrionik's guard. The glitterkind stretcher had been dropped a few dozen feet short of the fully constructed boom. The ullroct stood over the glitterkind the way a human warrior would protect a wounded comrade. It swung its staff once, twice, three times, missing the people but shattering a spear shaft and another time striking a tree trunk hard enough to make burning chunks of bark fly out.

Then suddenly Kyrionik saw them. Here and there, at the very edge of the plateau, lay wounded soldiers. A man with crumpled legs, a woman bleeding from the scalp, another woman whose right arm ended at the elbow. Once he saw the wounded, trembling and thrashing in pain, he saw the armored, unmoving dead, too.

The soldiers who were still standing, about ten in all, were trying to lunge close enough to the glitterkind to cut off a finger or a toe. They were trying to steal magic to save their comrades.

They leaped forward, only to dodge back as the staff swept by them. When the creature turned its weapon to the left, the soldiers on the right advanced. When it turned to the right, soldiers opposite tried to move in. But they couldn't get close enough to make a cut.

Then, unexpectedly, the ullroct went too far to the left, pursuing one of the soldiers an extra step. On the opposite side, a woman bent low and lunged toward the feet of the prone figure, sword held high.

The ullroct spun with shocking quickness, and its staff extended almost as fast. A feint. It struck the lunging woman on the top of her shoulder.

The blunt end of the staff plunged into her, snapping the leather strap that held her breastplate in place. Her face went slack.

Someone screamed in outrage, and Kyrionik thought it might have been himself. The ullroct swung its staff and, with a sudden flick, flung her body away.

One of the soldiers tried to duck, but he wasn't quick enough. The corpse hit him hard, carrying him over the edge of the cliff.

Morale broke. The other soldiers threw down their spears and ran. The ullroct pursued, slamming its staff down onto one of the fleeing humans, who died without a sound.

Shame and rage bloomed inside Kyrionik. These men and women were dying because of him. Because of his arrogance. He sprinted toward them with no clear idea of what he should do.

A soldier standing beside the boom shouted, then drew back his spear as if to hurl it at the glitterkind. The throw was another feint, but it was convincing enough that the ullroct stopped its pursuit to crouch protectively in front of the helpless giant.

The fleeing troops turned at the sound of the shout and saw that the spear wielder, having drawn the ullroct off, was facing it alone. He backed toward the edge of the cliff. Kyrionik suddenly realized there was a white plume on his helm.

That was Oblifell.

Its back to Kyrionik and the rest of the soldiers, the ullroct regained its feet. Oblifell edged away, stepping dangerously close to the edge of the cliff, then feinted another throw. The ullroct was ready to swat away any attack. Oblifell backed away two more steps, and the ullroct followed.

Kyrionik sprinted into the clearing, then leaped up onto the glitterkind's torso. Selsarim Lost, it was still awake—eyes open, mouth gaping.

It did not move. When Kyrionik ran across its chest and planted his boot on its face, it did not try to bite him in half.

Just as the ullroct bent down to grab Oblifell in one of those spidery hands, Kyrionik leaped from the top of the glitterkind forehead.

The creature was too big and too far away to hit its back, but he landed against its legs, the edge of his shield driving in hard to fold its knee.

Up close, Kyrionik could see that the ullroct's iron body was ridged in spiral patterns as though its limbs been formed by twisting them. What he'd taken for rust was actually patches of bristling hair, and that was where the flames seemed most fierce.

As they fell together, the ullroct's fire engulfed Kyrionik's shield, his arm, and the left side of his body. He was surprised that there was no pain, and then suddenly the pain was there, bright and hot and worse than anything he'd ever felt in his life.

The ullroct stumbled forward, close to the edge but not over it. It tried to right itself and the ground gave way. Without a sound, the creature fell out of sight.

Kyrionik's momentum nearly carried him over, too, but something caught hold of his leg and yanked him painfully back. Oblifell dragged him away from the cliff.

There was a loud splash. The ullroct had hit the water, and a plume of steam billowed over them, blowing into the jungle. Had the water doused its fire and destroyed it? Was it dead?

Oblifell kicked the burning shield away and began to slap Kyrionik's shoulder and rib cage. Mud. Oblifell was extinguishing the flames with sopping wet mud. Kyrionik jammed his burning left hand into the soil, flipping it over and back again to force cooling mud into the gauntlet.

A woman ran up with a bucket and began to pour the water into the gaps in his armor.

"Hold still, your virtue. We'll get you out of here. By the fallen gods, I knew you had valor, boy, but… You! Draw your dagger, and—"

"No!" Kyrionik forced himself to sit upright. The flames were out, but his arm and side still felt like they were burning. "No one is to touch the glitterkind."

The soldier stood nearby, dagger in hand. He looked from Kyrionik to Oblifell, frozen with indecision.

"Your virtue, your injuries—"

"Oblifell, an amateur's cut is what summoned the ullroct. Besides, there are many hurt worse than I am." He tried to clench his fist inside the gauntlet, but the pain was intense. He was going to be scarred for life.

Kyrionik stood, trying not to stagger from the pain. "We have to get everyone off the island. Can we lower the injured on the boom? They could be put in a skiff and transported to *Fair Season*—"

"Your virtue—"

"The others will have to strip off their armor and swim—"

"Kyrionik!"

He fell silent. Oblifell had never spoken his given name before.

"Your virtue, look!" Oblifell led him to the edge of the plateau.

Fair Season was aflame, its nose pointing into the air. A last pair of sailors leaped into the water, joining a half-dozen others swimming hard for the stair at the bottom of the cliff. Two were pulled under. Hunting jellies swarmed toward the others.

"It's climbing back up!"

The soldier who had doused the fire in Kyrionik's armor pointed down another section of cliff. At the same moment, Oblifell pointed in the opposite direction.

On the long slope at the northern end of the island, treetops trembled and shook. Something huge was tearing through the jungle, moving straight toward them. The jungle on the slope above also trembled as

Selso Rii's ullroct descended.

Three ullrocts. One creature could destroy them all, but they were facing three.

The sun touched the horizon. In that moment, a strange cry echoed out of the jungle. Kyrionik had never heard anything like it. It sounded like a flock of screeching birds mixed with chirping crickets, and it was deafening. That wasn't a sound that could be made by a single throat, or even a dozen. That was the sound of hundreds of swarming enemies out in the jungle.

None of them were going to get off this island alive.

CHAPTER TWENTY-THREE

Culzatik ward-Safroy defe-Safroy admir-Safroy hold-Safroy followed his bodyguard into the Upgarden gem shop, then nodded to Gurrishil, child of Garrisala, the owner. The elderly fellow beamed back in a near-perfect display of sincerity.

Gurrishil was one of the wealthiest stitches in the Safroy sail, and their families did a great deal of business together—Culzatik's father had even arranged for the man's grandson to serve on the flagship of the Salashi navy. It was a much-coveted position, bringing him into close contact with noble families with both money troubles and unwed children.

Many common folk hoped their descendants could shed their "child of" and take on a noble title, but Gurrishil was one of the few who might see it happen.

Until then, he was a Safroy stitch, and the well-guarded rooms inside his well-guarded shop on this well-guarded deck were perfect for clandestine meetings. If the old fellow was less gracious about letting Culzatik use his room than he would have been to his noble mother or father, well, that was to be expected. The heirs of noble families were notoriously frivolous with other people's belongings.

Gurrishil's attitude would change. Eventually.

A woman who stood six foot two, with prodigious shoulders and an even more prodigious belly, emerged from one of those private rooms. She had to be a bodyguard—no one else would be admitted to an Upgarden shop with a sword and buckler.

Right behind her came Essatreska admir-Phillien.

Culzatik couldn't hide his surprise. "What— Essatreska, my betrothed, I— What a surprise to find you here."

She smiled slightly, clearly pleased to make him uncomfortable. "You're surprised to chance upon me while shopping? Perhaps you don't know me as well as I'd thought."

Today, her dress was the color of pale roses, tailored to cover her lovely figure from ankle to jawline, and the fit was so snug that it showed off her every curve. She was still sporting yellow on her nails—expensive things take longer to fall out of fashion—but now her hands were painted with flowering vines. Her lovely black hair was no longer shaped like a candle flame. It had been oiled and twisted into a dozen slender braids, then tied to a wire frame to make a small cage atop her head. Inside the cage was a pair of stuffed songbirds. The only adornment on her face were two trails of painted pale blue tears, as though the beauty of that imaginary birdsong made her weep.

For her part, Essatreska peered down at his ink-stained fingers and scowled very slightly.

"Perhaps not," Culzatik agreed. "You look as if you're dressed for a party."

"Some of us simply like to look nice." She glanced down at his ring and the clasp of his robe. "You Safroys stick the bull's head on everything, don't you?"

"Everything except our spouses."

"This is lovely," said a voice from the back, "but too showy. I'd hoped to find something that looked showy without being showy, if you know what I mean."

As the sentence finished, the speaker emerged from the private room. It was Ponnalas admir-Phillien. He handed Illia, Gurrishil's daughter, a bracelet of coiled gold that did not look particularly showy at all.

"Hello, Ponnalas," Culzatik said.

The older man threw his arms into the air. "Culzatik! So good to see you, my boy."

"And you. Buying yourself a party favor? Gurrishil's work is amazing."

"So they tell me," Essatreska said with a hint of disapproval. She handed a diamond bracelet to a servant, who handed it to Illia. The proprietor's expression turned stoic. He wasn't accustomed to hearing his work insulted.

Illia was more diplomatic. "I'm sorry it wasn't to your liking, your virtue." Essatreska waved dismissively. "I'll take it anyway. Wrap it as a gift."

Illia nodded and smiled. Then she made a mistake. She glanced expectantly at Culzatik.

Manners can be complicated when one works in a business catering to the wealthy and powerful. Any noble, even one without the wealth and power of the Safroys behind him, can cause a hell of a lot of trouble when they perceive an insult or challenge.

And Culzatik was well known to be both Essatreska's betrothed and the heir to a fortune. In a circumstance like this, some might expect him to pay. But to glance at him as if waiting for him to make the offer? That was bad form. That was one step away from attempting to shame him into emptying his purse.

The moment passed and Culzatik did not make the offer. His family could better afford it than the Philliens, no matter what the growing rumors hinted, but he smiled pleasantly at Illia until she became embarrassed and slipped away, muttering about writing up a bill of sale.

Ponnalas, of course, was so caught up staring at the piece Essatreska had chosen that he missed it all. "Best not get anything for me," he said. "My daughter is showy enough for the both of us."

"Shopping together?" Culzatik asked.

"For today," the older man answered. "My daughter's bodyguard—the fellow who placed third in the tournament and is earning a top rate—has taken yet another personal day, so we have to share." He rolled his eyes at the inconvenience of it all, then leaned close to his daughter. "And I have much work still to do. Piles of it, my dear."

"We're just about done, Father."

Illia returned with the package and the note. Essatreska signed it and her servant pressed the family seal onto ink, then onto the paper. The package went to the servant. Ponnalas stared at it nervously, but Essatreska ignored him. "I will say that it's a surprise to see *you* here. I love to shop, but what use have you for Gurrishil's private viewing rooms?"

"I enjoy looking at beautiful things, my betrothed, although I suspect that seeing you has spoiled me for all this expensive jewelry." As they started to leave, Culzatik said, "Caflinna hasn't come over to see that book, Ponnalas. Did you forget to tell her?"

Ponnalas sighed. "My daughters," he said, and was gone.

* * *

FAY FOLLOWED MIRISHIYA OUT of the Undertower lift into Dawnshine. The Upgarden deck was no more than twenty-five feet over their heads, but it was early enough that the eastern sun shone slightly upward, casting shadows over their feet.

Despite appearances, Dawnshine was a prosperous deck. It was narrow and cramped, but the merchants living and working there either were hoping to move up into the most exclusive neighborhood in the city, or had made a niche for themselves as the equal of the Upgarden shops without the pretension.

The man they were going to see was in the export business, and very successful, too. It seemed unlikely to catch him there so early, but Mirishiya was convinced their trip would not be wasted.

The sign above the storefront they wanted read Long Diversion, and the proprietor was in his back office, although Fay had to produce his token to get the chubby assistant at the front to admit it.

The man who came out of the back was dressed well but not better than the clientele he'd expect to see, and his shoes had been chosen for comfort rather than style. His knuckles were scarred from years of hard labor, but his cheeks and midsection had grown soft. Apparently, his success was recent.

"Ah," he said in a way that suggested he was holding back his real opinion, "I'm Zikiriam admir-Vlosh tuto-Vlosh, the owner of this establishment. How can I help you?

Onderishta had taught Fay to keep his expression calm but sympathetic, and he did so now. "It's about the…item you sold at Suloh's Tower today."

"Ah. The bloodkind. Nothing illegal about that, is there? They're not people, are they?"

"No, nothing illegal about it," Fay said.

"It's about the boy you sent with it," Mirishiya said, demonstrating a good instinct for when to step in.

"Ah, yes, the boy I saved."

Mirishiya tilted her head. "But you're not the one who saved him, are you?"

Zikiriam admir-Vlosh tuto-Vlosh hesitated, then invited them into his office.

The space was spare. Except for a green carpet on the floor and a carved Harkan holy mask on the wall, it was as utilitarian as an office in Gray Flames. Zikiriam gestured that Fay and his apprentice should sit opposite his desk, then moved a stack of papers to one side. Then, without asking if they wanted any, he poured two cups of warm tea for them.

He finally sat down himself. "I did save that boy, for my part. I'm the one who brought him to the temple and got him the care he needed. I got him enrolled. But no, I'm not the one who drove off the bloodkind that was killing him."

"Who did?"

"A man I consider a friend," Zikiriam replied, "although I doubt he feels the same way about me. A man who saved my life and helped me create this business. A good man. I won't say anything to anyone who is trying to get him in trouble, right?"

"This is Kyrioc, child of No One, isn't it?"

"I won't help you against him. I just won't. I owe him too much."

"We don't want to collar him," Fay lied. "We're trying to help him. He's in trouble."

Zikiriam nodded. "He said as much to me this morning. He said he was being hunted."

"Do you see him often?"

"No." Zikiriam leaned forward and laid his fists on his desk. "Not for months. He came to me out of nowhere, without any warning, telling me he was being hunted. Then he saw a boy going under The Docks and somehow knew he was in danger. He went in to rescue the boy, and when he came out, he gave me a living bloodkind to sell and asked me to take responsibility for the boy."

Fay glanced at Mirishiya, and she glanced at him. She looked as confused as he felt. "Would you describe your friend?"

"Kyrioc? Tall, slender, strong. Needs a haircut. And he has a terrible scar on his face. Don't ask me how he got it. I never had the nerve to ask. That's the man you're looking for?"

"The description fits," Fay admitted. "But I confess that I'm confused by your story. Does every child who goes under The Docks disappear?"

Zikiriam pursed his lips. "Well, no. They dart in and out all the time. But we also know that some bloodkind live on this side of the wall. Presumably. How he knew that particular child... I've heard that Kyrioc lived on The Docks for a time, when I first brought him here, so maybe he's seen something I haven't."

Suddenly, there were too many potential lines of questioning. Fay had to restrain himself from chasing after them like a hound trying to catch butterflies. "Good sir, what did he want with the boy?"

"To question him," the older man said. "The boy was a messenger for one of the gangs in the city. The Pails. He thought the boy might know something."

"And he questioned the boy?" Fay asked. "Did you overhear them?"

At this, Zikiriam became uncomfortable. "Well, ah, I *could* have. I was standing just above them at the edge of the deck. I could have. But I had just been handed the bloodkind all wrapped up in a cloak, and...you know...I was so astonished that the whole world seemed to go away. A naked woman could have run by and I would have missed it." He glanced at Mirishiya. "Er, my apologies."

"No need," she responded calmly.

"I didn't look up again until Kyrioc was pressing the boy on me, too, telling me I needed to get him medical care and take him on as an apprentice. Which I did. You'll find him at Suloh's Tower, although I've forgotten the boy's name. Ask out front for it."

Of course, Mirishiya had already talked to the boy in the tower. That was how they'd gotten Zikiriam's name. "Thank you. We will."

"And...I think that's all I know. What sort of trouble brings you here asking about Kyrioc?"

"A woman was killed," Fay said, mainly to see Zikiriam's response. "His neighbor."

"And you think they're after him next? By the fallen gods, I told him I could put him someplace safe—I would have given him a berth on the *Quiet Speech*, for free, so he could sail around the Semprestian for six months—but he wouldn't have it."

In Fay's experience, getting out of Koh-Salash was the logical step after attacking the constables. The only ones who didn't were either too stupid to understand the consequences, too frightened to come out of hiding, or convinced they had nowhere else to go. He wasn't sure how Kyrioc fit into those categories, or if he fit at all. "How did you meet him?"

"A story!" Zikiriam jumped out of his chair and refilled their cups with more tepid tea. "I was a sea captain for many years, you know, before I became rich enough to pay others to sail for me, and people of the sea love good stories. So! This was late winter of last year. Spring was still weeks away. Right? I had pulled in to a little river inlet community to pick up that season's lion skins, which Harkan refugees in Smithwood and Ionelto absolutely have to have for their sons' transition to manhood, and there I met a funny little guy who swore he could direct me to a dragon's midden."

"Oh," Fay said. Zikiriam had so far seemed a reliable witness, but if he was going to start telling folk tales...

The former captain couldn't contain his grin. He gestured to the room around him. "Right?"

A tingle ran down Fay's back. A sea captain shipping goods to refugees in backwaters like Smithwood was not on the path to success. He'd be lucky if he could pay his crew.

"Anyway," Zikiriam continued, "the price was right because this was Harka, and everyone there is desperate for something, but it cost me just about everything I had. But they were beautiful." He cupped his hands in front of him as though holding his prize. "Gleaming, gorgeous yellow metal in the shape of massive turds.

"Now, a smart man would have just knifed the seller, kept his money, and sailed away, no questions asked. Unfortunately, I'm not a smart man. I'm an honest one. I paid the fellow and swore him to secrecy. But, as we pulled out of the inlet, a pirate's carrack came at us, tacking against the wind. I wanted to head northeast to the Free Cities, where the gold merchants compete ferociously, but the pirate stayed on our stern. Are you familiar with the exploits of the captain and crew of *Scream for Mercy*?"

Fay and Mirishiya shook their heads.

The captain spread his hands. "Not surprising, honestly. But among those of us who sail the waves, they were infamous.

"We had no choice but to turn westward, into the Parsu Deliverer, and flee for our lives. Not that we're cowards, you understand, but even if my ship had a full crew, the pirates would have outnumbered us three to two. Besides, I'm not much for fighting an enemy with archers in the rigging and the coin to arm every man and woman with a steel sword.

"The upshot is that they drove us out of the Semprestian into deep water. I had no charts for waters so far west. I never sailed there nor had any reason to. Worse, the weather gave me no stars to sail by. But I tried every trick I could think of, short of turning about and engaging my pursuer hand to hand. Nothing worked. As days of pursuit turned into weeks, I realized the Harkan had sold them word of our cargo, and they would follow us into the ghostkind-haunted lands of the west for that much gold.

"Now, you may be aware that there are volcanic islands out in the ocean. Not exactly an archipelago, you understand, but clusters here and there. By the time we spotted them, my crew was drinking their own piss—begging your pardon for the language—and were talking about dying quickly by sword rather than the slow agony of dehydration and seawater poisoning. I had a mind to restock at one of those islands and, while the pirates did the same, slip away eastward. So, we sailed around the largest of the islands, looking for a place among all those cliffs where a thirsty crew could come ashore.

"Late in the day, we had an unexpected boarder. No one knew where he'd come from at first, but his bare feet hit the boards with a loud *thunk*, and he was just standing there. There was a commotion, obviously, and the second mate charged with his knife drawn, but the boarder countered the mate's attack without hurting him, and I called for peace."

Here the old sea captain paused. Fay realized he was enjoying this.

"Our unexpected boarder was nothing impressive. His hair was long, matted, and filthy, with bits of greenery in it. He wore a girded cloth of a fabric I'd never seen before—something shimmery, like sharkskin—but it was in tatters. The only thing he had with him was a short length of black iron, barely as long as a truncheon.

"'Who are you,' I said, 'to come aboard my ship without permission?'

"He opened his mouth to answer, but it took a few seconds for the words to come. 'If you come to this island, this island will kill you all.'

"And that was all he said. The crew surrounded him, blades bared. They were about to cut him up and eat him, but I kept them steady. 'Without water,' I said, 'no sailor can live. And we don't have the time to search about, not with our enemy so close.'

"I pointed eastward, where Scream for Mercy held her position, waiting for us. I had no idea what they were doing for water themselves, but it spooked my crew just to mention it. But this boarder—who was Kyrioc, child of No One, as I'm sure you've guessed—peered across the waves at it. Then he said, simple as you please, 'If you promise to take me to Koh-Salash, I will kill everyone on that ship.'

"The crew just laughed, right? The first mate said there was a bounty on the captain, so he should take prisoners, too. Kyrioc shrugged and said it was 'acceptable.' The laughter faded a bit then, and I asked if he was mad or a fool.

"All he said was 'Delay the fight until after full nightfall, and give me something to eat. By morning, you'll have two ships. But first, you must get away from this island before it notices you.'

"Well, I don't mind saying that I took his advice. What did we have to lose? We moored at another island to the north, restocked our water from a little fall, and just before midnight were headed into deep water again. Kyrioc stood in the bow, directing us through the rocks, and the overcast night was so dark that I could only hear his voice. I couldn't see him.

"We were running before the wind while Scream for Mercy was reaching, so they caught up to us quickly. I heard their jeering before the twang of their bowstrings, and Kyrioc called for me to let them get close. A half-dozen of the crew, whether they were inspired or ashamed, appeared on deck with hatchets in hand, ready to join the fight, but Kyrioc told them to get below and keep out of his way."

Zikiriam paused. Now that he'd reached the climax of his tale, he looked a little lost. Fay felt Mirishiya glance at him, wondering why he didn't urge the man to continue, but silence was the best tool for that.

The sea captain spread his scarred hands. "I'm not telling this the way I normally do, you understand."

"How do you mean?"

"Well, if I'm telling this tale in a tavern or to a pretty girl, I embellish it. For one thing, I never tell anyone Kyrioc's name. He's always 'the mysterious boarder.' Partly out of respect for his privacy, you understand. Partly because I didn't know his name until days later. I'm not so sure it's his real name, anyway."

"Why not?"

Zikiriam shrugged. "Just a feeling. The way he said it. But if a man tells me his name is 'Pinch-Me Cock,' I'll say 'Pleased to meet you, Pinchy, my friend,' because why not? A person should be able to choose their own name, I say. So, it was just a feeling, and I didn't much care."

"And it makes a better story," Fay said, trying to get things back on track.

"You know what makes a great ending for this story?" Zikiriam said, leaning forward eagerly. "I tell them that when we finally arrived in Koh-Salash, delivering him back to his home port after so many weeks, I opened the berth and found him vanished. Sometime in the night, he had disappeared, just like a ghost. Oh, the ladies love that ending. If I think my audience is more conventional or sentimental, I'll describe a teary-eyed mother waiting at The Docks for him."

"But that's not what happened."

"Oh, no," Zikiriam said. "Not at all. We pulled into our slip. I offered him, once again, a share in the bounty for that pirate captain, or from the goods taken from his ship, or even just an honest job. He simply shook his head. All he took from me was a change of clothes and the meals we fed him aboard the ship. When he walked down the plank into the city, he didn't look back once."

"You were going to describe the fight," Mirishiya said.

"The fight is the best part of the story! Swift, bold strikes! One man against many! The pirate captain crippled! The pirate crew throwing down their weapons in terror! When I tell it, it's like an old tale of adventure.

"But the truth is I didn't see any of it. The night was darker than any I've seen before or since. The watch lanterns on *Scream for Mercy* seemed to wink out, as though a shroud had been thrown over them. I heard the clash of metal. I heard screaming. By the fallen gods, I heard screams that haunt my dreams to this day. But all I could see was growing darkness and the flicker of blue firelight."

"Blue?" Fay asked.

"Yes. I went to Suloh's Tower later to ask about blue flames. They can make them there, but it wasn't the same as the light I saw that night—icy blue fire that hovered in the darkness, while men and women screamed in terror and begged for their lives."

He looked around at his office as though it was evidence of something important, and perhaps it was. Kyrioc, child of No One—or whoever he was—had not just saved Zikiriam admir-Vlosh tuto-Vlosh's life that night. He'd changed it for the better. He'd made him a rich man.

Icy blue fire.

Zikiriam sighed. "Ruined."

Fay was surprised. "What was that? What was ruined?"

Zikiriam stared at his scarred hands. "Him. Kyrioc. The man who was trapped on that island for weeks or months. Whatever happened to him there, it ruined him."

* * *

ONDERISHTA SAT WITH HER eyes closed, reviewing everything she knew about the last few days. Where was Harl? Where was the package? Had that woman really been collected for her parts? And what was her relationship to that pawnbroker?

The curtain opened without any warning, and Culzatik entered. He glanced in the mirror, frowned, and tried to smooth his hair with one ink-stained hand. "Did she see you?"

He meant Essatreska, of course. "She did not, your virtue. Gurrishil brought me here before she arrived. I should say that I would be pleased to send you written reports—"

"I would be displeased to receive them," he said quickly. "Paper can be intercepted and altered. Face-to-face is more secure. Have you been putting those two apprentices to use?"

"I have, your virtue."

"Good. Keep them close and teach them. Trust them."

"Yes, your virtue."

"And please send the girl to me by the end of the day. I have a special task for her."

That was a surprise. Didn't the Safroys have a veritable army of people at their beck and call already? They were Onderishta's apprentices. Any tasks they needed to undertake should go through her.

But then, he had plans for her. "Do you intend to replace me, your virtue?"

"I do."

Onderishta could not have been more surprised if he'd sprouted wings. "I— I'm happy in my current occupation, your virtue. Haven't I served your family faithfully for many years?"

"Let's talk about it later. I hadn't planned to bring it up until after the Safroy family survived this threat. Acceptable?"

"Yes, your virtue," she said uncertainly.

"Good. Where do things stand?"

"A woman has turned up dead in Upgarden. I'm sure you've heard about it."

"Only the usual chancy gossip."

"In this case, the gossip is true. She was skinned and eviscerated as though being collected for a hospital. The medical bureaucracy thinks it's a trick to misdirect our investigation."

Culzatik nodded. "What do you think?"

"That she was placed on Harl's property so the scandal would deprive

216

him of the protection of his parsu."

"What about the package?"

Onderishta shrugged. "Either they found it or events made it unimportant. I figure it's the former, but I haven't heard enough to be sure. No one seems to be looking for it, at least."

"Do you think this corpse proves the package was what we think it is?"

What you think it is. "Not on its own, but lends weight to the theory."

"But you still think it could have been a delivery of white tar."

She sighed. Once upon a time, she could lie, blank-faced, to anyone. Now, even this boy could see through her. "It's possible, but I would be surprised. Harl has a little warehouse full of the stuff somewhere in the city, and more comes in every day. Would he go to such lengths for such a small amount? If he was hurting for money or if it was a brand-new special concentrate, maybe. Neither seems likely. Besides, Second Boar was paid a small fortune for that package, so I have my doubts that it could be tar."

Culzatik leaned back and rubbed his chin with an ink-stained hand. The ink was dry, thank the fallen gods. Onderishta had no intention of telling this well-heeled young man to wash his noble face.

"To appearances, then, Harl was expecting a delivery and he got two, neither of which he particularly wanted. And of course, the constables were right there to catch him."

"And several of his top heavies are still sitting in south tower cells. We're trying to track down the man who gave us the tip. All we know is that he's a Katr bodyguard for one of Harl's underlings. What we don't know if he was acting under orders or if he was betraying his employer."

"It's rare for a Katr to turn on his master, isn't it? All that honor and such?"

"Your virtue, if he's working for Harl's underlings, I'm guessing honor isn't his highest priority."

Culzatik smiled crookedly. "Did you know I made a study of bodyguards? The Free Cities have pit fighters, and they really hone their skills there. They also have that crazy pride that makes them fight to the death for some spoiled, snot-nosed Salashi heir. Usually, anyway. The Katr don't do that because their loyalties aren't for sale. Who serves and who commands is rigidly codified. So, I suspect that if a Katr is working for a bunch of low-level tar dealers, his honor is the only reason."

Onderishta couldn't imagine a concept of honor that allowed the selling of white tar to children, but at the same time, she couldn't see how her employer could have "made a study of bodyguards" and then hired a local woman who had placed near the bottom of the tournament and who went about armed with nothing but a pair of long knives.

However, it wasn't her place to question these things, even by her expression.

Onderishta said, "We're still hunting for Harl, although so many constables have taken his coin, it's hard to know who's tracking him and who's hiding him. And we're still trying to figure out who the scarred man is."

An odd look came over her employer's face. "What scarred man?"

She described him and his role in the raid at Harl's club, then his escape from the tower. Culzatik's narrow face darkened, and she decided not to mention the incident at Suloh's Tower with the bloodkind.

"I want to speak to this man."

"That's— Pardon me, your virtue, but that would be unwise."

A crooked smile came over his face. "Do you mean to forbid it?"

Yes. But she didn't dare say it aloud to this overconfident young man who'd lived his whole life up in the sunlight with his books. What did he know about the real Koh-Salash? What did he know about the way people lived inside the corpses? He didn't even have the common sense to hire a proper bodyguard. The skinny young woman who followed him around couldn't intimidate a greengrocer. "He's dangerous. Violent. He's probably the one who skinned that woman. He's definitely the man who delivered white tar to Harl. Besides, if the constables catch him on the street, after what he did in the tower—"

Culzatik shook his head. "I'm relying on you to prevent that. Have you heard about the man I chased out of my brother's funeral service?"

"Vaguely," she answered carefully. "This is the fellow who threw hot pepper into the eyes of the guards chasing him?"

As though enjoying a secret joke, Culzatik smiled again. "Perhaps. I wasn't there. But he had a scar, too." He laid his ink-stained hand on his face exactly where the Broken Man was scarred.

"You think they're the same?"

He shrugged. "Tell the constables whatever you have to, but bring him in alive. After I've met with him, we'll reassess."

"Is there anything else, your virtue?"

He sighed and affected a rueful smile. "I think we both know that's more than enough. Thank you, Onderishta."

They stood. "It is my pleasure to serve, your virtue. I'll send Mirishiya to your compound."

Onderishta pulled back the curtain and stepped into the main room of the shop. Custom required her employer to leave first if he wished, but she had a lot to do before that boy had her replaced.

CHAPTER TWENTY-FOUR

Tin *Pail had never* been to High Slope before. She'd never even gotten close enough to look at it. What would have been the point? The compounds in High Slope were for nobles… Actually, they were for rich nobles. People with noble blood who couldn't afford solid ground settled in The Folly or somewhere like that.

Now here she was, riding in a cart with Harl's head in a bag beside her, winding her way up The Boulevard. She'd left her brother back in Wild Dismal, looking after the white tar they'd taken from Harl's warehouse. Their bodyguard was with him mainly because, in this transition time, she was more worried about him than herself.

Soon, they would have to stick close. After today, she expected someone, somewhere would put a bounty on their heads.

It had better be a high one.

She nodded off, sleeping fitfully while the cart jolted and bounced. It had been a long night, stretching out into midmorning. Tin had a lot to do, and it wasn't the sort of work she could pawn off on her heavies. Or onto Wooden, for that matter. Preparations had to be made. First, High Slope. Second, Spillwater. Third, Low Apricot.

Then, if everything went according to plan, Koh-Salash would be hers. For as long as she could hold it.

She didn't realize she'd nodded off again until her driver said, "We're here, boss."

Tin took a deep breath, grabbed her bag, and hopped down from the cart. "Let's go."

She told the heavily armed and armored guard at the front gate that she had an important message from Harl. There was some fuss and delay about whether she needed to give it in person or whether she would be allowed to enter without being searched, but as she expected, they were too afraid of Harl's name to challenge his orders—even secondhand orders. Tin willingly turned her hammer over, and the house guard seemed pleased to have gotten that much of a concession from her.

The servant showing her the way was in a hurry, but Tin wasn't. She'd never seen so much decorated wood. Every wall was painted, every door carved with the most intricate designs: a sailing fleet, clasping lovers, twined jungle vines, stalks of wheat. And on the lintel above every door was the same mark, a mountain inside a circle.

Rueljun parsu-Lorrud ward-Lorrud defe-Lorrud admir-Lorrud hold-Lorrud was enjoying a late breakfast at a table set beneath an ancient apricot tree. Sitting with him was his wife, Luthella, and a young man with the same long, pointed nose and gloomy face as the old man. When the younger fellow saw Tin and her heavy approaching, he stood.

"Thank you, Uncle. I'm off to my appointment."

As the fellow passed, he kept his eyes downturned. Tin nearly laughed.

A man in a mail shirt entered from a second doorway. He walked gracefully, a machete in each hand. At his breast was a cloth insignia showing the encircled mountain. The Lorrud bodyguard.

The parsu of the Lorrud family was deep into old age. His hair had turned a dingy gray and the wattle at his throat hid the line of his jaw completely. His posture was hunched forward, like a scavenger bird, and he did not look comfortable as he turned toward her.

"What message could be so important that Harl interrupts my breakfast?"

"Only this, your virtue." Tin set the bag in the middle of the table, loosened the drawstrings, and let it drop, revealing Harl's swollen face.

Rueljun reeled back in his chair, his spoonful of stewed fruit clattering on his plate. He put his hands on the arms of his chair, as though about to rise up in anger, but instead let go with a helpless little tremor. The bodyguard stepped back three paces, his sword hand pressed over his mouth as though he were about to be ill. Only Luthella managed to keep her composure. She flinched in surprise, but only slightly. After a moment, she shrugged, spooned some jam onto a piece of bread, and continued her breakfast.

The parsu's voice was thin and strained. "What outrage is this, eh? What outrage is this?"

"Harl and me are making the rounds," Tin said. She pulled the bag over the head, cinched it, and tossed it to her heavy. "We're explaining how the world has changed, and helping people during a time when smart choices must be made."

"You're taking over for Harl," Luthella said.

"I am. You're going to support me the same way you supported him, and I'll be happy to tithe you like a proper stitch. And unlike Harl, I won't skim. I won't have to, since I won't be paying off our foreign friends."

Rueljun huffed. "Preposterous."

"We don't need coin," Luthella said mildly. "In fact, we don't even want it. We're too liquid as it is, and we don't dare spend the bulk of it. If we bought any more farmland, mines, ships, or trading houses, the High Watch would turn against us."

"Wouldn't like that," Rueljun muttered. "No, never."

Luthella folded her hands in her lap, a smile on her face. She was few years younger than her husband, and her eyes were large and expressive. Her hair was the color of steel, her gaze almost as cold and sharp.

She made Tin feel like a precocious child. Tin wasn't sure if she should admit that she admired the older woman or just plunge her thumb into one of those pretty eyes.

"What Harl brought us," Luthella continued, "was connections within the Carrig empire. Silks, peppercorns, aromatics— Have you seen the latest fad for steel jewelry? Rings and necklaces and such? We prompted that. You see, we import these goods at such reasonable prices and then sell them again at a slender profit or give them as gifts. Lavish gifts. To our friends."

Rueljun grunted. "It's the only way."

"Exactly, dear. Tell me, young woman, do you think the High Watch tolerates—*tolerated*, I suppose I should say—our support of a foreign gangster? They hate it. They really do. But they don't hate it as much as they love having nice things."

"Especially," the old man grunted, "when the nice things are right in their homes for guests to admire, while the gangster is out of sight, ruining some common person's life."

"Among the noble families, being a distribution point for splendor gives us a remarkable degree of influence. Young woman, can you keep those trade arrangements open?"

Just being asked was annoying. "No."

Luthella spread her palms. "Well, then."

Tin pulled out the young man's chair and sat. "You don't want money? All right, then. The stick." She tore off a piece of bread and spooned some of the stewed fruit onto it. The handle of the spoon was also marked with that Lorrud mountain. Maybe they did that so they could reclaim stolen property. "That pathetic mop handle that just left? Your nephew, yes?"

"My heir," Rueljun said with a dismissive wave of his hand.

"If we can't come to terms, or if you move against me, I'm going to destroy him."

The old man chuckled. "My nieces and nephews outnumber your pickpockets and bully boys. He can be replaced."

"Dear," Luthella said gently, "she's not talking about killing him."

The stewed fruit was delicious, as expected, but it was the bread that surprised Tin. It was the chewiest, freshest bread she'd ever had. "Wow. Delicious. Your wife is right. People die every day. But killing your heir wouldn't do me much good in the long term. No, I'd arrange to have him found naked, surrounded by empty jugs of brandy, a smear of white tar, and a dead orphan boy."

The old man huffed in surprise. "By the fallen gods—"

"And that would just be the start. A pair of constables I run would start spreading the rumor that Naufulin, child of Namfalis, the investigator your family controls, has covered up scenes like this before. Then a little sepulcher with four or five more bodies would be discovered, and your nephew's ring would be among them. He thinks he's lost it somewhere here in your compound, I expect, but I have it."

The old man glared at her, but Luthella kept smiling. The only evidence that she understood the threat she was facing was that she seemed to be studying Tin's face carefully for the first time. "Young woman, are you sure you want to make enemies of us?"

It was the older woman's first misstep, and it made Tin feel bold. She smiled crookedly. "I'm one of those *common people* who suffer out of your sight, so fuck you. Besides, we already have your nephew."

Luthella pursed her lips. "What do you mean?"

"He was supposed to meet someone at the south tower about Suloh's gift, yeah? Someone recommended him?" Both Luthella and Rueljun seemed shocked that Tin knew that. "Well, that invitation is counterfeit. I sent it. And by this time, he's tucked away in the back of a carriage somewhere, pissing his pants at the bared steel around him. If you two refuse my deal, you get the scandal instead. Or, I should say, the first scandal, because we can do it again with a Carrig merchant and a detailed map of the city walls, or maybe a map of the Steward-General's family compound. How much are your noble friends going to love your *nice things* when they think you're harboring spies and assassins?"

Rueljun leaned toward her. "I could have you—"

"Be quiet, dear," Luthella interjected.

Tin had them.

Luthella straightened her robe. For the first time since Harl's head had been put away, she looked uncomfortable. "You know how to wield a stick."

"But I haven't swung it yet," Tin said. She popped a small piece of bread in her mouth. Amazing. She was never going to enjoy the plain bread she got in the city again. "And I'm still offering the carrot. Harl has been bleeding this city dry for years. Gambling, white tar, whores, thieves, rackets, the whole deal. He's been shipping piles of gold back to Carrig, and what have we gotten out of it? Silks and spices bought at a discount for the benefit of the noble families. It's pathetic. It's practically treason. So. Here's how it's going to work from now on. You, Rueljun parsu-Lorrud ward-Lorrud defe-Lorrud admir-Lorrud hold-Lorrud, will be my parsu and I'll be one of the many humble stitches in your sail. I'll tithe to you, and in return—"

"Not from the white tar," Rueljun interrupted. "We don't take money from that. We don't want it."

Tin studied him a moment. He seemed to be sincere, and she stifled the urge to sneer. Did he think... No, it didn't matter what he thought. "And in return, you will do for us what you did for Harl: protect our people from the bureaucracy and the constables, help us secure deeds and titles that we need, and ensure that the High Watch does not make a serious effort to wreck our business. And don't worry about being *too liquid*. From now on, you'll be paying full price for the luxury goods that give you so much influence."

The old man's expression was sullen and resentful. He wasn't used to having terms dictated to him. "And if we decide to have you killed?"

Tin shrugged. "No one chases this prize without risking everything, and no one who does what I do expects to die quietly in their sleep, either, with lots of gray hair and little grandchildren. Someone will kill me. Maybe it will be you. Whoever does it will have to pay in blood and broken bones. I'm sure the High Watch will be overjoyed to see you ignite another Downscale War over your child-killing nephew and foreign gangster friends."

That, finally, ended the discussion.

"Three days," Luthella said. "If you're still alive in three days, and still in Harl's position, you'll become our stitch."

Rueljun sat upright. "My dear—"

"Three days," she said again, ignoring him. "You seem clever enough, but the Lorrud name goes all the way back to Selsarim. It means something. We can't just throw the full weight of our seal behind every boastful, ambitious criminal. Prove yourself capable of keeping your place *and keeping order*, and you'll be our stitch."

Tin hesitated, then pulled another knot from the loaf on the table. She stood. "Agreed. You'll have your nephew back in four days if I'm still alive and your word is good."

"It is." Luthella had regained her composure but not her smile. "You haven't told us your name."

"I'm called Tin Pail."

Rueljun looked confused, but his wife did not seem surprised. "Harl sent a message about you. He wanted Naufulin to mobilize the constables, flush you out, and hang you. But after that business in Upgarden with that harvested corpse, we weren't sure if we should act. And now we see that it's too late." She shrugged. "No great loss to the world. But… Tin Pail, you say? How prosaic."

Tin had never heard that word before in her life, but she got a sense of its meaning from the way Luthella said it. "Thank you."

* * *

THE FIRST THING RILISKA did when she woke was search the spa. As she'd hoped, there was a set of paints and brushes shoved into one of the cabinets, partially covered by some old linens. There was no yellow, of course, because that color was new, and the other colors were dry and cracked from having been locked away for so long. She would need a few drops of olive oil to make the red usable again, but the green and black needed only a drop of clean water each, and while the baths were dry, some of the fountains still worked.

She found the other kids at breakfast in a large room with mortared stone floors. She couldn't imagine what the room was for originally, but the stone felt nice against her bare feet. A little space was open at the end of the kids' table, and Riliska sat there.

Their meal was crackers and roasted pigskins. It tasted good, even if it was the kind of cheap food her mom said would pockmark her face. Also, it wasn't enough, but there were so many little ones that Riliska was afraid eating her fill would mean they went hungry. They looked like they went hungry all the time.

Grownups ate at another table on the far end of the room. They had real bread, fish preserves, and a crock of honey. The thought of salty fish reminded her of the Broken Man, but none of the heavies there looked like they might share.

When she finished eating, she offered to paint the nail of the little girl beside her. The girl couldn't have been older than five. She meekly offered up her hand.

The effect that one painted pinky nail—which Riliska made into a sleepy-eyed cat—had on the other kids was astonishing. They crowded around, jostling to be next. Riliska scolded a girl her own age after she pushed a little one, and the girl had the decency to blush.

After that, they were excited but orderly. Riliska explained the technique as it had been taught to her. Never move your wrist. Either make a short stroke with your fingers, or a long one with your whole arm. The kids mimed her movements, practicing with invisible brushes. A small boy brought a spoonful of oil from the grownup's table so she could use the red, too. The oldest boy brought her another plate with three crackers on it, and she said thank you.

It was fun. It had been a long time since she'd had other kids sitting close, paying attention to her. It was the best feeling in the world, and Riliska hoped it would never end.

Her hand and wrist got sore before she ran out of hands to paint, so she taught the boy who brought her extra food to do an owl.

A little girl no older than six approached Riliska. She'd gotten a happy kitten on her thumb, but now she looked frightened. "I don't think we're allowed," she said, displaying her hand.

Riliska glanced at the grownups. One was telling the others a story, and the others leaned forward, eyes wide and mouths gaping. They didn't seem to know the kids were there. "Why not?"

"Because."

Riliska had never had a sister, but she knew what to do. She put her arm around the little girl and turned her toward the distant grownups. "If it was forbidden, they would have stopped us, don't you think?"

The girl shrugged, then leaned against her, and Riliska felt an unfamiliar maternal kindness. The ache for her missing mother suddenly grew so strong that tears welled in her eyes.

It felt good to comfort someone smaller. She wished her mother would try it herself.

The door opened, and everyone stopped what they were doing. A big man with wild red hair entered the room. Tiny bells chimed as he walked. He shrugged out of his long, sleeveless coat with a fur collar—Riliska could see something long and heavy hanging inside—and hung it on a peg. His pale left cheek was swollen and there was a cut under his right eye. Someone had tried to beat him up.

The children were completely still, staring at the man as though he might pluck one out of the crowd and eat them. To her surprise, Riliska noticed the grownups had the same expression. They were scared of him too.

He moved to the grownup table. The heavies sitting there slid out of their chairs and moved away, not turning their backs until the red-haired man was seated. The man didn't seem to mind, but Riliska thought he looked lonely.

Rummaging through the paint set, Riliska pulled out the largest of the brushes. She couldn't imagine what it was used for. Her mother had taught her to make slender, delicate lines. Maybe it was an old set for a style that was out of fashion.

She brought the brush into the fountain and washed it in the icy trickle from the carved mouth in the wall. Then she fetched a linen from the cabinet where she'd found the paint set, and soaked that, too.

The moment before she returned to the big room, she had a momentary fear that the red-haired foreigner would have already left, but no, he was still there, chewing silently. Riliska hurried toward him. He wasn't ugly, but his pale pink skin made him look sickly. He gave her the same blank look he'd given the grownups when she approached the table.

"This is for you, good sir," she said, holding out the wet linen. "My mommy says that a cold compress keeps the swelling down. Men hit her sometimes, and she says this makes sure she stays pretty." The foreigner stared. She laid it gently on his cheek. "Not that you're pretty. I suppose you're not too bad-looking, for a foreigner, but my mom says we have to take all the help we can get." He didn't take the cloth from her, so she said, "Hold this, please."

He did. She smiled at him and held up the brush. "Don't worry. I just washed this." The nearest wooden plate had a clean spot on the corner. Riliska poured a drop of honey onto it, dipped the brush, then lifted it to his face.

"My mommy says that even small cuts can get infected, and doctors are expensive."

Riliska began to dab the honey onto the cut below his eye. The foreigner still hadn't spoken to her, and she had run out of ideas on how to make him start.

He stared at her as though she was a ghost.

This was one of the men who took her mother away. Maybe he knew where she was. Riliska wasn't sure how she could work her mother into the conversation again without directly asking to see her.

Better just to try. "Good sir," she said, "do you know—"

The door banged open, startling her. In walked the wild-eyed man with the steel chain around his neck. The one who had tortured Riliska's mom.

Others followed, but Riliska didn't look at them. She backed away quickly, her gaze on the floor.

"Get some sleep?" a woman asked.

"I did," the red-haired man answered as he stood. His voice sounded thick, like he was talking out of the back of his throat.

"Good. One more meeting. And I need you to be ready."

One of the gangsters brought the foreigner his odd coat and he put it on. Riliska risked a look at him. He was watching her, his eyes blank and his expression unreadable. He tore off a piece of bread with scarred, bloodied hands, then followed the others out the door.

Riliska had missed her chance.

* * *

"ARE THEY THERE?"

Tin waited for her heavy to answer. His name was Ink Mouse, and he was supposed to be Paper's cousin or something. At the moment, he was staring at the ground, lost in thought.

Wooden leaned forward and slapped the back of his head. Ink came to life and blurted, "What? Oh! Yes, boss. The last of them just arrived. Sorry. I was thinking about…"

He was thinking about Paper, of course. Tin had grown up with Paper Mouse. He'd once been a snotty kid trailing behind her and her brother, hoping for a leftover crust of bread. When Tin and Wooden had gone to sea, Paper had wept like a new-made orphan. When they'd returned, years later, with their Katr in tow, he'd fallen in behind them like an old soldier glad to march to war again.

But he was stupid enough to let that scarred pawnbroker stick him with his own knife when she needed him most, so fuck him. Who could she trust to take his place?

As they descended the stairs to the Spillwater deck, they came upon a group of young street toughs coming the other way. They were just stupid, swaggering kids—no older than twelve—but they reacted to her and her people the way she had in her day—they took on a tough posture and stood in the center of the stair for a moment too long, then got the fuck out of the way.

She fucking hated Spillwater. It was dark. It stank. The people were the dumbest assholes in the world. Mudside might have been a lawless hellhole of animals in human skin, but Spillwater, which stood just above, with its leaking overhead sewer pipes and copper-knot whores who'd gut you for a ragged cloak, was a place of vicious desperation and savagery.

This downcity shitpile was another reason she was glad Harl was dead. He'd let it fester. Tin was going to clean it up.

They reached the bottom of the stair and looked down the road at the crooked hovels, piles of trash, and puddles of murky water.

"Ugh," Wooden said, smoothing the cuff of his silk tunic. "This place."

Tin clapped him on the shoulder, and they walked around to the back of the stair.

They were on the southwestern corner of the Spillwater deck, far from the fresh air and daylight of the eastern edge of the city. A line of torches slanting upward caught her eye, and Tin stood for a moment, staring west toward Salash Hill.

Most goods that entered the city from the water came by way of The Docks, but for the most valuable cargo headed to the wealthiest merchants in Upgarden—and their noble customers—The Docks, with their thieving dockhands and corrupt constables, wasn't good enough.

For them, there was a back way—a steep stone road that went up Salash Hill directly to an Upgarden distribution point. It was always brightly lit and closely guarded. Even though it passed within ten feet of Wild Dismal, Tin had never been able to dip her hands into that trade.

She wondered whether Harl had managed what she could not.

At the edge of the Spillwater deck, she looked down into Mudside. A few torches burned there, mostly on the massive ribs of Yth's back and to the east along the spine. Evidence of life, of a kind.

Beside her was a squat, square building. It had been constructed not on the Spillwater deck itself but on a platform of normal wood that extended out over Mudside. The tar on the roof was still wet, but considering how quickly it had been slapped together, Tin was pleased.

Wooden passed her a clay oil lamp with a stubby wick at the end. Ink Mouse held an identical one, already lit. They touched wicks to share the flame.

Her bodyguard was as cool as ever. As for Wooden, his eyes were bright and his smile so wide, his mouth was hanging open. The only hint that he felt nervous was the way he absentmindedly stroked his steel chain.

Ink Mouse was sweating. If they survived the next few minutes, he was going back to grunt work. Coward's work.

As for Tin herself, this was the final test. She would take Harl's throne or die trying.

Her bodyguard pushed the door open. She followed him inside.

There was only a large single room a little over fifteen feet square. The wooden floor was bare. There were no cloths on the walls and no windows. The door and lintels had no carvings. The only openings came from the door, ill-fitting planks in the walls, and a smoke hole in the roof. There were benches along the wall and little oil lamps like the one Tin carried mounted on tiny shelves. The room was gloomy and the air close.

There were sixteen people inside. Tin knew the important ones. Immediately to her left was Dirty Straw, the youngest of Harl's lieutenants, along with three of his heavies. He was only a few years older than Tin, not yet thirty. He had earned his place by working out a new scheme for getting white tar off The Docks and into the city without attracting the attention of the cosh.

To his left was Cotton Stair, who had been Harl's top heavy for years before being trusted to run part of the city. Every member of his organization came up through the same street gang he did. They were all Stairs of one kind or another, and they valued loyalty and dim-witted brutality.

Standing in the far corner, almost directly opposite the door where Tin entered, was a group of four Carrig thugs. Their leader had fucked up in a big way and had been sent to his uncle in Koh-Salash, although it was unclear if that was punishment, apprenticeship, or a mixture of the two. Tin didn't know which were heavies and which the lieutenant. In their homeland, they did their fighting barehanded, although they were smart enough to be wearing hatchets and knives now.

And finally, with almost the entire right half of the room to herself, was Black Apricot, who had taken over for her sister when she'd been hanged. Tin Pail had always believed that gangsters didn't get to grow old, but Black was the exception. Her gray hair was cut very short, almost to her skull, and the sagging, wrinkled skin over her eyes could not disguise the shrewdness there. Her people had a ferocious loyalty to her, and Tin considered her the second most dangerous person in the room.

"By the fallen gods," Tin said, holding her lit lamp high. "It's dark in here."

Dirty Straw stepped toward her. "Who are you and what are you doing here?"

"That's Tin Pail," Black Apricot said. "Harl was planning to move you up in his organization, wasn't he? You brought the beetle system to Koh-Salash. But you fucked up the deal he set up for you. And that was after I told him word on the street was that you were pretty sharp." She clucked her tongue in disappointment.

Cotton Stair folded his massive arms across his chest. Dirty Straw narrowed his eyes. "Why did Harl call us here in secret? And why are you here?"

Tin smiled. "I'm here to bring Harl to the meeting."

At that, Wooden stepped forward and overturned the bag. Harl's rotting head made a sickening noise as it struck the floorboards. Then Wooden kicked it, sending it rolling across the floor to the Carrig gangsters.

The tallest and ugliest looked down at that gray sagging face and cried,

"Uncle Harl!"

That was the one. Tin threw the clay lamp with all her strength. It broke against his chest, flooding his throat and face with burning oil. Pain and shock made him inhale raw flame, and that was it. Once the fire had bent inward to his throat, nothing could save him short of a portion of glitterkind.

Wooden burst out laughing. She was a little envious of his ability to enjoy this sort of thing. To her it meant nothing, but it made him wildly happy. Maybe, when things were settled, she'd light people on fire for him just for fun.

When the heavies drew their weapons, so did Tin's bodyguard. Black Apricot immediately raised her hand. "Hold!" she commanded, and they did.

The Salashi gangsters did, at least. The three Carrig heavies screamed in rage and drew their hatchets. They did not take orders from Salashi.

Two threw their hatchets at Tin, and she just stood there while her bodyguard struck both out of the air with a swing of the handle of his glaive. Then, in one motion, he joined the two halves into one.

Knives in hand, the three Carrig heavies charged. Her bodyguard made short work of them.

The only sound in the room was the crackling of flames and the thrashing of Harl's nephew as he died. Cotton nudged one of his heavies, who put the man out of his misery with the blunt end of a hatchet.

Black Apricot chuckled. "Three killed with two strokes. So, it's true, then? You hired a foreigner with godkind magic?"

Black's own heavies stepped back in surprise, and so did the others. Dirty's lip was curled as though he smelled something awful. "How did you manage that?"

"Planning," Tin answered. "Here's the deal. The people of Koh-Salash are proud of the fact that they've never been conquered, and they say that because they don't know about assholes like Harl. The criminal underworld in this city was conquered decades ago, and our Carrig masters have been bleeding us white. No longer. I won't allow it."

Cotton snorted, then spoke for the first time. "*You* won't allow it? Are you taking over for Harl, then? I wouldn't follow this stripling here"—he pointed at Dirty with his thumb—"and you're even younger. If someone's taking over, it should be one of us."

"Yeah," Tin said. "It *should* have been one of you. Years ago. But you didn't, and now your chance is gone."

Dirty glanced at the burning body. The flames had spread to the floor around him and begun to climb the wall to the tarred roof. "We should have this conversation somewhere else."

"Why?" Tin asked mildly.

Black laughed harder. "Planning, eh?"

Tin shrugged and glanced at Wooden. He was grinning, but she only felt annoyed and impatient. "Let me make it simple. My people killed Harl. I have his latest shipment of white tar, and I have already taken control of his black-market medical operation." The lieutenants glanced at each other. Clearly, they had tried to find that information for themselves and failed. "I also have the support of his parsu, who will continue to watch over us as usual. If one of you really wanted to take over, you should have done all this for yourself."

"I couldn't," Dirty said. "I don't have enough heavies to take on Harl, not to mention the Amber Throne he represents. The Ancient Kings built that chair."

"And the Amber Throne has its Clutching Hand," Black said quietly. "Deadly assassins that can walk through walls, carrying blades no one can see. Have you planned a way to defy them, too?"

Tin shrugged. "I don't explain myself to my lieutenants…or to charred corpses"

Dirty and Cotton glanced nervously at the spreading flames. Time was running out.

"What do you want from us?" Black asked.

"First, I want to know who hired that pawnbroker to attack my people." Dirty, Cotton, and Black all exchanged confused looks. Whoever it was, they hid it well. "Scarred face? Worked at a pawnshop in Woodgarden? He exposed the site of Harl's black market doctors to the cosh."

Black pointed at the spreading flames. "He ran Woodgarden. You should have asked him. Besides, none of us would unleash the cosh on that scam. Take it over, sure. Hand it to the eye, never. We like money."

Tin shrugged. The fire was bright now, and the hole in the roof couldn't evacuate all the billowing black smoke. "In that case, we should do whatever it takes to keep business running as smoothly as possible. All you have to do is pledge your loyalty to me and make me believe it."

* * *

ONDERISHTA COULD SCARCELY BELIEVE IT.

Rumors were spreading among the constables that Harl was dead. Someone was walking around, showing his head to his people and demanding their loyalty.

Then they'd heard about this place.

It was a weaver's workshop. A family of half a dozen men and women lived and worked in the back and sold their cloth in the front. They were in The Folly, one of the city's "safe" neighborhoods. In fact, at that moment, Onderishta was standing only four blocks from her own little house. Just around the corner was Zetinna's favorite dumpling shop, and they walked right by this building to go there.

The workshop's front door was splashed with blood, and the rooms inside were a charnel house.

She sent four constables through the building to make sure it was safe, and their faces were ashen when they emerged. No one wanted to estimate the number of dead, but some, she was told, resembled Harl's top people.

Their first job was to reattach all those body parts and figure out if one of them was Harl himself.

Fay hurried around the corner, a doctor's assistant in tow. Onderishta knew her well. She was tall, athletic, and gorgeous, but she rarely looked anyone in the eye, and nothing seemed to upset her.

"Found her," Fay said, breathing hard.

The assistant, Adleri, child of Adlassa, spoke quietly. "You need me to put some bodies back together, right?"

"That's right. I'm going to come inside with you. Forgive me if I find it difficult."

Adleri took a lantern from Fay, then started toward the entrance. It didn't matter to her if someone else was uncomfortable.

Onderishta moved through the building slowly. There was no point in trying to count the bodies. Adleri would take care of that. Besides, it wasn't just limbs and heads lying about. Some of these people had been cut clean through their midsection. Some had been split collarbone to crotch.

What sort of weapon could cut through every bone in a man's ribcage in a single stroke? Only a ghostkind blade, and as far as she knew, there were none in the city. The last one had sailed away eight years earlier, in the hands of one of the guards of the Safroy heir, never to return.

As horrible as the smell and the sights were, the sound of rats crawling among the shadows was even worse.

Onderishta had not seen death like this since the invasion.

After studying six dead, graying faces, she had no doubt. Some were foreign friends, some Salashi, but these were Harl's most trusted bodyguards. The weavers who lived and worked here were nowhere in sight.

Onderishta surveyed the interior. The building was larger than she'd thought. What looked like a second warehouse next door was actually part of the same building. She found a small dining area and a row of beds—all mercifully empty—along with a dozen looms packed close together.

Beyond that was an open area with little to show how it had been used. There were pools of drying blood on the floor, but in several places, those irregular shapes had a long straight edge, as though the blood had spread against an object—like a crate—that had been removed later. She also found bloody bootprints near the loading bay. Something had been carried out of here. But what?

In a shadowy corner by the back wall, a small crate rested atop a stool. Onderishta pulled a hatchet from a support beam. There was no blood on the blade. Whoever had swung it had not had much luck. Onderishta levered the lid of the crate open with it.

Inside was a stack of oiled leather scraps, probably goatskin. She recognized them immediately—tar heads carried their drug of choice inside folded leather just like this.

"Shit."

Adleri glanced up. Onderishta shook her head, and the woman ignored her again.

Onderishta pushed open the loading dock door and stepped into the fresh air. Passersby craned their necks to see inside, so she slid the door shut quickly.

Her two apprentices run to her. Mirishiya grinned, showing her crooked teeth. "Can I go inside to investigate too? I've seen dead bodies before."

If she'd grown up an orphan and child burglar, Onderishta did not doubt it. "No, you can't. And stop smiling. Some of these onlookers might have family inside. You don't want them to think you're happy they've been cut apart, do you?"

Mirishiya blushed. "I don't want that."

"Good. Find Fay and bring him here." She ran off. To Trillistin, Onderishta said, "What about you? Do you want to go inside?"

"If you think it would help, I will."

He looked anxious, as though his reluctance might get him fired. She laid a hand on his shoulder to reassure him, then sent him into the crowd to seek witnesses.

Onderishta scanned the crowd. She saw a few familiar faces among the onlookers and knew the coming days would be full of neighbors carefully approaching her in cafes and on street corners, saying, *What was that the other day…*

Then she saw something she didn't expect. At the back of the crowd was a tall foreign man with a green scarf tied around his head and face. With his size, Onderishta thought he might have been a bodyguard. More than a few nobles lived on this deck, after all.

He might have been Bedler of Koh-Alzij, but Onderishta couldn't figure why he would be there.

Her thoughts were interrupted when Mirishiya returned with Fay. He asked, "What did you find?"

"What we found, aside from the corpses of Harl's top assholes, is his distribution point for white tar."

Fay's eyes went wide, while Mirishiya's narrowed. He was surprised. She was fascinated. "Here?" he exclaimed, then quickly lowered his voice. "In The Folly?"

The big guy with the green scarf was gone. "We're…" *four blocks from my house*, she almost said. It was appalling to think that Harl's people distributed their drugs from her safe, comfortable neighborhood, but who was she to be safe from his influence? Who was she to think his poison and his heavies would be quarantined in the poorer decks? She took a breath to compose herself. "We're lucky to have found this at all, considering that we've been searching everywhere from Low Apricot to Mudside for this fucking building. Except the contraband has already been moved out."

Fay scratched his head. "If there was a big fight here, Harl's first thought would be to hide his shit someplace else."

"If we're lucky," Onderishta said. Fay had heard the rumors, but he was still thinking about Harl as if he were untouchable. "If we're lucky, he's still out there for us to catch."

If not, there was more bloodshed on the way.

CHAPTER TWENTY-FIVE

Kyrioc felt hands clutching him and lashed out.

"Hey! Shh. Enough of that, now. We're trying to help."

He didn't recognize the voice, but no one put a knife into his belly or bashed his head, so he let his arms drop. They felt heavy and worthless, like long stockings full of mud.

Streams of sunlight shone onto the street beside him. When had daylight come? He was being helped out of a cart he did not recognize on a street that… He looked at the nearby buildings, but his vision was too blurry to make out details. "Who are you? Where…" His voice sounded dry and rasping.

"Never mind who I am," the strange voice said. "We're in Woodgarden. Don't you remember asking me to take you here?"

Kyrioc did not, in fact, remember that. He had lost a lot of blood. His heart fluttered and his head felt light. He wondered what else he'd said in his delirium and what secrets he'd revealed.

"Come on, Broken. I've got you."

That was the landlady's nephew. Kyrioc couldn't remember the boy's name.

The woman in the cart said, "All right, then," and clicked her tongue. Her cart started to roll away. Kyrioc tried to thank her, but his voice was too weak to be heard. The landlady's nephew relayed the message.

The boy helped him into the lobby. Several people called out, "Broken!" then asked what had happened. He needed a few seconds to realize they were referring to him.

Kyrioc's vision began to dim. Someone said, "He'll never make it to the third floor."

When Kyrioc woke again, he was lying on his back, being carried toward the pawnshop door. Eyalmati's rough voice echoed in the hallway.

"Kyrioc is here? Kyrioc, you let them steal my—" Then his tone changed completely. "Oh, my poor boy. Bring him inside! Bring him in!"

Kyrioc was carried into his room, then set on the floor. It took him a moment to realize all of the furniture was gone.

Eyalmati crouched over him, his flushed, puffy face twisted with concern. "By the fallen gods, this doesn't look good. A few inches one way, they would have missed you entirely. A few inches the other, and…well, I would never have found out what happened to you."

There was a crowd of people at Eyalmati's shoulder. They were mostly men with dirty faces and ragged clothes, but their expressions showed only concern.

"Should have taken him to the hospital," someone said.

"And paid with what? The place has been ransacked."

"No charity places nearby."

"Gotta clean him out and stitch him up."

Eyalmati sighed. "Can't. I used to have needle and stitches in that drawer, but…"

"My aunt's got some." That was the nephew again. Kyrioc saw the crowd ripple as he pushed his way through.

"Broth," Kyrioc said, and the others took up the call. The boy promised to return with a warm bowl.

"What can I do?" Eyalmati asked.

"I don't want," Kyrioc said, "to die with an audience."

The watching faces nodded and backed away, muttering in agreement.

He had never said a kind word to any of them. Not once. He had never even thought kindly of them. Every day, he'd walked through the crowd of unwashed men and thought they were just like him: broken, angry, and lost.

"Thank you," he croaked.

When they were gone, Eyalmati returned to his side. With trembling hands, he peeled back Kyrioc's vest and tunic, wiping at the sticky blood. "If I had a jug of something, I could disinfect this, but…"

Kyrioc grabbed his wrist. "There's a hidden panel in the sideboard beneath the counter. Right side. Take out the bundle inside and bring it to me, but whatever you do, don't open it."

Eyalmati stared at him a moment, his mouth working, as though he was about to protest. Instead, he stood and stumbled into the other room. Kyrioc could hear him fumbling around for far too long, while waves of pain flowed through him. He tried to press his hand against the wound, but his strength was fading.

Finally, an exclamation came from the next room, and Eyalmati shuffled back toward him, his trembling fingers picking at the laces. "They found all of my—"

"No," Kyrioc rasped. "Let me."

It took all of his willpower to focus on the way his fingers moved and the knot he needed to pick apart. Eyalmati held his own hands out, waggling his fingers as though he could help through sympathetic magic. Then it was open.

First, Kyrioc drew out a slender iron bar as long as the distance between the tip of his middle finger and the pulse point on his wrist. It was as black as an old skillet, but the surface was covered with rounded, oblong bumps that made it easy to grip. He set it onto his chest. Then he took out a piece of thin black leather and unfolded it.

Inside, no larger than a quarter of a grain of rice, was his last piece of glitterkind flesh.

Kyrioc pinched it between his bloody thumb and finger. It wouldn't be enough, but—

Eyalmati grabbed his wrist. "What is that?"

Kyrioc stared until he let go, then pushed the tiny grain deep into his wound. A flood of pleasure ran through him, followed by a pleasant stinging sensation as his flesh knitted together.

"How…" Eyalmati had a question but didn't seem to know how to ask it. "Where did *that* come from?"

"I brought it with me when I arrived in Koh-Salash," Kyrioc said. "I would never buy magic at the counter. Besides, we never had that much petty cash."

Eyalmati exhaled sharply. "This much is true. Now we have nothing."

"Floorboard," Kyrioc said. "Beneath the petty cash drawer."

The old man's eyes widened, and he practically leaped out of the room. After considerably less fumbling, he returned triumphant with a sack of coins in his trembling hands. "There must be a silver anchor's worth here! Did you know we were going to be robbed?"

Kyrioc shook his head. "I hid it from you, for those times when you empty the petty cash and leave me with nothing to run the shop."

Eyalmati looked crestfallen. "I do that?"

"Sometimes."

The landlady returned. The glitterkind magic had already faded, leaving behind a long cut that was not as deep as it had been, and a lot of pain. "When I was a girl," she said, brushing wisps of gray hair out of her eyes, "I joined the militia to fight the raiders from Koh-Benjatso. A lot of women did. Sometimes, my duties had me atop the wall, taking a hatchet to grappling lines, but most of my time was spent stitching Salashi fighters back together." She held up a needle and thread. "Do you trust me?"

"Do it."

First, she poured a bit of sharp brandy over the injury. Kyrioc bit back a cry. Passing the remains of the jug to Eyalmati, she said, "Dump out the extra somewhere, would you?" She didn't look at him as he took several deep swallows. His hands seemed steadier after.

Dabbing at Kyrioc's side, the landlady said, "This doesn't look so bad after all, Broken, but you've lost a lot of blood." Kyrioc clenched his teeth as the needle went into his skin and the gut pulled his wound closed. She didn't look up as she spoke. "Is anyone going to be looking for you?" Kyrioc nodded. "Then you shouldn't have come back here, should you?" He shook his head. The landlady kept stitching. "Busk, fetch some rags. We're taking the back stair, and I don't want to leave a trail of bloody footprints."

Darkness closed over Kyrioc again. He had just enough time and energy to take hold of his black iron staff before the world went away.

* * *

RILISKA HAD NOTHING TO DO.

Her paints had run dry, and while the other kids admired the work she'd done, they'd lost interest. The adults hadn't even noticed. Her popularity had drained away like water in a cracked bowl, and she still hadn't made friends with someone who could help her find her mother.

She spent most of her waking and sleeping hours in the baths. The other kids wouldn't enter because of the smell—it did smell like old wet clothes—so none of them knew about the hidden glitterkind child. No one had told Riliska to keep her a secret, but she did anyway. This was grownup business, and snooping into grownups' business was a good way to get hurt.

Besides, it was nice to have a secret.

She climbed over the side of the tub and crawled into the skywood slot beneath. The glitterkind child was still there. Riliska approached it.

Inch. That's what she called the little glitterkind, because the second time she visited, it seemed to have shrunk by an inch. Her friend Kyrioc had told her that glitterkind needed sunlight in order to grow properly. Riliska was glad that she didn't have the same weakness.

She whispered to it, telling it about her mommy and how they would soon be reunited. She also promised to find Inch a comfortable place to grow.

There was no response. There was never a response. Riliska fell quiet again. No one trusted her to run errands and she had no chores or lessons.

She wished she could sleep until evening meal, then sleep again until morning. Anything to fill the endless hours.

The old man who had shown them into the building had told her not to bother with the baths, and he was right. They were gross. He'd also said…

He'd said the caretaker stayed in the exercise room and he didn't like children.

But if the old man took care of the building, why did he call this other person a caretaker? Unless what he took care of was Inch.

It occurred to her that being near Inch could get her into serious trouble.

She walked through the building, visiting the empty spa and peering through the hole in the floor—it was daylight now, so she could see the empty plankway far below—then passing through the room where they ate, and looking out the windows. She was going to the exercise room because she wanted to see the sort of person who was supposed to be looking after Inch. Maybe she would ask him to do a better job.

It didn't bother her that she'd been told the caretaker didn't like children. In her experience, no one did.

But first, she wandered around the building to see if there was some reason to put it off. There wasn't.

The door to the exercise room creaked when she pulled it open. A large window that faced Suloh's hip bone brought in a lot of light, but it must not have been opened in a long time, because the room stank like moldy cloth. The floor was covered with a tattered mat, and a row of blunt metal swords leaned against the near wall. An armless wooden man on an iron base stood in the corner. His head, shoulders, and torso had been beaten almost into splinters.

The only place she couldn't see was the far corner, beside the window where the light couldn't reach. There was a long bench there, and a shadow—

The shadow moved. Riliska caught her breath as a figure stood off the bench and silently moved in front of the window. Backlit, the figure was hard to see clearly, but he was big and broad like a man. He wore steel. She'd never seen anyone in armor before, except the cosh.

Is this what he did all day? Sit quietly in the stink? No wonder he couldn't take care of Inch.

"Good sir? Aren't you lonely in here?"

The armored man laughed. A chill run through Riliska's blood, and she fled into the hall.

* * *

HARL WAS NOT FOUND among the dead.

That was good news as far as Onderishta was concerned, but she wouldn't be satisfied until she confirmed he was still alive.

It was one thing to arrest him. From a cell, Harl would play at being the boss, but his grip on the city would be weakened. The gangs would be weakened and the bureaucracy would be free to shut some of the worst brothels, casinos, and dealers.

But if Harl was dead, Koh-Salash might fall into a shadow civil war.

Adleri had finished her work with unexpected speed. Most of those inside the weaver's workshop had been killed with a single stroke, and only about half had their heads detached from their bodies. She found it easy to match them. The only body parts she could not account for were a left hand—and the bloody pawprints near the back door suggested a local mutt had stolen it—and a man's head.

She explained all this in the same bored tone that Onderishta would use to describe the weather. Onderishta thanked her with exacting politeness.

Then she hunted down the one body that was missing a head. He was short, with pale Carrig skin, and he might have been Harl. By the fallen gods, she hoped not, but it was possible.

Fay hurried toward her. "I didn't have much luck with the bystanders and the cafe employees. They were polite but all anyone would say was that a red-haired *foreigner*—with special emphasis on the word for my sake—drew a long-handled sword and entered the shop alone."

"Alone?"

"One man against more than a dozen. I think it's bullshit. You know what seems more likely? One of their own drugged a pot of tea or something and knocked them all out. Then this *foreigner* makes a show of drawing his weapon and marching in. One guy lifts an unconscious heavy, and the other chops him. *Thwack.*"

"Is that the sound effect for chopping a man in half?"

He shrugged. "That's what I'm going with."

"Red hair, you say?"

"And beard. He sounds like my buddy from High Apricot, Killer of Devils, who promised to turn over Second Boar's package."

"Promised the package but delivered something else." Onderishta looked over the crowd. Their numbers had dwindled, but there were no foreigners among them. Least of all a man with red hair. "I wonder what they promised our friend from the pawnshop."

"The boy is doing well," Fay said idly, as though the pawnshop broker was old news. "I was watching. He's got a knack for asking the right person and pretending to be interested. Plus, he's got the right skin color. I bet he comes back with something. How's the other?"

As though the question summoned her, Mirishiya emerged from the workshop with a small crate in her arms.

"You said I couldn't go inside, ma'am, and you were right, because I just wanted to see. It was selfish and this profession is about higher things. But I do want to help."

Fay grinned. "So, you thought up a better justification to do what you already wanted to do? You'll go far, little one."

The girl shifted uncomfortably, as though she was afraid of being dismissed. Onderishta spoke up. "Were you bothered by what you saw?"

Mirishiya looked up at her, then down at the lid of her crate. "I've seen worse, ma'am. Never so many at once, but definitely worse. And I found something unusual." She fumbled with the lid of the crate. Onderishta couldn't decide if she should buy her a sweet cake or send her back to the tower so she would disobey someone else. "I've also seen knife blades break in a fight. Cheap steel makes a cheap death." From the crate, Mirishiya drew out a knife handle. The blade had broken off only an inch past the grip. "But this isn't cheap steel at all. It's very good. And there are three of them. Also…"

The girl removed a hatchet handle. The blade had been cut through on a slant like a piece of melon.

Fay took it from her, then fished the other half out of the crate. They fit together perfectly. "I've never seen a hatchet break like this."

Onderishta scowled as she looked into the crate. The knives inside also looked like they'd been sliced in two. She thought again about the body inside that seemed to have been cut through the collarbone, breastbone, spine, and ribs.

Another ghostkind blade had come to Koh-Salash.

* * *

TIN SLEPT, BUT NOT well. She dreamed that Harl's lieutenants marched on Wild Dismal like four armies. Harl's nephew stood at the front, a charred corpse with a hatchet in each hand. When her own heavies saw the numbers, weapons, and discipline of the enemy, they fled like rats from a house fire. The entire deck was empty except her, her brother—who wouldn't stop admiring their enemies' army uniforms—and her bodyguard. Then the Katr shrugged, said, *Fuck honor*, and turned his blade toward Wooden.

She woke with her face drenched with sweat and her guts sick with worry.

It was daylight outside. A bowl of clean water had been brought to her room—*someone slipped into her bedroom while she slept and she hadn't noticed*. She gladly sponged the fear sweat from her skin.

Her plan was succeeding, even with this rushed timeline, but the closer she got, the shakier she felt.

No more.

She went to the window. The afternoon was fading, but the light from Suloh's pelvic bones was still strong. She was far from the activity of the city in here, hiding out in the shuttered spa where Harl had hidden his glitterkind. Safe. All she had to do was open the window and lean over the sill, and she would plummet a hundred feet into the black mud below.

The part of her that longed for that scared the shit out of her.

The truly strange thing was that it didn't matter. Either she threw herself out of this window, or some heavy knifed her in the back, or her own bodyguard—

Killer of Devils. That was his name. Yes, it was a boastful name—and boastful names were bad luck—but it didn't matter. If he brought her bad luck, at least she'd be free of this awful uncertainty.

She would make her name, spend a shitpile of gold, and then die violently, hopefully with her hammer buried in someone's skull. It was a good plan. The most difficult part, apparently, was convincing herself that it was working.

She closed the window and dressed in her plainest clothes. Today would be the last day of her life if she couldn't bring Harl's heavies into her organization. Her own people were next to worthless. But if her carefully planted seeds took root…

When she opened her bedroom door, she startled Ink Mouse. Apparently, he was supposed to be guarding her door.

"Awake already, boss?"

"I'm hungry," she said.

"Right away, boss. By the way, it worked," Ink said, grinning.

"Don't just say *It worked* to me, shitwit. What worked?"

"I'm sorry. The purge against the foreign friends. It started."

Well, who could have fucking called it? Harl's Salashi heavies had moved at her orders.

She had them.

"Good. I'm going to eat. Get that little girl we took with that pickpocket in Woodgarden. It's time I talked to her."

He hurried away. Tin returned to her room, slung on her belt, and tucked her hammer into the right side. The weight of it felt good.

A plate covered with fried lamb steak and a hunk of rough bread awaited her in the common room. The meat was cold but delicious. The bread only reminded her of the smell and taste of the loaf she'd eaten in High Slope. Was that why Harl made his headquarters in Upgarden? The food?

Surprisingly, the girl took longer to present than the meal, but when she appeared, she came running. Once she reached the middle of the room, she paused and looked around. There were a couple of beetles lying in the corner, whispering to each other, and a table of heavies playing cards. Her bodyg—Killer of Devils sat on a stool near the wall.

Tin was not going to shy from that name any longer. Killer of Devils.

Then the girl marched across the room and stood beside Tin's chair, waiting to be recognized.

While she chewed a mouthful of steak, Tin looked her over. Her cheeks were dirty and her shirt tattered, but that didn't look like a new development. Her mother must have given her a whole lot of neglect and not much else.

"Do you know why I called you here?" The girl shook her head. "I want to ask about your friend."

She furrowed her brow in confusion. "Do you mean the kids I painted? I just met them."

"I mean the man in the pawnshop."

Her smile was quick and bright. "Oh! You mean Broken."

"Why do you call him that?"

"It's his nickname. *The Broken Man*. I didn't give it to him, though."

"Who did? Why?"

The girl thought for a moment, then offered another bright smile. "I heard Old Inkiyenz say it first, I think. She's the little old lady who sells buns. I'm pretty sure Sintaree said it next. Then Young Inkiyenz. Young and Old aren't related, by the way. They just have the same name. The landlady's nephew said it a lot, but he likes to be mean. I don't know who started it, though. I think they called him *Broken* because he doesn't like to talk to people. Or look at them, really."

As far as Tin could tell, the girl was speaking openly and honestly, but nothing she said was remotely useful. "Do you know his real name?"

"Kyrioc, child of No One. I know that means he's an orphan. Isn't that sad?"

"Who does he work for?"

"Eyalmati, child of… I forgot."

Tin didn't recognize that name. Did Harl have operatives she didn't know about? "Who is he? Tell me about him."

"He's the owner of the pawnshop and he drinks a lot. Eyalmati used to give money to my mom, but she says he's too drunk for that now. He's hardly even in the shop anymore. It's usually Kyrioc all by himself, but I think he prefers it that way. I used to think he was an assassin in hiding or something, but…" She glanced over at the heavies, leaning against the wall and laughing, then at…at Killer of Devils, then at Tin herself. "But that's kid stuff. I don't think that anymore. Now I just think he's a sad person who forgets to be nice, sometimes. I…" She forced herself to say one thing instead of another. "I like him."

"Is Kyrioc your father?"

The girl shook her head, her expression serious. "My father was a gambler. He died when I was five."

Tin leaned back in her chair. What was this shit? This pawnbroker wanted this little girl, supposedly. That's what he'd told her beetle, and the beetle had no reason to lie. If he wasn't her father, what did he want? Who did he *really* work for?

Somehow, he must have figured out that she was living with the beetles, and he wanted the girl to lead him there.

The real question was how he'd kept such a low profile. Killer of Devils said the guy had godkind magic of a type he'd never seen before, and a guy like that doesn't work in a low-end pawnshop, buying stolen bracelets from whores. His name was common enough to be fake, and the *child of No One* bit made it impossible to check. It was all too convenient.

Someone was running a game on her. She needed to find out who.

"You've been bored here, haven't you?" Without waiting for a response, she waved Little Cinder over. "Put her to work." To Riliska, she said, "Eat until you're full. You'll need fuel for your fire." After the girl ran off, she gestured at Little Cinder. "Assign a heavy to follow her and make it someone quick and mean. If this pawnbroker shows up, he gets a knife in the back. No warning. No threats or challenges. Sudden, unexpected death. Pick someone looking to move up in the world. Send a beetle, too, in case the heavy fails. I'll want to know where he takes her."

Little nodded and approached the girl. She asked about her mommy, but he didn't answer.

Tin gestured to her bodyguard. He slid from his chair and fell in step behind her. One more conversation, then it was time to head for Upgarden to take command.

* * *

"YOU MUST BE FUCKING joking to come here. With him!"

At first, Kyrioc thought he was the unwelcome one, but the old fellow with the crooked back barely glanced at him.

His landlady said, "Keep your voice down, you miserable old— This man's been stabbed, and we need a place to hide him."

The crooked man squinted at Kyrioc's injury. "He needs a hospital."

"I can't afford a hospital," Eyalmati said. He was struggling to support his share of Kyrioc's weight. "I've been robbed of everything."

The crooked man's expression turned malicious. "So! Now you know what it's like to have someone steal from *you*!"

The landlady took hold of his collar and shook him like a blanket. "Don't you dare talk about me like a possession! He didn't steal me. You drove me away with your fussiness and hectoring. He was fun—actually fun!— until he drove me away too. I don't belong to either of you, and I never have. Now, are you going to help or do I have to get mean?"

"You broke my heart." The crooked old man sounded miserable. "I loved you."

"But not enough to change."

The anger drained out of him, and he studied Kyrioc's injury more closely. "Bring him in. But you two can't stay. It's too painful."

He stepped back, and Kyrioc was led to a low couch. The old man fussed about getting a blanket down first, then they all lowered him gently onto it.

The house was small and cluttered, with few windows to admit light. A pair of weak oil lamps provided the only light, but Kyrioc could see shelves filled with old clay jars, a charcoal grill, and a rack hung with greens several days past their prime.

"We couldn't stay even if we wanted to," the landlady said. Then she turned to Eyalmati. "The whole building knows who robbed you. Your parsu can get most of your money back, can't they?"

Eyalmati turned up his palms. "I'm not sure I still have a parsu. Stitches have to tithe."

"You've paid," Kyrioc said from the couch. "I made sure."

"By the fallen gods, you... Thank you."

The landlady straightened Eyalmati's collar. "You've been slipping pretty far this past year, you old boozer. You're barely aware of your surroundings most of the time. The cosh have been sniffing around about this one, too. We'll have to think up a story. Come on. You'll talk to your parsu about recovering your property, and I'll made sure you don't accidentally trip and fall into a tavern on the way."

The crooked old man closed and latched the door behind them, and quiet settled over the room. He fetched one of the lamps and set it on a table close to the couch. He began to gently probe Kyrioc's injury.

"That woman! So infuriating, and yet, when she asks for my help… My name is Pentulis, child of Penfilip."

"Kyrioc, child of No One."

"Hmf." Pentulis didn't think much of that answer. "Who gave you this wound?" When he didn't get an answer, he asked, "Where did you get the glitterkind flesh, then?" He smirked at Kyrioc's startled expression. "I worked in a hospital for thirty-five years, young man. You think I can't recognize the signs of supernatural healing?"

"It was the last of a supply that I carried with me for a long time."

Pentulis grunted and glanced at the left side of Kyrioc's face. "Not as long as you've had that scar, I'm guessing, or you wouldn't have the scar. Whose hand is that?"

Kyrioc slipped his left hand under the blanket. "I have a complicated history."

"Fine," Pentulis said. "Be that way if you must. I can show you a dye that will be a much closer match to your natural skin tone. Now the bad news. Yesseni is a charismatic woman, but she's terrible with a needle and gut. All these stitches are going to have to be redone, and the wound properly cleaned. It's going to hurt."

"Thank you."

Pentulis stood and took a pair of shears from a shelf. "Now, that is a proper response." He cut Kyrioc's shirt from the hem to the collar, then laid the flaps open.

And hesitated. He picked up the lamp to show the mass of scar tissue on Kyrioc's chest. There were old burns, healed slashing wounds, punctures, bite scars, and what looked like claw marks. Pentulis's expression was unreadable as he took it in.

Then he sighed. "Complicated history."

* * *

TIN ENTERED THE BATH with her hammer in hand.

Two men sat beside the drain. Their chairs were black iron and had shackles for their ankles and their thighs, and manacles for their wrists and upper arms. More treasures stolen from Harl's hideout in The Folly.

Both men breathed harder when she entered. The one she didn't recognize immediately began to plead with her, promising to answer every question or complete any task. The one she did recognize just kept saying, *Boss, I swear I swear, Boss,* over and over.

"Both of you shut up." They did. Wooden stood beside them, bared steel in his hands, and a bloodthirsty grin lighting up his face. It was only when she saw the knife that she realized the men were bleeding from cuts on their chests. "What have you found out?"

"Something amazing!" Wooden said, practically singing. "Nobody works for anyone else and no one is planning anything and no one knows anything except that they're really sorry."

Tin sighed and studied the two men. Strangely, they looked somewhat alike. They were both too old for the platform-hall clothes they were wearing and had physiques shaped more by drink than hard work. Both looked ready to do anything to save their own lives.

"This one," Wooden said, jerking his thumb at the stranger, "tells us his name is Haliyal, child of Hyordis."

"Well!" Tin exclaimed, surprised and a little angry. "A thief who goes by his family name! If you're so determined to rely on your elders, maybe we should pay them a visit. Maybe we should make them pay the debt you owe."

"But I'm not a thief!" the man wailed. "I didn't know we were stealing something. I mean, that she was going to steal something! I was out with a girl, and she said this guy had grabbed her ass, and that I should do something—"

Wooden lifted his knife. "It was her tit before."

Haliyal stopped blubbering, then broke down in tears. "I just wanted to get laid. I just… She told me to punch a guy and I did. I swear by the fallen gods I didn't know. I swear by Selsarim Lost."

Wooden laid the knife against his throat. "And who do you work for? Who planned it?"

"I work at a tannery. The girl might— It seemed so spur-of-the-moment!"

Tin kicked him, and the jolt made Wooden's knife graze the skin of his throat. Haliyal chirped in fear and tried to keep still. "What about the guy from the pawnshop?"

The prisoner looked from one face to the other as though he needed more explanation. "Who?"

"*Are you fucking playing with me?*" Tin roared. "How does the pawnshop broker fit into your plans? Did he hire you or did you hire him? Was he fucking the girl you were with? We know he arrived in the city a year ago. Where was he before that? Did he mention Carrig at all?"

"No, never! I don't know anything about any of that! I swear, I—"

"Shut the fuck up." She turned to her heavy, bound up beside him. "What about you, Wet? What do you have to say for yourself?"

Wet Cinder licked his dry lips. He was terrified too but trying his best to put on a brave front. "Magic, boss."

"*Magic, boss*?" She tightened her grip on her hammer. "Is that seriously all you have to say to me?"

"He used magic, boss. On me. I couldn't fight him."

Tin drew her forefinger across his narrow forehead, then wiped the sweat onto his clothes. "You couldn't fight him? Why? My bodyguard has godkind magic, and you could certainly fight him."

Wet glanced over at Killer of Devils as though he feared it was about to happen. "I'd never have a chance. He'd kill me."

"You helped a man break into my headquarters while you were on guard duty. Five lives were lost."

"Five? I thought—"

Tin slammed her hammer onto the top of his head, and by the fallen gods, it felt good. "Maybe now these fuckers will actually do some fucking guarding. As for you…"

Wooden stepped in front of her. His eyes were wide and his gaze intense, but he wasn't smiling.

She sighed. "Fine. Have your fun, but don't take too long. It's time we showed our faces in Upgarden."

That brought his smile back.

Tin headed toward the door. If she was going to take control of Harl's old headquarters, she needed to dress the part.

And maybe in the future they should do their interrogating in another room, drain or no drain. The screaming echoed too much with all these hard surfaces.

CHAPTER TWENTY-SIX

O**ver the next three** days, Kyrioc ate a lot of soup.

Pentulis came and went, often at odd hours of the night. He no longer worked in hospitals, but he did make himself available to examine injuries and illnesses. The second morning, after a long night on the deck somewhere, he'd sighed and unburdened himself.

Every time he was called out, no matter the hour or the condition of the patient, he was there to answer the same implicit question: *Should we spend coin at a hospital for this?* Whether it was fever, injured leg, vomiting child, or anything, really, they just wanted to know if he could fix it without having to turn their life savings over to the medical bureaucracy.

Kyrioc listened silently, thinking once again about the glitterkind ear Rulenya had hidden in the pawnshop. There was only so much healing magic to go around, and what they had was given to those who could pay. That had seemed like a perfectly reasonable solution when he was a boy in one of the richest families in the city.

"They're looking for you, you know."

Kyrioc waited for a clarification, but when none came, he had to ask. "Who?"

"Who? The ironshirts. The city constables," Pentulis said. "A shaggy-haired man with a scar on his face who injured half a dozen of their own. When Yesseni brought you here, I assumed you've been attacked by criminals."

"I was."

Pentulis chuckled. "Complicated history, then? Fair enough. You'll be safe here as long as you keep indoors. Another few days and you should be safe from infection. Oh, and I brought you this."

He set another crock full of broth on the table by Kyrioc. As before, it was a dark broth, but this one had rice and small bits of meat in it. Goat, by the smell. Kyrioc had hated goat as a boy.

The old man groaned as he settled onto his bed.

"Can I ask a question about hospitals? About donated parts?"

Without opening his eyes, Pentulis said, "If you like."

"How often do you get donations from children?"

The old man's eyes snapped open. "Why are you asking me that?" he snapped.

Kyrioc hadn't thought of it as some sort of accusation, but Pentulis seemed to have taken it as one. "A woman was murdered and collected. Her daughter might have been too, but I haven't seen evidence of it. Do hospitals take transplants from small children?"

"How small?"

"She was nine, I think."

Pentulis shook his head. "Too small. For children that young, their livers, hearts, and other parts are too small for anyone except other children, and glitterkind flesh doesn't always work correctly for them. The only parts that transplant well are the eyes and skin, but most people don't want to walk around with the skin of a child on their face, especially considering the history there."

Kyrioc had no idea what that history was, but he knew enough about people to assume it was ugly. "So, her eyes and skin would be of value, maybe, but little else?"

The answer, when it came, was little more than a grunt. Then: "You think she's been murdered and her parts have been sold?"

Kyrioc's eyes closed. At this early hour, he could hear nothing but his own breathing and the passage of the wind through the bare branches outside. He could remember so many things with terrible clarity—pain, fear, grief, helplessness at the death of someone close.

And Riliska's eyes lighting up after a bite of carrot.

The idea that she was dead now, cut up to patch some rich man's balding head, filled him with a fury he could not contain.

The iron staff he'd carried out of the pawnshop lay beside him. Taking it up, he felt the heat growing inside it. He was not going to give up on her. He would never give up on her until he knew for sure.

And if he had already failed her, Kyrioc would have to start killing and never stop until there was no one alive who remembered the Pails' names.

* * *

FAY RACED AROUND THE city, visiting each of the towers at least once a day. He even crossed the river to the Salashi living outside the gods' corpses to the north, checking in at the constable stations beyond the city.

Harl Sota List Im had vanished. Either the rumors were true and he was dead, or he had fled Koh-Salash.

Onderishta hoped he was hiding out somewhere, but Fay didn't believe it. A man like Harl had a reputation to protect. His only options were to fight to hold on to power or to run.

Extra constables watched The Docks, and while the risk was always there that they might be paid off to look the other way, he'd told them Harl would be fleeing the city with trunks full of coin. If there was one thing Fay had learned to rely on, it was the greed of his own constables. So far, though, nothing.

Fay sat in the high room of the south tower, thinking. Where else could he search for a rich Carrig?

"The bastard really is dead, isn't he?" he asked the empty room.

A tiny voice answered. "I think he is, yes."

Fay started. Mirishiya sat in the corner, a list of addresses on the table before her. It contained all of Harl's properties the bureaucracy knew about. "Oh! I didn't hear you come in. I thought you were still downstairs watching the interrogations."

"I spent the morning there, good sir. None of the prisoners talked, and the interrogator said the same thing each time. He seemed sort of bored by it all. Is he trying to make a personal connection with the prisoners?"

"He is," Fay answered, "but the fact that it doesn't work is no excuse to stop trying over and over and over." She smiled, showing those crooked teeth. Fay shrugged. "The principle works if it's applied properly." The problem was the interrogator himself. He liked his position and he had the connections to keep it. Only Onderishta could move him to a new position, and she didn't know he'd lost the knack.

"Sir, they're marshaling the constables."

Fay and Mirishiya rode the lift to the bottom of the tower. They found ironshirts rushing onto the Spillwater deck in full armor and shields.

"Captain!" Fay called, catching the commander's attention just as he was about to reach the door. "What's going on?"

The man smelled of spilled beer, but he, too, was well connected and impossible to oust. "Pirates, good sir," the captain bellowed. "Filthy Carrig pirated a ship right out of the dock." He immediately blushed and looked abashed. "Sorry, sir. No offense."

"We'll go together," Fay waved for his apprentice to follow, and they raced into the streets of Spillwater.

People came out of their homes to jeer or glare. Fay hated this neighborhood, and the locals hated the constables and anyone who traveled with them.

It was a short trip to The Docks, but Fay didn't have the patience to wait for the others. He ran ahead, crossing onto The Freightway, then down the stairs.

The sharp clanging of the bronze bell rang out. The navy was being called up. Fay pushed through the milling crowds, but they were all taller than him.

A stack of crates had been left on a cargo platform, and Fay clambered atop them. The ship, as expected, was tacking south into the wind. The Salashi flattered themselves a water-going people, but the naval yards at Vu-Timmer did not show any activity. Their spyglasses were probably pointed southward, watching for an invasion. A ship stolen in broad daylight…who could have expected that?

Of course, he himself had assigned extra constables here to make sure Harl didn't flee the city. He hoped they'd have a good reason why they let this happen.

There was a jostling mob on one of the quays, where a line of constables held the crowd back. Fay glanced down to make sure Mirishiya was close by, then plunged into the crowd, saying, "Government business, let me through," over and over.

People became harder to shift as he got closer to the front of the conflict. When he caught his first glimpse of a constable's helmet, a wiry shirtless man seized him by the arm.

"Here's another one of them! Another pirate late to the crime!"

"I'm an investigator," Fay snapped. "Stop acting like fools and—"

"He's trying to steal another ship!" a gravelly voice shouted from behind him. "Stop him!"

Fay was about to shout for them to get out of his way when he heard a high voice yell, "NO!"

He turned. Standing behind him was a weathered old sailor wearing what looked like salt-stained rags. He was holding bared steel, a short-bladed knife that was as broad as two thumbs and serrated partway down the spine. A working man's knife, not a fighting knife.

And the only thing between that blade and Fay was Mirishiya, standing with her arms splayed.

"No!" she shouted again. "Stop!"

The sailor looked bewildered by her. Fay grabbed her by the shoulders and pulled her behind him. "Don't you dare cut that child!"

At this, another sailor clasped his comrade's knife hand. Then it was over. The column of ironshirts had arrived. One glimpse at Fay's expression and the knife in the sailor's hand, and the captain's eyes narrowed.

To Fay, he said, "Something I can do for you, sir?"

"Clear this quay before these people do something stupid. You there"—Fay pointed at the man who had nearly killed him—"did you crew on the ship that was hijacked?"

"I did, good sir." The last two words seemed to have slipped out accidentally, and the sailor made a sour face.

"Is the captain here?"

"He's up in the city." No *good sir* this time.

"Well, maybe someone should go and tell him?"

Fay hurried away toward the end of the quay, and now the crowd made way. There were four bodies on the boards. Three were dressed as sailors, while the fourth wore a sensible blue tunic and trousers, like a merchant.

Two constables moved toward the fourth man as though they were about to pitch him into the water. The injured man protested weakly, clutching at his bloody stomach.

"Stop!" Fay called.

One of the constables trailed him. "It's the bloodkind, sir. They get under the docks somehow, and the blood sets them off somehow. We got to give them a little something to placate them somehow, or there will be an ugly fight once the sun sets. And this fellow can't tell us anything. He's speaking gibberish."

It was clear that there was more blood than could have come from these bodies. There was no point asking how many injured had already been thrown over. The constable would have simply lied about it.

Fay waved the men away, and they dropped the injured heavy. The man's face was pale and his hands paler. A hatchet lay beside him, but Fay doubted he had the strength to lift it, let alone attack.

He crouched beside the dying man. "How long have you been here in Koh-Salash?" he asked in Carrig.

The heavy blinked at him. "Three months. Just three months."

"Why were you and your friends in such a rush to leave?"

The man blinked slowly, then looked around at the ships, the sea, and the sky. "Your accent is shit."

"I wouldn't know. I was born here."

"There's no music in your words." The heavy coughed, straining the cords of his muscular neck. A dribble of blood appeared on his lip. "You grunt like these brownskins. Like hungry pigs." The heavy looked at him. "I was going to be rich. I was going to return home with a godwood ring on every finger."

"What happened?" The heavy didn't answer. "Why did your friends steal that ship and flee the city?" Still the man wouldn't answer. "Tell me your name. Mine is Fay Nog Fay."

"Nal At Isp," the man answered, almost out of habit. "Why should I tell you anything? Are you going to have me healed?"

"Hospitals are expensive," Fay said. "We don't pay to heal pirates."

That earned a crooked smile. "No, you hang them."

"Hanged? Pirates are hanged in the Free Cities. We burn them."

"*We*," the gangster muttered. "You are one of them, no matter what you look like. Golden on the outside, shit-brown underneath. And you have nothing to offer me but a quick death. Go fuck your whore of a mother."

Fay sighed. The man was baiting him, hoping to be put out of his misery. "Actually, there's something I can do for you. The Salashi are in love with the sea and with their ships. They're fast as hell, and mean about it. You heard the alarm, didn't you? Salashi cutters are going to run down that lumbering cargo ship your friends stole and put a few volleys into them. Anyone stupid enough to surrender gets the torch. You don't have any family on that ship, do you? Cousins, maybe? Brothers?"

"Fuck you."

Fay winced. "My condolences. They've lost you, and you're going to lose them."

Another hard cough brought blood to Nal's lips. "But you can fix it, yeah?"

"I can convince the captain to let the ship arrive in Carrig. Treat the pirates like cargo he has thoughtfully delivered, in the hopes of a substantial reward. But we can only stop those cutters while they're in hearing range of the bell, and if you help me. Why were you fleeing to the ship?"

"My brother?" Nal murmured. "You can see that he gets home?"

"If we act quickly."

"Why should I believe you?"

Fay spread his hands. "You are in the final moments of your life, and your brother is in danger. There's only one thing left you can do for him."

Nal's eyes closed. When he spoke, his words were thick. "In Low Apricot, there's a brothel called The Caves."

"That's Sen Pul Nat's property."

The heavy managed a sour smile. "Sen Pul Nat is dead, and so are most of his people. The survivors are heading home. Go to The Caves so that when the Clutching Hand seize your shriveled, hairless balls, you'll know why. That's all."

Fay stood and addressed the two ironshirts nearby. "Do what you have to."

He tilted his head to let Mirishiya know she should follow. As they walked away, they heard the dying man go into the water.

"Good sir?" Mirishiya asked. "What did he say?"

You are one of them, no matter what you look like.

"He gave us another errand to run." He stopped and spun on her. "And never, ever do that again. Do you hear? Never put yourself between me and a blade. You are a twelve-year-old girl. I'm the one who's supposed to die protecting you. Understand?"

"Yes, good sir." Her tone was resentful.

"Think of my reputation," he said, and she made an *ahh* sound of understanding. For all her time in Suloh's Tower learning figures and letters, she was still a street kid at heart.

"I wasn't afraid of that old man," she said. "He's what my auntie used to call a 'dog that's been fucked too many times.' He had to work up the courage to attack when your back was turned." She must have noticed the smile on Fay's face. "Er…excuse my language, good sir."

"By the fallen gods, don't talk that way around Onderishta. And never take it for granted that an armed man is harmless. Never. You can never really tell what a person is capable of."

* * *

KYRIOC SAT AT THE mouth of an alley across from Sailsday's Regret. His face was hidden by a deep hood, and his begging bowl sat empty before him. It was too early for a heavy crowd of dancers and musicians, but people stopped at cafes and tea shops, had their hands painted, or were just passing through.

The stairs down to Wild Dismal were right behind him.

Every time a passerby dropped a coin into his bowl, the youths loitering in the alley behind him sauntered out to take it. When a constable wandered by and told him to move along—begging was illegal inside the walls—one of those same youths slipped him a coin to look the other way. It didn't matter. He wasn't there for the money.

He was waiting for the beetles. Even if it took hours, one would have to pass through this intersection, and Kyrioc would be ready.

* * *

ONDERISHTA ARRIVED AT THE brothel well after Fay and the constables were in place. The captain looked relieved. He could finally move in.

As far as Onderishta knew, The Caves was the only building in all of Koh-Salash to have a round door. Well, a pair of them, since the entrance—which stood twelve feet in diameter—had two skywood doors that met in the middle. Each had a panel at the top and the bottom carved to show long, irregular fangs. Onderishta wasn't sure what fangs had to do with caves, but then, she'd never seen one. Still, it made the doorway seem like the entrance to a monster's belly.

Outside those doors stood two enormous guards with steel broadswords, which they held drawn and upright. That was illegal. Not even a licensed bodyguard was permitted to stand around with a bared long weapon, but the east tower received enough silver every month to turn a blind eye as long as the guards didn't do anything stupid.

Today, they appeared ready to do something stupid. Constables had been deployed outside the entrances to the building and around the perimeter in case someone was creative about escaping. But the guards stood in their place, swords held before them, as though those two men—big men, but just men after all—could hold off two dozen armed and armored constables.

She found Fay across the street, sharing a steamed bun with Mirishiya. "Where do things stand?"

"No one has come out. No one has gone in. But I guess we're ready to change that. Where's the boy?"

He meant the other apprentice, obviously. "Special errand. Think these assholes are going to make trouble?" She jerked her thumb at the two door guards.

Fay gave the rest of the bun to Mirishiya. "Let's find out."

When the ironshirts advanced, the guards immediately lowered their swords and opened the doors like they were welcoming paying customers.

Onderishta gestured, and a pair of constables shackled them. Then she waited while the ironshirts searched the building for belligerents.

Many were found. None were alive.

If Onderishta and Fay thought the scene at the weavers' workshop in The Folly was awful, this was worse. Inside The Cave, over the course of a three-hour reconnaissance, they found sixty-three bodies. Nine were men and women employed there. Seventeen were Salashi men and women armed with knives or hatchets and wearing thick leather vests. Thirty-seven were Carrig men and women dressed in the dark blue pants and tunics favored by the foreign friends.

And if the deaths in The Folly had been brutal but quick, served up with a single decisive stroke, these were messy and awful.

Corpses lay in heaps where they had been hacked apart in narrow halls. They lay dead in each other's arms, weapons in each other's hearts. They lay across bloody beds, expressions of surprise on their bloodless faces.

Onderishta felt sick to her stomach, and Fay was paler than usual. Mirishiya, in a small voice, said, "I didn't think this sort of thing happened."

"You can wait outside, if you like," Onderishta said, but the girl only shook her head stubbornly. Good for her. "All right. What do you make of all this, apprentice?"

Instead of speculating, the girl said, "I think we should talk to the owner."

"That's exactly right."

Like every brothel in the city, The Caves handled a lot of coin, and they took extreme measures to protect it. The constables, in searching the building, found no office or vault, no place where accounts could be recorded and balanced.

Fay turned to Mirishiya. "Well?"

After a few moments, she said, "I need to think like a thief." Mirishiya looked at the door, then the reception counter, then the long bar. She went behind the counter and found an empty cash drawer and a money slot beneath it. "There's a trapdoor," she said, which she found behind the bar. Opening it revealed a staircase down into darkness, and the strong scent of vinegar.

Onderishta called for a pair of constables with lanterns, then they descended into the dark. At the bottom, they found two shallow tubs beneath narrow chutes. Both were filled with cheap, watered-down vinegar.

"It's to clean the money," a voice called from the darkness. The constables turned, weapons ready, and Fay shone the lantern into the far end of the room.

It revealed a small Salashi woman in a plain dress and elaborate hairstyle. Her black hair curled around her head like a turban, and the pins that held it in place were glittering silver. She sat at a desk covered with ledgers, quill and ink pot beside her. A puddle of wax filled a candle tray beside her, and a lantern on a hook at her shoulder was dark.

"The vinegar, I mean. Some of those who come here... Well, I don't need to explain."

"Why are you sitting alone in the dark?" Onderishta asked.

"I was down here when the fighting started. I suppose I could have rushed upstairs and picked up a knife or something, but I didn't. I heard the screams. Blood dripped through the floorboards over there. Do you see it?" She made no move to indicate where *there* could be. "So, I stayed where I was until the candle burned down and the lantern ran out of oil. I guess I could have left when the light ran out, but I couldn't move. I'm not sure why."

The woman was in shock. Onderishta shined the light around the little basement, hoping to find an exit that would let this woman leave without passing through the charnel house above. There was none. "You work for Sen Pul Nat, don't you?"

"I don't think so," she answered. "I heard that he's dead, along with his uncle. Our foreign friends came here to destroy the place. To tear it up. We tried to stop them, but…"

Mirishiya's head quirked. She caught that the woman had already contradicted herself, which was a good sign. Now she needed to learn to hide her responses.

Onderishta set the lamp on the desk. The light fell on a tray filled with gold, but not gold coins. A closer look showed they golden brooches of the sort noble women might wear. One looked familiar. Onderishta picked it up and turned it over but couldn't recall where she'd seen it. "Like to pin your fancy robes with gold, eh?"

The woman shook her head. "I don't wear robes. Sen Pul Nat keeps them here. He trusts me. Trusted me, I mean."

"Where did he get them?"

"I never had the nerve to ask. But he sends them to his wife in Carrig."

"All right," Onderishta said. "Where's the coin?" The woman laid her hand on a strongbox beside her. It was not small. "Okay. Put the brooches and the ledgers inside, then give me the key. You're collared until this can all be sorted out."

She nodded meekly and did as she was told. Onderishta slipped the bulky iron key into her purse. To the constable, she said, "Tell me your name."

"Sempiris, child of Semlithic, good ma'am."

"Good. Sempiris, child of Semlithic, you and one of your comrades are going to see this strongbox and this prisoner to the south tower—"

"Low Apricot is an east tower deck," the man interrupted.

"But I work for the bureaucracy, and we go everywhere. Besides, of all the towers in the city, the east is the most rife with corruption…or do you want to dispute that?" He didn't. "See this box to the south tower and have the captain admit you to my office. You're to stay there until I relieve you, even if it takes a couple of days. Understand? When I relieve you, if this box has been broken open, or even if the lock has been scratched by picks, I'm going to have you collared. Yes, you, personally, even if your comrades made a show of blacking your eye and breaking your nose first."

"You can't—"

"Oh, shit," Fay interrupted. "Constable, you should not have said that."

Onderishta stepped close to the constable and lowered her voice. "Did you happen to notice the dead bodies upstairs? Did you see what those rooms looked like?"

"I did, ma'am."

"Have you ever seen anything like that in your life?"

"No, ma'am."

"I have. That's what a battlefield looks like after one side has fled. Koh-Salash is changing, and if you don't change with it, you and yours are going to suffer. Don't pick the losing side. Understand?"

"Yes, ma'am. South tower. Wait for you."

With a nod, Onderishta went up the stairs into the street. Fay and Mirishiya were close behind. "You were right, Fay. Harl is dead. He has to be, for someone to make a move like this. How long have the foreign friends been running the gangs in Koh-Salash?"

Fay shrugged. "No one's really sure when they took over. Longer than I've been alive."

"And now they've been purged."

Wiping his face with his hand, Fay said, "I suppose I should feel some kinship to those foreign friends since we share the same skin tone, but I'm not sorry to see them go."

"If they'd left on their own, I'd be cheering," Onderishta replied. "But the dead workers inside The Cave and down at the docks are a price we shouldn't have had to pay." And it was her fault. Hers and Fay's. If they'd collared Harl at his hammerball club…

Mirishiya spoke up. "How do we find the person who made us pay this price?"

Whoever it was, they had already been in hiding too long.

They stopped at three more brothels in Low Apricot, hoping to discover the name of the new boss. No one could answer. Eventually, they climbed up to High Apricot and stopped at several upscale platform halls.

Three managers claimed to know nothing. The others wouldn't even speak to them.

People were afraid, and Onderishta thought they were right to be.

Finally, they reached Sailsday's Regret. Tonight would not be a night for music and dancing, which meant the cafe tables were out. Since it was after dinnertime, Onderishta suggested they eat, and after they placed their order, she asked to speak to the manager.

"Ma'am, may I try this time?" Mirishiya asked.

Fay shrugged. Onderishta said, "We've been getting nowhere. Go ahead."

The food arrived before the manager did. They had crocks of pigeon stew with bread baked on top, and they dug in. The manager arrived when they were nearly finished. He was a short, balding man with an extravagant mustache. "Is something wrong with your meal?"

"Clearly not," Mirishiya said patiently. "However, due to the recent turmoil, my employers"—she gestured toward Fay and Onderishta—"have not been paid. The fellow who would normally handle things is currently sailing to Carrig. Obviously, this is unacceptable."

The manager removed a cloth from his pocket and patted away beads of sweat on his forehead. "I'm not sure why you bring your problem to me."

The girl shrugged. "We had to come somewhere. We also had to eat. This visit solves both problems. So, who should we talk to so we can rectify this accounting error?"

"But I don't know. I'm just the cafe manager."

Mirishiya sighed. "My employers do not work for free. If their services are no longer secure, and it gets around that you were the one who let them slip away—"

The manager opened his hands as if in prayer. "I'm not being coy. The turmoil is very recent, and word has not reached my office. All I know is that new bosses have stepped into the space where the old bosses were."

Mirishiya opened her mouth but Onderishta raised her hand. *Enough.* "Thank you," the girl said.

"I wish I knew more," the manager said with a little bow. "Please consider your meal on the house."

"No," Onderishta said firmly. "Bring us the bill."

The manager bowed again and left.

Fay was grinning. "Personal connection," he said. "Where did you learn to talk like that? No one *rectifies accounting errors* on the streets."

"In Suloh's Temple," Mirishiya said. "The tutors say things like that all day. I must hear *secure their services* fifty times a day. Ugh." She quirked her head at Onderishta. "You believed him?"

"I did. Also, he said *stepped into the space* and I don't think he was being figurative. We know where Harl's old space was."

After Onderishta paid, she stood and groaned at the pain in her feet. "I'm too old to be walking all over the city this way. Too old and too fat."

"Why don't you get some sleep?" Fay asked. "I can do reconnaissance."

"Thank you, Fay. Mirishiya, go to Suloh's Tower tonight. When Trillistin turns up, let him know I'll need his report tomorrow morning in the south tower."

They went their separate ways. Onderishta dropped a copper knot into the bowl of a hooded beggar for good luck—law be damned—then walked all the way back through both Apricot decks, Low Market, then into The Folly. Night had fallen by the time she reached home.

The house was empty.

She stared down at the empty bed, feeling lonely and forlorn. Keeping a marriage was difficult enough when both spouses spent time together and managed to speak a kind word once in a while. But when they didn't? Shit. Maybe her marriage was already over. Maybe the house would feel like this at the end of every day.

But no. Zetinna would never end things without a big, messy scene. Still, Onderishta couldn't help but wonder if one was coming and if she was as helpless to avoid it as she was to collar belligerents like Harl and his assholes.

She took a deep breath and shook out her limbs. She'd seen too many corpses these past few days. It was making her morose.

Back in the front room, she noticed a jug of clean water, a loaf of crusty bread, and a crock of spicy mashed olives waiting for her. Zetinna. She smiled, feeling loved and even lonelier, if that was possible. It was too late to go to the baths, but she washed at a basin, then collapsed into bed. Maybe Zetinna would come home early and wake her. It wouldn't happen, but it was a pleasant thought to take into dreams.

Onderishta woke to a darkness so complete, she thought she was still dreaming. Even with her window cloths across her shutters, the glow from Suloh's bones usually leaked through, but now there was nothing. She reached out across her bedcovers to the empty space beside her. Zetinna wasn't there. Not in itself a cause for alarm, but—

A length of cold metal gently touched the side of her jaw. For a moment, Onderishta thought her throat was about to be cut. She froze in fear.

But the length of metal didn't feel edged. In fact, it felt like the end of a metal bar.

"Don't move," a voice said. The metal lifted from her skin.

If he'd come to kill her, she would already be dying. If he intended to torture her for information, he would have abducted her and taken her to a secluded location. That left only one option. She slid her hand toward the knife mounted on her headboard.

"I want you to tell me what you know about the Pails."

Onderishta became still, her mind racing. "You mean the minor gang from Wild Dismal? Why? They're nobodies."

"They took someone. I'm trying to get her back."

The little girl. The cynic in her wanted to believe his concern was cover for a power play, but she didn't think so. "Try Wild Dismal."

"They've moved out. Even their messengers. I don't know where they are now."

"Whoever you're trying to get back is probably with their new boss. Someone took out Harl and purged his people, so the Pails probably turned over your missing friend to them."

The intruder was silent for a second. "The Pails are the ones who took out Harl."

Onderishta sat up, turning to face the direction of that soft, raw voice. Then she remembered she'd been told not to move. "They couldn't," she said. "It's not possible. They don't have the heavies."

"They have a Katr warrior with godkind magic and a ghostkind blade. He's worth a dozen street thugs, maybe more. The Pails arranged the raid at the hammerball courts, they made sure there was a collected body on site, and they've taken control of his black-market medical operation. I saw the glitterkind ear Harl gave them. It was no larger than a child's. They might have been Harl's underlings once, but no longer."

She had a dozen reasons not to believe him, but she did. To think that a bunch of minor heavies had glitterkind flesh and godkind magic…

Looking around at the inky darkness around her, she realized the Katr wasn't the only one with a gift from the fallen gods.

"Glitterkind flesh, eh?" Onderishta rubbed her face. This was confirmation of Culzatik's suspicions. "So, that woman who was cut open, Rulenya, child of Rashila, wasn't just killed for show? You think she was really collected?"

"Yes."

"Shit.

"That's why I have to find the Pails. I need them to tell me if the daughter was collected too."

Onderishta didn't have to think about that for long. "She wasn't. At least, I don't think she was. The discovery of that body was a scandal and made Harl's parsu withhold support when he needed it most. If there had been a child's body, too, it would have triggered another Downscale War. They can't risk it. No, the girl almost certainly wasn't collected. She might have been murdered, but it's more likely that they sold her to a workshop, or they put her to work for them."

Whoever was crouching in the darkness made no response, and Onderishta could not begin to guess what he was thinking.

"I know who you are," she said. The realization struck her suddenly. "You're the pawnbroker. Kyrioc, child of No One. But that name's bullshit, right? You're just hiding your connections. Tell me your real name."

"The Broken Man. And you still haven't told me where to find the Pails."

His voice sounded subtly different. More alive somehow. Onderishta was right. It wasn't a pretense. He really was searching for the little girl.

"The Upgarden hammerball courts were Harl's public throne, and his replacement will want to sit where he sat." She called up her courage. "You know, you were smart to hide yourself after putting my constables in the hospital. I'm going to find you, and no matter what tricks you have, I'm going to put a collar on you."

"Before you do, visit the medical bureaucrats and find out what happens to a glitterkind that has been cut too deeply and too often. Don't let them brush you off with a vague answer. Make them tell. Everyone in this city depends on it."

"Wait. If the whole city is in danger, I need to know— We need your help!"

The pitch darkness moved away like a blowing fog. Once again, Suloh's dim glow shone through her window shutters. Onderishta lunged for the headboard and drew the knife, but she did not stand.

She heard the front door open and close. Perhaps the intruder was gone. Perhaps she was safe again.

The Pails. The pawnshop broker. The Katr informant. The mislaid package. The harvested woman. The workshop filled with heavies who'd been killed with a single stroke. The murder and expulsion of the foreign friends. It all came together, now that she knew the northerner had godkind magic.

She hurried into the front room to make sure that Zetinna wasn't lying dead on the floor but she was nowhere in sight. She was fine. Presumably.

Onderishta's knees suddenly felt weak, and she gripped the edge of the table to keep from falling over. The bark of laughter that escaped her was so sharp that she frightened herself. The knife clattered against the floor.

He could have killed her easily. So easily.

What time was it? She threw back the shutters. Zetinna could judge the lateness of the hour by the stars, but she wasn't here.

Thank the fallen gods.

The hour didn't matter. She wasn't going to sleep tonight. Maybe she would never be able to sleep here again.

Dressing quickly, she hurried outside and lit her lantern from the flame of the oil lamp at the intersection. Then, bared knife in hand, she hurried toward Gray Flames and the medical bureaucrats there.

CHAPTER TWENTY-SEVEN

Kyrioc *circled the block* around Harl's hammerball courts twice, searching for the exit Harl used to escape the constables. He didn't find it, but he did notice a constable watching him closely. Kyrioc was still dressed in his funeral black—the cloth torn from his fight with the Katr—and Pentulis's ancient cloak, both of which were out of place among the nobles and merchants in this neighborhood. After his second circuit, an ironshirt pushed off from the lamppost toward him, and Kyrioc went down the long stairs into High Apricot.

Everywhere he looked, he saw children, but none of them looked like the beetles the Pails employed. Either their clothes were too fine, or they chattered too much, or they seemed to have nothing to do.

The Pails were working Riliska, or they had sold her. All he had to do was find someone to ask, and he would know where to find her. Simple.

He traveled the length of High Apricot and spotted no one. Descending to Low Apricot, where the platform halls and cafes gave way to casinos and brothels, he found a few likely candidates, but it quickly became clear that they were pickpockets and petty thieves, not messengers.

In Low Market, he finally spotted one. A boy at least two years younger than Riliska hurried around a corner with a wooden doll in his hand. Kyrioc immediately recognized it from the shelves of the warehouse in Wild Dismal. In the boy's other hand, he held a rag doll.

Ducking his head as he hurried past a pair of constables, Kyrioc fell into step behind the beetle and followed him into the maze of planks, platforms, and shops.

* * *

"FEEL HOW HEAVY THIS IS?"

Riliska accepted the doll from Bonsital, one of the other beetles. They were about the same age, but Bonsital talked as though Riliska was a little child.

The doll was like the ones she'd seen on the shelves of the warehouse. Bonsital had just gone into a carpet shop with a stained, ratty old rag doll. She'd emerged with this wooden one.

"There's coin inside," the girl whispered. "But you must never open it. Not ever. They skin you for real if you do. For real. Just peel you. Then they go after your family."

Goosebumps ran down Riliska's neck. She'd seen the way those heavies had stared at her, especially the one with the steel chain. She believed it.

"Watch," Bonsital said, pulling her out of sight between two rain barrels.

Another beetle—this one no older than seven, Riliska thought—came down the plankway and hurried to a noodle shop. He was holding a rag doll. When the woman behind the counter saw him, she grabbed the boy's arm and dragged him into the back.

Then she scanned the street.

Riliska looked at her feet, careful not to make eye contact. "What's in the rag doll?"

"One of these," Bonsital said, waggling the little wooden doll back and forth, "but it's empty. Also some white tar, I think. This is our job. This is what keeps our families safe."

The two of them slipped out of their hiding space, hid from a tall man in a black cloak, then climbed down a flight of stairs. It was time for the next delivery.

* * *

ONDERISHTA WAS LATE FOR her own meeting, but she found Fay, Mirishiya, and Trillistin deep in conversation when she arrived. She hurried into the council room and set her empty lantern on the desk. Fay glanced at it, then studied her face. He was clearly concerned.

"Well," he said, nodding at the lantern, "so much for getting a good night's rest."

"I'm sorry I'm late," Onderishta said, gasping a little from the effort of hurrying up the stairs. "Bureaucrats can be infuriating."

They laughed. Trillistin jumped up from his chair to pull one out for her, then poured her tea from the pot. It had gone cool, but it was welcome nonetheless.

"Are you hungry, boss?" Fay asked.

"After, after," she said. "Trillistin, what have you found out?"

He stood and clasped his hands behind his back. The Safroys' servants addressed their masters the same way. "I sought out Jallientus, child of Jalliusha, in Suloh's Tower and befriended him there. It took some time, but eventually he trusted me enough to describe his life as he lived it before he was taken into the tower. He told me he was a 'beetle' in the employ of a local gangster. A courier."

Fay turned to Onderishta. "I've heard of this, haven't I?"

She shrugged. "Child messengers are common in Koh-Kaulma and Koh-Benjatso, but I didn't know the practice had spread here. Continue."

Trillistin nodded. "According to Jallientus, it's common for Harl's couriers to be collared by the ironshirts. Coin and white tar are taken from them, and costs are high. The Pails use a different system, something they learned when they sailed around the Semprestian when they were young. They use children, called beetles, to deliver drugs and money, and they're almost never intercepted. The beetles live with the heavies, sleeping together in..." He hesitated. "Filth," he said, looking uncomfortable, as though describing the problem made him complicit. "They sleep in filth. Jallientus described spilled chamber pots, sheets that were never washed, cheap food, no schooling, no...no care. No one talks to them except to scold them or give them orders. No one looks out for them. No one cares."

"Whose kids are these?" Fay asked. "Their own?"

"They come from gambling houses," Trillistin said. "Casinos, dice alleys, card shops—" He saw Fay was about to interrupt again, and hurried to his point. "Their parents get deep into debt, and the Pails take their children as payment."

Fay's mouth hung open, and Onderishta grimaced. Of all the vices the criminals of Koh-Salash unleashed on the city, gambling was considered the least harmful. Now they were a means to steal children? "You're talking about slavery."

"I am," Trillistin said. "The kids are kept in line with threats against them and their families. Jallientus only accepted a place in the tower because his bosses think he's dead."

"And these children," Onderishta said, "are just running through the streets with white tar? And gold coin?"

"Stuffed into dolls," Trillistin said. "Yes. From what Jallientus told me, no one ever pays attention to them because they look like orphans."

Fay turned to Onderishta. "And no one gives a shit. By the fallen gods, I hate this fucking city sometimes."

"Have you discovered anything else?" Onderishta asked.

The boy frowned. "I tried to find more beetles to talk to, but—"

"You mean out in the city?"

"Well, yes."

"Okay," Onderishta said. "Don't do that again—ever—unless I tell you it's all right. But you did good." She downed the last of her tea. "My turn. I had an unwelcome visitor last night, in my home. It was the pawnbroker who fought his way out of the tower."

"Kyrioc?" Fay blurted out.

"If that's his real name." She told them about their conversation.

There was silence for a few moments. "That explains a lot," Fay finally said, "except why now?"

"The package that was stolen at Sailsday's Regret. Our pawnbroker friend claims that it contained a tiny glitterkind ear."

Fay stood out of his chair as though he were about run out of the room to retrieve it, then sat again. "That's confirmation, if we believe him."

"I do," Onderishta said. "The Pails proved themselves capable by bringing Harl this beetle system that's been operating under our noses for who knows how long, so he offers them a chance to move up into black-market medical care. But Harl thinks this delivery is too important to trust to the beetles and insists on using one of his heavies, which draws the wrong sort of attention."

"The courier gets robbed, right? By the woman who lived in that hovel with the little girl."

"I doubt she realized just how valuable that score was until after. She was too smart to hide it in her shabby room, so she goes to the pawnshop next door. Remember the robe we found that was torn open at the seams? Harl orders the Pails to recover his property and sends one of his people along to babysit. They track down the woman, grab her and the daughter, then retrieve the package from the pawnshop."

Fay nodded. "The Pails knew Harl would blame them for the failed exchange, and so they struck him before he could strike them."

"First they took the point to Second Boar," Onderishta said, "then they delivered the collected corpse of that woman at exactly the same moment that we were conducting our raid."

"They must have something against that pawnshop asshole, too."

"Maybe." Onderishta rubbed her chin. "Maybe they didn't want another magical asshole running around the city. Or maybe they didn't even know who he was. Maybe he was just a guy who saw the package and who could be manipulated into running this errand."

"So, why did he come to you?"

"He wants the little girl."

"I'm sorry," Fay said, "but I don't believe it. I can't. The man's been in the city for one year, so he's not her father. Is he risking his life for one random little girl when the city's gangs are up for grabs and a piece of glitterkind worth five Harkan regents is in play? A man who can fight his way out of the south tower? It can't be that simple. He must be playing a game of his own."

"Excuse me," Mirishiya said. The apprentices had been silent—as they should be—while Onderishta and Fay talked, but the girl had seized on the first pause. "Do you think this piece of glitterkind came from the Lost Ward?"

Trillistin leaned forward. "What's the Lost Ward?"

Mirishiya was surprised he didn't know. "A story I've heard all my life— a glitterkind went missing from the home of a noble family—ward-nobles, I mean—and ended up in some slum. The whole thing was hushed up. In the story, anyone who was sick or injured could cure themselves just by kissing the Lost Ward on the lips. It had been kissed so many times that it had shrunk to the size of a little doll, but it still had the brand of its noble family on it."

"What brand?" Onderishta snapped.

"It's different every time the story's told," the girl said, more quietly. "Sometimes it's a mountain, sometimes an eagle or a bull."

A bull. The symbol of the Safroy family.

Onderishta laid her fists on the table before her. "All right. No one is to talk about this Lost Ward business outside of this room. Understand? If anyone asks, tell them our investigation is incomplete. Rumors of a Lost Ward have been around since I was small, and nothing ever comes of it. Talking about it now will make people think we've lost our minds. Trillistin, come here." She opened a chest on the shelf behind her. Once she found the token she was looking for, she pressed it into the boy's hand. "Take this to Gray Flames. Do you know my boss's name? It's Hulmanis defe-Firos. Show this at the gate and you'll be taken to his office. He needs to know about the beetles, and you're going to tell him. He should know about good work you did." She tousled his close-cropped hair.

"Thank you," he said.

"If the ear is small…" Fay said, letting his voice trail off. "That's dangerous, isn't it?"

Trillistin moved slowly, hoping to overhear her answer. Onderishta gestured for him to sit. "That's why I was late. It took all morning to bully the medical bureaucrats to tell me exactly what will happen if a glitterkind is cut too often or too deeply. The pawnbroker insisted I needed to know. He said it could cost the life of every living soul in Koh-Salash."

All three stared at her expectantly. She began to explain what she'd learned.

* * *

THE CROWDS HELPED.

The beetle moved through Low Market, and as Kyrioc followed, he stayed in the shadows of the decks above as much as possible. His cloak of mirrors wouldn't work in full daylight, but the daylight couldn't touch him here, and the crowds of shoppers and sellers made the magic stronger.

But the boy was quick and darted through a crowd the way only small children could. Kyrioc tried to keep pace, but pushing through traffic—or drawing attention to himself in any way—was risky. His cloak made people see what they expected, not what was there. Whenever he did something unexpected, even if it did nothing more than make someone look twice, it weakened the magic of the cloak.

Then, as he hurried through an intersection, someone on a platform above moved something suddenly—a huge placard or a hanging canvas— and a shaft of sunlight fell directly onto Kyrioc. His cloak of mirrors vanished like a wisp of fog.

A pair of ironshirts standing guard on the cross street glanced at him, then looked again. At the same moment, the boy ducked into an alleyway.

Slipping into an ironmonger's shop, Kyrioc pressed his fingers to his lips, vaulted the counter, and ducked into the back. The man at the counter called for him to halt, but Kyrioc had already reached the alley.

Alarmed by the shopkeeper's cry, the boy turned around as Kyrioc ducked around the corner of the building. The stamp of small feet running on wood sounded out. The boy sprinted straight toward another shop door.

The street was narrow and the windows on the right had been shuttered. Kyrioc leaped for the balcony and pulled himself up, then slipped through a broken shutter.

The place smelled like decomposing rat. The back wall was stained with piss streaks and the floor covered by broken crates, crooked shelving, and pigeon shit.

Peering through a crack in the shutter, Kyrioc saw the constables emerge from the ironmonger's shop. They looked around, then started down the alley in the opposite direction from the boy.

Kyrioc hurried to the end of the building. The door the boy had run for was shut tight. When he appeared, Kyrioc would have to move quickly from his hiding place to keep up.

Someone passed very close to the gap in the shutter. Kyrioc stepped back, a floorboard creaking under his tread. The door latch rattled, but it was rotten and wouldn't release. A booted foot smashed the door inward, and the constables who had followed him into the ironmonger's shop forced their way through.

"This is him," the lead said. He was about Kyrioc's age, and had the flattened nose of a fighter. "This is the asshole that broke my cousin's knee."

The one behind him was bigger. "He's gonna look good in a collar." Both men drew their truncheons.

Kyrioc stepped away from the daylight streaming through the door.

The ironshirts grinned confidently. They were armed and armored. He was not. They thought they had every advantage.

As the first constable stepped forward, he swung his truncheon downward in a swift diagonal stroke. Kyrioc pivoted inside the swing, caught the constable's wrist, and flipped him to the floor.

The noise of his armored form striking the boards was gigantic. Kyrioc had to hurry. He sidestepped the second constable, kicking low. The man landed atop his partner. Both cried out, but the fellow on the bottom got the worst of it.

Kyrioc quickly stomped on the big one's ankle. He howled, rolling over and trying to clutch at his injured leg despite his bulky breastplate.

The first ironshirt had already scrambled onto his hands and knees, truncheon still in his grip. Kyrioc stomped on his hand, breaking three of his fingers. This one didn't cry out—he was too much of a fighter for that—but the expression on his face showed he was beaten and knew it. He expected to die.

Stripping off their helmets, Kyrioc struck each on the side of the jaw. They slumped to the floor, helpless and dazed. The effect wouldn't last long but it was the best he could do. He wasn't going to waste the lives of honest constables. Not today.

He hurried back to the bright side of the room, wondering if the boy had already left. As he approached the shutter, the shop door swung outward and the boy stepped out, looking warily in every direction. He'd exchanged his rag doll for a second wooden one. The boy hurried away. Kyrioc yanked open the shutter and vaulted over the balcony rail.

Only to find two more ironshirts waiting for him. Both were lanky, with knife scars on their faces. "Well, well," the tall one said. "Black Apricot is paying for scar-faced men. Looks like we get an extra visit to the brothel this week." They didn't draw their truncheons, because they were already holding bared knives. "Come peacefully, and live."

Kyrioc slid the Childfall Staff from his belt.

It was almost a foot long when he held it at his side, but a second later, when the grinning constables tried to flank him, it was as long as a soldier's broadsword.

He left their corpses, armor crushed and flesh burning, in the alley.

Kyrioc ran around the curving plankway, sliding his weapon—once again reduced to the length of his hand—back into his belt. He was in pursuit of the beetle, yes, but he also needed to burn off the flood of shameful joy that welled within him.

He had wasted lives again. For seven years, he had survived by bringing death to enemy and prey, until the desire to take life had become a living thing inside him. A dragon. He'd hoped he could leave the dragon on Vu-Dolmont, but that was a fool's wish and he knew it.

He'd also hoped the dragon would slumber on the horde of lives he had already fed it.

It had, if uneasily.

But he was wasting lives again, one after another. And now that his enemies knew about his cloaks, his chances of slipping away unnoticed with Riliska were dwindling. To free his friend, he was going to have to *fight*.

And that thought made his dragon stir.

He spotted the beetle—those little wooden dolls clutched to his chest—creeping warily toward two figures at the top of a distant stair. One was a hulking man with hands like sledges, and the other was a small, lithe woman holding a slender spear.

Weapons of that length were illegal inside city limits, with very few exceptions, so she must have been a licensed bodyguard. Judging by the way the pickpockets and other alley rats averted their eyes, the beetle was her charge.

The bodyguards led the child down the stair, and Kyrioc followed as closely as he could. The farther down they went, the deeper the shadows, until they reached the bare wood and endless twilight of the bottom of Koh-Salash.

It felt good to be out of the daylight. Kyrioc summoned his cloak of mirrors and hunched his shoulders to match the crowd of drinkers huddled beneath the stairs. Down here, there was nothing but forgotten people and heavy plankways built for transporting goods to upcity shops.

A carriage pulled by two horses came around a cluster of wooden pylons, and the boy clambered inside. The carriage driver heard the door click shut and snapped the reins, riding off toward the south.

Kyrioc followed.

CHAPTER TWENTY-EIGHT

The idea was Trillistin's.

Onderishta marveled at the simplicity of it. She had never considered the idea that growing up as a servant in a noble house—even a minor one—would have trained him to quiet deception, but it made sense. What else could explain the boy's devious mind?

Mirishiya and three constables poured water over their heads, then stumbled down a set of stairs from High Apricot into Wild Dismal. They didn't run. They wheezed and reeled as though they were exhausted, chasing a little thief and pushing themselves to the limits of their endurance.

The heavies standing guard on the Pails' warehouse loved it. They looked at the drenched faces, the men with their mouths hanging open, and the exaggerated slow-motion strides of the armored constables, and jeered.

"Make them work for it, girl!"

"Better pick up the pace, fat asses!"

"That little girl is shaming you. *Shaming* you!"

When one of the heavies offered to help Mirishiya—and she told them to fuck off—they laughed at her impertinence. Onderishta knew they wouldn't have found Trillistin so amusing, even if he could swear naturally, which he couldn't.

At the main doors, Mirishiya sprinted away at the same moment the constables, no longer pretending to be exhausted, rushed the door.

A dozen more ironshirts were a block behind, and they weren't playacting. The first three hit the doors before they could be barred and held them open until the main force arrived.

By the fallen gods, it was good work and a much-needed victory. Onderishta clapped Trillistin's shoulder and marched down the street to take possession of everything the Pails owned in this world.

* * *

KILLER OF DEVILS DID not like loitering in Wild Dismal, but his employer said it was necessary, and it was not his duty to argue. At least her younger brother was well hidden while overseeing his new responsibilities.

But Tin could not abandon the warehouse without first collecting her records, her surgeon, and the coin she kept there. Her new role as the head of the syndicate had already earned twice the coin she had saved, but Killer's employer was not wasteful or extravagant. What she had acquired, she would keep.

That included her old headquarters.

"It kept us safe for six years," she had said. "It's my home."

"A castle is only as safe as the troops guarding it."

She had nodded thoughtfully, then begun plans to relocate. Killer was simultaneously glad and disappointed. The great tribal leaders he had known in his youth, commanders of legions of fierce warriors, had rarely been open to good counsel.

Killer was glad his employer valued his opinion. It disappointed him that she was making the smart, safe move. The longer it took for this woman and her brother to be taken from this world, the longer he would be stuck in this doomed city.

The narcotics had already been relocated, along with the dolls the beetles used to hide the money. But the surgeon Harl had used—an elderly Carrig—had either fled the city or died in The Caves. Tin needed her addict.

A roar of laughter sounded from outside. While Killer strained to hear what the heavies were yelling, Tin shoved High Cap toward the door. "Fetch my doctor and follow."

He hurried away.

Tin muscled her leather satchel over her shoulder. It bulged with coin, mostly copper knots and sails. She would not travel quickly with that load.

Then she surprised him. "Killer of Devils," she said—it was only the second time she had said his name aloud—"do you remember the emergency exit I showed you on your first day here?"

He did. In the back room, Killer tilted the shelves, then lifted the trapdoor beneath, revealing a set of stairs. When he stepped on them, his weight lowered the far end until it struck a public stair down into Shadetree.

He led the way into safety.

* * *

NIGHT FELL AS THE beetle's carriage passed into Spillwater. Kyrioc quickened his pace to close the gap between them, in case his quarry began to weave through the streets.

In his youth, the leaking sewer lines that gave the Spillwater deck its name had kept him from coming to the south end of downcity, but since his return, he'd passed through several times. The houses had been built of cast-off wood and tarred skins, and the plankways creaked under his tread. Rotting garbage and other random trash had been arranged into impromptu basins and gutters, to capture the splash and flow from leaking pipes, some of which fell all the way from Dawnshine. The stench was like poison.

Shadowy forms moved furtively down alleys, heading for the stairs and lifts that would take them upcity for their night's occupation. There were a few honest folk down on this deck, but they didn't survive long.

After only three blocks, the carriage turned eastward, then northward, onto another descending ramp. There was only one district below and it was, if possible, even more hellish than this one. Mudside.

When they descended far enough to be even with the top of the inner wall, they hit a guard station. This post wasn't controlled by ordinary constables. Salashi soldiers armed with pikes and bearing full helms forged into devil faces stood here. The carriage needed only to pause briefly.

Kyrioc—once he called up his cloak of mirrors—was waved through.

Coming back the other way would be complicated. The damned could descend, but they were no longer welcome above.

Farther down, at the edges of the plankway, there were two torches and two stools and two men to sit on them. Both were inches from a hundred-foot plunge into the muck below. Machetes rested on their laps. The carriage barely slowed as one of the men lit a taper from his torch and transferred the flame to the carriage lantern.

With a nod of gratitude, the driver headed down into the darkness.

Kyrioc shuffled his step, hung his head, and called up his cloak of mirrors again. Most of those who entered Mudside were driven there by debt, addiction, or other calamity. He played the part. The heavies glared but did not address him.

The carriage pulled farther away with each second.

There were five more pairs of torches on the road down to Mudside, each well guarded. Kyrioc kept to the center of the plankway, where the light from the torches was dimmest. The heavies watched him but did not challenge him or try to shake him down. He was just another of life's losers falling out of the world.

The carriage slowed as the ramp descended to the top of Yth's ribs. This far downcity, torches and lanterns burned everywhere, but there were few moving figures and only one moving light. Eventually, that light made its way to Yth's last rib, then turned westward toward the spine. The dim lantern vanished as it passed behind a building.

Kyrioc made his inexorable way forward. Without a carriage on the road, the heavies guarding it had no interest in anything but throwing dice. The air reeked of overturned chamber pots. The stink of the leaking sewer pipes that gave the Spillwater deck its name was concentrated here, because this was where those leaks drained to. The heat of the summer's day lingered, and the inner wall, the decks above, and Salash Hill blocked the ocean breezes that might have brought relief.

But from the vantage point of the ramp, Kyrioc could look across the open space, here at the bottom of this doomed city, and see the outline of Yth's skeleton told with pinpricks of firelight. It would have been beautiful, if the air had not made every pore and follicle on his body feel foul.

At the last rib, when Kyrioc turned to follow the path of the beetle's carriage, the last two guards took hold of their machetes.

"This ain't for you. Get down in the muck." They pointed northward.

On the far side of Yth's last rib was a set of stairs leading downward. Kyrioc could see nothing down there, not firelight, not movement. He could only hear the trickle of flowing water, and the sound of someone far away pleading for mercy.

The southernmost edge of Low Market, built upon Yth's hipbones, stood about a third of a mile away. As far as Kyrioc could see, on this level, only the long, firelit god's spine connected the place he stood with that neighborhood. There might have been plankways down in the muck and darkness, but he couldn't see them.

"Get down the stairs," the heavy called to him, "or we'll throw you down."

Kyrioc descended. After two dozen stairs, he was out of the torchlight. He dropped his cloak of mirrors.

If he found Riliska here, he had few choices for getting her out: down the spine to the dubious safety of Low Market, descend into the sewage-soaked mud, or return the way he came, either fighting or in disguise. He had no plan and no need for one.

He crept back up the stairs. The heavies had moved back to the light of their torches. Inside his cloak of shadows, he slipped past them.

In Mudside, each rib was its own small district. The eastern end of this rib curved upward and ended far above the northern edge of Woodgarden.

However, the back of the bone had sunk so deep into the mud that the rib stood barely fifty feet above it.

Here, the gangsters of Koh-Salash had built a miniature deck, over three hundred feet wide and more than eight hundred feet long, from the road to Yth's spine.

But Kyrioc could not find the carriage. If it had ridden all the way to the spine, he'd have no idea where to search. North back to Low Market? South toward one of the other ribs or even Yth's skull?

No, the route was too circuitous. This had to be the carriage's destination. Kyrioc spun about. There was a small open stadium with a sandy pit in the middle, but it was in such disrepair that he doubted anyone had fought there in years.

Across the street from it was a row of rotting vendors' stalls built around brick ovens.

Wood had also rotted in the dueling yard, the barrack, the workshop, and the low apartment buildings near the spine. Some time earlier—more than a decade, Kyrioc thought—this place had hosted gladiatorial combat where the constables and bureaucracy could not interfere.

Not only were the buildings falling apart, they'd been cannibalized, too. Planks had been stripped...

Kyrioc stopped. He could peer into all the buildings except the workshop. It hadn't been stripped.

He loosened a broken shutter and peered inside. It was nearly pitch-dark, but the magic of his cloak let him see the faint outlines of benches and work stations. He stepped away and noticed the shutters on the next window didn't match the one beside him.

The other buildings had been cannibalized for this one.

Kyrioc circled three sides of the building—the northern end extended beyond the edge of the deck. There were only two doors and no guards. The small side door was either locked or jammed. The front double doors were as big as the warehouse doors in the Pails' headquarters in Wild Dismal, and they were large enough to admit a horse-drawn carriage.

That's when he noticed faint sweep marks on the front approach. There was no trace of carriage wheels or hooves, but the dirt and grime had been swept recently.

Kyrioc pressed his ear to the jamb. At first, he heard nothing. Then there was a nicker, and a human voice murmuring as if in greeting. Other voices responded. They didn't sound kind. The building was guarded, but the guards were inside.

He circled to the side of the building facing the spine. The double doors faced the street to the south, and the small door hung in the eastern wall.

Once, the whole of Yth's rib had been covered with a smooth deck of ordinary wood, but in the years since, small stumps had burst through. Even all the way down in the dark, Yth's bounty grew.

Kyrioc willed the Childfall Staff to stretch to the length of a quarterstaff, then he wedged one end into a notch where two stumps stood close to each other. Bracing himself, he willed it to extend farther, straining against its growing weight until it was long enough to rest on the edge of the roof.

Hooking his ankles around the rough surface of the staff, he climbed. It bent slightly under his weight, but it bent slightly—though never more than that—under almost any weight. Kyrioc would have preferred to reduce the angle of his ascent so he could walk up—being able to move quickly off the ground had saved his life many times in his exile—but the staff would have been too heavy to manage quietly.

What he found on the roof surprised him. The roof was slanted toward the north and had been re-tarred recently. If the sides of the building made it look derelict, the top was pristine. Someone had spent time and money to make sure the filthy runoff from the decks above could not get inside.

The Childfall Staff had become wedged between two roof slats, but at Kyrioc's touch, it grew narrow enough to pull free. Then he lifted it, struggling to keep the far end from dragging on the deck or slamming against the building while he shrank it to a manageable weight.

There was a hatch on the northern end of the roof, and it was unlocked. Kyrioc descended into a small room. Long brooms stood in the corner, and the shelves were lined with buckets of tar.

The room opened onto a catwalk. A dim lantern burned at the southern end of the building. He crept close enough to see the horses still hitched to the carriage, and the carriage driver playing cards with three heavies.

Kyrioc crept to the northwestern corner of the catwalk and descended a spiral stair. It creaked but no one noticed. He reached the workshop floor, but the stairs continued down.

Basements were not a common feature in the architecture of Koh-Salash. Light shone from somewhere below, and Kyrioc headed toward it.

The stair ended in a large room lit by a single lantern turned down so low, it barely glowed. The walls had been scrubbed clean—in fact, the sting of vinegar was still sharp, and bucket and brush still stood in the corner.

Then Kyrioc noticed a row of tables and the large glass tank against the far wall.

All three tables had bodies on them, each covered with a long cloth.

The two nearest were full-grown adults, but the third was smaller. Kyrioc's hair stood on end and his stomach felt leaden. Who was under that cloth?

He forced himself to walk to the nearest body, forced himself to touch the edge of the cloth, forced himself to lift it.

Forced himself to look.

It was a young man, not particularly large or handsome, but very dead. His skin was quite pale. It took Kyrioc a moment to realize he was Carrig. His eyes had been taken. Lifting the cloth higher revealed that his abdomen had been emptied.

The second body was like the first, but female. She, too, had been opened and emptied.

Finally, he approached the last table. The figure looked so small…as small as Riliska.

Kyrioc couldn't bring himself to lift the cloth from the end, so he moved to the side and raised it there.

A tiny hand. The nails and fingers had been painted. He touched the cool, dead flesh and saw that the face Riliska had painted onto his nail still remained. What's more, it matched. Riliska had done this child's art, too.

Goosebumps ran down his back, and the dragon inside him stirred.

Was it her?

From the child's wrist and upward, there was nothing but exposed meat. This little one had been skinned.

Her hand must have been too complicated to cut, and with that thought, Kyrioc moved to the head of the table and lifted the cloth to reveal the head.

It wasn't Riliska. Her face was intact from the chin to her hairline, and it wasn't her. The Pails had taken her eyes, her scalp, and her skin but, it seemed, not her organs.

Kyrioc went to the tank against the wall. Mesh bags hung in the cloudy water. The largest held folded skin. Long black hairs floated out from it. Of course. A Salashi might take a Carrig liver or eye, but they didn't want a patch of pale skin on their dark one, not if they didn't have to. And what would be smoother and more attractive than the skin of a child?

Taking a deep, shuddering breath, Kyrioc laid a trembling hand on the side of the tank. Little children, skinned… In all the years he'd spent in exile, he'd seen unbelievable suffering and faced innumerable hardships. He'd done things to survive that filled him with shame even now.

But no one was killing these children to survive. They were doing it for a little extra coin. The Pails had protection rackets, casinos, white tar, brothels, and more, probably, but it wasn't enough.

Kyrioc's skin was flushed, his senses fully alert. The urgency to find

Riliska reopened within him like the door of a furnace. Would she be next? Was she already dead?

He opened a door to reveal a broad hallway filled with thick copper piping as wide as a loaf of bread. They came upward, curling like the pipes of a still. At three intervals were broad copper junctions, like curving tubs. Each tub had a small plugged drain on the bottom and a sealed nozzle entry at the top. A faint bubbling sound came from them. Water traps. Whatever was being vented was being filtered through water to clean it first. After the third copper box, the outflowing pipe led back along the ceiling of the hall, presumably to vent out the northern side of the building.

The acrid smell made Kyrioc queasy. At the end of the hallway was another catwalk, but this one was made of skywood—no creaking planks here. He leaned forward.

The pipes originated from a huge copper kettle—about four feet across—that was round and flat like a bun someone had sat on. A low fire made it burble gently.

Three children in brown smocks walked in circles around it, stirring the contents with long skywood paddles. Standing against the wall were two heavies. One had a billy club tethered to his wrist, flipping it back and forth in a bored way. The other looked to be asleep with his eyes open. Unlike the children, they wore silk masks over their noses and mouths.

To the left was a long table. A half-dozen children—all about the same age as Riliska—stood around it, pulling small brown stones from a bowl in the center and laying them in a vise. The children were wearing leather mittens, and that's when he realized they were not stones at all.

Those were ulund nuts, although they were larger than the ones he'd seen on Vu-Dolmont. The children scraped the insides of those broken shells, smearing the sticky resin and cluster of white seeds into a little bowl.

After that, he knew, the bowls would be emptied into the kettle and cooked into white tar.

There was something familiar about one of the girls at the table. Kyrioc could only see the top of her head but—

Then she turned toward him to stop a smaller child who was about to touch his mitten to his nose, and Kyrioc could see that she did not look like Riliska at all.

"What the fuck are you doing?"

The sudden shout startled everyone, including Kyrioc. Wooden Pail stormed out from beneath the catwalk and rounded on one of the children.

"It was time to add wood to the fire, sir," the child said. His voice was so faint, he was difficult to hear. The boy glanced at the heavies. "He told me to—"

"I don't fucking care!" Wooden shouted, bending low to move his face close to the boy's. "Do you know what happens if this shit cooks over? Well? Speak up!"

"The fumes will kill us all?"

"A cookover will ruin the whole batch! And we're not adding water to cool it down, because that shit has to be carried all the way down here. Now pull out that piece of firewood. *Right now!*"

The boy glanced at the nearest heavy, then stretched his hand toward the fire. A piece of wood jutted from the flames, and the fire slowly crawled up its length. The boy stuck his bare hand in quickly and yanked it out. The burning hunk of wood clattered onto the floor, and the boy cried out and clutched his wrist.

"Oh, look at this," Wooden said, "a new generation of martyrs. You"— he pointed at the heavy who'd been fidgeting with his billy club—"take this kid in the back and clean him up. I don't want to hear him crying."

The heavy shrugged, lightly rapped the boy on the top of his head with the club, and took his arm. The blow was not enough to harm the kid but painful enough to frighten him. He fell quiet as the man dragged him around the kettle, through the dark, empty space to the right, and into another little room.

Kyrioc followed.

His skin was tingling. He felt as though he was standing on the edge of a precipice, and if he just leaned out far enough, he would plummet with no way to stop himself, and damnation take those below.

CHAPTER TWENTY-NINE

Kyrioc descended a ladder* in the darkness. The only lights were on the far side of the kettle—which threw its shadow over him—and a lantern in the side office where the heavy had led the boy. Its wick was set so low that only shadows seemed to move within.

The little boy whimpered quietly. The man told him to shut up. Kyrioc moved toward them, feeling as though he was floating like a ghost.

The heavy had settled onto a stool with his back to the door. He lifted a jug of brandy and pulled the boy's burned hand toward him.

"This is going to hurt, but it'll hurt more if you noise at me." He poured the brandy on the boy's fingertips. The boy shuddered and bared his teeth but stayed silent. By the fallen gods, he couldn't have been older than seven.

There were three more children lying in a bed of rags in the room. All were between four and six, and they were filthy. The chamber pot in the corner brimmed over.

The small children turned their attention to Kyrioc standing in the doorway. Then the injured boy looked up at him.

Kyrioc had dropped his cloak of shadows without realizing it, but it didn't matter. In this moment, very few things did.

The heavy glanced over his shoulder, then smiled. "Hello, friend," he said, his hand groping for his billy club.

Kyrioc slammed the iron staff onto the top of his head.

The heavy grunted loudly and collapsed.

"You better not be touching those kids again," Wooden called from the other room. "You can't afford them."

Kyrioc put his finger to his lips and waved the boy with the burned hand toward the other children. They stared at him with terrified expressions. He doused the lantern and summoned his cloak of shadows.

Two heavies approached from the far side of the kettle, knives drawn. Kyrioc knew they would see only inky darkness, so he stood in the doorway and watched them creep forward, fear and confusion on their faces.

If they ran, Kyrioc would let them live. Only if they ran.

They crept forward like goats to a pit trap.

Wooden followed, head tilted like a curious dog. He raised his lantern, angling the mirror to shine into the doorway.

That bright, focused light made Kyrioc's cloak retreat, so he pivoted out of the doorway and dropped it. He cocked his arm back, ready to lay the first blow the moment a face appeared. If it was the tall heavy, he'd aim for the throat. The short one would take it on his forehead. *You can't afford them*, Wooden had said, and the terrible rage Kyrioc was trying to keep in check thrashed inside him.

He had to keep control. He was only going to kill these men.

The first lunged through the door and thrust to the side, straight at Kyrioc. Had he seen something, or was it a lucky guess? Kyrioc's swing, already in progress, altered to meet the attack, slamming the man's wrist against the wall as the blade caught the edge of Kyrioc's vest.

The knife clattered to the floor. The second rushed in, point forward, and shoved the first toward him.

Kyrioc went flat against the wall, letting the heavy fall past. The second man brought his knife up, but Kyrioc caught his wrist and kicked the inside of his knee.

The man went down with a pitiful cry. The first dove for the knife he'd dropped. Kyrioc crushed his skull in one swift strike.

The second called for help.

Kyrioc bolted through the doorway. Wooden was already sprinting around the kettle toward a ladder on the far side of the room. The children immediately ducked beneath the furniture. "Guards!" Wooden shrieked. "Guards!"

Kyrioc pursued, feeling like a hound eager to taste blood.

Wooden reached the ladder but didn't have time to climb it. He flung the lantern at Kyrioc.

He could have dodged it easily, but it would have smashed on the floor near the children, the kettle, and all that white tar. Kyrioc twisted and caught the lantern's handle as it flew past.

Then Wooden was on him, slashing with his long knife.

The attacks were swift and savage. Kyrioc leaned away from the first one, but the tip of the knife still caught him on the chin. He dodged the second completely, and parried the third with such force, the weapon flew from Wooden's hand. Wooden froze, suddenly unsure what do to. Kyrioc kicked him, hard, in the crotch.

He stumbled but didn't go down, so Kyrioc slammed the Childfall Staff against the side of his jaw.

From the mezzanine above, a voice called, "Boss? Did you shout for us?"

"Cookover!" Kyrioc shrieked, trying to match Wooden's panicked voice. He dragged Wooden under the catwalk out of sight. "Cookover! Help!" He coughed and hacked, making choking noises high in his throat.

The voice above cursed in surprise and fear. Kyrioc promised himself that if any of Wooden's heavies came down the ladder to help the kids, he would let them live. He would have to fight them, probably break some of their bones, but he wouldn't waste their lives.

Kyrioc listened to several sets of retreating footsteps.

Wooden writhed on the floor. "Wait here," Kyrioc said, then slammed his iron staff onto the man's ankle. While the gangster choked out a scream, Kyrioc carried the lantern to the dark office.

The heavy with the ruined knee had gotten to his feet, although he could only put weight on one of them. His left hand braced against the table and his right held his knife.

"Keep back!" he barked, sweat pouring down his face. "Or I'll take the point to you."

Kyrioc stamped, feinting at the man. The heavy shifted his balance in response, put too much weight on his injured leg, and collapsed with a cry of pain. Kyrioc kicked the knife away and rolled him over, clearing a path to the door.

"Wait out there with the others."

The kids scampered past.

The heavy held up his empty hands, pleading silently.

Kyrioc hungered to take his life. He could have spent hours on it. No bloodkind could have savored a feast as much as Kyrioc would enjoy killing this man.

But the children in the other room needed help, and they would lead him to Riliska. Kyrioc smashed the man's skull with merciful swiftness.

The kids waited for him in the main room. "I'll be right back," he said, then went upstairs. The guards were gone but the carriage driver had just finished harnessing the horses. Maybe it was more than his life was worth to return without them, cookover or not.

While he backed the horses toward the front doors, Kyrioc came up behind him, spun him around, and struck him in the throat. Then he shoved the driver through the open doors. He fell onto the street, clutching at his throat and trying to breathe through a crushed windpipe. Someone nearby cursed in terror. Someone else shouted, "Cookover!" More footsteps led away.

Kyrioc tied the horses again, shushed them, and returned to the kids.

"Are there any other kids nearby?" They shook their heads. "Okay. Can you guys find me some rope?"

Three ran off. One older boy had an odd look in his eye. It was part anger, part sadness, and Kyrioc couldn't read it.

The blankets on the children's beds stank of piss, but they were large and without holes. Kyrioc threw the three largest onto the catwalk. Then he dragged the two smaller corpses into the main room. Wooden Pail was utterly still and his face ashen, except for the discoloration at the base of his jaw where it was broken. He'd fainted. Kyrioc helped himself to their purses and money belts.

By then, the children had returned with a coil of rope at least fifty feet long. While Kyrioc tied a loop around a dead man's chest, he heard a light step behind him. He pivoted away.

The boy with the unreadable expression lost his balance and fell over the heavy's corpse. He dropped Wooden's knife.

A second slower, and Kyrioc would have had a blade in his kidney.

The boy cursed, grabbed the knife again, and attacked, slashing wildly. Kyrioc caught his wrist and lifted him off the ground. The boy spit and cursed, kicking his small feet. The blade slipped from his grasp. "I'll kill you! Kill you!"

Kyrioc set him down and picked up the knife. The boy stared at the metal point and fell quiet. "Why?"

"You think you can fuck with the Pails? One of us is gonna kill you, and I hope it's me. It's gonna be me!"

"You don't have to be his slave anymore."

"Fuck you! You don't scare me!"

Kyrioc got down on one knee so they were eye to eye. "I'm not trying to. All I want is a little girl they took. Nothing more." The boy's expression didn't change. "None of you have to return to the Pails if you don't want to—"

"I do! I'm loyal!"

"Then you can save Wooden's life." He offered Wooden's knife to the boy, handle first. The boy didn't take it. "Maybe you'll get a reward. Take this to Tin and tell her I want to exchange her brother for Riliska, child of Rulenya. No tricks. No one gets hurt any more than they already are. No one needs to know. All I want is the girl, unharmed."

"Why?"

"I owe a debt."

"You're going to pay this debt with your life!"

"Yes," Kyrioc said. "If I have to, then yes." Kyrioc pulled the knife back. "Talk to Tin Pail first. If you tell the heavies on the street outside, or the cosh on her payroll, or anyone, I'll kill him. Even if it looks like I would die too, I'll kill him. The exchange will happen at Sailsday's Regret at dawn. If anyone comes for me before then, he dies. Got that?"

He jutted out his tiny chin. "I'm a fucking *beetle*. I can deliver a secret message. No one will even see me from when I leave here till I speak to my boss." Nodding, Kyrioc extended the knife again. The boy snatched it and ran for the ladder. "No one can follow me, either. You think you can trick me to take you to my boss, but I would never! You just try!"

He reached the top of the ladder and sprinted away.

Wooden groaned as he started waking. His complexion was no longer ashen. The children backed away. Kyrioc walked toward the worktable. When Wooden saw him, he tried to crawl away, steel chain rattling, but that made his ankle flare with pain. He wailed and fell still, his long, slender fingers probing the swelling on the side of his face.

Kyrioc took a bowl of ulund nuts and resin from the table, along with one of the leather mittens. They were too small, but he slipped two fingers into one.

He stood before Wooden. "Nice clothes."

Wooden writhed and tried to cry for help. Kyrioc shushed him and knelt. Wooden tried to push his hands away, but he didn't have the strength.

"Do you know how much it hurts to ride in a bouncing, jolting carriage with broken bones?" Wooden didn't stop struggling, but he seemed to lose his enthusiasm for it. Kyrioc scooped resin and white seed from the bowl and smeared it onto Wooden's lips.

The injured man's eyes rolled, and his breathing came harder, his nostrils flaring with each breath. Kyrioc touched the smeared leather to Wooden's nose just as he sucked in air, and little flecks of resin and seed flew up into his sinuses.

"That should do it," he said, standing.

Wooden's gaze became unfocused. He slumped to the ground.

Kyrioc turned to the children and opened one of the dead men's purses. Copper coins glittered in the lantern light, alongside a few bits of silver. He drew out the largest silver coin he could see—a beam—and held it up. The children gawped at it.

"Do you know the girl I'm looking for? Her name is Riliska." The children shook their heads. Kyrioc knelt and took the oldest girl's hand. It had been painted with curving green vines with the face of a red cat on her pinky nail. Then he touched a few of the other kids' hands. They lifted them to show the art.

He raised his own left hand. The art Riliska had painted there had faded over the last few days, but not by much. "Do you know where I can find her? You won't have to go there with me."

The children all looked at each other, their expressions closed and careful. Finally, the two oldest nodded.

"Thank you. Are you hungry?"

* * *

KILLER OF DEVILS DID not usually follow beetles into the Pails' hideaway, but there was something about the boy's body language that caught his attention. Beetles typically skulked and cringed, but this one charged across the empty plaza like a bull.

Killer himself was just returning from a meeting with Black Apricot to arrange a secure transfer of funds. Tin Pail suspected Black was the most likely candidate to move against her, but the older woman was polite and businesslike. She did not even try to buy his loyalty.

In all, a rather dull errand.

But that running boy intrigued him. As Killer stepped onto the long plankway that connected the plaza to the spa, he raised his arm. The guards at the entrance made the beetle wait.

"Sir," the child said impatiently, "I have a big message for Tin Pail. I can't tell no one else."

"Of course. Let's go together." The child considered that, then nodded. Killer fought the urge to smile. "Tell me your name."

"Hoppila, child of Uzwillia, sir, but I'll take a street name soon. I'm hoping to become a Pail, if the boss will let me."

"What name will you choose, if you can become a Pail?"

"It's hard to decide, sir, because it's a choice that follows you. You don't want to be a grown man with a name only a little child would like. Maybe Cracked Pail? Or Shiny Pail? Picking *Silver* would be like bragging about how rich I plan to get, but *Shiny* sort of hints that without being too obvious, if you see what I mean."

This time, Killer could not hide his smile. When he had been exiled from his homeland, his own son had been slightly older than this boy, and he had been just as serious. "I think I do."

"But my favorite at the moment is Blue Pail. I like that one because when my mother was still alive, she would take me to the edge of the deck to look at the sky. She loved that color. Good sir, do you think that's a little kid's name? Do you think I'd regret it when I'm grown?"

"I cannot speak for you, but I would cherish it."

"Thank you, good sir." Hoppila wiggled his fingers, clearly anxious about something. "Good sir, I got an urgent message."

"We will run together."

* * *

TIN PAIL PACED BACK and forth in her bedroom, fighting the urge to close the shutters every time she passed them. This was the largest, most comfortable bedroom in the building—a suite for wealthy guests, and she was sure that decrepit old bed had seen its share of fat merchants and underage whores.

But that was long ago. This place was hers now, just like the hammerball court in Upgarden, the tar cookery in Mudside, the black-market medical staff, and a thousand other little ventures. It didn't matter what had been there before. Now it was hers.

All she had to do was hold on to it.

Looking eastward over the city walls, she could see the moonlit Timmer Strait. The watchfires and patrolling soldiers were only a few hundred feet away, and she wondered about those archers. If she stood at the window, could one of them spot her, nock, bend, and hit their target at this extraordinary range?

Not normally, but nothing about these times was normal. She had her bodyguard—*Killer of Devils*, she thought, remembering her decision to speak his name boldly. And then there was the asshole. The pawnbroker.

Who knew how many others were out there and what they could do? The Clutching Hand were supposed to have spellkind weapons. What if they were already inside the city, ready to take the point to her?

If she closed these shutters, she'd be surrendering to her fear. Worse, it would be an absurd fear—a fear of spells or whatever. If she gave in to it now, she'd never stop.

Because one thing was sure—someone was going to try to take the point to her.

She'd won over Harl's Salashi heavies, but using them to purge the foreign friends had been costly. She was shorthanded while Harl's lieutenants were at full strength. Yes, she'd backed them down in the burning room, but they wouldn't stay backed down. They were going to come after her.

So would the cosh. And then, when word reached Carrig, the Amber Throne would move against her.

Tin laid her hand on the hammer. Harl had gone about unarmed, but Tin didn't dare. Not yet.

She imagined, once again, fighting alongside her brother in some brothel or casino—him slashing wildly, her smashing in skulls. When that day came, it would be glorious, but she wanted it to be years away. On the day she went down fighting, she wanted to be as rich as a Harkan emperor, wearing gold on every limb.

Her plan to deal with the Amber Throne required a few peaceful months of business as usual downcity so that the cosh, the eye, and the High Watch would be invested in her. For that, she needed the support of Harl's lieutenants.

It'd be a bitter pill for them. She wasn't even twenty-eight yet, younger than any of them. As far as they were concerned, she hadn't paid her dues, and the big project Harl gave her went to shit before it began.

Never mind that Harl had set up that stupid exchange. Blame rolled downcity.

So, they would test her.

She had to be ready. She had to recognize where that first provocation came from and respond with speed and intelligence. And she had to be mean about it.

That was the way to win their trust and respect. After, she'd talk about how they were going to defy the Amber Throne. Together. How they'd split the money that used to float away across the Semprestian.

If she couldn't manage that, she and her brother were doomed.

There was a light knock on the door. Tin's stomach grumbled. She was still waiting for her evening meal. This was a good spot to lie low, but with all the coming and going, they were bound to attract attention. Either this had to become her official headquarters—which meant hiding the glitterkind elsewhere—or she'd have to move soon.

She opened her door and saw Wool Cap standing in the hall. "Message, boss. Beetle says it's urgent."

She hurried to the dining hall. Everyone was gathered there, waiting beside empty tables.

The hall—the place they ate—smelled moldy and dank. Fuck this place. Time to move. If she had to, she'd return to her warehouse in Wild Dismal and work from Harl's hammerball club.

Her club. *Her club.*

"Where's the food?"

Wool looked uncomfortable. "We sent a couple guys to get it, but they're worried about poison, so they're being careful."

Tin shrugged. If she was going to die, she didn't want to do it clutching her guts while she shit blood. Checking for poison was fine by her.

Killer of Devils stood in the middle of the room with the beetle beside him. The boy looked anxious. When she nodded, he lifted his shirt and removed a bundle hidden on his back.

"Boss," he said, unwrapping it, "I'm sorry, but your brother's been made hostage." Then he threw back the cloth and revealed Wooden's steel knife.

Tin stared at it, then at the boy. Here it was. Already. "From the beginning."

CHAPTER THIRTY

Riliska *knew something was* wrong when the room went quiet.

It didn't happen suddenly. The beetles were always silent. The kids in Riliska's neighborhood screeched and cried and laughed, but the beetles were too frightened to speak aloud with heavies around.

It was the gangsters who were talking—complaining, mostly, because they were hungry. More than a few had been drinking, and Riliska didn't need anyone to tell her how dangerous that could be. But when the grownups fell silent, everyone turned toward the boss.

Tin Pail was standing at a high spot on the sloping floor, talking to one of their own. He was about Riliska's age—she had painted a bear's face on the big knuckle of his left hand, and he had called it a wolf. She hadn't argued. Beyond that, he was one of the kids who never spoke with her. He seemed to have no friends, but that didn't mean he was bad, just quiet.

"How many guards?" Tin suddenly yelled. "How many guards did we have on the building and the approach?"

The red-haired barbarian answered, his voice sounding utterly calm. "Half again what Harl placed there."

"How many attacked the building?" Tin shouted at the boy.

The beetle—Riliska didn't know his name—could be heard clearly when he answered. "One."

Voices were lower after that. Riliska knew something big was happening, but she didn't dare leave her chair to move closer. Curiosity was dangerous.

Then Tin looked right at her.

Riliska's blood ran cold. It was a big room, and she was as far from the boss as she could get without going into the hall. She couldn't have been the one Tin was looking at. It must have been someone else.

But there she was, staring directly at her.

* * *

KILLER OF DEVILS AGREED with his employer. Yes, it was bullshit. The hostage exchange was a pretense.

"It has to be," Tin said, pacing back and forth. "All those ulund nuts and a whole fucking kettle full of white tar. And the money my brother was collecting? He should have had a satchel full of silver in his belt. No. Fuck, no. He wanted something else. Did he follow you? Did you lead him here?"

Little Hoppila pulled himself up to his full height. "Never. I know what I'm supposed to do."

"But you couldn't stick a fucking knife in his back! You're old enough to take the point to someone when they're not looking, aren't you?"

"I tried! He…" The boy swallowed, looking nervous. "It was like he knew."

"It is the same man," Killer said, "and he has his own godkind magic."

"Like yours?"

He shook his head, making the bells in his beard chime. "No. He carries darkness with him like a cloud, a trick I have never heard of before."

Tin paced back and forth. The room was full of children and half-drunk street heavies, but it was so quiet, Killer could hear her harsh, ragged breathing. "This is bullshit. A guy like this doesn't just fall out of the rafters. Who is he? Where does he come from? He can't be one of the Clutching Hand. They carry spellkind weapons and they're all Carrig, aren't they? Our guy is Salashi. Don't the Clutching Hand recruit from Carrig slums and orphanages?"

"I do not know for certain," Killer answered.

"This asshole didn't have any kind of weapon?"

"An iron bar," the beetle answered.

"Against me, he had none but what he took from those he fought," Killer answered.

"Shit. He can't be one of the Clutching Hand. They couldn't have reacted to Harl's death so fast. And who is he working for? Cotton Stair only hires other Stairs, so probably not him. Unless he went for an independent contractor. Dirty Straw is ambitious, you can tell that by looking at him, but he…"

"He would not come sideways, with an obviously false demand for an exchange."

"Exactly. He'd just take the point to Wooden and display him somewhere public, because he has no fucking imagination. Black Apricot is clever enough to make a move like this, and Low Market is the most lucrative deck in the city. She could afford to hire someone. But how could she have known ahead of time?"

She had jumped ahead and Killer could not follow. His expression must have shown his confusion, because she scowled.

"This asshole's been on the fringes of our business for days now. He wanted the package Harl was delivering to us, so he sent two of his people to grab it—the nail-painter and the creep too stupid to use a street name while he's stealing shit. When they got caught, he came after them. To protect the members of his crew? Fuck that. Not those two fuckups. He was after the glitterkind. And what did we do? We're shorthanded, so we *brought the painter's kid into our organization*. She's seen the inside of our operation, and he knows it. You think he wants some kid? Fuck that. He's after that glitterkind. The whole thing."

Killer of Devils felt an unexpected tingle of excitement. This was a war council. After so many months of living like a gangster, he finally had the chance to wage the war he was meant for. He might finally have a chance for honor.

Tin shouted, "You! Beetle!"

Hoppila stood tall, proud to stand beside her.

She grabbed him under the arms and threw him through the window.

The boy vanished into the darkness with no sound other than a gasp of surprise. One of the smaller children screamed. When Killer glanced toward the sound, he saw the girl at the center of this mess—Riliska was her name?—rush to comfort the child.

And to hush her so she would not draw the attention of their boss.

"Hear me!" Tin shouted to the room. The assembled gangsters, both her own people and those who had flocked to her after she supplanted Harl, stared in shocked silence. "Everyone keeps saying this asshole has magic! Everyone keeps saying they *tried* to kill him but couldn't. Well, I don't give a shit. There is no magic in the world that can protect you from a knife in the heart, and killing assholes is *what you are here to do*. When an enemy shows their face, I will be right beside you, hammer in hand. *Every motherfucker piles on*, no shirking, no excuses, or I'll kill you myself. Now get ready! We have an asshole that needs to be murdered."

Killer of Devils barely heard her. He stared at the darkness beyond the window.

In this city, children fell from stairs and platforms every day. Sometimes, they hit lower decks and made a mess. Sometimes, they missed the decks and vanished into the mud and shit beneath the city. That beetle, whose name Killer had already forgotten, would be the latter. That eager, loyal boy who had hoped to become a Pail like his boss...

Honor had brought Killer to this. He had sworn to serve, and that oath brought him to this moment.

Wool Cap approached. "Boss, should we send heavies to stake out High Apricot?"

"Send five."

"That's all?"

"Make them runners, not fighters," Tin said. "I don't believe for a second that he's going to make the exchange at a platform hall, but we should have someone there to let us know if he's stupid enough to show up. No, I think he's coming here and he's not going to wait. Move people into position to defend *this* place. What about this kid he's supposed to be asking for?"

Wool Cap peered across the room at the table where the beetles were sitting, but his expression was not hopeful. Killer stepped forward. "I know the child he means. Should I ready her to make the exchange?"

"You fucking should not," Tin said. "We're not making any exchange with anyone." She paused for a moment, biting her lip and rubbing her thumb against her first two fingers as if she were holding a coin. She was feeling vulnerable, and like any threatened animal, she was ready to drive off her enemy with a display of savagery. She looked up. "My doctor is in the basement, yeah?"

* * *

FAY DIDN'T MEAN TO grunt, but grunt he did. He flushed with embarrassment when Onderishta asked him what was wrong.

"Give me a moment."

Several days before, Onderishta had put constables on the couriers who delivered glitterkind portions. Based on what they discovered, it had seemed a waste of their time. The couriers came and went, under guard, between the three reputable courier companies and the hospitals. No extra portions were kept on site. The couriers were not waylaid. They made no detours. Not once.

And along with each speck of enchanted flesh was an authentication sheet. This was no mere wooden token. It was made of a special parchment with silk threads patterned through it, and it was signed by the bureaucrat who had personally cut and measured the portion. That sheet, with that signature, was like a writ from the Steward-General. No one questioned it, because no one thought they had reason to.

Again, it was Trillistin who spotted their error. Onderishta and Fay both assumed that underworld contraband—even magical contraband— would be diverted and sold to underworld dealers like any smuggled good. Trillistin pointed out that if Harl or the Pails wanted to make real money and keep it secret, they would have to sell to the best hospitals in Koh-Salash.

And all those hospitals cared about was that sheet.

So, Fay and a half-dozen constables had marched into Gray Flames, kicked open the medical bureaucrat's offices, and crated up three months' worth of sheets. Now he and Onderishta were going through them, looking for irregularities.

And damned if he hadn't found one.

An hour later, when Fay and Onderishta were trying to decide the best way to break up the scheme, their friend the medical bureaucrat burst into the room. His mouth gaped—obviously, he had a prepared speech ready—but as soon as he saw the stacks of authentication sheets, he lunged for them. The constable who followed him up the stairs had to restrain him.

"Those are stolen!" the medical inspector shouted. "I could have you—Constable, arrest these two *immediately*." The ironshirt rolled his eyes. He didn't even let go of the bureaucrat's arm. "I assure you I have the authority—"

"Not here, you don't," Onderishta said calmly. "In this room, I outrank you. Now, will you give me your name?"

The bureaucrat wrenched his arm out of the constable's grip. His ridiculous tall hat didn't even fall askew. Fay wondered how many pins he used to hold it on. "You must be insane. I'm the senior undersecretary to the chancellor of the medical inspections division. I have the ear of two members of the High Watch through blood relation alone. Do you have any comprehension of how sensitive that material is? I think not, if you're asking for my *name*. What will *you* say when I bring you up on charges of theft and misappropriation of state secrets?"

"What will I say?" Onderishta drained the last of her tea and winced at the bitter dregs. "Nothing, except that you were right about one thing—there is no black-market hospital operating in the city. However, my second will say plenty about how you have allowed, through avarice or incompetence, a black-market medical *supplier* to operate right under your nose."

Before the bureaucrat could launch into another tirade, Fay spoke up. "Do you know a medical inspector named Pelkusut tuto-Liyulsik?" From the man's expression, it was obvious he did. Fay felt a flutter in his stomach. He was honestly nervous about confronting this fool. This dangerously powerful fool. "Would you say he's a vigorous worker?"

"No," the bureaucrat answered. "Competent, yes. He wouldn't be in his position if he weren't. But he's methodical, almost to a fault. Apparently, he has a second cousin on the High Watch and he's leery of making an error."

Fay laid his palms on two stacks of authentication sheets. "Then why is he your most productive employee? He has slivered fifteen percent more glitterkind portions than the next highest coworker. No response? I have another question. Have you changed your ink recently?"

"I... What do you mean?"

That was it. The bureaucrat was flummoxed and buying time. Fay had him. "Your ink. Did you change it seven weeks ago?"

"We did. We were asked to cut our budget. The paper, obviously, has to be just so to prevent forgeries, but we switched to a cheaper ink."

"I know. It's how we caught them." Fay took the top sheet from the two stacks beneath his hand. "See this signature here? The ink is a bit gray, just like the signatures in the other stacks." He held up the sheet from the smaller stack. "But this one is very dark. Expensive, like all the signatures from before the change, but it's only ten days old. See? You switched the ink but the forgers didn't. Maybe they didn't know. Maybe you forgot to sell that information to them."

"Wait a minute, now—"

Onderishta stood. "Collar him."

The constable shoved the bureaucrat against the wall, then pulled off his hat. It fell to the floor in a clatter of pins, unleashing a long, lustrous fall of hair. It was so lovely, Fay almost laughed. Why couldn't he have hair like that?

"No," the bureaucrat said, "wait..."

"Wait for what?" Onderishta said, coming around her desk. "You think we only collar poor people? We fucking love throwing one of you rich creeps in jail. Tell us your name."

The bureaucrat winced as he shifted his manacled hands. The ironshirt must have strained his shoulder. "You don't understand—"

"Security of the slivered portions," Fay interrupted, "relies on affidavits and signatures from high officials, and the names of those officials are kept secret, even if they're not the ones doing the cutting."

The bureaucrat said nothing. Onderishta practically barked at him. "Right?"

The man stood up straight, shaking his hair out of his eyes. "It keeps our families safe."

"That's not really a concern for you anymore. You're out."

The skin on Fay's back tingled. This bureaucrat with the access to the High Watch was finished.

"If you let me go," the bureaucrat said, "I'll get to the bottom of this. I'll drag Pelkusut into my office—"

"And blow the whole investigation," Onderishta said, "perhaps deliberately. This black market was set up by the Amber Throne and is run by downcity Salashi heavies. You can't threaten them with *scandal*. And that's why you're going into a cell. We need to keep you someplace where you can't shit in our pantry."

"This… This isn't permitted."

"Fay, tell the man what investigators do."

"Find the truth."

Onderishta stared at the man as though her gaze could set him on fire. "That's right. Now, maybe you've heard that I visited your offices in Gray Flames recently to find out what *actually happens* when a glitterkind is cut too much."

"That, too, was improper."

She nodded. "And they told me about the ullroct. The ullroct is a creature of the Ancient Kings, is it not? One of their servants?"

The inspector shook his hair out of his eyes again. He obviously didn't want to answer. "That's what the histories teach."

"I know what the histories teach," Onderishta snapped. "I apprenticed at Suloh's Tower too. There, I learned that ullroct either fed upon or protected the glitterkind—scholars were unsure—but the good folks at your office seemed pretty certain it was the latter." The medical inspector nodded. "So, don't refer me to the tower when I ask you this next question. Are you ready?"

He didn't respond at first. The constable shook his manacles and he seemed to shrink, just a little. "I'm ready."

"What are the glitterkind? What is their purpose? In Suloh's Tower, I was taught that all magic has a purpose, so obviously they can't be like the bushes and trees, springing from the ground and growing in the sun. What are they for?"

The medical inspector sighed. "To be honest, I don't know. No one knows, except for the Ancient Kings themselves, and they are not here to answer questions."

Onderishta sat back in her chair. "For now."

There was a sharp knock on the door, then it opened. The tower captain strode in, took in the scene, then shrugged. "Two messengers have arrived. They say they can speak to no one other than Onderishta."

Two children of about eight shuffled into the room. They were dirty and underfed, and they looked as if they cut each other's hair with dull knives. They didn't even glance at the manacled bureaucrat. They looked at Fay, then Onderishta.

"We have two messages. First, the Broken Man needs one good constable and thirty comp'tent ones to go to Low Market to save the life of a little girl. You can also collar anyone in the Pails' secret hideout, if you want to. He said I should take you to him. If you agree to that, as a thank-you, my sister will lead you to the biggest tar cooker in the city. There's a tank with collected parts there, too. He says you wouldn't need more than a dozen cosh for that job, but you have to hurry. The building won't be empty for long."

"This tank with collected parts," the bureaucrat said, "is it full of viscous…er, thick liquid?" The two children nodded. He turned to Fay and Onderishta. "I can help."

"Agreed." Onderishta gestured at the constable. He began to remove the bureaucrat's manacles.

Fay had a bad feeling about that plan. "Kids, is this cookery in Spillwater?"

The smaller child shook her head. "Mudside."

Before the bureaucrat could protest, Onderishta pointed a finger at him. "You'll stay close and stay quiet." He closed his mouth. She turned to Fay. "What do you think?"

The question startled him. After his failure at the hammerball court, did she really trust him? Did he trust himself?

To be honest, he still wasn't keen on running errands for criminals, but when it came to gang wars, the only side he was on was Onderishta's. If this Broken Man—this Kyrioc—led him to the Pails and helped him round up their operation, there was nothing to stop Fay from collaring him, too.

He turned to the children. "You work for him?"

They shook their heads gravely. "He set us free."

Huh. Fay wasn't sure what he thought about that. "Boss, this asshole can pitch himself off an upcity deck for all I care, but if he'll take us to Harl, the Pails, or whoever is running things, we should go."

She nodded. "All right. I'll take our bureaucrat down to Mudside. You take the Pails."

"What? Boss, that doesn't make sense. I'm just your second. This should be your collar."

Onderishta sighed. "It's time for you to make a name for yourself. I want you secure in your position, just in case. Besides, I'm taking the dangerous task. You get the prestigious one."

"I'm not doing this for prestige."

"If you were, you wouldn't be working with me. Still, prestige is useful. It's another kind of coin, to be spent at need." Onderishta addressed the two children. "We accept the terms of the message. Which of you will lead me to Mudside?"

The smallest child raised her hand. "I will."

Onderishta bent down to her. "Would you like to stop for a honey cake on the way?"

The child's expression remained grave. "Maybe after. We really should hurry."

With a shrug, Onderishta turned toward the captain, ordered him to gather a dozen constables, and they left. That left Fay alone with the older messenger. "I'm not a constable, but I'll play the role of the good one. And all our constables are competent. Are you going to lead me to the hideout?"

She shook her head. "To the Broken Man."

Of course she was. This Broken Man, whoever he *really* was, wasn't asking Fay to fetch the girl for him. He planned to take part and probably thought he'd be in charge.

The girl led him to the Spillwater deck. The plaza outside the tower was well lit and well patrolled, but they moved quickly into the shadowy streets beyond. Fay realized he'd left the tower to meet with a dangerous criminal with nothing more than a belt knife and a hooded lantern, and he was not what you'd call a fighter. Was he being led to his death?

They came to the mouth of an alleyway, and Fay saw a figure sitting at the reins of a ruined two-horse carriage. From what he could tell by his lantern light, it had been a decent-enough vehicle once, but the roof was gone, as though it had rammed full speed into a lowering portcullis. Four splintered supports for the missing roof rose above the bed, with nothing above.

Three of those supports had bundles tied to them. At first, Fay wasn't sure what they were—they were wrapped in damp blankets and quite bulky—until he saw one move.

People. Those were people.

The driver himself was a hunched figure in a hooded cloak. He looked like something out of a play, as if a specter had risen from the mud below the city to deliver a message of doom.

"Where are the constables?"

Fay felt goosebumps down his back but did his best to hide them. The voice that came from that hood was rough—as though the speaker rarely talked—and hollow. It was the voice of a ghost, a person who had already died but didn't know it.

"If we're going to Low Market, we need constables from the east tower. That's their jurisdiction."

The hood turned to the girl. "You know where to wait." She ran off. To

Fay, he said, "Let's go."

The stink of putrefying flesh wafted over Fay. At least one of the bodies in the carriage was dead.

Or the Broken Man was.

Fay shook off those superstitions. Onderishta entrusted this mission to him. He hooded his lantern and climbed in.

The Broken Man flicked the reins, and they started off.

* * *

RILISKA FELT A SHIVER when the red-bearded man began to walk toward her. She tried to tell herself that whatever he was doing, it had nothing to do with her, but this time she couldn't lie to herself. Maybe because he looked only at her.

There was nowhere to run. Riliska patted the hair of the little girl who had screamed, then stood away from the table. Her mouth was dry.

She had just seen a boy her own age thrown through a window. It didn't seem real, but it was. It might even happen again, and to her.

"Good sir," she said, her voice clear in the quiet room, "are you going to…"

She fell silent, as though speaking the words would be like daring him to do it.

He shook his head, making tiny chiming sounds. "I am not. Come."

Riliska followed him, then glanced back at the table of children. The little one she'd been comforting seemed on the verge of crying again. Riliska waved goodbye. The girl waved back.

As Riliska and the red-bearded man came to the door, two heavies—although they were so skinny, Riliska did not think they deserved the name—pushed a wheeled cart into the room. A large cloth covered the mound on top. Food had arrived.

A cheer rose from the room and the northerner wasted no time. He tore the cloth off the top, revealing a huge stack of rolled buns. The cheering lost its enthusiasm, but the northerner took two and offered one to Riliska.

"Thank you," she said, and took a bite. It was filled with sweetened pork and it was good.

Heavies surged toward the food with a lot of shoving and yelling. Riliska hustled into the hall and the northerner shut the door. It did not muffle the voices much.

Riliska flinched as she remembered the way the boy gasped in surprise as he went through the window. She never wanted to go into that room again.

Maybe they had finally realized that she should be sent back to her mother. That thought, along with the food, made her feel almost cheerful. She glanced at the red-bearded man again. They were walking side by side down a long hall. She marveled at the number of scars on his arms.

"Why do you wear bells in your hair?" she asked, since asking about his scars might remind him of bad things.

"They represent something sacred," he answered. "Do you understand this word?"

"Oh, yes," Riliska assured him, but on considering it, she said, "or maybe not." He smiled at her and she asked, "Do you have any kids?"

That ruined the smile. "Yes, I do."

"Are they here?"

"They are far away and I may never see them again."

His voice sounded weird, and Riliska figured he was feeling the adult version of her own unhappiness. She'd been separated from her mother for *days* now, and it was *awful*. Of course he sounded weird.

She laid her hand on his arm. "Why?"

He stopped walking, and so did she. One of the tiny bells in his hair fell against his ear, making a single pleasing *ting*. "For honor. Do not worry. You are Salashi, descended from the people of Selsarim, and I know you have no understanding of that particular word."

"Um, doesn't it mean *being a good person*?"

He knelt so that his face was at the same height as hers, which meant her hand fell from his arm. His wild hair and beard hid most of his face, but Riliska was surprised to see that his skin was sort of red too, and spiderwebbed with scars on the left side. "Among my people, it does not. It has nothing to do with being good or bad. It means to always do what you have promised to do, to keep every oath, and to follow the rules that have been set for you. No excuses may be made. If the rules and your oaths urge you toward good, then you are a good person. If they urge you the other way, then you are not. But there is no other worthwhile measure of a human being. There is no other way to know if you can be trusted."

"I think I understand," Riliska said, "but it sounds terrible. What if you want to be a good person?"

"Then you must take care in the oaths you swear and the allegiances you make."

He was looking at her with a serious expression, as though there were something he wanted her to understand. It was almost as if he were sending a message. Was he trying to say he was a good person forced to do bad things?

Maybe he just felt sad.

Riliska gently laid her hand on his cheek. The northerner looked surprised just before she did it, but he did not pull away or stop her. Riliska wondered what his real name was. She knew what people called him, but that couldn't have been his real, actual name.

Then his expression went blank and he stood tall. "Come along, child," he said. They went down a flight of stairs into the cobwebbed darkness of the lowest level.

CHAPTER THIRTY-ONE

The room the doctor had chosen for herself was rancid, cramped, and airless. Killer of Devils could not understand why she had settled there until he saw the piles of leather packets. She was an addict, and this room was at the end of a long corridor. If someone came for her, she would have ample warning. What she would do with that warning, Killer could not guess, but his time with the Pails meant time with addicts, and their paranoia could be all-consuming.

Surveying the room a second time, he realized it had once contained cleaning supplies. Now it held only the doctor's blades, her cot, her bloodstained table, and a pot brimming with old chicken bones and excrement.

"I don't have a tank here," the doctor said from her cot. "I thought I explained all this. We can't preserve anything."

Killer spoke Harkan better than Salashi, so he switched to that language. "This one is not for the tank. Tin Pail does not want to sell her. She is for revenge." If she was truly a doctor, she would have had to learn that language.

With a groan, the doctor sat up. She switched to Harkan, too. "Fine. Eyes and skin, then?"

"That is what Tin Pail wants."

"Fine," the doctor said again. Then she switched back to Salashi. "Up onto the table, little one. Let's look you over."

Riliska approached it hesitantly, then glanced back at Killer as though hoping he would take her somewhere nicer.

The doctor lifted her onto the table. "You were supposed to have a bath first, but I suppose it doesn't matter."

Killer realized he was still standing in the doorway, and he had no idea why. His duty was done. There was no reason to linger. The way the girl stared at him, imploring his help, made his skin prickle.

This was who he was now. This was his role in an evil world.

The doctor said, in Harkan, "You know, a lot of people think being a doctor means you're soft-hearted. Maybe you thought that yourself. I hear it all the time. 'How good you are to help people in need,' 'How kind you are to take care of the sick and injured,' and all that. And sure, it's nice to help people, but I was well paid, too. I guess what people don't understand is that most of my patients mean nothing to me. A lot of doctors are like that. The soft-hearted ones usually don't last. Do you know why?"

"I do not."

She continued her examination of the girl while she talked, although Killer was not sure why she bothered. "Because the most important part of our work involves cutting people apart. Slicing flesh, even when you're trying to save lives, can be harrowing for the weak-hearted. We have to be as hard and smooth as slate so the blood just washes off. I like to think we're similar to warriors in that way."

She smiled at him over her shoulder, showing those stained lips. Eight hells, she was making a pass at him.

"Perhaps we are more alike than we seem," he said.

Because why should they not be? Both worked for the same criminal in a doomed, depraved city. Both were engaged in the same cruel tasks. Why should he not fuck this unfeeling addict in her reeking abattoir? Why should he not fuck her beside the bloody corpse of this child?

This was the place his honor had taken him.

The girl still stared at him, imploring his help with her expression, while the doctor pushed her flat on the table and strapped her in place. Killer of Devils did nothing, because nothing was what he was required to do.

* * *

KYRIOC SAID NOTHING AS they rode through Spillwater toward the east tower. He had already scouted the Pails' hideout, but only briefly and from a safe distance. A band of ironshirts, mobilized quickly like an army, would almost certainly draw the attention of the people they were hunting. All the Pails had to do was draw back the plankway that connected their deck from the rest of the city, and the constables would have one option. Wait them out.

Only this broken carriage, and Tin's concern for her brother, that might keep the plankway in place.

As they approached the east tower, the bureaucrat leaped from the carriage.

"Secrecy," Kyrioc said, voice still raw from lack of use. "All is lost without it." The bureaucrat rolled his eyes. "Please."

* * *

RILISKA HAD NEVER MET a doctor before, but if they were all like this, she never wanted to meet another. The woman smelled awful and she was strong—stronger than any tar head had a right to be.

Riliska's legs were strapped down first so she couldn't kick. Then her hands. A sob escaped her, as surprising as it was embarrassing.

Never once had Riliska stopped being afraid, not from the moment she saw the man with the crazy smile pinching her mother's nostrils shut, but she'd done her best to hold it in.

Now—right now—this doctor was making her helpless, and that brought all her panic and loneliness up, and she couldn't hold it in any more.

Riliska wailed her terror and loss. They were going to do something huge and unthinkable to her. It would be so far beyond the petty cruelties she'd endured so far that she couldn't even imagine it. She only knew it would be awful beyond her experience.

But most of all, Riliska was afraid for her mother. If she died here, how would her mother know what became of her?

Now would have been the time for the doctor to say something comforting, but instead she lay a strap across Riliska's forehead. Before she was fully immobilized, Riliska managed to glance at the big, red-haired man. No one else could save her, but he only stood in the doorway, as still as a broom handle leaning against a wall.

But he wouldn't do anything, because he wasn't a good person. He was only honorable.

Her screaming turned raw as the doctor pulled the strap over her chin and mouth, muffling her. She could only breathe through her nose, and her skin was so hot and her heart racing so fast that she couldn't catch her breath. She was going to suffocate. She was!

Somewhere, out of sight, she heard clinking metal. The doctor had picked up an instrument.

* * *

FAY KNEW THE NIGHT captain of the east tower slightly, but it was enough. The man was ambitious. So, when Fay turned up in the middle of the night for a secret raid on a gangster hideout, the captain was happy to call up his ironshirts.

Fay had hoped the captain would recognize the location the Broken Man had given him, but he didn't. Low Market, which was the bulk of the east tower's responsibilities, was made up of four centuries' worth of decks, platforms, plankways, and footbridges, many abandoned and reclaimed, burned and rebuilt several times over.

The ironshirts would leave the tower in groups of two to five, some casually, some rushing as though headed for trouble, some dressed like they were sneaking out for drinks. They would change back into uniform, if necessary, and meet at the rally point Kyrioc recommended.

Where Kyrioc waited.

If they realized the cart held dead bodies, they'd collar him and they wouldn't be gentle about it. If they recognized him as the man who put six constables in the hospital, they might throw him off a deck. The ironshirts Kyrioc attacked worked out of the south tower, but they were still constables.

Fay wasn't worried. As long as he kept a reasonable distance between the ironshirts and his informant, he could keep the collar off this Broken Man until he'd led them to the Pails' hideout.

After that, he didn't care what the cosh did to the man who'd broken into his boss's home.

* * *

CULZATIK STOOD IN THE dark room, breathing in the musty air. It had been a long time since he'd come in here… A year? No, two years, maybe a little more. He'd told himself he would stop doing this, and he had.

But after Kyrionik's service and the sighting of that scarred man who looked so much like him, the urge to return to his older brother's bedroom had built until he couldn't resist it any longer.

The bedsheets. The practice weapons. The boots. Everything the Safroy family had kept of his brother's was still here, but the servants had let a thin layer of dust accumulate. He'd have to have a word.

After another few moments, he went into the hall, lit his candle, then returned to the room and set it on the desk. He couldn't sleep, so he might as well not-sleep in here. It occurred to him suddenly that his parents might clear the room out now that Kyrionik's services were finished. He'd gone missing. They waited the required time. They'd held the service. He was legally deceased.

It was time to say goodbye—past time, really—but Culzatik wasn't ready.

The door opened slowly. Culzatik looked up and saw a familiar figure lean in. His father.

He braced himself to hear the inevitable bark of aggravation and disappointment. Culzatik was supposed to be asleep. If he'd kept up his sword practice, he'd be too tired to wander the compound at night. And so on. He'd heard it all before.

But his father didn't say any of that. Instead, he stepped into the room and quietly shut the door. He was not wearing armor, of course, but he was wearing a steel bracer on his left arm. He was a fighting man, and wearing metal seemed to bring him comfort.

"I come here sometimes too" was all he said.

Culzatik was so astonished that he didn't trust himself to speak, but some answer had to be made. "I didn't know that."

"He was my son. We can't…"

Whatever he was thinking, he couldn't say it.

"Father, that man in black at the funeral, the one I chased?" Culzatik knew this was a mistake. He knew he should shut up, but he couldn't. The urge to speak was irresistible. "I didn't see a knife. You know that. What I saw was Kyrionik. He looked *so much* like him. Just…the way he stood, and moved. Scars covered his face, but I could have sworn…" He took a deep, shuddering breath. "I'm sorry. I know it's ridiculous. I know it can't be him. But right there, in that moment, it seemed undeniable."

It was time for Father to lose his temper. It was time for a slap, or a roaring tirade in the quiet hours of this sleeping house.

Instead, his father sighed. "When I was a young man, I made a name for myself with my tenacity. Do you know that story?"

It was a strange question to ask. Of course he'd heard the story. His father's carrack had been attacked by two pirate ships hoping to ransom the Safroy heir. His father knew that if he surrendered, he would have been spared, but the guards, servants, and crew would have been slaughtered.

So, he'd fought, long past the hope of capture and ransom, until he was wielding his sword with his right and holding in his guts with his left. The pirates broke and ran, losing one of their ships, and Father survived only because one of his servants had been entrusted with a nugget of glitterkind flesh. According to the story, she had shoved it directly into his slashed gut wound.

Then Culzatik realized why his father was asking this question. "I've heard it, but not from you."

"I'm not a storyteller," his father said simply. "But holding on, never giving up…it's a fine quality in battle, but maybe not in grief."

"It would be easier," Culzatik said, "and less painful if you could let him go. But you don't want it to be easier. And you don't want the pain to lessen."

His father looked at him, stone-faced, and nodded three times. Then he moved to the table by the bed and picked up an iridescent blue ammonite shell. He wiped the dust from it. "This was a gift from the girl he loved."

Culzatik hadn't known that, either. The shell had been on display there for years, and he'd thought it was just another trinket. "Not Essatreska."

"No. He didn't like Essatreska any more than you do. This was someone else. His mother knew her name, I believe, but I don't pry."

The urge to sit and talk with this girl—well, a young woman by now—was powerful. He let it pass. "Was she at the service? She should have been."

"Many people were there. I don't know."

Silence.

"Why was that Carrig Tower Apostle there? Do you know the woman I mean?" Father shook his head. "She wore a red bonnet, which is religious garb for nuns who worship the Ancient Kings."

"Ah. The Carrig heretic. They're looking to seize power, and your mother is going to give them silver and weapons. We've been hearing rumbling of another attack on Koh-Salash—another attempt to drive us out—and your mother believes a homegrown insurrection will keep their armies at home. Better for the Carrig to kill each other than to sail here to kill us."

"Aren't the Apostles a minority?"

"In Carrig? Yes, but they're a majority in other places, praying for the return of the Ancient Kings, which they have been predicting for generations and will probably keep predicting for generations more. But minorities can wield power. The Salashi nobles are a minority."

That was something Culzatik wouldn't soon forget. "Father, I know I'm not him"—Culzatik suddenly couldn't say Kyrionik's name—"and I'll never measure up to him, but I promise to do what I can for this family."

"Of course you measure up. You take after your mother. And, like your mother, I'll never understand you." There was silence for a moment, and Culzatik didn't know what to say. He'd always believed his father hated him. "But you're my son."

Culzatik had a sudden urge to invite his father into the library but he squashed it. Instead, he sat quietly, enjoying the moment.

Then he said, "I can't let go either. I keep hoping that Kyrionik is going to return and fight for this family the way he was born to do."

* * *

KYRIOC WAITED INSIDE HIS cloak of shadows at the mouth of an alley. There were no vagrants, but the stink of human excrement was still fresh, and gnawed bones littered the planking. They'd been cleared out, and recently.

His back to an abandoned candle shop, he looked over the long ramp that led to the northern edge of Low Apricot. The spa at the end of the long plankway behind him had faux columns constructed with skywood facing, six stories, and a peaked roof with three chimneys and a water inlet. Fancy. It would have been an exclusive destination once, and the shops that sprang up around it would have served both the spa and its wealthy clientele.

But like every fashionable place, it would have become unfashionable. Then, isolated as it was, it would have died, and scavengers would have moved in.

Three heavies wearing expensive leather boots and black cloaks came around the corner. All were slender and loose-limbed, moving with the grace of sprinters. They kept a wary eye. On their last patrol, they'd driven off a pair of drunks.

The smallest ran into certain buildings as they circled around, then emerged a moment later. Kyrioc had already shadowed them twice on their circuit. In this deck, where the only light came from a few cheap torches at the edge of the plaza and Suloh's bones far above, no one even noticed his cloak of shadows.

The people he waited for were another matter.

When the heavies finished checking the buildings, they moved on. Kyrioc returned across the plankway. The horses and shattered carriage remained where he had hobbled them, in a Low Apricot alleyway out of sight.

The Carrig bureaucrat had arrived. He'd wisely left the constables at some distance. Wooden moaned softly. The ulund was wearing off.

He could make all the noise he wanted in a few minutes.

"The constables are close?"

The bureaucrat nodded. "But not too close. If they knew what you had here, they'd collar you."

Kyrioc almost said, *They could try*. Then he remembered how many ironshirts he'd asked for.

But he needed them. Kyrioc had asked for an exchange in a public place, but he had no intention of conducting one there. If Tin Pail was naive enough to believe him, she and her heavies would stream across that narrow plankway into the plaza, and it would be easy for him to blend in. Then, when they hit Low Apricot, the constables would collar them while Kyrioc slipped away with Riliska in the confusion.

Except he didn't believe Tin Pail was naive. Not for one moment.

He needed a distraction so he could slip into her crowd of heavies, where his cloak of mirrors would have its full effect.

The constables and the heavies, well, they didn't mean anything to him. The heavies could all be collared, or the ironshirts might take bribes and walk away, or they might all kill each other. It didn't matter as long as he got Riliska to safety.

He shrugged off the cloak he had taken from the cookhouse and offered it to the bureaucrat. "The beetles have seen me wearing this."

"Except you're a head taller than I am," the bureaucrat said. "More. Won't they notice?"

"You'll be up here, driving the cart. People see what they expect to see."

The bureaucrat stared up at him. He was obviously still afraid, but he was doing his best to hide it. He hadn't accepted the cloak. "My name is Fay Nog Fay. What's yours?"

This again. "Kyrioc, child of No One. But you already know that."

"I do," Fay answered. "When all this is over, you're going to answer for what you did in south tower."

It took boldness to say that. Kyrioc felt a surge of admiration for him, along with a pang of sorrow. Kyrioc had been bold, once.

"We can settle that after the girl is safe and you have as many of the Pails' people as you can catch. Deal?"

In truth, Kyrioc had no idea how he would settle anything. As long as Riliska was safe, being arrested and sent to the mines for ten years—or simply hanged—would be a tolerable way to end his life. Or he could use his cloaks to escape the city. Both options seemed equally appealing.

But if he let the constables take him, his old identity might be uncovered. He could not face that. Not now. Not ever.

Kyrioc had no idea what he would do when this was over. Everything after rescuing Riliska was a void. Blackness. He couldn't return to the pawnshop. He had nowhere to live and no reason to do anything. His future was emptiness.

And that was fine. It didn't matter.

Fay accepted the dead man's cloak. "Deal."

Kyrioc told him about the heavies in the plaza. "They're here to kill the driver of this cart and recover this asshole alive. Can the constables move in and take them quietly?"

"No," the bureaucrat answered. "The heavies shout and the constables shout back. They push each other around. It's always like that. Always."

Kyrioc was hoping this task could be turned over to someone who would not have to waste more lives. "I'll clear them out."

The bureaucrat picked up on his reluctance but misread his reason for it. "Can you? All those thugs? Because I'm risking my life here."

"Do you want to call a constable to take your place?"

No sooner had he asked the question than Wooden moaned.

The bureaucrat sighed. "It would never work. An honest constable would never hold a gangster for ransom, and a dishonest one can't be trusted. It has to be me."

"Then put this on."

Kyrioc pulled a flat wooden panel from the bed of the broken carriage. It had been part of the roof, with two short, curving pieces of the support still attached. He turned it so the curved supports pointed toward Fay.

The bureaucrat understood immediately. He draped the curving pieces onto his shoulders so the wooden panel hung on him like a chest plate, then tied it in place with the cloak.

"When you see the next patrol come through, do a slow count to twenty, then drive the cart up. The constables should be behind you, but stay out of sight for as long as possible."

Fay looked down as he tied a knot in his cloak. Kyrioc stepped back and called up his cloak of shadow.

* * *

COLD SUNSHINE LIKED THIS new boss. She was hard, like the thugs he grew up with, and he'd do anything to impress her.

For the moment, that meant patrolling this plaza. The other two men in his team were older, so he was the one who did the extra running, dodging into the abandoned buildings to check on the heavies stationed there. He tried to play it cool—perfectly willing to do the extra work without seeming puppy-dog eager, but the guys acted like they were looking down on him anyway. Like he was the junior.

Which was okay, because someday they would fuck something up, and Tin Pail would decide they needed to have the point taken to them. And she would give that job to Cold.

Wool Cap jerked his thumb toward the plankway. Time for another patrol. The heavies started the night at the edges of the spa platform, staring across the gulf at nothing. Hours later, they looked tired and bored. Only Tin Pail's endless pacing, hammer in hand, kept them from sitting or wandering back inside.

But not Cold Sunshine. At the jerk of Wool's thumb, he was on the plankway, heading toward the plaza again. His partners kept up, mostly. Cold was careful not to act like he wanted to show them up, even though he was doing exactly that.

The plaza across the gap was deserted but half the torches were lit. Wool Cap had told them to look for a shadow that seemed out of place—either much darker than it should be or cast by something they couldn't see.

That meant magic, and Cold could tell his partners weren't happy about it. Cold himself thought it was bullshit. Godkind blessings were one thing. They were gifts from the dead gods. They didn't even count as magic, because they were really real.

Other kinds, though? Witchy-tale stuff for little kids.

He checked for weird shadows anyway, because he wanted to prove he could be relied on, whatever his personal feelings.

He turned right at the platform, hustling along the edge. "Kid," said one of the others. It didn't matter which. He was getting too far ahead. They thought he had to be reined in. He slowed down, not to be controlled by them in any way—fuck them—but because Cold didn't want word getting around that he was careless.

They came to the shop where the first team of heavies lay in wait. Cold headed for the door, taking care to step onto the floor near the walls, where the boards would be less likely to squeak. If he wasn't allowed to kill anyone, he could at least enjoy sneaking up on them, hand on knife. For practice.

The interior of the shop was dark and quiet. The heavies didn't react to his approach. Goosebumps ran down Cold's arms. Had he finally snuck up on them? They were at his mercy. "Anything to report?"

They didn't stir.

Several things happened at once. Cold realized he could smell blood and shit, and had been smelling it since he passed through the door, but he'd been too excited to notice.

He also sensed someone behind him.

In that brief moment, Cold knew he was never going to get his chance to murder someone, because he was going to experience it from the other side. In this room of corpses, he was the victim.

Just before the iron struck his skull, he felt a powerful sense of loss. What a waste his death was going to be. His killer wouldn't even see his expression.

* * *

TIN'S RESTLESSNESS HAD PASSED. The jumbled emotions she'd felt when she'd heard her brother had been taken—fear for his safety, rage at the challenge to her authority, worry that her own people would turn on her—had finally run out like water in a cracked tub.

What she had left was annoyance.

The asshole who took her brother was making her wait. She hated waiting. She wanted sleep, another meal, a jug of brandy or a trip to the baths. Anything but this fucking waiting.

It was wearing her heavies out, too. She wanted them alert and dangerous, but their energy was flagging. The ones who liked to drink through the night were sweating, and the others clearly just wanted somewhere to sit.

And her fucking bodyguard was somewhere inside the building, probably sulking over that little girl. He'd turned pale at that order. For a moment, Tin thought she might have finally pushed him too far.

But no. He had his honor, which meant he was hers.

Morale. That was the problem. Their morale was dropping. She told Wool Cap to find a jug of brandy and pour cups out for the heavies. He suggested they set benches against the side of the building so they could relax in shifts. She agreed.

There was a collective sigh when word got around. They didn't dare complain openly, but they were grateful that she thought about their comfort.

Fuck them. She didn't give a shit about their sore feet or tired eyes. She wanted them ready to fight.

* * *

KYRIOC TOOK THE CLOAK from the man he'd killed. By the fallen gods, he was so *young*.

It was a pointless waste of a life, but the only way to Riliska led through a pile of corpses.

He put on the cloak and summoned his cloak of mirrors.

Stolen hood pulled low, he ran into the street. If only he'd had the time to steal the kid's boots, too, assuming he could make them fit.

The two heavies jogged to catch up, their attention worrying his magic. He focused his will on it.

"Kid," one of the heavies called. They wanted him to slow down, which meant his cloak was holding. The heavy called to him again, this time with a weary tone, as though he was tired of chasing after a runaway child. Kyrioc didn't pull farther ahead, but he did maintain his distance as he ducked into the next building, and the next.

The teams were all dead, of course. If there was one thing Kyrioc was good at, it was creeping up on someone in the dark and bashing in their skulls. When he entered each building, he called, "Anything to report?" just as the boy had, because the more he behaved like the kid he'd replaced, the stronger his cloak would be.

Then he came to the edge of the ramp where the bureaucrat was waiting with the cart. Kyrioc dared a glance to the side but saw nothing but shadow.

Good. Fay was well hidden. Or it was bad, because he was not there and was not coming, and Kyrioc would never make it to the spa under the gaze of so many enemies.

It didn't matter. He would go where he needed to go, do what he had to do, to see Riliska safe.

* * *

JUST AS TIN THOUGHT the patrol was taking too long, a figure appeared in the plaza. For a moment, she didn't recognize him, but that was the cloak she'd given to the sly, skinny kid who couldn't stop touching his knife, so—yeah, that was him. The others were close behind.

They made their way onto the plankway, crossing the long, narrow path back toward headquarters. Everyone was watching them now— there was nothing else to look at, after all—and Tin realized the sly kid looked more hunched over than when he left, and maybe it was someone else wearing that—

"There!"

Wool Cap pointed to the western edge of the plaza, where a cart driven by two horses came slowly into view. She recognized the horses and their rigging, even at this distance. They were the ones that went back and forth to Harl's supposedly safe tar cookery in Mudside, but it was all fucked up.

Her patrol crossed onto the spa deck, mixing with the rest of the heavies, but she wasn't paying attention to them anymore. No one was. Her people had gotten off the benches and moved toward the edge of the deck, watching the slow progress of the wrecked carriage, with the sound of the horses' hooves echoing across the gap.

She couldn't see the driver clearly. He was wearing the same sort of cloak her people wore when they wanted to be anonymous, probably stolen from one of her brother's useless guards. She should have sent Killer of Devils with him, despite Harl's security arrangements. It was fucking Mudside.

And there was something piled in the back.

She pushed through the crowd to her archer and found him straining to string his bow. His arrows lay on a little table beside him. Some had broad, barbed heads. Some had slender points. Some had oil-soaked rags tied just behind the head.

"Tell me what you see."

The archer finally got his bow strung, then peered across the gap. "Two horses, one driver, three bundles in the back. The driver looks like a little guy, but with a quiet wind I could hit him square in the chest from here."

Tin was glad he sounded so confident. "Tell me about the bundles."

"They're wrapped in blankets. Tied to the support posts. Maybe man-sized."

Her brother.

"Good," she said. "Be ready." He picked up the arrow with the broadest head and widest barbs, then kissed it.

Tin snapped her fingers and moved to the edge of the plankway. Wool Cap was ready. He removed the flag from his belt and handed it to her. Tin unfurled it slowly, watching the horses make their inexorable passage across the plaza. God, they were slower than her own people. She'd intended to wait for the carriage to reach the mouth of the plankway, but fuck it. She hated waiting.

It was time for her teams to move against this asshole. She raised the flag above her head and waved it back and forth.

CHAPTER THIRTY-TWO

When Fay saw the waving flag, an icy shiver ran through him. The Broken Man had promised to clear the plaza, and although Fay had no reason to trust him, he had.

No one rushed at him. No one shouted at him to stay where he was. Kyrioc, child of No One, had done it.

Still, it gave him goosebumps to see someone give the order to kill him.

After a few more moments of nothing, the crowd on the deck in front of the spa became uneasy. Someone's plan hadn't gone off, and Fay wasn't keen to find out what they would try next.

He pressed the wooden shell against his chest. Only constables were entitled to a steel breastplate, but maybe he should have borrowed one.

"Hey, asshole!"

For one absurd moment, Fay wanted to protest that he was just standing in for the asshole. The voice came from the middle of the crowd, and there was no way to tell who was speaking. It was a woman's voice, though, harsh and raw.

"Send over the girl!" he shouted. "Let's make this trade!"

"Tell me who you work for!" the woman called back.

Fay was stymied for a moment. It hadn't occurred to him that the Broken Man, as he called himself, was *working* for someone. Had Fay been tricked—once again—into doing some ganglord's dirty work? The thought made him flush with anger.

Fuck it. He had a role, and he was going to stick with it. "I work for Riliska, child of Rulenya."

There was a murmur from across the way. They didn't like his answer, but it wasn't Fay's job to make assholes like him.

The woman called again, "All right, little petal. All right. At least tell us your name."

"Broken Man," he shouted back. "Let's make this trade! Send over—
Fay heard a whistling sound.

* * *

TIN SAW THE DRIVER reel and tumble backward out of his seat.

"Center apple," the archer said proudly. Whatever she was paying him, he'd earned it.

"All right," she said to Wool Cap. "Let's get a team of six and—"

Wool pointed toward the plaza. "Shit."

The man across the way was climbing to his feet. His hood had fallen back, and even at this distance she could see he wasn't Salashi. He had a Carrig's complexion. One of Harl's people. That's who the scarred asshole had been working for all along—the foreign friends.

Fine. No, actually it was better than fine, because now she wasn't annoyed. She was pissed off. And that made her strong.

"Hey!" the carriage driver shouted. "Try that shit again, and I will burn your brother alive! I came here to make a trade! Send out the girl, and no more bullshit!"

Tin gritted her teeth. *No more bullshit*, he'd said. To her! *No more bullshit.*

"Boss," the archer said nervously, "he must be wearing armor. I have arrows that—"

"Shut the fuck up," she snapped. "Time for Plan C. Send the girl."

* * *

KYRIOC'S HEART LEAPED. *SEND the girl.*

He'd taken a space in the back of the crowd, as far from the lanterns as he could get. He glanced at the spa's front door, but it stayed closed. Riliska should be stepping through it any moment now.

In that moment, it became absolutely clear what he should do. The void he'd imagined once Riliska was safe suddenly wasn't so black anymore. He could picture it as easily as he could picture the coming dawn. Riliska would walk across the plankway to the bureaucrat, who would scoop her up and carry her away. Then constables would surge out of their hiding places.

When they did, Kyrioc was going kill Tin Pail so she could never do this again. After that, he'd murder as many of these assholes as he could.

And if that meant that Kyrioc took the point or was thrown off the platform, so be it. It would be better than returning to a life that meant absolutely nothing to him.

Was this happiness? Was this relief? Had he fought and killed until he finally redeemed one of his many mistakes?

Still, the door didn't open. The heavies were turned toward the plaza. At the back of the crowd, Kyrioc couldn't see what they were looking at, but he thought he could hear the scuffle of soft footfalls.

Riliska was already on the plankway. Tin had kept her close, where no one could see her in the press of bodies.

That was a smart move. If Kyrioc had realized she was there...

Not that it mattered now. He straightened to see over the crowd, holding tight to his cloak of mirrors. A woman beside him with a scar across her face glanced at him, then looked away.

Kyrioc could see nothing. He climbed onto the bench, standing well above the others.

A little girl walked with a shuttered lantern in both hands. She was almost to the far side, scurrying along with quick, tiny, furtive steps.

He'd never seen Riliska walk that way before.

For a moment, he considered shouting to Fay that they'd sent an imposter, but he supposed it didn't matter. If they weren't sending her across the plankway, she was somewhere in the building. While the heavies were wasting time out here, he'd find her and free her.

"Can you see him?" one of the heavies asked. "I can't see that far. Can you see him?"

The tall woman beside him said, "Fuck, yes."

"Tell me," the squinting man said. "Tell me what he does when he finds out."

Goosebumps ran down Kyrioc's back, and the emptiness inside him swallowed all happiness and hope.

* * *

FAY FELT AS LIGHT as smoke. The thin trickle of blood running down his belly was proof the asshole had tried to kill him. If their broadhead arrow had struck with the grain of his wooden panel instead of across it, he would have suffered more than this pinprick. Much more.

Still, he was alive, and he wasn't even angry. It seemed odd that he would feel nothing more than a vague amazement. Was there something wrong with him? Why wasn't he filled with righteous outrage, anger, and bloodlust? He was pretty sure those were the normal feelings people were supposed to have. He hoped they'd show up soon.

As he rocked the arrowhead back and forth, working it out of his wooden breastplate, he watched a child approach with a lantern. It was thoroughly shrouded and heavy enough that she had to carry it with both hands.

Was this the child that Kyrioc, child of No One, had gone to such trouble for? She looked quite ordinary—half-starved and undergrown, with a yellow tinge to her complexion that suggested she wasn't eating well. Fay saw dozens like her running the alleys of Koh-Salash. It had never occurred to him that he should take up arms for them.

A tiny prick of shame made his heart skip. Why was he chasing Harl when he could have been doing something for this child and the others like her?

The girl stopped some feet away from him, as though she did not expect to be taken to safety.

"You're not Riliska, child of Rulenya, are you?"

The little girl shook her head solemnly, then lifted the lantern.

Fay realized the heavy shroud that blocked most of the light was some kind of wet leather. Inside the wick chamber, two small, slightly scorched spheres dangled a few inches from the flame.

Goosebumps ran down the back of Fay's neck.

"Where is Riliska, child of Rulenya?"

The child looked down at the deck.

"Hey, asshole!"

The woman who had been shouting at him had moved to the edge of the crowd. Everyone else positioned themselves as though she were a fire keeping them warm. Constables and bureaucrats, including Fay, stood around Onderishta the same way. That had to be Tin Pail.

She was dressed in the sober green of a magistrate, which had been the uniform for ambitious gangsters for a generation, but she held a hammer in her hand. Not a knife or hatchet. A hammer.

Tin pointed at the little girl with her weapon. "She's right there. Do you see her? Right. There. See, you can't collect little kids, not for most things. Their hearts and livers and shit are too small. But their eyes are good and so is their skin. Oh, man, a child's skin is like a sheet of solid gold, even for kids living rough. Upcity assholes pay big for unblemished skin or a scalp full of hair.

"And yet, I'm wasting her skin and eyes on you. And you know why? Because fuck you. You take my brother? You fuck with my family? Well, *that* is what's going to happen to you and everyone you love if you don't return my brother unharmed *RIGHT N—*"

There was a commotion in the crowd beside her. One of the heavies snatched an arrow from a little table, then lit it on a torch. The archer—the man who'd just tried to kill Fay, he guessed—moved to challenge him, but in a sudden movement that Fay couldn't quite follow, the heavy took the bow into his own hands and sent the archer rolling toward the edge of the deck.

There was a cry of outrage from the other thugs as they rushed to save him.

In one swift, effortless motion, the heavy nocked the burning arrow, drew it all the way back, and released it.

Right at Fay.

He could hear it coming, and because of the flame, he could see its path, too. Fay dove out of the cart.

The arrow struck one of the bodies in the back of the carriage. Fay realized it would have missed him by several feet. And maybe they weren't aiming at him this time.

A terrible moan of pain came from beneath that blanket, and the cloth began to burn brightly, as though it had been soaked in oil. In moments, the entire carriage was ablaze. The horses bolted.

Panicked horses pulling a blazing carriage through the wooden streets of Koh-Salash could do no one any good.

He took the whistle from his pocket and blew three short blasts. The constables would be swarming in once they saw that fire, but he gave the order anyway, if only to preserve the illusion that he was still in charge.

Fay turned to the little girl, still standing nervously at the edge of the plankway, ghastly lantern in her trembling hand.

"Set that down," he said. "Come here. You don't have to do this anymore."

* * *

BEFORE HIS ARROW STRUCK, Kyrioc plucked four more off the table. The archer lay half on the edge of the deck, clinging with one leg and one arm. His eyes were as big as apricots. A woman bent low to pull him back, and Kyrioc jabbed her below the ear with an arrow. She flinched away, so the strike wasn't deep, but her reaction made her fall against the archer, and they plunged into the darkness together.

Inside Kyrioc, the dragon was wide awake.

He spun, nocked an arrow, and loosed it on a half-draw. It slid between the ribs of a man just a few feet away. Kyrioc loosed again, puncturing the kidney of another heavy between himself and Tin Pail. The gangsters fell back in a blind panic—the wrong thing to do when facing an archer, especially one close enough to spit on, but these were just street thugs. They had no real training or discipline, just dull sadism.

His third shot passed through the throat of a slender woman holding a curved knife, then lodged in the right lung of the man behind her. Both toppled to the deck.

Revealing Tin Pail. The one who'd ordered Riliska's death. The one who'd ruined everything.

He nocked his last arrow and shot it on the half-draw, a quick sharp shot aimed directly at her eye.

Without flinching, she swung her hammer, deflecting the splintered shaft over her head.

Kyrioc couldn't tell if she was lucky or good, but it didn't matter. He reached for more arrows, but one of the heavies had enough initiative to kick the table. The arrows scattered across the deck. He drew the bowstring, and even though he clearly had no arrow nocked, she ducked low and fell back into the crowd.

All their attention was on him now. It was like a gale-force wind against his magic. He was going to lose his cloak of mirrors, so he released it, revealing himself for the first time.

The heavies fell back again, this time in awe. He heard someone mutter, "Shitfire." It didn't matter who.

Nothing mattered. Riliska was dead.

Riliska was dead.

If Kyrioc had spoken up for her when she needed him—during a petty dispute over a fucking wax tablet—she would be safe right now. If he were a better person, he would be spending this very moment with her in his little room, helping her plan her mother's funeral and promising to look after her.

He was not that person. He was this one. The past could never be changed. No one knew that better than him. The best Kyrioc could hope for was that this time, no more innocents would have to pay for his sins.

The heavies stared at him with open terror, but Tin Pail did not look impressed. She glanced at the far plaza as the bureaucrat blew a whistle, then turned her attention back to him.

"You're full of surprises, aren't you? I'm flattered. Whoever hired you must have really laid out some gold. Tell me who you're working for."

Kyrioc didn't answer.

"Never mind. I already know you're working for the Amber Throne. Not at first, though, right? But when I sent you to Harl, you warned him. Helped him get away. So, our foreign friends reached out to you. How much are they paying you?"

Kyrioc didn't answer.

"Look where you are. Do you think you can survive this fight? Against all of us? Tell me what they're paying you. I'll pay a quarter of that, and you'll actually live to spend it. All you have to do is tell me where to find your contact. Well?"

Kyrioc didn't answer.

"I don't get you. You haven't made a stupid move before this, so what the fuck? I'm offering to pay you and let you live."

"You have nothing I want," Kyrioc said. "Not anymore."

"Because of the girl? Bullshit. You're not doing all of this because of some worthless orphaned kid. That's bullshit. Why her? Why this one little girl?"

The death of a single child is like the end of the world.

Kyrioc said, "She was my neighbor."

Tin's lip curled in anger. She thought he was taunting her.

None of that mattered. He threw the bow over his shoulder. It missed the deck behind him and fell silently through the darkness, without even the *click* of wood impacting wood to mark its passing.

Into nothingness. That was how Kyrioc felt. He had not been able to imagine what the world would be like when he rescued Riliska, but the thought of failure had been unbearable.

Now that moment had come, and it was more than he could stand. He wanted to tear off all his skin. He wanted to set fire to himself with his self-hatred. He wanted to be someone, anyone, else.

One kind act at the right moment would have saved Riliska's life, but he had been incapable of it. She'd been doomed from the moment they met.

He should have wept in shame, but it was too late for that.

He had nothing left but the urge to die.

But first, he was going to kill every last one of these motherfuckers.

* * *

KILLER OF DEVILS SAT alone in the spa, thinking about the rolling green fields of his homeland. The Katr were famously generous with invited guests, and infamously harsh on unwelcome invaders. As a boy, Killer had met many foreigners and had liked most of them.

Still, when the lonelto raiders had paddled into the river mouth beside his village, he had taken up his grandfather's spear and helped to drive them away. Young he may have been, but he fought with distinction.

That was the day he had earned his name. It had opened doors for him, first for his studies in the priesthood, then the halls of the clan chiefs. Everything he had done since had been won through hard work and iron will, but the opportunities would never have come without that day and that name. *Killer of Devils.*

But what was it worth now?

He thought again of that little girl, so desperate to be reunited with her mother. He thought again of the way she had trusted him when he led her into the doctor's basement of horrors…

It was too much. He was trapped in this city, serving these masters.

For centuries, his people had believed it was blasphemy to live among the corpses of the gods. But when other nations had joined forces to drive the Salashi out, his refused. The Katr believed the gods themselves would make their displeasure known.

Well, they had waited more than four hundred years for the gods' vengeance, and Killer suspected they were waiting for the wrong thing. The gods did not have to rain fire and pestilence among the Salashi. They only needed to let them live inside this hell, while they slowly strangled whatever decency and vitality fled Selsarim all those years before. If the people here were doomed, they were doomed to become uncaring monsters who skinned children alive for spite.

Killer could not simply walk away from the oaths that bound him to the Pails, but he could be freed of them. Death would do it, and for the first time in his life, he was ready—no, eager—for death to claim him.

But it could not be at his own hand, or with his assistance. He needed to find a fight he could not win, and he needed to find that fight as soon as possible, because his time was over.

He heard three faint whistle blasts. The cosh were coming. Killer of Devils took up his ghostkind blade and headed for the exit, wondering how many of them he would have to kill before they finally brought him down.

* * *

TIN JUST STOOD THERE, watching this fucking guy with the scar on his face, as he stared at her like she was a broken bottle of brandy. Like she was a mess that needed to be wiped up.

Wooden was dead. She hadn't really believed the broker would bring him. She'd been sure that was fake. But with that agonizing cry from the burning carriage—a voice she recognized instantly—she realized she'd played this all wrong. She had tried to be smart, but she'd overthought it.

Her brother was dead.

And it was this asshole's fault.

She'd offered him money and his life—neither of which she would have actually given him—for the name of the person running him, but he'd just stared. He was still acting like the orphan girl was his sole reason for being there.

Which was bullshit.

The broker drew a slender iron rod from his left sleeve. It was no longer than his forearm—not even as long as a truncheon—and covered with little oblong ridges. She'd never seen a weapon like it.

Idiot. She wasn't afraid of him. If she was going to die fighting, best to lose to an asshole with magic behind him. But she was the boss now, and she didn't have to be in the front. First, she was going to let her people take a few pieces of him.

But they were just standing around like shitwits.

"WHAT THE FUCK ARE YOU WAITING FOR?"

The heavies surged forward.

Wool Cap caught her elbow. "Boss!"

He didn't have to point. She turned toward the plaza, where constables had begun to gather in ranks. The asshole who'd pretended to be the broker was watching her. He was definitely another Carrig invader, come to undermine her city from within the bureaucracy. She wondered how much the Amber Throne was paying him and how many more there were like him. And he was giving orders to the fucking cosh.

"Spring the plank," she said, as the first constables stepped onto the plankway.

Wool went pale. "Boss, the cosh are already…"

"Fuck this," she said. She knelt at the edge of the spot where the plankway met the spa deck. The handle beneath wouldn't budge.

The hinge was made of wood, like every fucking thing in this city. Tin raised her hammer and struck it once, twice, three times.

Something broke off and fell into the darkness. The whole plankway shuddered. The skywood hinge made a sound like a lonely ghost. Wool Cap stood at the edge of the deck, waving for the cosh to go back. Then the plankway groaned and dropped a few inches. One of the ironshirts lost her balance and fell off the edge. The rest scrambled back to the safety of the plaza.

Some didn't make it. When the plankway finally dropped from beneath them with the sound of a dying whale, two reached for safety, caught nothing, and fell out of sight.

"Three constables," Wool said. "Three. You're going to start a new Downscale War."

The truce that had followed the last Downscale War was nothing but appeasement to foreign invaders. The days when Salashi heavies appeased invaders and collaborators was over. She turned Wool toward the broker and shoved him forward. "Get in there and fight!"

CHAPTER THIRTY-THREE

The *Childfall Staff felt* cold in Kyrioc's hands.

The first of the heavies shouted a battle cry and lunged with a knife.

Kyrioc met her with a blow to the forehead. She crumpled backward into the path of the thugs behind her.

He called up his cloak of iron, then stepped forward, lashing out with his staff. He kept his weapon short for close quarters and struck swiftly against skulls, collarbones, and wrists. His weapon felt as light as a reed, but it struck with the force of a sledgehammer.

And it was growing warmer.

* * *

KILLER OF DEVILS STEPPED outside. The walkway that connected to the rest of the city was gone, and the constables were stuck on the far side.

He suddenly felt very tired.

Someone nearby was fighting. Killer hopped onto a bench by the wall and peered over the heavies.

At the edge of the platform, the pawnshop broker was facing down three dozen thugs. Some were the useless street-corner blunderers Tin had brought from Wild Dismal. Some were the slightly less useless bullies she had skimmed from Harl. None seemed eager to engage the scarred man in his tattered funeral clothes.

Killer was about to take over when three heavies charged together. The broker lashed out so quickly, Killer could barely see the motion. Eight hells, Killer had fought the man and knew he was quick, but not that quick.

The broker stepped forward, clearing space with his length of iron. It seemed an odd choice of weapons until Killer realized that it was growing longer with each strike. Then, when another heavy lunged, it shortened again to deliver a close knock to the skull.

Magic. The broker had a magic weapon.

What fool would sell an enchanted weapon in a Woodgarden pawnshop? It did not matter. The broker was tearing through the heavies, blocking knife strikes with his left arm—strikes that should have drawn blood but did not—kicking at knees and ankles when the thug looked unbalanced, and breaking bones with that changeable iron truncheon.

His movements were fluid, quick, and unpredictable. He pivoted first in one direction, then another, one moment turning his back on an enemy, then spinning around to bash anyone who dared come close.

The iron staff burst into flames.

The heavies fell back, amazed. The broker—Killer needed to learn that man's name—stood still, breathing heavily, the flames washing over his hand without any seeming effect.

The man summoned that shadow cloud again. It was smaller and more diffuse than before, but it had the desired effect. The heavies gasped and fell back farther. Then the shadow was gone, and the scarred man seemed to transform before their eyes. For a moment, he looked like Tin Pail, but only for a moment.

Then Killer noticed the expression on the broker's face. This scarred man was also seeking death, and like Killer, he was going to kill as many as he could before it came to him.

They were practically brothers.

There was another flurry of attacks, and this time, one of the heavies slashed high with his knife, above the stranger's arm. The blade struck the scarred part of the broker's face, but it did not glance off completely. A thin red line appeared on the man's jawline, and a tiny seep of blood appeared.

Whatever magic protected him, it was wearing down.

Then Tin Pail shoved a heavy toward the broker, shouting that she was going to have to do their jobs for them. That Killer could not allow.

* * *

THERE WERE TOO MANY of them, and this was taking too long.

Kyrioc's cloak of iron had already deflected three killing strokes, but every blow weakened it, and the heavies' edges had begun to draw blood. No matter how hard Kyrioc concentrated, his cloak was becoming thin.

Screaming, the heavies surged again, hatchets high and knives low. When they withdrew, three more lay on the deck, one moaning in pain.

Tiny flames ran the length of the Childfall Staff. The heavies glanced down at it, clearly terrified, but they did not break and run. They were still more afraid of their boss than of him.

Kyrioc tried to rush them, but they fell back while others went for his flank. He pivoted, then pivoted again, reaching out with the Childfall Staff. The heavies only gave him more space.

And they didn't know it, but they were killing him with every pause. The Childfall Staff drew its magic from his life force, and he could already feel himself becoming vague and unfocused.

The Staff was powerful. His cloaks were powerful. Together, they were a fire that would consume his entire soul.

With his cloak failing and his ultimate target safe behind her mob of thugs, Kyrioc's sole hope lay in breaking the heavies' morale. Which should have happened already. He couldn't imagine what she'd done to inspire and terrify them this way.

Maybe if Riliska were alive—and he were fighting for her—he'd get the surge of vitality he needed to survive this.

But she wasn't, and there was no need for him to survive. He just needed to waste as many lives as he could before darkness claimed him.

* * *

THE IRONSHIRTS HAD BLOCKED the horses' flight and were now frantically cutting them free of the burning carriage.

The captain stormed up to Fay, his face red. Before he could speak, Fay said, "Have them push the carriage away from the buildings. The skywood deck won't burn, but—"

"I don't need advice on fighting a fucking fire from the likes of you." The captain bared his teeth like an angry dog. "We're *constables*. We fight fires twice a week. But you do need to... I just lost three good people and I don't mean to lose more. Why didn't you tell me these assholes would threaten another Downscale War?"

They didn't have time for this. "Threaten? Captain, a new Downscale War just started. You have to decide what you're going to do about it. You can withdraw to your tower, staying safe for the rest of the night—until one of your superiors explains that it's time to retire your commission—or you can take out your anger on the person responsible." The captain looked surprised at this. "Now, are you going to retreat, or are you going to hit back so hard, no one ever dares test you again?"

The captain looked guilty, as though just realizing that he'd been shouting at the wrong person. He glanced around, suddenly aware of how many eyes were on him. "We're certainly not going to *retreat*."

"Glad to hear it," Fay said, surprised at how mild he sounded. "Now we have to find a way across this gap, and quickly."

"Quickly? Why don't we turn this into a siege and wait them out? They're trapped."

Fay didn't believe that. This Tin Pail wasn't stupid. "Captain, I want to be inside that building within the hour. But first, send me six of your fastest people."

* * *

WHEN KILLER OF DEVILS reached his employer, she had arranged a half-dozen of her heavies into a wedge, with the man at the point holding a table like a battering ram and the heavies behind holding a pair of benches. Tin stood in the center, hammer in hand.

Killer pushed through the side of the wedge and pulled his employer out of it. "You are not doing this."

"Fuck that," she spat. "I'm not afraid of this asshole."

"You are the boss."

She bared her teeth. "If it's gotta happen, this asshole might as well be the one."

Suddenly it made sense. "Is that why? You want a glorious death? I thought you planned to sit on the throne of the underworld, not throw your life away."

Tin blinked as though she was surprised to hear it stated so baldly. "I'm not afraid."

Killer knew she would keep repeating that. It was the most important thing she knew about herself. "This is what it means to sit upon a throne. You have people to deal with these problems. Glory is for underlings. What you have is power. Act like it."

"Even if we kill this asshole," she said, sounding strained and unhappy, "the cosh are coming. We can't—"

"You should slip away with everything of value before they seize it. Leave the asshole to me."

Gritting her teeth, Tin looked away. Then she nodded. She grabbed the nearest heavy and led him into the spa.

"You."

The woman Killer addressed was barely over five feet tall, and her arms were as slender as broom handles. She had lingered in the back of the pack because she was not made for fighting.

Killer had better uses for her.

* * *

KYRIOC CRIED OUT WHEN he saw Tin run inside. He had crippled and killed her thugs, but just as he was getting close, he was losing her.

"You can't escape!" he shouted, his voice hoarse. "Not from me!"

Anger surged through him, and the Childfall Staff burned brighter. He extended his weapon to the length of a long sword, then charged at the heavies blocking the door.

They gave ground but not much. One parried with a wooden bench, but it burst into a spray of splinters and the man fell back.

Then someone struck him hard on the side with something large and blunt. Kyrioc hit the deck and rolled. A heavy rushed him. A smash on the ankle drove him and his companions back.

Bracing the staff against the wooden deck, Kyrioc pushed himself to his feet.

The heavies gasped and drew back, their eyes wide. They stared at the deck where he had fallen.

"That's skywood," one muttered.

Glancing down, Kyrioc saw that a tiny tongue of flame on the spot where he'd braced his staff. Skywood was supposed to be proof against fire, but the unnatural flame of his staff was spreading slowly along the grain.

Kyrioc touched the little flames with the Childfall Staff. The fire let itself be gathered up like cobwebs on a broomstick.

The heavies fled into the building.

All that remained between him and the front door were the Katr barbarian and his ghostkind weapon.

* * *

KILLER OF DEVILS SURVEYED his opponent. The pawnbroker was bleeding from more than a half-dozen shallow cuts on his face, arms, and back. Whatever godkind gift he possessed, it had not made him invulnerable.

It was disappointing. Still, he would test himself against this man. If he won, his renown would increase. If he failed, he would be free of this oath. Either would mean victory.

"Have you truly done all this for the life of one orphaned girl?"

Killer received no answer. He nodded toward the dead and injured lying on the platform. More than two dozen bodies lay there, either writhing in pain or unable to feel it. "You have godkind magic," Killer said.

The man hesitated before answering. "I do."

"You are an avatar. Like me."

"I am."

"You must tell me which god has given you this magic. It is no secret that I bear the gift of Asca, goddess of the home and hearth. My magic is rare but not unknown. You, however, bear gifts that I have never heard of before, even in rumor. Tell me of them."

The man stared without answering.

"There are more children inside, my friend. They need rescuing as well." Killer expected some response, but his words vanished like lantern light shining at the night sky. "Tell me your name. Tell me the name of your weapon."

He was asking too many questions. It did not feel right. It felt like weakness. But he got the response he wanted.

"This is the Childfall Staff," the stranger said. The weapon was now as long as a quarterstaff, but the flames had died. "My name is Kyrioc, child of No One."

That did not feel right, either. "That is not your real name."

"The Broken Man."

Killer nodded. "Yes. That is the name that suits you." He almost said, *That is the name of the one who could kill me*, but he did not think the broker would understand. "I am called Killer of Devils. This"—he hefted his polearm—"well, the warrior I took it from tried to teach me its name. It sounded like 'Wish Emdue Lock'."

"Wi'shem Dulahc," the Broken Man said.

"Yes!" Killer exclaimed. "Those were his words!"

"It means *Cleaver of Bonds*."

Killer glanced at his weapon. "I wish it could live up to that name, but no matter. My friend, if circumstances were otherwise, I would take you out and get you roaring drunk to repay you for that information."

There was no change in the man's expression. "You work for a woman who enslaves and murders children."

Yes, he did.

"As I said, if circumstances were otherwise. I think you can release me from this oath, but I must make you earn it. And, if you manage to kill me and set me free, I will bestow upon you a great gift."

"I don't want anything from you."

"You will want this." There was a great deal of commotion on the plaza across the gap. The constables were busy, and the last thing Killer wanted was interference from the local authorities. "Follow me."

He went into the building, leaving the doors standing open.

* * *

THE NORTHERNER'S WORDS MEANT nothing. He was just another liar in a city full of them.

The building was dark. Kyrioc called up his cloak of shadows to see the outlines of the interior. There was no one in sight, not even the Katr he was supposed to be following.

Glancing back, he saw constables bustling in the plaza across the gap. He'd brought them to distract Tin and her heavies, but it had been for nothing. Riliska was already dead.

Riliska.

She was in there, somewhere. Her skinned, eyeless corpse was lying in a room in that building, and for a moment, Kyrioc thought the northerner might be leading him to her. Cruelty was its own purpose for these assholes. It delighted them.

The northerner knew Riliska had been murdered, but he still talked as though he and Kyrioc were comrades. After Kyrioc killed him, he'd kill Tin Pail. After that, nothing would matter.

He entered the building.

The entry hall was decorated with panels carved with symbols of nobility: the flower of ice, vigilant stag, sleeping crane, unfinished tower...

And the Safroy bull. He stopped looking after that.

There were no people, only a faint glimmer from a door that stood ajar and a sound of heavy sliding. He approached it, stalking down a long, dark hallway. Narrow doors stood on either side. He opened the nearest, revealing spacious sleeping quarters. It was empty. He opened the next and the next, progressing down the hall.

As Kyrioc checked the final room, a flash of movement made him raise his staff in a quick parry. He batted the northerner's thrusting ghostkind blade upward and over his shoulder. Kyrioc fell back, swinging for the man's ankle, but the Katr leaped lightly forward and body-checked him.

Kyrioc fell through the door into the lighted room. He hit hard and rolled to his feet. The floor was stone—just like home, he thought. The light was so bright, it dazzled him and burned away his cloak of shadows.

The room had once been a bath. The floors were mortared stone, with a broad, shallow tub in the center and two fountains shaped like sailing ships. Except everything was bone-dry, the mortar was cracked, and the tub filled with trash. The drain stank of urine.

Around the rim of the tub stood another dozen heavies, knives bared. Beside each was either a lantern with the hood flung open or a lit torch. The room blazed with firelight. Kyrioc tried to call up his cloak of iron, but it was too bright.

He had no protective magic here.

"Good!" Killer of Devils followed him into the room. One of the heavies slammed the door behind him. "Where is your cloud of shadow now, Broken Man? Where is the secret armor that blunts edges? Where is your false face?"

Kyrioc had been deprived of his cloaks and was surrounded by enemies. He should have been afraid, but he'd honestly expected to die outside. Living a few extra moments to die here felt like a gift.

"You see?" the northerner said. "The godkind blessings that made him so formidable in the shadows have deserted him in the light."

The heavies circled, squeezed the handles of their knives, and twirled their clubs. They were finding their courage again.

The northerner bowed very slightly. "I know you want to kill me, my friend. But as I said, you have to earn it."

CHAPTER THIRTY-FOUR

Whi le *Killer spoke, he* saw the stranger's weapon slowly growing beyond the length of a quarterstaff, and when the first heavy screamed out a battle cry to nerve himself up to attack, the Broken Man made a backhanded swing at the nearest lantern.

Killer lunged to intercept, deflecting the staff with the back of his ghostkind blade. The heavies would do the fighting for now, while he protected the lights that protected them.

The broker was already moving to the side as the screaming heavy rushed forward, his confederates close behind. Holding the iron staff in the same grip that Killer himself used, he slammed the screaming man on the side of the head. The heavy collapsed, tripping one of his friends and making the other hop awkwardly over his pulped skull.

The next strike hit the leaping thug on the ankle and dropped him, howling, in front of the others.

Then they surged toward him. Flashing knives caught his shoulder and forearm, scoring small wounds that would not amount to much on their own, but the Broken Man kept circling, attacking furiously and knocking heavies into each other.

But they were getting wise to the tactic. The next heavy to go down found himself dragged away by his friends while others tried to flank.

The broker circled back, his staff much shorter now, almost back to the length of a baton. A man with an axe handle charged in, screaming. The Broken Man quickly deflected the attack, then laid a stroke against the back of the man's skull as he passed. Two women rushed in with knives, and he struck one on the wrist as though swatting a fly, then—

Killer of Devils came out of his trance and leaped forward. As he did, the stranger landed a straight thrusting kick into the stomach of the second woman, sending her flying backward. Killer barely arrived in time to catch her before she toppled a standing lantern.

She fell to her knees and retched into the trash-clogged drain. Killer ignored her, interested only in the broker. The man struck quickly—wrist, ankle, skull—moving from target to target, evading many of their attacks with nothing but reflex and training.

It was the most beautiful thing Killer had ever seen.

Could Killer himself, deprived of his godkind blessing, have lasted so long against so many? He wasn't sure.

One of the injured heavies lunged with a knife. Killer would have thought it a near miss, except the Broken Man stumbled slightly as he moved away.

Enough. Killer stepped forward, raising his weapon.

The heavies saw him and backed away, which was all the warning the stranger needed. He pivoted.

Killer's gift told him the Broken Man would parry his stroke, but the dirt was full of warriors who tried to block ghostkind steel. Cleaver of Bonds had cut through them all.

He had a wide grip and shifted his weight to add power to his downward stroke. The Broken Man raised the Childfall Staff over his head with both hands.

It seemed a shame to destroy it.

The ghostkind blade struck.

Then rebounded back.

The reverberations of the clash echoed in the stone room, but everything else was still. Killer was so astonished, he almost laughed. Had he finally found a weapon—and a wielder—to match him?

The stranger inclined his head in the direction of the Killer's blade.

The ghostkind blade was notched.

Until that moment, Killer thought that was impossible.

"All of you," Killer shouted, "get the fuck out!"

* * *

KYRIOC WELCOMED THE LOOKS the injured heavies gave him as they limped away. He wanted their hatred. He was starving for it.

The first thing the northerner did was tip a water barrel into the stone pool. It burst open. Then he toppled the lit torches into it. They were quickly extinguished in the wet trash. As he circled the room, he turned the lantern flames low.

"All of them," the northerner said, and the heavies began to take away their dead, too.

Of the enemies Kyrioc had dropped, only four lives had been wasted. He wished he'd gotten more, but without his cloaks…

Riliska was dead and Tin Pail had escaped.

His hands shook with fury. At himself. At Tin Pail. At the constables and bureaucrats that allowed people like Tin Pail to exist. At everyone who had ever played a part in the Pail's crew, like this Killer of Devils.

He couldn't waste all their lives—he was exhausted and had lost too much blood—but maybe he could manage one more.

Riliska was dead.

He'd be with her soon.

Kyrioc sighed. He'd fulfilled his promise to Aratill. He'd mourned those lost on Vu-Dolmont. And he'd failed the one person he should never have failed.

He was ready.

But this northerner had set Tin Pail free. Kyrioc forced himself to stand up straight. One more. Just one more life to throw away.

After dropping a hood over the last lantern, Killer of Devils shrugged out of his long coat. He moved to the center of the room, tiny chimes ringing. The sound was lovely and delicate in this terrible place.

His expression was strange. For a moment, Kyrioc thought it echoed what he was feeling himself—a desperate, aching emptiness that yearned to make death, and to have death made upon it.

In the dim, Kyrioc called up his cloak of iron one last time.

* * *

KILLER OF DEVILS STARED at the Broken Man, and he stared back. The light was dim enough for the stranger to summon his magic but not so dim that Killer was blinded.

Killer could not have set aside his own gift even if he wanted to, and thought it fitting to leave his opponent equally empowered.

He had never in his life felt this way before a fight. A sort of hopeful resignation had come over him. Honor required him to fight at his utmost, but this contest, against this man, was an opportunity he was unlikely to find again. If he died here, he could hold his head high while feasting in the halls of his ancestors, whatever his crimes.

Death would bring no loss. His family was forbidden to him. The godkind gifts he possessed, meant to benefit his people, instead benefited their enemy. Even his legendary ghostkind weapon, won after such terrible trials, did not serve the Katr any longer.

He was dead in all the ways that mattered except one. Now it was up to this stranger to make it real.

Killer waited until he saw the tiniest flicker in the broker's expression. Then he struck.

The clash was loud in the stone chamber. Killer did not check to see what damage, if any, he was doing to his weapon. If the Broken Man killed him, he'd rather his blade be ruined than fall into Salashi hands.

As before, the stranger was startlingly fast. Killer's gift told him what his opponents intended in the moment the thought entered their minds, but he could barely dodge and deflect the Broken Man's strokes.

But there was less power behind them. The fight had weakened his enemy more than he'd expected.

Still, Killer found himself mostly on the defensive. The stranger used both ends of his staff to equal effect, taking aim at Killer's legs as often as his head. He attacked everywhere with great ferocity.

But Killer managed, barely, to keep ahead and to make the occasional counterstroke. The Broken Man was an evasive fighter. Even with his gift, Killer's strokes were a few inches off target.

It was a difficult, maddening fight. Killer thought he could outlast his enemy—simply parry and dodge for however long it took for his opponent to tire himself out—but that was a coward's stratagem. He could not rely wholly on his gift to win this fight, or else the victory would belong to Asca, not to him. He would never have earned his weapon nor his gift if he fought that way.

He dropped to one knee, deflecting a horizontal stroke with the back of his ghostkind blade. Then, with the handle of his own weapon, he struck the injury just above the Broken Man's left hip.

The stranger gasped and stumbled backward. Killer sprang upward to press the attack, but the Broken Man recovered too quickly, moving sideways and swinging low. Killer managed to dodge the attack against his knee, but he lost his balance and hit the ground rolling.

When he regained his feet, he saw that the stranger's weapon was growing longer.

Killer had no choice. He charged, letting Asca's gift guide his dodges and parries. The Broken Man backpedaled, pivoting to the left or the right, trying to keep beyond the range of Killer's weapon. He swung his iron staff with incredible speed, as though the added length had not added weight to it.

But even if the stranger had been uninjured, he could not back away as fast as Killer could advance, especially since Killer could anticipate every feint. The Childfall Staff withdrew, becoming shorter with every parry.

Then the stranger did something so simple and quick that Killer could not react in time. He braced his Childfall Staff against the floor.

Killer tried to twist out of the way, but the staff caught his shoulder, making him spin and fall onto his back.

This was it, he thought. This was the moment when he would be freed.

But the Broken Man's weariness had caught up to him. His follow-up stroke was just slow enough for Killer to roll out of the way. Instead, the Childfall Staff struck the haft of his polearm, which broke in half in a hail of splinters, with the steel blade spinning out of his grip.

"*Yes!*" Killer cried, unable to contain his excitement. Another warrior, disarmed so thoroughly, would have fumbled for his knife, giving his foe time to make another attack. But Killer leaped forward and slammed his elbow into the man's face.

Together, they fell into the pool. The Broken Man landed on his back— Killer's weight added to his—and hit his head on the stone. That alone would have been enough to kill most enemies, but his magic must have blunted the blow.

The Childfall Staff landed hard against the bottom of the pool and the edge, warped very slightly, then rebounded out of the Broken Man's grip. It landed in a clatter on the stone deck somewhere behind him.

Killer of Devils was on top of his enemy, which gave him an advantage he would not surrender quickly. He knelt on the stranger's left arm, then leaned down hard on his right. The man writhed and kicked to no effect.

Killer's first three punches seemed to have little effect. The Broken Man's skin did not feel metallic, but there was a little glint of the color of iron at each impact. The glint grew fainter with each blow, until a punch to the side of the face made the man's eyes roll back and his limbs lose all strength. Blood ran from the Broken Man's mouth, and his body lay nerveless on the stone floor.

The fight was over.

Leaning back, Killer had to admit that he was disappointed. This was not the enemy that was going to free him from his bonds. After this, he would have to return to Tin Pail, wherever she was, and continue to obey her orders. He was going to have to continue murdering in her name in this doomed corpse of a city.

"You failed me."

He punched the Broken Man one more time.

"You were supposed to free me from this oath. I cannot do it myself, and... No matter. I have not been challenged so thoroughly since I received this gift. Your ancestors will welcome you with pride."

He stood and looked around. The bladed end of his ghostkind weapon lay in the corner of the room, much farther away than he would have suspected. His gift told him his opponent would not be moving for a while, so he went to it.

The blade was deeply notched in a half-dozen places, and the tip was curled. If he had not seen it for himself, Killer would not have believed it. According to legend, no power humankind possessed could affect ghostkind steel, either to damage or repair it.

He looked again at the Childfall Staff now lying at the edge of the pool. He had thought it a poor weapon at first. His people preferred edges and points. Blunt weapons were for children's training. Still, if it had the power to do *this*...

There was a story behind this weapon, of this Killer was sure, but he would not learn it today.

There was also a story behind a pawnshop broker who could fight like a ghostkind knight, but the stories of dead men were for the dead to enjoy. Killer would hear it, someday, when it was his turn to die.

"I will give you ghostkind steel to ease you from this world," he said. The Broken Man was slowly coming to consciousness. He almost certainly did not hear what Killer had said about his failure, which was for the best. It was undignified to chastise a defeated foe. "You have earned it. This is the last time this weapon will be used in battle, and you will have the honor of dying from it." Then, in case the man missed it the first time, he said, "Your ancestors will be proud."

He hopped down into the pool and stood over the stranger's body. The man tried to move, but he could barely drag his arms along the floor. "Riliska" was all he said.

Killer of Devils hesitated. This broker was a man of power, and they sometimes had their uses. Even if the Broken Man could not be brought into the Pails' service, it would have pleased Killer to know he was out in the world somewhere.

But Tin had ordered him killed.

"I wish I could spare you, my friend. There are so few of us carrying these gifts that it seems a shame to destroy one. And I admit that I admire your willingness to help these children." The stranger stirred, as though any mention of the children galvanized him. "Unfortunately, someone else must save them. My employer has ordered your death, and your godkind magic, while powerful, was no match for mine."

"You..." the man croaked, his voice weak and rough. "You're wrong."

"Am I? Tell me how, and since these will be your last words, make them memorable."

The pawnbroker pursed his lips, trying to get his lips and tongue to work correctly.

337

"You're right that I have godkind magic," the Broken Man said, "but you haven't seen it yet."

The Broken Man seized Killer's ankle with a hand that was as cold as a plunge into an icy river.

CHAPTER THIRTY-FIVE

The year 395 of the New Calendar, eight years earlier.

* * *

AS THE SUN SANK below the horizon, the jungles of Vu-Dolmont trembled. The glitterkind bellowed out their breathless, unceasing distress call. A chorus of shrieking voices from some unknown enemy shook the leaves, and ullrocts moved toward the ruins of Childfall, their burning bodies setting the wilderness ablaze.

Trails of black smoke rose from the treetops, marking their progress.

Aratill charged into the clearing. His helm and spear were gone. His bald head was bright red and slick with sweat, and his bull's-head shield was held high. "The creature is not far behind! Your virtue, we must get you away from the glitterkind."

Kyrionik looked around the plateau. Four of his guard lay sprawled on the ground, injured. Besides Aratill and Oblifell, there were eight others still unharmed. Where were the rest? "But the injured—"

"We swore an oath to your mother and father that we would preserve your life. I mean to keep that oath. Now give the order to form up, your virtue."

One of the soldiers leaned over the cliff's edge. "It will soon be upon us!"

Kyrionik ran beside him. The ullroct he had shoved into the water was nearly halfway up, its burning iron fingers gouging deep into the rock as it climbed.

A wounded soldier pressed the butt of his spear into the ground and hoisted himself upright. "Your virtue, it has been an honor to serve. My sword, please, sir."

The man trembled as he clutched at his spear, broken leg dangling. Sweat poured over his face. Kyrionik didn't even know his name.

Aratill pulled the man's sword from its sheath.

The injured man thanked him and, with a trembling hand, took the blade and plunged it into the dirt. Then he shouted "Koh-Salash!" and threw himself over the cliff.

"No!" Kyrionik tried to catch him, but it was too late. He leaned out and saw the falling soldier strike the climbing ullroct on the shoulder. Both plummeted into the waters below.

Aratill caught Kyrionik's arm. "If the fall didn't kill it the first time, half the fall won't do the job now. We need to go."

The woman with the missing hand stumbled to the cliff's edge. She drew her sword and plunged it into the dirt beside the first. "If it tries to get back up, I'll knock it down again. Live, your virtue, in honor of your mother."

Her face was turning gray and she did not appear to have much life left in her.

She needed a doctor, but Kyrionik had ordered their doctor to stay on *Fair Season*. Another mistake.

"Thank you." He turned to Aratill. "You're right. We'll form up, evade the ullrocts in the jungle, then find shelter for the night."

Oblifell stared up the slope at the impenetrable green. "I don't like the sound of those…whatever they are."

"I don't know what they are either," Aratill said, "but I still choose them over those fucking ullrocts. Pardon me, your virtue."

Kyrionik had finally discovered what could break Aratill's unbreakable composure. "Spear formation, heading upslope to the southeast. I'll take point."

Aratill raised his hand. "With respect, your virtue, I'll take point."

"I'll take the rearguard," Oblifell said. "You two take the captain's shoulder."

The soldiers fell in behind Aratill as they struck out through the jungle. Kyrionik spared one last look back.

The one-armed soldier stood waiting at the edge of the cliff, staring down into the billows of steam, waiting to throw her life away.

The infernal chorus of birdlike shrieking grew louder. Whatever was making that sound, it was moving toward them. If they were lucky, the ullrocts would be distracted by the sound and the humankind would slip away to safety.

But where? Without *Fair Season*, they had no way off the island, not unless one of Aratill's soldiers knew how to build a boat with a real hull.

Hunting jellies would pull a raft apart.

That was a problem for another day. They had to survive this one first.

Aratill marched along the slope, barely moving uphill at all. They weren't quick, but they were as quick as they could be, weaving through the trees and trying not to foul their spearpoints in the heavy underbrush.

The ullrocts certainly couldn't see them in this jungle cover, but could they track them by smell? By the sound of their armor?

Kyrionik's left arm and side were painful and inflamed, but he still wished the others were faster. The man in front of him stumbled and braced himself with the butt of his spear. In the practice yard of Kyrionik's family compound, that would have earned him a swat from Aratill. Out here in the real world, in the face of a rout, no one cared.

It occurred to him, quite suddenly, that he was never going to see his family's compound again. Never eat olives at breakfast with his mother, never train with his brothers, never visit his sister's grave. He'd never again see the girl he loved, or the girl his parents had arranged for him to marry. He'd never play chainball with his friends. He'd never sit in the temple and read in the light cast by Suloh's teeth.

How strange that, in this place at this moment, he should remember the distinctive echo that his footsteps made in the hall outside his bedroom. He would never make that sound again.

And it was all his fault. Selso Rii may have been the one who cut the glitterkind arm, and Shulipik may have been lax in his duty to prevent that, but Kyrionik had been in charge. If there was one thing a First Labor was supposed to teach young nobles, it was that the one in charge cannot expect to take the credit for their successes if they're not ready to take the blame for failure.

Everything Kyrionik had believed about himself was wrong. He'd thought he was destined to be a great man, but instead he was going to die here—along with his whole expedition—where no one could recover his bones. In his arrogance, he thought he could place his mother in the Steward-General's chair. Now he would never see her again.

The man in front of him stepped on a log. It rolled under his boot and he pitched to the side, falling off balance. Kyrionik leaped forward to steady him, dropping his spear in the process. The weapon bounced down the slope into a thicket. One of the soldiers quickly fetched it for him.

With a flush of shame, Kyrionik returned his focus to the here and now. "Thank you, your virtue," the soldier said, but Kyrionik could only nod in return. He didn't trust himself to speak. He knew he would apologize, and he might not be able to stop.

The shriekers were louder than ever now, but now the sound came from behind them.

"We're all relying on each other now," Oblifell said from the back of the line, "so why don't we try, just try, to move quietly in this fucking jungle. I realize you're all wearing steel and the ground is an inch thick with dead plant matter, but let's not make it any easier for those assholes than it has to be." He glanced back. "Left forty degrees."

Aratill changed course, moving uphill at a forty-degree angle. Their progress slowed, but if Oblifell thought it necessary, it must have been.

They crept through the wilderness, bracing their boots against tree trunks more than they trod on the ground, because the slope was becoming increasingly steep and there was no surer footing, even if it sometimes made the slender trees shudder and rustle.

After half an hour, Kyrionik no longer felt that the soldiers in front of him were slowing him down. In fact, he felt as if he might collapse at any moment. Aratill had told him many times that endurance came with years of grinding effort, and he was still too young to have acquired his full share. Still, he said nothing. Someone was going to call for a rest but it would not be him. Too many had already sacrificed their lives for his sake.

The sound the swarm of shriekers made—assuming it was a swarm and not a single creature with a thousand throats—changed abruptly. They didn't like the ullrocts either, Kyrionik guessed. Maybe they'd killed one. Maybe.

By now, the sun was nearly gone, and the only dim light they had was from the darkening sky above, and the foliage above cast heavy shadows. Kyrionik hoped they would find a place to stop soon. An unoccupied fortress with fresh water, full rations, and clean bedding would be perfect.

Aratill seemed to have read his mind. In a low voice, he said, "The other side of the ridge should have some sort of shelter, even if it's just an overhang." He had to pause between words as he gasped for air. He was exhausted too. "If nothing else, it'll let us put the hill between ourselves and these creatures."

"Can we see how much farther, captain?" a soldier asked. "The light is failing."

"We cannot. We'll stop in the jungle if it gets so dark that we risk walking off a cliff."

A boom echoed over the island like thunder. Far below them to the northwest, a huge bloom of silver fire rose above the ruins of Childfall. Had the shriekers destroyed one of the ullrocts? Had the ullrocts deployed some new weapon?

It hardly mattered. The sound of the shriekers, whatever they were, moved away. The wind, which had grown quiet during the long sunset, began to rustle the leaves again, hiding the metal-on-metal noises of their armor and their harsh breath.

For a moment, Kyrionik dared to hope they might get away.

A burning tree passed overhead. It was as slender as a spear, and the plume of fire at the leafy end smelled like a campfire. It landed atop a stand of trees, embers falling among the dead foliage below.

Oblifell moved upslope alongside them. "I have unsurprising news. One ullroct, at least, is following us."

Looking at the growing flames, Aratill said, "And it's trying to cut us off."

Oblifell pointed to the soldiers who had fallen in at Aratill's shoulder. "You two stick with the captain. The rest of you are on me. Elxaris, take rearguard."

Elxaris was a woman of about thirty who had a slight dent in her helm. "What's our mission?"

"We're going to search the jungle below for a stand of trees that would make a suitable sailing galleon."

She smiled ruefully and glanced at Kyrionik. "I understand."

Kyrionik felt a sudden chill. "I don't. Why are you splitting off? We need you."

Oblifell only bowed. "It's been an honor, your virtue. Please survive, so that our oaths to your noble mother will be upheld."

He glanced at Aratill. They nodded to one another, making brief eye contact, then Oblifell peeled off, moving southward down the slope. The guard moved quickly, stamping their feet and thumping their shields against the trees to make the branches rattle.

When Aratill spoke, his voice was tight. "Let's move double-time so we don't get cut off by that fire."

"Aratill, we can't let him go off alone."

The captain didn't answer. No one seemed to be listening to Kyrionik now. To the soldiers, Aratill said, "If our young noble will not come on his own, you two will carry him."

The two soldiers turned to Kyrionik, but he sprang up the hill between them. Aratill had already begun to climb again, now moving more slowly because they had to go straight up to avoid the growing fire.

"Aratill, this isn't right. We can't... I've known you two my whole life. I don't want... You didn't even get to say goodbye."

"We said our goodbyes before the mission," Aratill said, his voice strained and edging toward anger. "We say them before every mission, your virtue, in anticipation of this moment."

"But your husband—"

"Others have already sacrificed more than a loved one, your virtue, and there may be more sacrifices to come." Aratill began to move more quickly, his anger giving him strength. "We are men and women of honor, and we hold our oaths above all else. For the love of your noble mother—and for you, too, although you still don't seem to understand that—we do what honor demands to see you reach home again, alive."

Kyrionik's immediate impulse was to apologize, but he stopped himself before the words escaped. An apology would be insulting, and he didn't want to insult this man. "I didn't want that."

"And yet you have it, without asking. Will you swear to do what Oblifell has asked? In honor of those who have already given their lives, and those who may soon, will you swear to do everything you can to return safely to Koh-Salash?"

"I swear," Kyrionik said, "on my family name, that I will do what I must to return safely to Koh-Salash."

"Thank you, your virtue. If—"

There was a sudden crashing sound from behind. A column of dark smoke moved through the jungle, battering trees aside and setting the detritus on the forest floor alight. It moved almost due south, along the rim of the island.

It had to be chasing Oblifell and his soldiers.

The wind blew embers directly toward them. Soon, they would be fleeing an advancing wall of fire.

Aratill began to climb again.

"Captain."

One of the soldiers had stopped and stood upright. He looked left, toward the center of the island, but in the twilight, Kyrionik was unsure what had alarmed him. There was a fallen tree, older and more substantial than most of the trees on the island, laid across the slope. Thickets grew nearby, as they did in any place where the canopy had a sudden gap, and there was a growing shadow in the trees beyond.

Then the darkness moved, and Kyrionik realized that it was not back among the trees but squatting right there on the log itself, a strange shape of glossy darkness that reflected the orange light of the darkening, firelit sky like polished obsidian. Kyrionik could not imagine what he was looking at.

It moved again, raising upright. Suddenly, Kyrionik could make out a head with a long beak, and a pair of arms, and a pair of legs.

But the proportions seemed all wrong. The limbs were too long and gangly, the torso too flat, the head…

"Selsarim Lost," Aratill said. "Shadowkind."

In that moment, as goosebumps ran down his back, Kyrionik realized he was not looking at some strange armor. It was flesh. Not flesh like his own dark skin, or even the darker skin of traders from the southern ends of the crumbling Harkan empire. This was like shadow made solid, except the twilight reflected off it like glass. This was a devourer of light and life straight out of myth.

It opened its mouth, and the same loud bird-like shrieking that they'd heard echoing through the jungle erupted from inside it. A moment later, dozens of answering cries resounded.

The shadowkind spread its arms, showing vestigial wings and outsized claws darker than the space between the stars, and charged at them, mouth gaping.

Without a moment's thought, Kyrionik hurled his spear, piercing the creature's belly as it leaped at the nearest guard. It stumbled against a tree, clutched at the shaft, then toppled down the hill, dead.

Aratill took Kyrionik's arm and nudged him up the slope. "Well thrown, your virtue."

"Thank you." The young noble began to scramble up the hill. "I'm just glad we have found an enemy who dislikes being stabbed as much as I do."

One of the soldiers guffawed, and Kyrionik experienced a strange, light-headed thrill. It was something Oblifell might have said, if he hadn't given his life so Kyrionik could delay his own death by a quarter hour. Kyrionik didn't feel courageous, but he knew how to pretend. All he had to do was mimic those around him.

The flames crackled and roared to the right and behind them. On the left, the shrieking of the shadowkind—by the fallen gods, who knew there were still such things in the world—grew louder.

"They're driving us toward the flame!" one of the soldiers cried.

Aratill kept his voice low. "Don't shout about it, you fool."

They climbed. Kyrionik felt naked without his spear and shield, but he didn't draw his sword. He needed both hands for climbing.

Glancing back, he saw Aratill and his two guards falling behind. Then he saw the shadowkind were moving from tree to tree, bounding up the slope with terrifying ease.

Kyrionik drew his sword. "Look to the north." His voice sounded surprisingly calm. He slid down the hill, letting the three with spears form the front line, with Aratill at the highest point. There was no reason to climb farther when the shadowkind could outpace them so easily.

How many creatures there were, he could not be sure—their bodies seemed to meld together—but there had to be at least a dozen. The shadowkind shrieked as they came, their harsh, ugly voices making the hairs on the back of Kyrionik's neck stand up. Someone shouted, "Koh-Salash!" and the others, Kyrionik included, joined in.

Then the spearpoints found their first marks, and the battle began.

The shadowkind were silent during the fight itself. Kyrionik could clearly hear the thump of body against shield, the sound of steel slicing into shadow-flesh, and the scrape of claws on steel armor.

He leaped forward, plunging the point of his sword into a creature that slipped between the spears, then hurried upslope to keep three more from circling Aratill's flank.

He fought as he had been trained: to use the point where he could, to attack from a guard position—even though his shield had been lost—to make horizontal and diagonal cuts at the enemy's face and belly, to grab the end of his blade with his left gauntlet and bear the enemy to the ground before skewering them.

He had to be careful not to get so excited that he swung too early. Wait for the right moment, then move hard and fast. Two came at him at once, and he managed a crosscut that struck them both. One died with its claws scrabbling at his helm. It managed to prick his nose, but it was a tiny wound—meaningless—which the enemy purchased with its life.

When the creatures stopped trying to get around the soldiers, Kyrionik moved to the guard's shoulders and stabbed over their shields. The shadowkind were not strong, but they were quick and numerous. They tried to dodge inside the range of the spears and push through, isolating the humans, but they could not score enough hits against their well-armored, well-trained foes.

Then the soldier at the bottom of the slope cried out, staggered, and slipped, falling onto his back. Three shadowkind leaped onto him, digging at his helm.

Kyrionik pivoted and, with a long downhill step, sent a sword thrust through one neck into a second ribcage. The soldier screamed, and the last creature leaped at Kyrionik.

Aratill's spearpoint plunged through its collarbone, and it flopped onto the jungle floor. Ten enemies—perhaps more—lay strewn about them, and from the sound of the shrieking, more were coming.

"Fuck!" the wounded soldier shouted. Blood flowed from his helm. "My eyes! I'm blind."

The other soldier wiped his spearpoint clean. "They tried to do the same to me."

Kyrionik tasted blood from the cut on the end of his nose and shuddered.

"Help me to my feet," the wounded man said. Aratill pulled him upright. Kyrionik could only stare at the bloody holes behind his face guard. He'd seen bodies gutted and beheaded, but this made his skin crawl.

The blind man cast aside his shivered spear and drew his sword. "It would be best if you moved away from me now. The enemy is coming, and I'll be swinging at every footstep I hear."

Aratill clapped him on the shoulder. "Strength to your arm. You'll be remembered."

"Captain, I go into the next world with shadowkind blood on the end of my blade. I'm content. Live a long life, your virtue."

Aratill started up the slope, but Kyrionik quickly overtook him. Surely, the top of the slope was near. Surely.

The wind blew smoke into their lungs. Kyrionik could not help but cough—he was working too hard not to breathe deeply. Behind him, he could hear Aratill and the last soldier coughing, too. The fire was blazing.

Then, suddenly, Kyrionik saw clouds lit by the vanished sun. The jungle thinned ahead. He hurried up the slope, pleased that it was less steep here, and found himself at the top of the ridge. Finally.

But the other side of the ridge was not what he'd hoped. Instead of another long, tree-covered slope, hopefully with a few tumbled boulders that would protect his back while he made a stand, he found a sheer cliff.

The valley below looked like an endless void—he thought he could leap into it and fall forever—until he realized he was seeing the sky reflected in a still pool more than a hundred feet below. Even without his armor, a plunge from this height would hill him, no matter how deep it was.

Looking northward, toward the sound of the shadowkind cries, he saw that the ridge rose higher, curving to the right and dropping again well past the midpoint, long after the still waters ended and the valley floor rose again.

To the south, the ridge sank toward the ocean, and the valley floor rose to meet it. Perhaps three miles away, the ridge and the floor were close enough for him to jump, assuming the fire racing uphill didn't cut him off first.

Then Kyrionik looked over the long, broad valley below—a few hundred square miles of it—and he saw something no one had could have expected.

There, in the valley below, was a massive skeleton made of pale white bone.

It wasn't made of skywood like Yth, and it didn't glow like Suloh did, but otherwise, the size and shape of the bones were very like the skeletons of Koh-Salash.

When the gods were killed a millennium before, their blasted skeletons fell in many places in the world. Suloh and Yth in the Straits of Timmer. Indib lay outside Selsarim. Asca fell in the far north, in the lands that the ghostkind have taken from the Katr tribes. Others were thought long lost, either at the bottom of the ocean or in remote lands where humankind never trod.

One lay here, in a place no humankind could settle.

Of course, the gods granted gifts.

What gift could this god offer, and could it save them?

Kyrionik heard a cry of pain and distress behind him. He turned, sword at the ready, and saw Aratill only a few yards down the slope. The second soldier was nowhere to be seen.

Dark shapes moved between the trees.

"Your virtue, make for the southern end of the ridge. Look to your belt pouch for—"

A sudden, screeching cry sounded out, followed by a noise like hail. The shadowkind were hurling stones against Aratill's shield and armor, and while he protected his face, three more ascended the hill toward the ridge.

Kyrionik rushed to meet them. He couldn't flee southward with the shadowkind right on his heels—they would overtake him in ten paces—but he could make use of the advantage the slope provided.

He cut downward at the shadowkind as they leaped up at him.

Aratill cursed as his spear shattered and he toppled onto his back. Dark shapes fell atop him.

"NO!" Forgetting his oath, Kyrionik rushed toward his teacher, but shadowkind immediately circled above him on the hill. Before he could take three steps, he was hard pressed from above, with no shield except the lower cannon on his injured left arm.

Aratill cried out, and Kyrionik dared a glance at him. His bodyguard's shield was also gone, but his left gauntlet shielded his face. With his right hand, he slashed at shadowkind throats with his dagger.

Instinctively, Kyrionik felt an attack coming, and he jerked his head back. A slender claw slipped through his face guard and gouged his cheek to the bone.

He cried out in pain and frustration, then grabbed that arm and severed it, shoving the shrieking shadowkind back toward its fellows to trip them up.

It wasn't enough. There were few shadowkind left, but they were close. Kyrionik gripped his sword point in his burned left hand and swung out like a quarterstaff, bashing the creatures with what strength remained in him. He maneuvered again toward the top of the hill, keeping his enemies bunched before him, their claws digging for gaps at his elbows, throat, and eyes.

Then Aratill was there, with a hoarse cry of "Koh-Salash!" His face was turned toward Kyrionik, but the streaks of blood flowing out of his helm showed that he could see nothing. His eyes were bloody holes. Arms outstretched, Aratill collided hard with the four remaining shadowkind, driving them to the edge of the precipice.

Then over it.

Aratill went with them, plummeting into the darkness without a sound.

Kyrionik stood beside the cliff, frozen with shock. Aratill was gone. He was all alone on this island, except for the ullrocts and the shadowkind and who knows what other enemies out of ancient myths.

He realized his sword was gone, and he had no idea what had happened to it.

More enemies were coming. The winds out of the west were blowing the fires uphill, and the fire to the south stood like a bright barrier.

Kyrionik sprinted southward along the top of the ridge. Tongues of windblown flame stretched toward the edge of the precipice, and he ran through them, his face turned away, with all the speed his aching legs could manage.

The blast of heat was oppressive, scorching his entire body through his plate. Once clear, he cast aside his helm to beat out the flames in his hair, but his clothes did not seem to have ignited. Unbuckling his breastplate, he cast it over the cliff, then the rest of his armor, piece by piece, as he hurried away from the flames and shadows.

A burning tree fell behind him, and Kyrionik could hear the frustrated cries of the shadowkind. They had been cut off by the fire.

There was barely any glow left in the sky, and barely any strength left in him. The burns on his left side and the deep cut on his face seemed to be stealing his life away. If the flames hadn't been so close, he might have collapsed right there.

What had Aratill said about a pouch at his belt?

There was a pouch there, made of calfskin. Kyrionik squinted at it in the firelight. It was Aratill's change purse, something he'd carried for years. When had he hooked it to Kyrionik's belt?

It contained no coin, but there was something round and soft inside. Kyrionik took it out.

It was a small bluish white nugget, no bigger than the last knuckle on Kyrionik's thumb, and it glittered in the firelight.

Aratill had gone against his orders and cut a piece of glitterkind flesh for him. It was enough, with the prudent cutting tools of a Salashi bureaucrat, for a hundred transplants of skin, eye, or liver. Without healthy transplants, it might be enough to close his wounds.

A terrible wave of grief and bitterness came over him, and Kyrionik nearly threw himself on the ground and wept.

...the death of a single child is like the end of the world.

So many lost. All had been children once, and many had children of their own. Now they were gone.

But he had sworn an oath to Aratill, his bodyguard, teacher, and friend. He would not allow his own death to be added to that tally. He would survive and return to Koh-Salash.

The stars began to appear through the smoke.

Glancing down in the valley, Kyrionik could see the gigantic white bones against the dark valley floor, almost as if they were glowing. The skeleton had a thick barrel chest and huge hands. The back of its skull was long and tapering, like the bill of a bird.

Suddenly, Kyrionik knew whose bones they were. He'd seen that figure in many times in old manuscripts.

It was Morlin, the god of death.

Time to discover what gifts he might take from it.

CHAPTER THIRTY-SIX

The Katr warrior's life force flooded into Kyrioc like rainwater into parched earth.

The gift of Morlin, god of death, long forsworn, filled him.

With the stolen life force came the dizzying rush of the Katr's memories: a quiet village on the calm Timmer Sea, training sessions with an older man that were little more than daily beatings, quietly eating salt pork beside a fire with his mother, the ritual clubbing of an oath-breaker before he was banished, riding a borrowed horse across the misty grasslands with the gigantic skeleton of Asca coming into view, bitter winds and punishing winters, the moment when he and his new bride shared their true names, the shock and grief of having his oath given to the Pails, the disgust he felt the first time he saw Koh-Salash from the water, the shame of doing the Pails' dirty work…

Not every humankind had a soul, but Killer of Devils had a substantial one. Kyrioc drank it down along with his life force and felt his strength renewed.

Killer of Devils's weapon clanged against the stone floor, then he fell sideways against the edge of the pool. Kyrioc held on. He wasn't sure he could break that grip even if he'd wanted to.

Because he was killing, but he was not wasting the man's life. He was *feasting* again. There was a deep, vicious pleasure in taking everything a person has, even their memories of their mother.

Kyrioc brimmed with that pleasure. He was drunk with savage joy. By the fallen gods, Kyrioc hadn't felt this good since he returned to Koh-Salash.

Why had he denied himself? His exhaustion was gone. He could feel his mind focusing and his wounds closing. All the northerner's memories were his. He knew the man's secret name, and his wife's, too.

He ached to shout it out. It wasn't enough to defeat an enemy. Kyrioc wanted to shame them, smash all they once had, and hound them into the next world. He wanted to destroy them in every way possible.

Then it happened. He felt Morlin's touch once more.

The god of death was not truly dead—none of them were—and when Kyrioc used Morlin's gift to drink life, the god's death dream intruded onto his thoughts.

It was a dream of desolation. Blasted landscapes. Dying suns. Caustic oceans. A world without life of any kind, where the only souls left to take would be the other godkind themselves, until starvation reduced Morlin to dust.

Oblivion to the world and to the self.

...the death of a single child is like the end of the world.

Kyrioc immediately let go of Killer of Devils. The flood of stolen life stopped. The visions stopped. The healing of his wounds stopped. All that remained was feral delight at the power he'd taken, and the furious ache to drain the last dregs of the Katr's life.

Instead, Kyrioc moved away.

Selsarim Lost, what had he done? He'd sworn to accept death before using Morlin's gift again, especially here in the city. If he became Morlin's instrument among so many innocent lives...

Kyrioc staggered to his feet. He was still hurting, still exhausted, though he was no longer deliriously close to death. The urge to take the northerner's hand and drain the last of his life away was almost unbearable. Part of him was sure he could never *really* resist it. And once he started to feed again, the transformation...

He'd tried to leave his godkind gift on Vu-Dolmont. He'd tried. But he'd called on it again, just as he knew he would. He didn't have the strength to resist, so why bother?

He held up his hands. They glowed slightly.

Savage triumph turned to hopelessness. He had broken his vow to reject Morlin's gift. He had failed to protect his friend. What had he truly accomplished?

Riliska was dead.

This city. Those without conscience acted with impunity. The rest were helpless to respond. The only ones who slept safely were the rich, secure behind their walls. Nations all along the Timmer and Semprestian Seas thought Koh-Salash was doomed, and they were right, but not because of the vengeance of the gods. The Salashi people were doomed because of who they were and what they allowed to happen here.

They were doomed because a tiny child could be murdered and no one cared but him. The death of one child...

Kyrioc should have been angry, but he didn't have the heart anymore. He was sick of Koh-Salash and the vicious way people lived here. He wanted the city gone. Swept away. If the children of this city weren't safe, there should be no city.

Then he realized that if anyone could rid the world of this doomed, blasphemous place, it was him. He bore the gift of Morlin, the god of death. If he began killing downcity—taking only those who truly deserved it, devouring them instead of wasting their deaths—he would first transform into the Telmein Griavus again, then manifest the Crown of Night. Morlin's avatar would once again walk among humankind.

The Salashi would have to abandon their homeland once again, only this time, they would not be driven out by a ghostkind army. They'd be driven out by the godkind.

If the death of a single child was like the end of the world, let the world end.

He picked up the Childfall Staff, shrank it down, and slid it into his belt. The weapon was no longer necessary, but it was too powerful to cast aside. The northerner was practically a corpse already, but there was no point in wasting what he had left—

Footsteps echoed from the other side of the door. Kyrioc left the northerner where he lay. Why bother to take a tiny, final sip when new corpses brimming with life were close?

The door opened just as Kyrioc reached it. Six heavies stood on the other side. Kyrioc caught hold of the wrists of the two in front. Glowing flesh shone through the ripped, bloody sleeves of his funeral clothes, and his new victims cried out in terror.

Their life flowed into him, although their souls were thin, like drops of rancid oil atop a water jug. He took their fears, their triumphs, and their sadistic pleasures. And because he wanted them—because he chose to use his power not from the bleary desperation at the edge of death but from a genuine desire to kill—he emptied them quickly, the way a hungry owl gulped down a rat.

His body shone like a bonfire through white-tinted glass. One of the heavies swung his hatchet, but Kyrioc caught his wrist as easily as an adult would wrench a treat from a toddler.

Another man tried to run, but Kyrioc grabbed his greasy braid and yanked him back, catching hold of his throat.

Their lives and souls flowed into him. He realized he was laughing. As the two heavies sank to the floor, nerveless, Kyrioc's body glowed like a beacon. The two remaining thugs cried out and fell back, then sprinted down the hall and, at the first intersection, ran in different directions.

As the second pair of heavies fell to the floor, dead, Kyrioc's glow winked out. He raised his hands. They were darkness. Void. His flesh had become inky nothingness. He drew all light into himself.

Strength flowed through him. He felt faster than ever. Had he been injured before? Exhausted? That had been another life, when he was still humankind. The power was his to keep, until he released it or he let it fade. He would do neither.

He would become the Telmein Griavus, the avatar of the god of death, once more, and it would happen soon. He hadn't even taken five full lives. The transformation was happening more quickly than ever.

How many more did he need to make the Crown of Night spark to existence? One? A hundred? He didn't know, but it would happen. Today.

And once his crown was in place, his transformation would be complete. He would continue the work he had been remade for.

You don't exactly look like a respectable *person.*

No.

He put that memory away. He didn't deserve it, and it didn't matter. He had surrendered to his gift. His old life was done.

He heard shouting and running feet. Kyrioc floated down the hall, the soles of his boots a quarter-inch off the ground.

* * *

THE BUILDING HAD BECOME eerily quiet. Tin had heard screams earlier, and she'd hoped someone was killing that asshole pawnbroker, but there were too many, with too many different voices.

When Tin and her heavy approached the gym, they found a half-dozen heavies there. They stood outside the door, lightly but insistently rapping on it.

"What the fuck is all this?"

They spun as though expecting an attack, then bowed their heads. "Boss, the guy in there barred the door!"

"What are you trying to do? Escape?"

"Boss," a tall man in the back of the group said, "this guy... Even his weapon is magic."

"I saw him out on the platform," Tin said. "Bleeding. If he bleeds, he can be killed."

"Your northman thought so too."

Shit. Had that fucking pawnbroker taken out Killer of Devils? Really?

"So, don't fight him. Hide in a doorway or something and knife him when he passes." They didn't seem enthusiastic. "What the fuck do you think you're going to do next? Work for another boss? Don't you fucking believe it. Fuck this up and you'll be lucky to be wading through piss at a tannery. We are gangland heavies. When we see something we want, we take it. Someone punches us, we knife them. If you can't do that, you might as well be scrubbing shitstains in a laundry like a petal. Now go knife this fucker in the back. And remember, he can disguise himself!"

They went. Not enthusiastically, but they went. The heavy she'd brought with her almost went with them.

If Tin believed a word she'd said, she should have gone too. Next time.

She banged on the door. "Open this right fucking now. I'm the one paying your—"

The bolt slid back. Tin opened the door, then helped the heavy pull the cart into the room. Just a few hours before, this cart had been loaded with buns. Now it strained and creaked under the weight of a dozen little strong boxes filled with Harl's—no, fuck that, *her*—coin. "Shut that," she said. Her heavy bolted the door. "Unload."

The little gym hadn't changed. The thick coil of rope sat beside the hole in the floor. A few practice weapons leaned against the wall, and in the darkest corner stood the man in armor.

The glitterkind child lay at his feet. Tin touched the leather packet tucked into her belt. She'd remembered to grab the ear but had completely forgotten the child it came from.

"Lot of commotion out there." His voice was clear and lovely, like a minstrel's.

"Join in any time," Tin said.

He did not pick up the ghostkind weapon leaning against the wall. "I'm here for the glitterkind."

Tin pulled the end of the rope out of the coil. The iron hook tied there seemed sturdy enough. "Well, wrap it in a sling or something. We're getting out."

"No."

Tin looked up, startled.

The man had picked up his weapon.

Until she'd met Killer, Tin had never seen a ghostkind blade. Now there were two under her own roof. And while she was sure her bodyguard could cut this fool into pieces, he wasn't here. All she had were her hammer and an underling in a dirty shirt, neither of which could stand against that alien steel.

"Fuck that," she said. "It's mine. I'm taking it."

"Harl may have called me a caretaker, but this ward is mine. If you think you can take it..." The armored man stepped forward, his black braids obscuring his shadowed face, and snatched the leather packet from Tin's belt. He threw it in the corner beside the glitterkind. "... try."

In that moment, Tin knew she was finished. All her ambition and careful planning had put her at the top of the slope, and being on top sucked. This city had taken her parents, her brother, and now her fucking pride.

Wooden. Her little brother was dead, and so were her ambitions. She'd misread the situation and fucked everything up. Maybe she should have felt more than disappointment that her plans had come to shit—he was her brother, after all—but she didn't.

Istliani, child of Maliakis, Wooden had been born. Maybe Tin would reclaim her family name, too, when she fled.

Because this city was going to kill her if she stayed.

"Get this fucking cart hooked on," she told her heavy. Together, they lowered the empty cart through the hole until the rope went slack. Then Tin climbed on. "When I get below, I'll unhook the cart and twirl the rope. That's your signal to lower the first strongbox. You follow the last one."

With a wary glance at the armored man, the heavy nodded. Tin started down the rope, wondering if one of these assholes planned to cut it and drop her through the darkness to her death.

CHAPTER THIRTY-SEVEN

Turning a corner, Kyrioc heard the slow, careful exhalations of frightened people trying to control their breath. More heavies lay in wait in the doorway ahead.

His cloak of shadows came easily. The two magics had little to do with each other, but his cloaks responded to power. He moved forward slowly, enjoying the thrill of stalking his victims.

The cloud of darkness preceded him through the doorway. When his would-be assassins recognized it, they fled. Kyrioc seized the nearest by the back of his neck.

The flood of the man's blood-drenched memories ran through him. They tasted sweet, but even sweeter were the last moments of his life. This was a cold-blooded killer. His soul may have been a tiny, shriveled thing, but his horror was delicious.

Kyrioc's cloak of shadows expanded. The Crown of Night was almost ready to manifest. He only needed more lives.

The other heavy sprinted into a darkened hall. A predator's grim satisfaction made Kyrioc's skin tingle. He had been ashamed of this feeling on Vu-Dolmont, but Koh-Salash was not a place for mercy.

Riliska was—

Just the thought of her spurred a memory from one of his victims— Riliska was strapped to a table, tears streaming down her cheeks. Kyrioc wasn't sure whose memory it was, but it filled him with rage.

He'd tried to be a better man. He'd tried to live the way humankind lived, and what had it gotten him?

The heavy fled down a flight of stairs into the servants' area. She was a good runner, but she wasn't fast enough.

Kyrioc was through with being a person. He was going to feed his gift until his transformation was complete, then he'd try living as a monster.

* * *

TIN HATED THE STINK. The river was supposed to wash all this out to sea, but it didn't work and no one cared.

The chamber pot stink got in her hair, up her nostrils, inside her clothes. She could imagine it touching her eyes and filling her mouth and lungs. Flies buzzed everywhere, and hordes of rats swim-scurried through the filth. It was revolting.

The platform at the bottom of the rope was twenty feet by twenty feet and stood on stilts about three feet above the wet, black muck. She would have bet anything that it had once stood much higher. There was no rail, but there was a gangway to a drawbridge, which dropped from her side. From there, it was a straight shot to Low Market.

Little light from Suloh's bones reached this place. She could barely see the deck's edges. Darkness hid this place and there was no way to get to it without wading through raw sewage. Someone'd have to be pretty fucking motivated for that.

When she was ready to get out, she only needed to lower the drawbridge. She'd hire or steal a carriage and lie low in an empty house she knew about in Shadetree. Then goodbye to Koh-Salash, the heavies, cosh, and the eye. And dying in a glorious fight. Hello, mansion in the Free Cities.

With this much money, she could die of old age on a bed of silken pillows. Why not?

The second strongbox appeared. Tin unhooked it, then twirled the rope three times. The hook retreated into the darkness above. That peddler up there had better speed it up. When dawn came, she was leaving no matter what she had to leave behind.

A boom of wood striking wood sounded in the darkness, and Tin knew what it was immediately. Someone had dropped the drawbridge—her drawbridge—which they could only have done from her side.

She drew her hammer.

So much for that Free Cities mansion.

So much for those silken pillows.

Tin moved down the gangway toward the sound. Who was she kidding, anyway? She'd been born a street rat in Wild Dismal, and all this ambition had made her forget that she was a thief and killer. She was born to fight.

Hard-soled footsteps approached, and Tin knew it was the cosh before they emerged from the gloom. There were six, all breathing hard as though they'd run a long way. The shortest, a woman with a long scar on the side of her nose, was covered in filth.

She must have been pretty fucking motivated.

"My cousin was on that plankway," she said.

Tin remembered her own brother's screams. "So?"

The cosh drew their truncheons.

The moment had finally come. She could have fought the broker or the glitterkind caretaker, but she'd passed those deaths up. But fighting alone against six constables? This was the death she'd long hoped for. The only thing that could have made it better was an audience.

Tin would just have to kill enough of them to make it a story worth telling.

"I know your cousin," Tin lied. "I saw him shit himself when he fell."

The constables broke formation to rush at her.

Tin was fast, her hammer already in its downward stroke, aiming for the skull of the nearest cosh. One tried to grab her wrist, but she powered through.

Something struck the side of her face. Dazed, she didn't see where her blow fell. Armored bodies slammed into her and pinned her to the deck. A knee dropped onto her arm and the hammer was ripped from her grasp. Tin couldn't see anything but the steel breastplate pressing against the side of her face.

Now she just had to wait for them to beat her to death. One swing. That's all she could get. Shit. She should have—

"That asshole broke my arm!"

No. No no no no no. Had her stroke missed? Because if Tin missed with her only attack, she was going to die here all alone without taking *anyone* with her.

She writhed and kicked, struggling to break free. In response, one kicked the side of her head. Bright lights exploded inside Tin's head, and she fell into darkness, thinking she would never wake again.

She was wrong. When consciousness returned, she found herself collared and bound. Her jaw was broken, too. She couldn't even curse at the ironshirts. Not that they were paying attention to her.

"It all goes to the captain," someone said.

"But—"

"I've never held out before and I'm not about to start. He'll decide how much coin is for Gray Flames, the grieving families, and our finder's share. I ain't stiffing the rest of our tower just because we got lucky."

"You're right. It was nice to think about, but you're right."

"Well, well!"

"Selsarim Lost, someone up there likes us."

Tin heard a strongbox drop into the cart.

"How do we get them to like us again?"

"Oh, shit! I think I saw her give the signal."

"There it goes! How long should we wait for the next box?"

"I'm staying until they start dropping bodies."

Tin tried to turn toward them, but the pain was too intense.

"Someone's finally coming around."

The shit-covered woman knelt beside her, bared knife in hand. Finally, the time had come, and they'd made sure she was awake for it.

"The easiest thing in the world would be for me to cut your throat and roll you into the shit. No one would ever find you and no one would ever know. But I'm not going to do that. We're going to haul you up to the tower. You know what they do to murderers, right?"

Pitch and flame.

"Pitch and flame, asshole. I'm going bring the families of the constables you killed to watch you burn, and I'm packing a fucking picnic."

* * *

THE TELMEIN GRIAVUS MOVED through the darkness, letting the delicious anticipation of the chase play out. His victim looked back as she fled, her face beautiful with terror.

Suddenly, he couldn't bear it any longer. He bounded toward her. In a panic, she accidentally stepped into a stairwell and tumbled into darkness.

The Telmein Griavus swept after her, angry that she might have died and denied him a meal. Koh-Salash was full of humankind, and he wanted all of them. Death spared no one.

He found her sprawled at the bottom of the stair, leg broken but alive. The hunt had ended. He seized her by the throat.

Stolen memories flashed through his thoughts: beatings received and given, knives in the dark, petals cowering in their shops, cheap brandy guzzled by the jug every night. A shitty life, with almost no trace of a soul clinging to it, but invigorating all the same.

A familiar feeling came over him. So soon?

He dropped his cloak of shadows just as the Crown of Night sparked to life.

It would not last long. He hadn't yet taken enough lives to sustain it, but it had been more than a year since it manifested on the deck of that pirate ship, and he could feel it close to the surface, eager to rise into the world.

The wise would bow before him. The foolish would try to flee and be devoured. Rich and poor, adult and child—how he had always longed to taste the lives of children!—all would be pulled into the void. The Telmein Griavus would establish the kingdom on Salash Hill that was always meant to be here. A kingdom of the dead.

The end of the era of humankind was about to begin.

And for one moment, the Crown of Night cast its icy blue firelight all around him.

There was a tiny gasp behind him. The Telmein Griavus turned and saw a small figure standing at the end of the hall.

It was Riliska, child of Rulenya, her dirty cheeks streaked with tears.

* * *

THE WARRIOR WITH THE bells in his hair couldn't promise to come back for Riliska, but he said someone would come. He told her to wait.

And she did…until she couldn't bear to be in the same room as the doctor's raw, bloody corpse. Then she ran into the hall.

Where she entered a nightmare.

She'd heard stories about winters in the lands to the north and south, when water got so cold it turned into stone, but she had never really believed it until she'd felt that blast of cold air in the corridor. She thought she herself might turn into stone.

Then she saw it, a figure made of darkness, as if someone had cut a humankind-shaped hole in the air to reveal the nothing behind the world. No light could touch it, not even the crown of blue fire that hovered six inches above its head.

That was the source of the cold. It was drawing in every scrap of heat in the hallway, including the heat of her own body. She could feel it pulling at her.

A shudder ran through her body. All her life, she'd been surrounded by those who could—and often did—hurt her. Bigger than her. Stronger than her.

But the figure before her was as far beyond the fuddled men who visited her mom that it felt as though she was discovering the *real and true* amount of pain that the universe was waiting to give her.

Riliska must have made some small noise, because the darkness turned toward her.

And she recognized him: The tall lean figure, hunched over as though in sorrow. The strange shape of its head, like a shadow cast by a man with shaggy hair. The way it looked at her…

She spoke without thinking. "Good sir?"

The blue flames winked out and the inky darkness floated away from the figure like smoke. She was right. Beneath that strange, terrifying figure was Kyrioc, child of No One, the only friend she had in the world.

* * *

THINGS HAPPENED QUICKLY ONCE the captain committed to the work. He barked out orders and his constables got things done.

It was an impressive and intimidating spectacle. Fay had never seen military drills, but he expected they looked something like this, although probably without the bloodthirsty expressions.

Three of their own had been killed. They were not playing by the old rules anymore.

A team of constables returned with two women in a long cart. They were city engineers, a mother-and-daughter team, who specialized in repairing plankways.

Just as the elder was explaining that the only replacement wood long enough was in a warehouse way out in The Folly, another crowd of ironshirts returned with a long plankway of ordinary wood they'd obviously torn out of the structure of Low Market.

"What did you do?" the younger engineer began to shout. "What— You can't just take the city apart! Do you know the penalty for stealing a plankway?"

"I'll pay it," the captain snapped. "If the High Watch wants to put a noose around my neck for the choices I make tonight, so be it. And your objection has been noted. Now, is it long enough?"

"It's not my objection that—"

"Is it long enough?" the captain insisted.

"It is," the older engineer said.

They returned to their work, arranging ropes and pulleys, then shifting the stolen plankway into position to span the gap.

The captain approached Fay. "We'll secure the building then send for you. Until then, wait—"

"I'm going with you."

"It could get bloody."

"I'm going. I don't have to be first, but I'm going."

* * *

KYRIOC SAW THE TERROR in Riliska's face and immediately released the power he was holding. Morlin's gift evaporated, and he was left with nothing but pain, exhaustion, and bone-deep shame.

For a moment, he thought she might be a ghost. But no. Her chest moved as she panted in fear. And her eyes…

It seemed impossible, but Riliska was still alive.

I will bestow upon you a great gift.

This was what the northerner meant. But Kyrioc, in his despair, had turned to killing instead of searching for her. He'd given up on her again.

When he spoke, his voice was barely above a whisper. "I'm sor—"

She took a step toward him, and Kyrioc imagined the Telmein Griavus seizing hold of her and draining her life away. "No," he said, stepping back. "I'm not safe."

Her upper lip trembled. "Did you come to save me?"

He had. Of course he had. But he couldn't say that aloud. It would have made him seem like a good person, and the worst kind of lie is the one you tell with the truth.

"Did you?" she asked again. Her whole body trembled. Kyrioc wasn't sure if she was afraid of him or—

She ran to him. He dropped to one knee. She threw herself against him, striking open wounds on his side and back. He made no sound.

He expected her to cry, to let the fear and terror of the last few days flood out of her in tears. She didn't. Instead, her tiny rib cage shook as she took deep, shuddering breaths.

A few seconds later, she was done. "I know a way out, but we need to find the red-haired man. He did a bad thing to save me."

Shouting and footsteps came from above, although it sounded far away. The little bureaucrat had finally arrived with his constables.

Kyrioc lifted Riliska in his arms, then leaned the Childfall Staff, now as long as a sword, against the wall. "Don't be afraid," he whispered as he pulled his cloak of shadow around them.

CHAPTER THIRTY-EIGHT

Riliska heard voices but she couldn't see a thing. She wrapped her arms around Kyrioc's neck while he ran. It felt nice. She knew they weren't safe, but she felt safe anyway.

"Hide," he whispered, and set her down. A moment later, the darkness seemed to fold into his body. They were in a tiny storeroom full of musty folded blankets.

He slipped away, with a lopsided shuffling walk she'd never seen from him before. After a moment, he opened a door—she recognized it; they'd come to the baths—and closed it behind him.

A moment later, one of the Pails' heavies came around the corner. He moved with the same shuffling step, but his had a spring in it.

* * *

"NEED THE BARBARIAN," KYRIOC said as he shuffled into the room. He'd only seen the man's stride for a few steps, but it was enough for his cloak of mirrors. The heavies let him enter the bath without challenge.

There was another round of shouting from outside. "We should check," one of the heavies said, but no one moved to do so. Eight…no, nine of the Pails' heavies paced the room restlessly. They were trapped and they didn't know what to do.

Kyrioc kept his head down and shuffled to the northerner lying half-slumped against the edge of the pool. He looked like he was sleeping. A quick check showed his pulse was still strong.

One of the heavies approached. "Need him for what?" she snapped.

Damn. Kyrioc thought he'd timed things too tightly, but—

"Hey, everyone!" They turned toward the doorway. The man Kyrioc was imitating shuffled in. He was holding the Childfall Staff. "Look what I fou—

"

"It's him!"

"Don't give him a chance!"

Maybe, if the heavy had dropped the staff and raised his hands, the others would have spared him. Maybe. Instead, he clutched it against his chest as though he was afraid they'd steal it.

Kyrioc didn't watch him die. He grabbed the northerner's wrist and lifted him up. The effort made his side ache and his vision go fuzzy, but it passed once the man was on his shoulders. Morlin's gift had brought him back from the brink of death, but he wasn't anywhere near his full strength.

The pounding was accompanied by the sound of splintering wood. The ironshirts were breaking through.

"Why isn't he changing back?" was the last thing Kyrioc heard before he slipped away.

He was breathing hard before he reached the first bend in the hall. If Riliska's escape route was far away, he might not make it. Luckily, she ran to meet him rather than hide as he'd asked.

"This way!"

He followed. Streams of blood ran down Kyrioc's legs. Pain and exhaustion made it hard for him to focus, but for the moment, he didn't need to. He only needed to stay upright, put one foot after another, and follow Riliska.

They came to a door, finally, but it was barred. Riliska raised her tiny fist to knock, withdrew. She was afraid to make noise. Kyrioc kicked the door.

"Go away!" a voice called from inside.

The sound of stamping feet and shouting sounded above. Several voices began to scream in pain. Kyrioc kicked again, harder.

"Go a— Who is it?"

"Killer of Devils," Kyrioc answered.

The bar slid back and the door began to open. Kyrioc kicked it again, making it swing wide. The man on the other side—one of the Pails' heavies, in threadbare, ill-fitting magistrate's clothing—fell backward over a cart. Both toppled.

Strongboxes hit the floor hard. One broke open, spilling bright silver coins. Riliska gasped.

Then Kyrioc saw the hole in the floor and the rope coiled beside it. This had once been a gym of some kind, with weighted practice weapons and an armored target dummy in the corner, but someone had cut through the floor. The heavy, the strongboxes, and the rope made it clear what was happening. Tin Pail waited at the bottom of that hole, rescuing her money instead of her people.

Kyrioc had promised to murder her, too, but it didn't seem important now. His first goal was to get Riliska to safety. Once that was done, he'd worry about who needed killing.

He set the Katr down. "Fill your pockets," Kyrioc said. "And his, too. He's going to need someone to take care of him."

Riliska dove at the spilled coins.

The heavy didn't challenge them. He dropped the rope down the hole, clutching it to his breast like a beloved child. Then, with a wary look at Kyrioc, he leaned toward a cloth-covered bundle on the floor—something so small Kyrioc hadn't noticed it before—and picked up a leather packet.

The practice dummy in the corner moved. Kyrioc grabbed Riliska and dragged her back against the wall. Steel flashed.

Kyrioc covered Riliska's eyes. The dead man's leg slid over the edge of the hole, and the weight dragged him through. The man in armor, braids spilling from his full helm, tapped the severed head with the flat of his weapon. It dropped into the hole too.

By the fallen gods, Kyrioc recognized that notched ghostkind weapon.

* * *

WHEN THE CONSTABLES CROSSED, the captain went first. Fay's bodyguards—two had been assigned—put him at the back of the line.

Fay saw nothing but the aftermath. Heavies sprawled on the floor, moaning in pain, collars binding their necks and hands. Tin Pail was gone, and so was her red-haired barbarian.

The Broken Man was nowhere in sight either.

"All low-level nobodies so far," the captain said, "many already dead."

Fay nodded. Constables were working their way down the hall, opening doors one at a time, shields held high.

"Collar them," the captain called, "but don't kill them. You know what this lot has coming to them."

The ironshirts answered with bitter laughter. *Pitch and flame.* The dead heavies were the lucky ones.

His bodyguards scowled at a blank spot on the wall. "Irritated, are you?" They looked surprised, as though he'd read their minds with a magic trick. "If you come with me, we might find a few higher-level targets to collar."

They nodded eagerly and he led them down a flight of stairs. If Tin Pail had an escape route, it had to be downward.

Just as they reached an intersection, they heard the distinctive sound of a door being kicked open. The constables moved toward it double-time. They were as quiet as possible, shields and truncheons at the ready as they surged into the room. Fay could see nothing but the straps holding their breastplates in place.

"You're all collared!" the taller bodyguard shouted.

Blood sprayed onto Fay's face, splashing into his open mouth. He stumbled back, momentarily blinded. Then someone collided with him, knocking him into a pile of wooden practice swords. When he wiped his eyes clear, he saw a blade stuck deep into the door where he'd been standing. Kyrioc, child of No One, had pushed him to safety.

The Broken Man had saved his life.

The blade withdrew. His would-be killer was dressed head-to-toe in steel armor that gleamed even in the dim lantern light, and his head was covered in a helm that obscured his face. Thick black braids hung through the gap at the bottom.

And he was carrying a ghostkind weapon.

Fay glanced at his bodyguards, both stone dead on the floor. The one on the right had been cut through his steel helmet. The one on the left had been cut through the sternum from collarbone to armpit, and his thick steel breastplate had split as easily as his flesh.

Both had been killed with a single stroke.

"Shulipik! Shulipik tuto-Beskeroth, stop!" the Broken Man said. "He's not a threat to you."

The armored man tilted his head. "How do you know my name?"

"You don't recognize me?"

"Kyrionik?" the armored man said. "Of course! I could sense someone nearby had eaten glitterkind flesh, but I didn't know it was you."

"Shulipik, how did you get off Vu-Dolmont?"

Shulipik lifted his helm's face guard, but the lantern was behind him and his features were hidden in shadow. "I arranged for my cousin to follow *Fair Season*." He shrugged. "I got my prize." He gestured toward a cloth-covered bundle.

Fay felt a chill. What prize could he be talking about? Unless it was the child-sized figure wrapped in that cloth.

"No," the Broken Man said, more forcefully this time. "I saw you killed. The ullroct caved in your ribcage."

"I took precautions."

* * *

FOR SO MANY YEARS, Kyrioc had believed all those deaths on Vu-Dolmont were his fault. So many years.

"You did it," Kyrioc said. "Those deaths are on your head."

"I didn't know," Shulipik answered, his voice low. "I didn't know what would happen. I wanted… I had a tumor. For all my skills in battle, I had a tumor no doctor could treat, and the bureaucracy would never sliver a dose large enough to save me."

"So, you cut one for yourself."

"I'd planned to take a finger. Just one. But once I saw all those giants, I got greedy and cut too much. Ate too much." He picked up the lantern and removed his helm. The light struck his face. The bureaucrat cursed in surprise. Riliska cringed and hid her eyes.

Kyrioc was not surprised by what he saw.

The shape of Shulipik's face was still recognizable, but his flesh was murky and translucent, like sewer water thickened into aspic. His eyes were dark, sunken pits without whites or irises. He still had a head, with a nose, mouth, and hair. But he no longer looked as if he was made of humankind flesh.

He held up the lantern so it fell fully on Kyrioc. "We have both changed." He gestured toward the covered bundle. "The giant your people carried down the hill at Vu-Dolmont is right there. How many backs did you need to bear that load? Now look at it."

Kyrioc glanced at Fay, who scrambled forward and yanked the cloth away.

It was the smallest glitterkind he had ever seen, not even three feet from heel to crown. And it was down here, far from daylight and growing green things.

The bureaucrat's face turned ashen. Kyrioc's stomach felt like lead. He had to get Riliska away from this thing.

"My cousin…" Shulipik said. "We had to convince Harl that it would be cheaper to pay us than to steal the giant from us, but my cousin took the point before Harl saw reason." He sighed. "I cured my tumor. I became rich. But still, I have regrets. So many regrets. The gods are evil, you know."

The sudden change startled Kyrioc. "What?"

"A millennium ago, humankind sided with the godkind and spellkind against the Ancient Kings of the Walking Towers, but we were wrong. They could have wiped us out. I'm not sure why they didn't. Still, the Salashi people have done a pretty good job making sure the gods can't return before the Ancient Kings do."

"Shulipik, what the fuck are you talking about?"

He looked at Kyrioc as though he was waking from a dream. "I'm warning you that war— No, something worse than war is coming. The fight between the godkind and the Ancient Kings threw down mountains and shattered continents. Armies fell like wheat before the scythe. I know. I shared the glitterkinds' visions. Soon, it will begin again. I'm warning you that things are going to get worse, especially for someone like her."

He swung his polearm toward Riliska, the point inches from her throat. She gasped.

Kyrioc couldn't tell if it was a threat or not, but he couldn't take the risk. He crouched, his hand falling onto a knife in a dead constable's belt, then leaped.

Despite his armor, Shulipik was quick, but he wasn't as quick as Kyrioc. Before he could even step back, the constable's knife sank deep into his eye. The blade did not slide in as easily as it should have. Shulipik's grotesque translucent flesh was dense, even in his eye socket and brain.

His mailed fist struck Kyrioc's ribs with strength no dead man should have had in him. Kyrioc fell into a stack of practice swords. He rolled onto his back, clutching at the cracked bones in his side.

"I suppose you think you owed me that," Shulipik said. He pulled the knife out of his head—the blade did not have a drop of blood on it—and dropped it through the hole. "But I wish you hadn't. I'm sorry, little noble, for leaving you behind. I thought you died."

"I did."

Shulipik shrugged and swung his ghostkind blade in a short, downward chop onto the tiny glitterkind child, then snatched something from the ground. A finger. It was the smallest finger from the glitterkind's tiny hand.

The glitterkind child opened its eyes and mouth. A wordless bellow of pain and fear echoed out it. Kyrioc knew that cry all too well. He'd heard one exactly like it on his first day on Vu-Dolmont.

He forced himself to stand, although unsteadily. "Put it back."

A wry smile crossed Shulipik's face, as though he was a boy who'd been caught acting naughty. He popped the finger into his mouth and stepped back.

He vanished through the hole in the floor.

"What do we do?" Fay called, panicking. By his expression, Kyrioc could tell he understood the danger. "What do we do?"

Just as he was about to answer, Kyrioc saw a leather packet on the floor. Before he could even completely remember why he recognized it, he cut the knot.

Inside was the glitterkind ear. He laid it on the glitterkind's shoulder.

When it touched the creature's skin, the bellowing cry faltered and its eyes fluttered. Kyrioc dared to hope it would be enough to send it back to sleep, but its eyes opened again, and the bellow returned. It was quieter but still slowly building.

"We need more," Kyrioc said, searching the floor.

Fay did the same. "There is no more. There is no more!"

"Yes, there is," came a small voice from behind.

Kyrioc spun toward Riliska. An ullroct was coming. He needed to get her way from here.

"Where?" Fay called.

* * *

ONCE AGAIN, FAY WAS following a criminal's lead, but what choice did he have? The child was fast and knew the way. Fay sprinted hard, the glitterkind cry echoing in his skull. The Broken Man followed too, but he was too injured to run. Did this little beetle understand the danger? How could she?

He wasn't sure he understood, either. Ullrocts were supposed to be giants who stole or protected naughty children, depending on the tale. As a boy in Suloh's Tower, he'd seen wood prints of them, but it had never occurred to him that they were real.

This was his chance to see one, apparently. And if he did, it would destroy him.

As they turned a corner, a constable spotted them. "Sir!" she called. "Where are your bodyguards?"

It hadn't occurred to him that he could run into stray heavies with bared knives and nothing to lose. He didn't know what to do about that, so he did nothing. The constable ran after him. "What's that noise?"

The girl led them to a filthy storeroom that smelled of blood and rotting flesh. A flayed woman lay on the floor. As Fay's gorge rose up, he heard the constable behind him dry-heave.

The girl, Riliska, kept her gaze averted. "This way! See?"

She pointed to a shelf on the wall. The constable grabbed a lantern and brought it closer. Fay had never seen so much glass in one place in his life. They were jars the size of his fist, each stoppered with cork and wax and filled with a cloudy liquid. Lying on the bottom of the nearest like a gigantic gory tadpole was a single human eye.

"By the fallen gods," the constable said.

Fay took the lantern while she went away to be sick.

"I know," Riliska said. "I had to look at them for a really long time. But do you see it, floating at the top of the water?"

Fay leaned closer. A fleck of something white, no larger than a grain a rice, floated at the rim of the glass.

"Constable!"

Fay loaded jars into her arms. When she had as much as she could carry, he loaded the Broken Man, then himself. It would have been faster to bring the glitterkind here, but no one dared touch it in its current state.

A sound like a vat of cold water hitting a red-hot anvil sounded, and a wave of cold swept over them. They had to hurry.

"Lead the way."

She did, and opened the gym door for them. "Hurry!"

A terrible white light that obliterated shadow shone from a slender column of blue-white that blasted upward from the glitterkind child's abdomen. It had already burned through the ceiling.

A light like that could shine on the whole city.

Fay squinted against that terrible brilliance and knelt beside the creature's head. Where the light struck the glitterkind, a spray of rainbow colors reflected as if from a thousand tiny prisms. Fay found it beautiful beyond words. He drew his knife—he couldn't remember the last time he'd done that—and began to pry open the jars.

The constable knelt beside him, jars spilling from her arms like apples. By the fallen gods, he hadn't realized she was so young. They were still opening jars when Kyrioc caught up to them.

"What's happening here, please?" the constable asked.

Kyrioc answered. "It's summoning an ullroct to protect it. The ullroct will kill every living thing it can find, and no weapon forged by humankind can harm it."

Fay stuck his finger Into one of the open jars to draw out the sliver of ghostkind flesh, but it was as elusive as a shard of eggshell. And as disgusting as the contents of the jar looked, touching it was worse. The liquid was thick and sticky like mucus.

He finally trapped the piece of flesh against the rim of the glass and slid it free. Unlike the ear, which had been soft like firm dough, this felt spongy, and he had to smear it onto the glitterkind's forehead to get it off his finger.

The bit of flesh was quickly absorbed into the creature's body like a stone sinking into mud, but it had no effect on the column of light or the ear-shattering cry of fear and distress.

This wasn't going to work.

"Pry the rest of these lids off," he said, "then get the girl and these two out of here. Make sure Onderishta gets a good look at them both. And be respectful. The one in black saved my life, and the northerner gave us Harl. Quickly."

He peered into another jar, trying to spot the piece of glitterkind within. He was forced to turn his back to the creature just to squint inside.

371

The little girl approached with a jar of her own and dribbled it onto the glitterkind's face. The drops stuck like water on a waxed cloth. Fay shielded his eyes and saw the viscous part of the liquid absorbed into the creature's flesh. What appeared to be clean water drained off.

He immediately stopped fishing for the cut flesh. If he poured some of this slime into its open mouth, would it swallow or drown?

Fuck it. Its eyes were open. Maybe that meant it could take a drink.

He poured a dollop of thick liquid into the glitterkind's open mouth. He expected, if nothing else, that it would interrupt that awful bellow of distress, but the noise didn't change. Magic, not breath, made that sound. He poured the rest in.

There was still a human eyeball in the bottom. It was probably impolite to feed it to the creature, but it was coated with the stuff. He laid it onto the glitterkind's shoulder and watched the slime slowly flow into the body.

The column seemed to grow brighter. It had become thick several feet above them, as though something was forming inside that light.

The ironshirt finished opening the last of the jars. "Go!"

She had to yell. "I should stay to help!"

Fay shook his head. Help what? He'd already failed. "Get them out!"

She and Kyrioc lifted the northerner and went. Fay didn't watch. He poured another jar into the glitterkind's open mouth.

It occurred to him that he was going to die here. He wondered if he'd get a good look at the ullroct, and if it would resemble those wood prints. They had given him nightmares.

The glitterkind's mouth was full, so he started dribbling the liquid onto its skin.

His family would mourn, then move on. The work he might have done would fall to someone else. All his memories and experience would vanish. It seemed like such a stupid waste.

But he didn't run. He'd chosen to stay and give his life for a city he loved but that didn't love him back, because that was what was needed. No one could have been more surprised than him.

The liquid in the glitterkind's mouth had turned to water. He tilted its head to let it flow out, then righted it again. No more time for niceties. He emptied two jars into the creature's open mouth, holding back only the eyes, which he laid across its chest like a necklace of bloody trophies.

He hoped the ironshirt survived to tell Onderishta what he'd done, so she could explain to his family. Would they think he was a hero? He didn't feel like one.

He dumped clean water from the glitterkind's mouth three more times before he filled it with the last of his jars. The strange cry never lessened or lost its note of fear and pain, and while the column had stopped growing thicker, it had not shrunk, either. Fay set the empty jars upside down on the crook of the creature's arms and legs so it could absorb every drop.

After that, he had nothing else.

He closed his eyes against the column of light. *Little noble*, the armored man had said. *Shulipik. Kyrionik. Vu-Dolmont.* By the fallen gods, there was a story there. He hoped Onderishta could work it all out.

He held its tiny hand. It looked like a child, but he knew it had once been three times his size. A giant. Then it had come to Koh-Salash, and like so many others, it had been slowly whittled down to *this*.

"I'm sorry." His voice was drowned out by the creature's distress call. He couldn't even hear himself. He placed his hand, still slimy from the jar, onto the glitterkind's forehead. The viscous liquid slid down his hand into the tiny figure.

Suddenly, the noise and light ceased, leaving only echoes and blinding afterimages. Fay opened his eyes to darkness and silence. It had stopped. Everything had stopped.

For a moment, he thought the ullroct had come. He rubbed his eyes, trying to clear the spots from them so he could see the monster of legend before it killed him.

Nothing happened. His eyes slowly adjusted. The jars were empty. Clear water puddled on the planks. Dawn light was visible through the hole in the floor.

Through the hole in the ceiling, he saw the spot where the column of light struck the edge of Suloh's pelvic bone. The rest of the god's bones glowed, as always, like orange gemstone, but in that spot, it had been gouged and blackened.

"I hope no one blames me for that."

Fay began to laugh so hard, he had lie back until the fit passed. He laughed to relieve stress. He laughed because he had survived against all odds. He laughed because no one would believe this story.

Snatching up the blanket Shulipik had used to cover the glitterkind, he wrapped it loosely, letting eyeballs and jars hit the floorboards. He lifted it and hurried out of the building.

The dead lay where they'd fallen. The living were gone. The captain had moved his people and prisoners out of harm's way. Good.

Dawn warmed him as he crossed the makeshift plankway back to the plaza. He was tempted to open the blanket. It was common knowledge that glitterkind thrived on sunlight. Still, he didn't dare. A person could get knifed for walking the streets with a bulging purse. With this...

This treasure felt as light as a feather.

Someone would be coming. That magical shitshow must have looked like the end of the world to the High Watch. Even now, a few looky-loos loitered at the edges of the plaza: a pair of crooked-back old women, a great big wrestler type with a green scarf on his head, a chubby young girl holding a basket of steamed buns. Fay couldn't help but wonder what they thought of a man fleeing the scene with a child-sized bundle in his arms.

He had to get to the south tower, lock himself in an upper room, and send for a pair of medical bureaucrats. Maybe they'd let him explain himself without collaring him first. He even had enough copper sails to hire a cart.

He hurried toward Low Market. The next few days were going to be interesting.

CHAPTER THIRTY-NINE

O nderishta *wouldn't believe it* until she saw it.

"This way," Mirishiya called needlessly. They rounded a corner into the usual bustle of Low Market traffic: shoppers, delivery boys, private guards, and hawking merchants. The jostling. The noise. The smells. The midmorning sun was high enough that the shadows of the decks above crept eastward toward them.

She bulled through until she reached a wall of mournful ironshirts out of the east tower. They were blocking an alley between a cloth-and-dye place and a shop that sold cheap clay cups. At her approach, one of the constables called into the alley.

The captain of the east tower rushed to her. "We *will* find who did this."

"Let me through. I have to see."

He ushered her through the line. Onderishta waved for Mirishiya to keep back, then noticed the girl had tears on her cheeks. Onderishta's were still dry.

The alley ran north and south, and there were decks above. No light from Suloh's bones or the ever-moving sun touched this place. The ironshirts had set up four lanterns amidst the trash.

In the center, well lit from all sides, was the body of Fay Nog Fay. He lay on his stomach, his left hand resting by his hip, his right stretched above his head. That position could only mean one thing—his killer had dragged his dead body into the alley by his hand.

The back of Fay's skull had been bashed in.

Hulmanis defe-Firos, Onderishta's own boss, pushed through the wall of ironshirts and hurried toward her. For ten years, the man hadn't left his office in Gray Flames for anything but a home-cooked meal, but he was here now. She was so grateful that she almost told him so.

"Selsarim Lost," Hulmanis muttered, "he was wearing his grays."

Which meant it should have been obvious that he was a bureaucrat, which meant the local assholes should have let him pass because they should have known he was *off-fucking-limits*. "His purse is still tucked into his belt," Onderishta said.

Hulmanis might have been highborn, but he'd spent years doing actual investigative work. He knew what that meant. Rubbing the stubble on his chin, he sighed. "I'm going to be running this investigation—"

"Sir, you haven't actually investigated anything in more than a decade." It was a risky thing to say to a superior of noble blood, but at the moment, Onderishta did not care.

"Which is why I want you by my side. Not as a second, sent to run down preliminary bullshit and keep the constables on task. I want you with me every moment, seeing what I see, hearing what I hear. Any thoughts, you tell me and me alone. Onderishta, you're the best investigator the city has, but I can open doors that you cannot."

She knelt beside Fay's body. There was the curve of his shoulder. There was the upturned palm of his hand, smeared with dirt. There was the curve of his calf, which ached when he climbed too many stairs. There was the mass of matted hair and bloody gore where his self used to live. By the fallen gods, the world was diminished without him.

No, she could not run the investigation, because she would burn down the whole city to find his killer. "Thank you, sir."

One of the ironshirts broke from the others and approached, making an effort to catch Onderishta's attention. She was young and pretty in a plain, muscular way. She reminded Onderishta of her wife when they'd first met, all those years ago, before the accident. A new wave of sadness came over her.

"I was there," the constable said. "He saved us all."

Onderishta nodded, tears finally welling up. She took a deep breath and clenched her jaw, because she didn't trust what she might say next.

"Excuse me! Excuse me, let me through!" It was Trillistin, and he was drenched in sweat. "Ma'am, you're wanted in High Slope. The Steward-General is arresting the Safroys for treason."

* * *

CULZATIK WARD-SAFROY DEFE-SAFROY admir-Safroy hold-Safroy was hiding in his own home...

There was a spot on the roof of the library that was accessible by ladder, although no one ventured up there but him. It overlooked the Timmer, which made it a pleasant place to get lost in a book.

That's what he was pretending to do now.

A steel helmet appeared at the top of the ladder, then turned to show a scowling face. "He's here." He climbed onto the roof as quickly as his armor would allow.

Culzatik was mildly surprised to see a sword at his hip where his truncheon should be. "What's going on?" he asked, snapping his book shut.

The next face to appear belonged to Pinfilas parsu-Yares ward-Yares admir-Yares tuto-Yares hold-Yares. He was an Elder of the High Watch, and he'd never had an original thought in his life. However, his ideas had come from reasonably intelligent people, which put him head and shoulders above the rest of his faction.

And there was no cause for him to be wandering the Safroy compound. Culzatik moved toward him.

The constable laid his hand on his sword. His expression was murderous.

Aziatil was suddenly between them. Like a good bodyguard, she was always close, but he never had to think about her.

"I wouldn't," Culzatik said. The constable glanced at him, then at small, slender Aziatil. The corner of his mouth curled.

"Come down here," Pinfilas said, and he wasn't speaking to Culzatik. The constable hopped onto the ladder and went down.

Culzatik followed. Aziatil startled them all by hopping down beside him.

Pinfilas used a more respectful tone when he spoke to Culzatik. "Your virtue, I'm afraid you and your bodyguard must disarm."

"No." Culzatik had no intention of following illegal orders, not here in his own home.

Pinfilas had two constables with him. They shifted their stances as though about to move for her, but the noble shook his head. There was no legal difference between attacking a bodyguard and attacking the noble they protected, and Pinfilas was the type to observe the legal niceties. "If you would."

Culzatik let them lead him though the compound. Furniture was upended. Servants stood in doorways, whispering. Untended fires burned low. It looked like the aftermath of a robbery.

The family sitting room was not for the family. It was a place to entertain guests, and currently it was crowded enough for a political luncheon.

Except that Culzatik's mother, father, and little brother were down on the parquet with their bodyguards and servants, while a group of gray-haired nobles and their functionaries stood up among the couches and tables.

Essatreska was there. "Please, your virtue, I would like to be free again," she said to a tall, elderly man with a magnificent head of gray hair. He accepted a document from her. She turned around so he could sign on her back. The old fellow seemed quite conscious of how close her rear end came to him.

She took the signed document with a smirk, then moved toward her father, who looked dismayed and alarmed.

Billentik rushed toward Culzatik. "Where have you—"

Culzatik stopped him with a gesture. "Essatreska, my betrothed, I didn't realize you were here."

"You've lost the right to call me that," she answered, then pursed her lips to blow the signature dry.

"Our advocate hasn't even seen the dissolution agreement you just signed," Mother said, stepping forward.

"A cancelled betrothal is the least of your worries!" the old man snapped.

Culzatik suddenly recognized him. It was Evenset defe-Presse admir-Presse hold-Presse, the Steward-General of Koh-Salash. The most powerful person in the city, and a political enemy of the Safroy family.

"I ask again, will you disarm?" Evenset asked. "Will you allow these medical inspectors access to your wards?"

"I answer again," Mother said evenly, "not without formal charges. And we will only give access to the family inspectors. So, again, where are the family inspectors?"

Clearly, the Steward-General was tired of the conversation. "In irons," he said, with the dramatic timing of a stage actor. No wonder the nobles voted for him. He glanced over his shoulder at a distinguished woman in green. No one would mistake her for a gangster in magistrate's colors. She was the real thing. "Along with your investigator. Which is how you will soon be, now that widespread rumors of your corruption have been thoroughly substantiated. After the incident in Low Market, the mad scramble your people have been conducting to retrieve your lost ward, and finding your husband here in full steel armor—"

"Stop there," Mother said. Evenset, the most powerful man in the city, did. She looked back at Father, who was indeed dressed in full armor. "Do we have a missing ward?"

"I checked the moment the alarm was raised," Father said. "We do not."

"Hah!" Evenset called. "Then why are you dressed for war, if not to recover your lost ward?"

Father bared his teeth. "Didn't you see that column of light? Every citizen—"

Mother laid a gentle hand on his arm. "He's not a ward-family. He

378

doesn't know what that light meant." She turned to a servant. "Get my investigator."

The constables at the door glanced at the magistrate. She nodded, and they allowed the servant to pass.

"So, I'm supposed to have a secret fourth ward, then, is that it?" Mother said. "With gangsters slivering portions, for some reason?"

"For money," Evenset said. "We've all heard rumors of your debts. You haven't even been paying this lovely child's bride price."

Essatreska smirked at Culzatik, as though daring him to say she'd asked him to delay payment. Ponnalas stepped around his daughter. "That's... That's not true!"

No one paid attention to him.

The door opened behind the Steward-General, and Onderishta was brought in. She held her head high, despite the heavy iron collar around her neck. Mother took a step forward, then stopped herself, clenching her hands at her side to control her anger. "Onderishta, can you give us a brief report, please?"

The investigator walked down to the parquet and cleared her throat. "My second and I were investigating rumors that a new figure had taken over the gangs of Koh-Salash. I went after a tar cookery while he raided their reputed hideout. There was a glitterkind on site, and one of the heavies cut it too deeply. I don't know why. Fay, my second, sent everyone away while he..."

Her voice broke, and she took a moment to collect herself. Mother said, "So, he saved us all." Onderishta nodded. "What then?"

"Someone bashed in his skull and dumped him in an alley."

"Oh, no!" Culzatik cried. "Onderishta, I'm so sorry."

"You don't fool me," Evenset proclaimed. "Bring in the evidence!" Constables rushed from the room. "I find it telling that the moment this foreign ganglord was killed, your people went into a frenzy to reclaim his glitterkind. And when the medical bureaucrats tried to intervene, they were threatened with *prison*. I wonder what connections my investigator will find between this murdered foreign ganglord and your own murdered *foreign* investigator, hmm?"

At that, Onderishta's hands began to tremble with rage.

Mother became calmer. "Let's see this evidence."

There was a commotion as people began to push into the room. "This was found," Evenset said, "in the street—the street, mind you—in Gray Flames. And it's been branded with the Safroy mark."

The top medical inspector in the city, a woman who lived in her office, came through the crowd. She was ashen. Beside her were two constables pushing a tiny wheeled cart. A tiny, shrouded figure lay upon it.

Silence fell over the room. The inspector ordered the constables to lower the table onto the parquet. When the Steward-General began to object, she snapped, "It must feel the sunlight *right now*." Then she drew back the shroud.

Goosebumps ran down Culzatik's back when he saw just how small the glitterkind was.

There was pandemonium for nearly half a minute. Even Pinfilas leaped down with surprising spryness for a man his age to help push the cart to the sunny balcony.

Evenset looked confused. He'd expected outrage, not panic. With a glance back at the other members of the High Watch who'd come to support him—none of them ward-families, obviously—he cleared his throat and tried to take control of the scene. "And you can see the Safroy mark! That's treason!"

With the glitterkind positioned in the sun, the medical inspector bent low to look behind its ear. "Yes, there's a Safroy bull here."

Pinfilas's head quirked in surprise. Mother sidestepped to see for herself. "Indeed, there is a Safroy bull. But there's one problem, General. We don't mark our wards with a bull." The room became still. "Billentik, take the inspector—and only the inspector—to see the wards so she can confirm the brands don't match." They hurried away.

Evenset looked suddenly wary. Pinfilas approached so he could speak in a low voice. "General, we Yares didn't brand our ward with the soaring gull. The brand is secret."

"What, then?" Evenset demanded. Pinfilas's expression had stolen all his authority. "Is it fake?"

"If you had spoken with the Safroys' assigned medical inspectors," Mother interrupted, "instead of collaring them, they could have cleared this up in a moment. Instead, you show up with wild accusations and fabricated evidence trying to trick a magistrate into charging me with treason."

"*Trick*? Now, see here! I would never... It wouldn't even occur to me."

"Then who would believe we put the Safroy bull on our wards?"

"Essatreska," Culzatik said. "Where are you going?"

All eyes turned toward the Phillien family. Ponnalas and Caflinna were in the same place, but Essatreska and her bodyguard were slinking toward the door.

"Come forward," Evenset said. She did, then adopted a demure pose. Evenset sighed. "How could this lovely creature—"

Culzatik interrupted. "*You Safroys put a bull on everything*, she says. It's like a joke between us: pin, belt buckle, shield. *You Safroys put a bull on everything.* One time, she asked if we put them on our wards, too. The way she said it made me a little uncomfortable, so I lied."

Evenset snorted. "You can't mean that this child—"

Culzatik walked toward her. "Ponnalas, hasn't Essatreska's bodyguard taken a lot of personal days lately? Bedler's always away, isn't he?"

"Sen Pul Nat," Onderishta said. Everyone turned to her. "He ran a brothel and casino called The Caves, and there was a box of jewelry in his countinghouse. I knew I recognized the pieces, but until now, I didn't realize where. I've seen her wearing them. Once we show them around a few Upgarden shops, I'm sure we'll find out who made them and who bought them."

"But it didn't work, did it, Essatreska?" Culzatik stood beside her now. "You knew there was a Lost Ward in the city, but no matter who you bribed, you couldn't get close to it. Then all this shit rained down, and your bodyguard finally saw his chance—a man carrying a glitterkind through the plankways of Koh-Salash, and I'll bet he already had that iron brand in his pocket. I'll bet he carried it everywhere. All he needed to do was seize that ward and mark it with the bull, and the only thing standing in his way was an honorable man who'd just averted a city-wide catastrophe." Culzatik looked at Bedler and said, "Onderishta, do you think Fay's wound would match the maul that Bedler—"

Bedler's fist smashed him in the middle of his face, but Culzatik was expecting it and rolled with the punch. From the floor, he said, "Alive."

In a single motion, Aziatil drew her long knives and slashed both of Bedler's biceps. Then she plunged the points into his calves. His hammer, only half-drawn, clattered to the floor and he fell on top of it.

Just like that, Bedler was done. Culzatik got to his feet and nodded his thanks to Aziatil. She pretended not to notice.

Everyone was staring at Essatreska. For the first time since Culzatik met her, she seemed vulnerable. "I didn't mean for things to go so far."

Ponnalas seized his daughter's arm. "What have you done? Why?"

She opened her mouth but couldn't make words come out, so Culzatik said, "Pride. She loved the idea of marrying my brother but thought I was a poor substitute. Besides, with the dissolution signed before formal treason charges, any penalties would be paid to her before the High Watch could…"

Evenset seized the document from her and tore it apart. Mother advanced on Ponnalas, teeth bared, but Culzatik waved her off. To his surprise, she stopped. "Someone take this collar off my investigator," he said to no one in particular.

"By the fallen gods," Evenset said, "if I'd realized..." He looked around. Pinfilas had already left, and so had the other members of the High Watch.

"It was me!" Bedler called. "I did everything. Essatreska didn't know. I pressed the brand to the glitterkind. I stole her jewelry to... She had nothing to do with it."

The magistrate managed a thin smile. "You really get your money's worth with these Free Cities bodyguards."

Culzatik turned to the Steward-General. "I'm satisfied by his confession. Aren't you? Good. I'm glad. But it would be better for everyone if he didn't stand trial." To Bedler, he said, "The drop from that balcony is about twenty-five feet."

Bedler thought about that for a moment, but only a moment. He struggled to his feet and began limping toward the rail. He took a green scarf from his pocket and tied it over his eyes like a blindfold.

Mother ordered Billentik to set up their spare scale for the new glitterkind. When the head medical inspector offered to help, no one dared object.

Culzatik walked toward Ponnalas and his two daughters. Essatreska wore a stunned smile, as if she'd only just realized how close she came to execution. Ponnalas was sweating. Culzatik smiled and laid a hand on his shoulder. Then he turned to the youngest daughter, Caflinna.

"You never came over to see my new copy of *The Kings of Koh-Benjatso and Their Wars*."

Caflinna squeezed her bodyguard's hand. She squeezed back. "I wanted to."

Mother had come close. "Come visit tomorrow," Culzatik said. "You, too, Ponnalas. You can borrow it, and we could talk. Maybe even make a new arrangement that would unite our families peacefully."

Ponnalas looked so grateful that he could weep.

Onderishta approached, rubbing her neck where the collar had pinched. "That man killed Fay, and he's not going to stand trial? He gets to punish himself?"

"I'm sorry," Culzatik said. "He deserves the pitch and flame, but a trial would ruin the Phillien family, and we need them."

The look she gave Culzatik was stony. Then she picked Bedler's maul off the floor and started after him.

"Perhaps we should clear this room," Mother said, and they were nearly through the door when they heard the blow fall.

Culzatik retreated to his library, but he couldn't focus. Instead, he sat and looked out over the Timmer as night fell.

The stars were bright when Onderishta returned. She still wore her stony expression. Culzatik wasn't sure if she was grieving or angry with him. Or both. She carried a long, wrapped bundle.

"They found iron shavings beneath Bedler's bed. He's been posthumously convicted of branding the glitterkind and of Fay's murder."

"Good."

"Mirishiya planted that evidence, didn't she? That's why you asked me to take on a burglar. That was the errand she ran for you."

"You went to the Phillien compound?"

"Trillistin was there. I knew he came from a servant's family, but I didn't know which one. He warned the Philliens about the treason charges, didn't he?"

"He did. If the Philliens were ruined in a scandal, his mother would have been cast out of the kitchens. And he's the reason that Essatreska and Bedler were right here when everything went wrong for them. He was only protecting his mother."

Onderishta looked over the dark waters. "I'm keeping her. He's going back to the tower. He's a smart kid, but I can't have apprentices who spill secrets, even for their mother's sake." There was a pause. "Did you know Bedler was going to kill Fay?"

"I didn't. I swear it."

"But you put a Phillien spy inside my investigation."

"The one doesn't connect with the other." He sounded surer than he felt.

She stared at him for a moment. "We picked up that scarred fellow you wanted to talk to—the Broken Man—but he slipped away from thirty constables with a little girl and an unconscious man. Don't ask me how. All we have is his weapon."

She laid the bundle on the table and unwrapped it. It was a rough iron bar as long as his arm.

Culzatik was disappointed, but he wasn't sure why. "I still want to talk to him, if you get another chance." She nodded. "Onderishta, there should be a service for Fay. A ceremony. The man saved all of us. The next Mourning Day is a long way off, but the whole city should stand for him."

She didn't respond immediately. "Your virtue, you were very clever."

"What do you mean?"

"The problem with being clever is that it gets good people killed. Next time, don't be clever. Be smart."

She left.

Culzatik sat for a moment, then surged to his feet. Who was she to speak to him this way? *Be smart*? Hadn't he just upended a scheme to have his mother executed for treason? The Safroys had a fourth ward now—

one they couldn't sliver for a generation, but still. The Steward-General had just made a fool of himself, moving Mother's faction closer to winning back control of the High Watch.

The Safroys were one of the oldest families in Koh-Salash, and he hadn't just saved them from scorn and ruin. He'd turned things to their advantage. Which was supposed to be his role in life. Yes, it was a shame that a man had lost his life, but it was hardly Culzatik's fault that Bedler was such a fool.

Besides, what was one commoner's life—a man who wasn't even Salashi—against the dignity of the Safroy name?

A shadow passed over him, plunging him into utter darkness. No stars, no glow of Suloh's bones, not even the lantern at the end of the table was visible. Culzatik cried out in sudden terror...

Then it passed, and the dim light of the Salashi night returned.

The length of iron on the table before him was gone.

CHAPTER FORTY

R**iliska stirred the honey** into the bowl of water, then used the stick to lay a drop onto Killer of Devils's lips.

He did not respond. She did it again.

They were still in the ruined Temple of Yth down in Woodgarden. Kyrioc had led her here in the early hours of the morning, then gone away again. Most of the other beetles were already here, the crumbs of a dozen buns scattered around them. Since then, Kyrioc had left and returned several times.

To her surprise, one of the younger boys gave Riliska a hug when she first arrived. Three of the others fetched breakfast for her. Now it was nighttime and she was hungry again, but she didn't know how much silver the other kids had left, and she didn't want to ask. The way they looked at her—as though she were special because of the awful things that happened to her—made her want to cry.

The temple itself covered less than half a block and was surrounded by three-story buildings on three sides. The only roof was a length of canvas Kyrioc had bought or stolen, and only the unconscious barbarian—and Riliska, his friend—took shelter beneath it. The others huddled at the tumbled-down stone walls.

There was a commotion outside. She set her bowl and stirring stick down as the first of the teenagers reached the temple arch. It was the same crowd she'd seen before in the alleys—mean, rough-talking boys with knives in their pockets. The first, a tall one with a scarred lip, held an oversized wine jug.

"What the fuck?" he said when he saw the beetles. He jerked his thumb over his shoulder, toward the street. "You kids get the—"

"Shh," Riliska said. "You'll wake him."

He was so surprised to be shushed that he forgot to be angry. "Wake who?"

"Killer of Devils," she said, and pointed.

The boy lifted his lantern. The others behind him whispered among themselves while his mouth fell open. They crowded into the doorway to see.

They had no way to know that Killer was not asleep and could not have roused himself if he'd been set on fire. It didn't matter. They saw him and fled.

"You handled that well," Kyrioc said.

Riliska shrugged. Kyrioc stood near the canvas, another sack of bread and carrots in hand, and she had no idea how he'd gotten there without her noticing. Kyrioc knew how to do things, and Riliska wanted to learn them too. "It won't work next time. We need to find a place. And I'm going to need a new paint set so we can make more money."

He knelt beside her, looking exhausted. "This is going to be our place. For all of us. And you're not going to need to make money any longer. That man there"—he pointed to the Katr—"when he's restored to health, will help. We're going to look after you."

"But what about my mommy?"

Riliska already knew the answer, but it felt too big to accept.

Kyrioc's eyes became sad and he touched her cheek. Riliska took a step forward and buried her face in his shoulder. She could smell old blood on his clothes, but she didn't know if it was his or someone else's.

So much blood had been shed over the last few days, it was silly to think her mommy would come through unhurt. Tears welled in her eyes.

He put his arms around her.

Riliska was hungry. She was tired. She was thirsty. She had dirt on her hands and face and her back prickled from dry sweat. Kyrioc had promised to look after her, which meant he promised to take care of all of those things.

But for now, they could start with this.

.

ABOUT THE AUTHOR

Child of Fire, Harry Connolly's debut novel and the first in the Twenty Palaces series, was named to *Publishers Weekly's* Best 100 Novels of 2009. The sequel, *Game of Cages*, was released in 2010 and the third book, *Circle of Enemies*, came out in 2011, as did a prequel (cleverly) titled *Twenty Palaces*.

King Khan, a pulp adventure novel based on the role-playing game *Spirit of the Century*, was released in 2013 by game company Evil Hat.

Later in 2013, Harry ran a Kickstarter for his apocalyptic epic fantasy trilogy, *The Great Way*, which was released in 2015. As stretch goals for that project, he published his pacifist urban fantasy *A Key, an Egg, an Unfortunate Remark*, and the short fiction collection *Bad Little Girls Die Horrible Deaths and Other Tales of Dark Fantasy*, which includes the Twenty Palaces short story "The Homemade Mask."

Harry lives in Seattle with his beloved wife, his beloved son, and his beloved library system. You can find him online at: www.harryjconnolly.com

Praise for the Twenty Palaces novels:

"[*Child of Fire*] is excellent reading and has a lot of things I love in a book: a truly dark and sinister world, delicious tension and suspense, violence so gritty you'll get something in your eye just reading it, and a gorgeously flawed protagonist. Take this one to the checkout counter. Seriously." — Jim Butcher

"Connolly doesn't shy away from tackling big philosophical issues . . . amid gory action scenes and plenty of rapid-fire sardonic dialogue."—*Publishers Weekly* (starred review), on *Game of Cages*

"An edge-of-the-seat read! Ray Lilly is the new high-water mark of paranormal noir." — Charles Stross

CPSIA information can be obtained
at www.ICGtesting.com
Printed in the USA
LVHW111627061020
667983LV00020B/2875